{ THE SATURDAY WIFE }

The Saturday Wife

{ NAOMI RAGEN }

ST. MARTIN'S GRIFFIN

New York

THE SATURDAY WIFE. Copyright © 2007 by Naomi Ragen. All rights reserved. Printed in the United States of America. For information, address St. Martin's Press, 175 Fifth Avenue, New York, N.Y. 10010.

www.stmartins.com

Book design by Mary A. Wirth

Library of Congress Cataloging-in-Publication Data

Ragen, Naomi.
　　The Saturday wife / Naomi Ragen.—1st St. Martin's Griffin ed.
　　　　p. cm.
　　ISBN-13: 978-0-312-35239-4
　　ISBN-10: 0-312-35239-5
　　1. Jewish women—Fiction. 2. Rabbis' spouses—Fiction. 3. Marriage—Fiction.
4. Jewish fiction. I. Title.

PS3568.A4118 S28 2007
813'.54—dc22

2007016179

10 9 8 7 6 5 4 3 2

Dedicated, with love, to
Hallel, Hillel, Ariella, Manny, Yotam, Elon, Aviyah, Matan, and Eliora
for bringing more joy and laughter into my life
than I ever imagined possible

✎ ACKNOWLEDGMENTS ✎

*T*he genesis of any book is a strange and mysterious process. I would like to thank, equally and profoundly, the blonde in the miniskirt and tank top who got up onstage to dance with the toddlers during a Kosher Club week in the Dominican Republic, and Gustave Flaubert for writing *Madame Bovary,* which I took along with me on vacation. The confluence of these two is truly responsible for this book.

I would also like to thank the approximately ten thousand members of my e-mail list (www.naomiragen.com) for responding so generously to my request for help with my research. The hundreds of e-mails I received describing actual Bar and Bat Mitzvas and weddings, as well as shul wars and stories of rabbis, their wives, and their congregations, were wonderful, and I've used them all (well, almost). Without this input, the book you read wouldn't have been the same. I especially thank the wonderful rabbis and rabbis' wives who wrote me, as well as the intrepid and talented bloggers, the incomparable Renegade Rebbitzen and Ezer K'negdo, and others for information and inspiration.

As for those few on my e-mail list who wrote me nasty letters declining to participate until they knew more about how I was planning to use this material, I hope you are now feeling satisfied that you cannot be held responsible.

I thank my agent, Lisa Bankoff, for her unending support and encouragement through this and many other projects.

I thank my talented and very patient editor, Jennifer Weis of St. Martin's Press, for her enormous help and editorial guidance, as well as for suggesting in the back of a New York taxi that I make my main character a rabbi's wife. It has made all the difference.

I thank my son Asher for taking time off from finishing his doctorate at Harvard (I had to get that in) to read and comment on this book.

I thank my dear husband, Alex, for telling me jokes for the last thirty-six years. I finally got to use a few. If you don't think they're funny, his e-mail address is available.

Naomi Ragen
JERUSALEM, 2007

If we disregard due proportion by giving anything what is too much for it . . . the consequence is always shipwreck.

—PLATO

PROLOGUE

*I*t is not an easy thing for an Orthodox Jewish girl to be saddled with the name of a Gentile temptress responsible for destroying a famous Jewish hero. When Delilah's father filled in her name on the Hebrew Academy day school application form, the rabbi/administrator assumed it was a mistake, a feeble attempt on the part of some clueless, nonreligious Jew to find a Hebrew equivalent for Delia or Dorothy:

"You are aware, Mr. Goldgrab, that, in the Bible, Delilah seduced Samson and is considered a wicked whore by our sages?" he pointed out, as gently as he could.

"Well, now, you don't say?" Delilah's father drawled, his six-foot-two-inch frame towering over the little man, who nervously clutched his skullcap. "Just so happens it was my mother's name."

Our first meeting with Delilah was in second grade out on the punchball fields of the Hebrew Academy of Cedar Heights on Long Island. Punchball was a Jewish girl's baseball without the bat. You just made the hardest fist you could and *wham!*—started to run. When you hit that rubber ball, you took out all your anger, all your angst, all your frustration. You ran and ran and ran and ran, hoping you'd hit it hard enough so that no one could catch it or you and send you back to first base—or, worse, throw you out of the game altogether.

The privilege of hitting the punchball was not to be taken for granted. Each recess, teams were picked anew by captains, who were, by mutual agreement, the prettiest and richest girls in the class. Everyone who wanted to play lined up and just waited for the magic summons. And as in life, some girls—like rich, snobby Hadassah Mittelman—were always the captains, and some girls, like me, were never asked to play. Never.

We knew who we were and finally slipped away. But there were others—like Delilah—who sometimes made it in. Girls like her always had it the hardest. To *almost* make it was a far crueler fate that to be permanently relieved of hope.

The world was a simple place back then, neatly divided between those of us who got the little blue admission cards in the mail at the start of each new term because our parents had paid the full tuition and those who got them at the last minute, only after much parental groveling and pleading had pried them from the tightfisted grip of the merciless rabbi/administrator in charge. It was a world divided between those who had cashmere sweaters and indulgent fathers who dropped them off at school in their big cars because they lived in even more upscale neighborhoods farther out on the island and those who shivered in scratchy wool on public buses coming from the opposite direction.

Delilah took the bus, but she also had a cashmere sweater, the most glorious color pink, that seemed to float around her shoulders like angel hair. Rumor had it that her mother had actually knitted it for her from scratch, a rumor that cruelly denied her the status conferred by ownership.

This was no doubt true. Mrs. Goldgrab was a woman of scary heaviness, with bad skin and glasses with rhinestone frames that made her eyes contract into hard river stones. She worked a forty-hour week in some low-level office job that computers have permanently wiped off the employment map, and in her spare time, was a seething cauldron of unfulfilled social ambitions, thwarted at every turn by impassable roadblocks. One of the largest was her husband: a tall, lanky man with a shocking Texas accent who worked as a mechanic in a local car repair shop. If anyone ever ran into him in his uniform and mentioned it, Delilah was mortified. Over the years, she adopted the same attitude toward him as her mother: he was something she had to put up with, but he wasn't an asset.

From the beginning, Mrs. Goldgrab had plans for Delilah. Big plans. She wanted her to be popular with the right girls. To be invited to their birthday parties. She hoped to be able to drop her off at Tudor mansions in Woodmere and be casually invited in for coffee, where she would chitchat with the mothers who wore pearls and Ann Taylor suits even on weekends, women who existed—along with the longed-for invitations— only in her lower-middle-class imagination. Even Hadassah's mother wore jeans on weekends. And no one wanted to chitchat with Mrs. Goldgrab, not even her husband.

We always envied Delilah that sweater—to this day. Except that now we understand it had meant nothing to her. What she had wanted was a store-bought sweater, the kind Hadassah Mittelman wore. In fact, she wanted to *be* Hadassah Mittelman, the rabbi's beautiful daughter, who lived in a house with a full suit of armor standing in her hallway, guarding the grand staircase upstairs to her designer bedroom, with its ruffled canopy bed. Delilah didn't want to visit that house. She wanted to move in. Maybe we all did in those days. The difference was that Delilah never got over it.

So before you judge her for the horrible things she did, please try to re- member this: All Delilah Goldgrab Levi ever really wanted was to be in- cluded when they called out the names of those who were allowed to play.

{ ONE }

The thing people never understood about Delilah was that she always
considered herself the victim of a painfully disadvantaged childhood,
something that mystified her hardworking, upwardly mobile parents.
There were few who knew how deeply she mourned her endless humilia-
tions: winter clothes chosen from picked-over reduced racks in January
sales instead of shiny new in autumn; a sweet sixteen celebrated in a bowl-
ing alley instead of in a hotel with a live band; Passover seders at home prepared by her sweating mother instead of in the dining room of exclusive
resorts; summers lying on the public beach instead of trips to Israel and
Europe. A childhood of last year's Nikes, drugstore sunglasses, fifteen-
dollar haircuts, and do-it-yourself French manicures whose white line was
always crooked. . . .

On the rare occasions that she sat in self-judgment, such as before the
Yom Kippur fast, she never felt these longings marked her as selfish, materialistic, or shallow. On the contrary, she considered herself an idealist,

someone focused on the really important things in life: true happiness, true love. As she saw it, she was simply being honest with herself. And someone who "really loved her" would be the kind of person who would stop at nothing to help her overcome the trauma of her youth, her mother's cheap fashion accessories—those fake pearls, those nine-karat gold amethyst rings. Someone who "really loved her" would understand and appreciate how profoundly she needed a house, not an apartment, preferably with a swimming pool, in addition to business-class jaunts to five-star resorts in the Caribbean and Hawaii.

She felt this way despite all the best efforts of our synagogue and schooling to convince us of the fleeting worth of material things, as opposed to the eternal reward—in this life and the next—of spiritual attainments.

In general, Delilah's relationship to religion was somewhat complex. She wasn't a natural rebel. She actually loved the elaborate meals, the dressing up for the synagogue, the socializing afterward. On the other hand, she absolutely refused to accept the fact that bearded rabbis had the right to decide for her how long her skirts and sleeves would be, what she could and couldn't read, or watch on TV or in the movies, or what kind of dates she could have (i.e., serious ones, leading to early marriages, as opposed to frivolous recreational ones like riding roller coasters in Playland).

Like most people, she snipped and tugged and restitched her religion to make it a more comfortable fit. She didn't feel guilty about this. Why should she, she told herself, when the rabbis themselves had done a good deal of tailoring? Take the relationship between the sexes. On the one hand, the Bible taught that men and women were both created in God's image as equals, but on the other, Jewish law was male chauvinist in the extreme, notwithstanding millennia of rabbinical apologetics to disprove the obvious.

Men were the leaders, high priests, rabbis, judges. While rabbis claimed that they were simply expounding on eternal laws derived from God-given sacred texts, the laws always seemed to come out to the men's advantage. For example, sitting shiva. During the seven days of mourning for a parent, wife, or child, rabbinical law said a man wasn't permitted to do anything; he had to be served and taken care of. But if a woman was sitting shiva—surprise!—the same law said she was allowed to get up and wash the floor and cook dinner.

Despite these feelings, Delilah never considered herself a feminist, refusing to join those of us who railed against being banned from donning a prayer shawl and phylacteries or from learning Talmud. She'd just roll her eyes and yawn. "That's all I need. More religious obligations."

The biblical heroines she admired were not the tough, powerful matriarchs, but Esther, who'd soaked in precious bath oils for six months, mesmerizing the king and becoming queen of Persia; and Abigail, who sent war-weary King David camel-loads of food and drink, thereby giving her tightfisted husband, Nabal, a fatal heart attack, thus leaving herself rich and free to marry David, which she was only too happy to do. To Delilah's thinking, these were stories with a deeply spiritual message for women.

Betty Friedan and Simone de Beauvoir bored her. Equal wages were all right, but it was better if your husband earned enough so that you never, ever had to work if you didn't want to. Truth be told, her vision of the perfect world would have been a party in *Gone with the Wind* where women wore ball gowns to barbecues and men brought them plates of delicious food; a place where all women had to do was smile and be pretty and men fell all over themselves to please and amuse them.

All through high school, Delilah was in training for this role. If only you could have seen her then: those manicured toenails with the red polish so carefully applied, those tanned slim thighs, the blond hair braided in cornrows with turquoise beads, the tiny bathing suit like two slashes of color, the eyes that flashed at you like tanzanite, deep blue flecked with gold. She was so deliciously slim, so adorably sexy, it made you stop and stare, the way one stares at a flashy lightning storm or a gaudy tropical sunset. And she knew it.

How could she not? Men and boys flocked around her, and she giggled and flirted indiscriminately with all of them, even the young Puerto Rican janitors hired to clean the floors and bathrooms of the Hebrew Academy of Cedar Heights.

"Everyone does exactly as they please," she'd say cryptically, tossing her head. "Even the ones who parade around showing off their holiness with all those head coverings and fringed garments, yarmulkes and wigs. Secretly, they also do exactly what they want and find excuses afterward." When we protested mildly, she told us to grow up.

While we had all more or less decided by the end of high school what we wanted to be, Delilah remained vague. Her mother wanted her to take some education courses and become a teacher. But something as small and unimaginative as that wouldn't suit her at all, she said. Besides, she didn't like the outfits or the hair and makeup that went with it. You couldn't get away with much in front of a class full of yeshiva kids with a rabbi/principal peeking in on you every few hours. And what if the kids asked you questions, let's say, about the Resurrection of the Dead? Or if the Messiah was coming? She knew she was supposed to believe with perfect faith, but honestly, she had never been able to get her head around such ideas. What, would they come out of their graves, like in *The Night of the Living Dead*? Or like that mangled factory-worker who comes knocking on his parents' door in *The Monkey's Curse*?

And this Messiah. Did he know he was the Messiah? A person is born, gets toilet trained, eats hamburgers, and then—what, finds out he's going to bring peace to the world and change all human life as we know it? Would it be like Moses and the burning bush, where you are just minding your own business trying to keep the sheep from falling off a cliff when God suddenly calls your name and gives you your assignment? But then, how could you tell it was true and you weren't just another candidate for lithium?

She could always be a public school teacher, she supposed. But everyone knew the Teachers' Union stuck new teachers in hellholes in Brooklyn and the South Bronx, places where a white Jewish blonde getting into a new car was like waving a red flag in front of a bull. She tried to envision herself like Michelle Pfeiffer in that movie where she gets all the drug-addicted Puerto Ricans to become honor students because she's so tough, but kind and she really, really believes in them. But she couldn't imagine working in a public school and not wearing pants, which the rabbis absolutely forbade and which she still hadn't figured a way around. Michelle could never have worked those miracles in a skirt with all that sitting up on the desk with her legs crossed.

The decision to enroll at Bernstein Women's College, affiliated with the well-known Bernstein Rabbinical College, had been made after long discussions with friends and counselors. Although the tuition was thousands of dollars a year and she could have gone to any city college for free, she was advised by all that she wouldn't like city colleges. They were too big, too impersonal, full of public high school riffraff. There was no social life. The bottom line was she was afraid to venture out, despite her bravado, from the sheltered yeshiva day school environment she had known, to face the real world, where her new sophistication would be laughed at by hip young New Yorkers who slept together and indulged in drugs and all kinds of other perversions she could only just imagine with equal parts loathing and envy.

But there was one thing you had to give Bernstein, the one true incontrovertible fact which made all those student loans a worthwhile investment: it was turning out to be one, long *shidduch* date.

Everyone was a matchmaker: the girls, the teachers, the teacher's cousins, the girls' cousins. It was the official bride pool for Bernstein Rabbinical College as well as Yeshiva University, with its well-regarded medical and law school, a fact well-known to all the parents shouldering the burden of their daughters' unjustified and outlandish tuition.

Many of the girls were out-of-towners from tiny Jewish communities where available religious Jewish men were either under ten or over forty. Enrolling at Bernstein rescued them from horrible Young Israel weekends in Catskill hotels and being relentlessly pursued by the proverbial kosher butcher from Milwaukee: over thirty, overweight, and oversexed. Here, in a relaxed and respectable atmosphere, every Ruchie could find her Moishe. And vice versa.

The out-of-towners were usually the sheltered daughters of rabbis, pretty and sweet and innocent, with very little dating experience. Most of them had endured at least a year of long-distance courtships in which relatives and friends and professionals had found matches for them in places like Monsey, Brooklyn, or Baltimore. The dates arranged necessitated expensive cross-country plane trips, a situation that understandably left most of them languishing in solitary gloom on Saturday nights. When they moved into the dorms at Bernstein, they thought they'd died and gone to heaven.

In contrast, the native New Yorkers, used to a plethora of possibilities, found the fix-ups from Bernstein and Yeshiva University left much to be desired. Most of the guys were short and pale and wore glasses. They showed up dressed like they were on their way to a Rabbinical Council of America convention. Moreover, most were victims of severe rabbinical brainwashing on the subject of physical contact with the opposite sex outside of marriage. The *negiah*, or "touching" laws, were basically one loud NO! NOT ANYPLACE, ANY TIME, ANY BODY PART, UNDER ANY CIRCUMSTANCES! This left some of the young men severely challenged on this subject, making Delilah feel as if she had a rare communicable disease. Even the most adventurous managed little more than casually stretching an arm out onto the back of her subway seat.

Gee, that was a thrill.

Some, at least, had looked normal enough: a crocheted skullcap, a nice sweater over an open-collared shirt. There was one universal problem, though. Anyone willing to be fixed up was almost always someone who couldn't find a date on his own. And for good reason.

Delilah kept on going, though, always allowing herself to be persuaded by the hard or soft sell of the people who were setting her up, that this one "was different." And why shouldn't she trust them? After all, they had nothing to gain from making her miserable. In fact, most of them were involved in matchmaking because they considered it a good deed. Indeed, there is a widely held belief among religious Jews that achieving three successful matches earns one a free entry pass to the best neighborhoods in the World to Come.

The system in Bernstein worked this way: The guys would come into the dorm lobby and give their name and the name of the girl they were taking out to the housemother, who would then call up to the girl's room, announcing him. The girl would then come down to the lobby and tell the housemother the name of the boy. Sometimes, seeing the girl who spoke his name, the boy would sit perfectly still until he could quietly slip out the front door.

It was quite a show. When she had nothing better to do on a Saturday night, Delilah delighted in hanging around the lobby to watch. Which is how she got involved with Yitzie Polinsky.

The boy was striking: tall and very slim, with broad shoulders and thick rock-star hair that fell adorably over his eyes. He wore a dark skullcap that melted right in and was hardly noticeable at all. His jeans were faded in all the right places, and to top it off he had on a black turtleneck and a kind of bomber jacket of brown leather.

You could tell the housemother didn't approve at all. But when he gave her his name, her eyes lit up: the son of the very famous Rabbi Menachem Polinsky of Crown Heights. The housemother pushed her reading glasses to the top of her gray wig, looked him over again, lips pursed, and then shrugged. Allowances had to be made. She called up to the girl.

Delilah recognized her name: Penina Gwertzman, a cute little out-of-towner from Kansas or some other impossibly goyish place. Petite, with long dark hair and an ample figure, she was from a very religious family and had been carefully brought up. Yitzie wasn't her type at all. He was Delilah's type.

She watched as Yitzie's eyes took in Penina's body in long, slow strokes. Satisfied, he smiled and got up, sauntering over to her, his hands in his pockets. The nearer he got, the more Penina tugged nervously at her long pleated skirt, as if willing it to grow a few more inches.

What a waste, Delilah thought, watching them walk out together into the night, already making plans.

{ T W O }

*I*n the morning, Delilah made inquiries. "I heard Penina went out last night with Yitzie Polinsky," she mentioned casually to her roommate, Rivkie. "How did it go?"

Rivkie, who had not a suspicious bone in her body and who considered any kind of gossip a mortal sin and so never listened to or repeated anything of value, said she thought she'd heard something not so good about it. Coming from such a source, Delilah knew it was going to be major, major breaking news.

She knocked on a few doors of reliable yentas and got the goods: a disastrous date that had ended scandalously, with tears and angry phone calls and possible repercussions for Yitzie, who was slated to follow in his father's footsteps, if only he could shed his yeshiva-bum reputation.

Yes! Delilah thought, thrilled.

She settled her face into the right lines of worry and concern and knocked on Penina's door. "I just heard. Are you all right?"

The girl's big, obviously cried-out eyes, welled. "Does everybody know?"

Delilah took a step back. "No! It's just that I happened to be waiting down in the lobby and saw him come in. I mean, that leather jacket. . . . He looked a little dangerous to me, so I asked to make sure you were OK."

Penina's face was stiff.

"It's just . . . I've had some bad experiences myself."

The girl suddenly melted into an angry puddle of damp emotions.

"It wasn't my fault!!" she cried passionately. "They told me he was a brilliant Torah scholar from a very important family, who was going to take over his father's congregation one day soon." She blinked and two large tears rolled down her fresh pink cheeks.

Delilah caught her breath in joy. "What . . . did something . . . happen?"

"He said he was taking me to the Village. I didn't know what village! I thought he meant Boro Park. But it wasn't. . . . I didn't see a single Jew. Then he took me inside some restaurant. But it wasn't a kosher deli or anything. It was really dark. And I didn't see anybody eating, or smell pickles—you know. It smelled like . . . liquor. There was a stage, and some girl with very uncombed frizzy hair was singing! Imagine, Yitzie Polinsky—the son of Rebbe Polinsky, who everyone calls a saint, who is known to be so stringently pious people are terrified of him and they worship him—imagine *his son listening to a woman's voice*, which everybody knows is forbidden! Anyway, we sat down at this little table. I couldn't see a thing. So"—she wiped her eyes, taking a deep breath—"at first I thought I was imagining it, but then I realized he had his hand on my knee. And then he put his other hand on my shoulder, and his fingers started playing with my hair and then moved underneath my collar. . . ."

Delilah bit the inside of her cheek, handing the girl a tissue. "Oh!" She shook her head in outraged sympathy. "The creep." She waited impatiently what she hoped was a suitable moment of commiseration. "And then what happened?" she asked eagerly.

Penina's eyes looked up over the tissue with sudden suspicion. "What do you mean? Of course I told him to take me back immediately!"

"Oh, yes. Of course, of course! That's exactly what I . . . thought. Meant. I mean, what else could you do? Did he?"

Penina stared down at the tissue, then blew her nose again miserably. "He said he had to make a phone call first. I waited and waited, but he never came back. I wound up paying the check, and I didn't even have enough money left to take a taxi! I had to use the subway. I was petrified!" She sobbed.

Delilah made an O with her lips and held it. "I have a good mind to call him up and tell him off. You wouldn't happen to have his phone number, would you?"

"You would do that? For me? But we hardly even know each other!"

"Doesn't our holy Torah tell us, 'Before a blind man put no obstacle'? It's my sacred religious duty. We wouldn't want another innocent young girl to go out and have such an experience, would we? I mean, he has to be stopped!"

Penina blinked. "Sharona Gottleib fixed me up. She said her grandmother was friends with his grandmother. . . . I'll never speak to her again!"

Delilah sighed heavily. "I understand." She patted the girl's soft white hand with its little fourteen-carat birthstone ring from Mommy and Daddy. "I will talk to Sharona. Trust me, I know exactly how to handle this."

Penina stared at her, her eyes welling once again. "You would do that? For me? Meet with him and tell him off?"

Delilah patted the little hand. *"Kol Yisrael aravim zeh le zeh."* All Israel is responsible one for the other.

~⸰ ⸰~

She found out where his father's shul was and arranged to sleep over at a friend's house nearby. She wore a demure outfit that covered everything. Still, she sensed the cold eyes of matronly disapproval pointed like lasers at the top of her blond head to the bottom of her spiked heels as she walked down the narrow aisle of the women's section in Reb Menachem Polinsky's synagogue. She took a seat near the high *mechitzah*—the religiously mandated barrier piously separating the men from the women. It ran the entire length of the synagogue, giving the men almost the entire room, and confining the women to a small, cramped space. As usual, the more Orthodox the synagogue, the more demeaning and uncomfortable the women's section. Still, she was just grateful that at least she was in the same room with Yitzie, as some stringency kings had created synagogues where the women were shunted off to side rooms in completely different parts of the building, where only a handful could see or hear anything. Discreetly, she lifted the little curtain and peered inside at the men's section.

There he was, dressed in the traditional Hasidic Sabbath outfit: the satin waistcoat with its braided string belt that separated his holy upper body from his profane lower half, the dark, wide-brimmed hat. He wore a magnificent prayer shawl over his shoulders. His father, the old man with the white beard who stood at the center at the bimah, seemed to be running the place, the way everyone was falling all over themselves to be respectful to him.

Well, well, she thought. A real saint.

She waited for him in the room where they served the kiddush—the traditional after-prayer refreshments—but the synagogue was so over-the-top *frum,* it had separate rooms for men and women. So she waited outside. He came out, a few paces behind his father, surrounded by men. But when he saw her, he lifted his head and a secret look passed between them.

She called him that night. She was the blonde who had been standing outside his father's synagogue, she told him, and she had something she needed to talk to him about. They agreed to meet in the Village. When he showed up, he was again dressed in his leather jacket.

"I'm just here to tell you what a bum you are" was her opening line.

"You're fast. Usually, it takes women at least one date to find that out." He smiled.

"That girl you dumped last Saturday night? Well, she happens to be a friend of mine."

"She was pretty anxious to get rid of me. So I helped her out."

"You stuck her with the check and left her stranded."

"What happened to women's lib? Don't you girls carry cabfare?"

"She only had enough left for the subway, you creep." She laughed.

He took a step closer. "And you came here to tell me off, is that right?"

"Well, what other reason could I have?" she asked demurely, lowering her eyes.

He took her arm and tucked it between his bended elbow, patting her hand. The forbidden feel of his male skin against hers was exciting, as well as the fact that he'd done it on his own, without asking permission. Some of her other dates had actually asked straight out, "How religious are you?" Idiots. What did they expect a girl to do, give them a road map and a list of directions? To tell them, Not religious at all, just do anything you want? Her answer was always the same: "Very." The date ahead never failed to be a disaster.

Yitzie thrilled her. They met in places she had never been. Top of the Sixes, where she ordered her first daiquiri, which made her feel all warm and happy. Avant-garde movie theaters showing films by Godard that were so shocking and lewd she'd once actually run from the theater. To make it up to her, he'd bought her tickets to the opera at Lincoln Center. Orchestra seats. She'd worn a very form-fitting dress covered with silver glitter with a high collar of white silk and matching white cuffs, which she'd sneaked past the dorm mother under her prim black winter coat. She'd piled her hair on top of her head. Later, while she was in the lobby waiting for him to get her a Coke, two obviously tipsy middle-aged men had approached her with lewd smiles, about to say something when Yitzie showed up and they steered abruptly in the opposite direction. She looked at herself in the glass windows of the lobby. She looked ravishing and a bit slutty, she thought, wavering between embarrassment and delight.

She was in Yitzie's spell, or maybe he was in hers, she couldn't decide. He graduated slowly from slinging his hand across her shoulders in the secluded booths of dark little bars, to twining his fingers through her hair, to grasping her waist as they walked, slightly tipsy, down the streets of Manhattan. And then he began to pick her up in a car.

They drove out to the Rockaways and parked by the deserted summer bungalows. When he'd first suggested it, she'd told herself he was being romantic. She envisioned holding hands and watching the waves roll in while he whispered compliments into her pink little ears. The first time he kissed her, his tongue pressing between her teeth, she was so busy gagging she didn't feel his hand wander under her skirt. She was wearing a girdle and stockings, more solid than a chastity belt. But his hands moved so quickly. She couldn't believe someone could actually unhook a bra without having to put his hands under her blouse—which she would *never* have allowed, of course—but there she was, unhooked.

All the while, he kept telling her how beautiful she was—how irresistible, how much he loved her—in this slow, worshipful, sweet voice. She was deeply conflicted, part of her giving in immediately, the other part shocked and outraged and threatened.

Then something happened, physically, she hadn't expected. She felt all her juices begin to flow, inexorable and unstoppable. She felt light-headed and strange. Not herself. And the space they were in felt safe and private.

Who was to know? She let her arms fall to her sides, letting him use his hands on her as one lets a musician play an instrument: She watched, thrilling to the chords that resonated within her, absolutely new. She throbbed with a deep, resounding bass.

Her classes at Bernstein became a vague hum. She'd finally enrolled in the associate program to become a dental hygienist, enjoying the idea of leaning over strange men and telling them to open wide, but the classes were a bore. She could barely keep her eyes open through Dental Hygiene Theory I, Dental Materials, Infection and Immunity, Ezekiel and Gaonic Literature II. All she wanted to do was close them and dream of the night to come.

Things progressed rapidly. Yitzie was like a drug. He was everything she really wanted. Exciting and unconventional, but from a good family who had *yichus* and money. She daydreamed of how this was all going to end with a marriage proposal. They were, after all, so "good together." They had so much in common. She knew she could keep him happy.

But whenever he wanted to take it up the final notch, explore the last frontier, she kept pushing him away, adamantly refusing to go that extra step that would mark her forever as an uncapped bottle of Coke, as a rebbitzin once told them in high school. A girl who had lost all her fizz before her wedding night.

The laws of the Torah about maintaining virginity—as taught in yeshiva—were uncompromising. A girl who willingly bedded a man was a whore. And even if she was forced into it, she still had to marry the creep and he wasn't allowed to divorce her, ever. That was a punishment for the rapist, her rabbis had explained, never really getting into why a girl would want to be tied to such a man the rest of her life. If you pushed them on it, they'd get all excited, and finally shout at you that a woman's position during biblical times made it imperative for her to have a husband, and who would marry a deflowered, single girl?

Where it all got really sticky, as far as she could see, was when you decided to marry someone other than your lover. If the husband was clueless, expecting you to be a virgin and found out otherwise, he was within his legal right to throw you out without a dime. Which is why in biblical times the girl's parents saved the sheet from the marriage bed to display to town elders should just such a problem arise. Nowadays, though, DNA testing made presenting the bloody sheet as proof of virginity a bit more tricky. So Delilah knew she had to be cautious.

But she was in love with him. And he—he was . . . ? She couldn't make up her mind.

Sometimes he seemed totally enthusiastic, like a rabid sports fan fanatically immersed in witnessing the achievement of that last winning goal. And sometimes he seemed distracted, even bored. Sometimes he said hurtful things, like, "Another blintz, another inch," pinching her flesh in various places. His moodiness confused and depressed her. It took quite a bit of self-coaching for her to talk herself out of her bouts of pessimism and fright. She was, however, successful. She planned their future. He had no interest in taking over his father's congregation, which was fine with her, because she had no interest at all in being a rabbi's wife.

The mere sound of the Yiddish term *rebbitzin* filled her with distaste and dread, conjuring up images of overweight Jewesses in bad wigs wearing dowdy calf-length skirts and long-sleeved polyester blouses. She remembered the rabbis' wives who had been her teachers in yeshiva high school, those mirthless paragons of virtue dedicated to squeezing out and discarding the last ounce of joy from living, the way you squeezed a sweet orange, leaving behind only the empty bitter shell. God, God, God, and more God, combined with a life of doing *chesed*—good deeds—i.e., distasteful and inconvenient favors for ungrateful people you hardly knew and who would never reciprocate. That was the ideal of Jewish life according to her pious teachers, who, if they had had a magic wand, would have waved it over all twenty of them as they sat in class, turning their clothes navy blue, their hair into long braids, and their thoughts to bearded rabbinical students who would touch them only two weeks out of the month until they got pregnant, and then it was anybody's guess.

Only Rebbitzin Hamesh, her teacher for Jewish thought, filled her with admiration. While she viewed with pity her excess weight, her stiffly sprayed, formally coiffed wigs, and her matronly clothes and thick ankles, she nevertheless found her witty and charming in a pale-lipped pious way. Delilah was certain Rebbitzin Hamesh would wind up in heaven with a rich reward.

Once, Rebbitzin Hamesh invited the girls over on a Friday night. She'd worn a blue-velvet ankle-length housecoat and an elaborate head scarf. The house had been well swept with colorful touches, surprisingly beautiful rugs in bright greens and reds on the floors and walls. The house had smelled of roast chicken and warm sweet apple kugel. There had been a large lovely china closet filled with beautiful silver ritual objects. And

Rebbitzin Hamesh had not looked miserable or tasteless as she sat there with her ankles crossed, her clean cheeks shining like ripe apples as she read her prayer book and waited for her husband to return from synagogue with her well-scrubbed children.

But it had been so quiet, so very, very quiet. Like being in paradise already. Or like being dead. Rebbitzin Hamesh, Delilah thought, was too young for this kind of life. Anyone under eighty was too young. And that, Delilah decided, was the problem with worrying about earning your heavenly reward too early. It was then she made up her mind to live until she died. Rewards in the Afterlife, Heaven or Hell, were hard to imagine, let alone sacrifice the here and now for. It was like that television show, *Let's Make a Deal*. Do you trade the perfectly fine refrigerator you have in your hand for curtain number three, which might or might not have a new car, thereby risking getting stuck with a broken-down wagon filled with straw? Ah, the eternal question.

One night, Yitzie took her to a friend's apartment "for a Chanukah party." It was in an apartment house in Kew Gardens. No one answered the door when they knocked. Surprisingly, she saw he had a key. When he opened the door, there was no menorah. No latkes. No dreidels. No friends. They were alone together.

By the light of the menorah he dug up somewhere in a closet ("Otherwise, I'm leaving!") he sat down beside her on the very worn but comfortable old sofa, where he piously reminded her of the Jewish custom of relaxing while the candles still burned. He apologized for upsetting her. And then, almost more quickly than she could have imagined, things got completely out of hand. She didn't even recognize herself, the feelings streaming through her like a tsunami breaking through, washing out her brain like some flimsy beach structure that just floated out to sea, unpinned from its moorings. His clothes were everywhere. His hands were everywhere. And then, suddenly, her clothes were everywhere too. It was all happening so fast, she wasn't even sure she knew, exactly, what was going on. At least, that is what she told herself then, and later. She felt stunned, enthralled, humiliated, embarrassed, curious. When it was over, she stood up, looking down at the couch pillows. She touched them. Were they damp, dry? Were the stains old, new?

Frantically, she pulled on her clothes.

Afterward, Yitzie was very romantic, very concerned. On the way back to Bernstein, he stopped a block away. There, in the shadowed alleyway of an office tower, he held her close and kissed her just the way she'd always imagined in her fantasies. Yet, alone, sitting on her dorm-room bed, she felt a sense of deep shock and horror.

She undressed and took a shower, fingering her body tenderly, as if it belonged to someone else, someone childish and vulnerable. She examined herself, her clothing, the dark blue skirt, the white lamb's-wool sweater. She was not in any pain; still, the idea of what might have happened was profoundly terrifying to her.

Was it a sin? she wondered. And if so, which one?

She was free and single. And sex without marriage wasn't actually forbidden anywhere, as far as she could tell, whatever blather they'd thrown at her in high school. True, she hadn't gone to the ritual baths, but that was more Yitzie's problem than hers, sin-wise. She began to calm down, soaping herself and standing in the downpour of lovely hot water until all her bad thoughts just washed away. It was just nature taking its course. She shrugged, a secret little smile curling her lips as she allowed herself to think, How lovely! How lovely! And now that they had *done it* (she began to convince herself of that fact, although she was by no means sure; it had all happened so fast, and she was so totally inexperienced), she was now certain, beyond a doubt, that chuppah and *kedushin*—a marriage canopy and a sacred wedding ceremony—were on the horizon, the next step for the two of them.

She would be Mrs. Yitzie Polinsky, daughter-in-law of the renowned Torah sage Rebbe Menachem Polinsky of Crown Heights. And Yitzie? He would find his place in law or accounting or be taken in by one of his father's wealthy Hasidim as a trainee and later a partner in some lucrative import-export business. There would be a lovely home in Jamaica Estates, one of those mock Tudors that Donald Trump's father had put up and that were going for a million or more these days. They'd put in a swimming pool—she had to have a swimming pool—and beautiful Henredon French country-style furniture. She already had a scrapbook filled with ads for exactly the pieces she wanted. She'd have a large china closet filled with wonderful silver ritual objects, and all those creamy, gold-edged porcelain pieces made especially for Jews by Lenox: the seder plate, the kiddush cup, all of which would never be used and would pass untouched to her children, who would also never use them. She'd have a charge account in Lord & Taylor and Macy's. And they'd have great sex and a house filled with little yeshiva boys and pretty yeshiva girls. And everyone who'd been unkind to her in high school would eat their hearts out.

So she didn't object when Yitzie suggested another "party" at the same friend's house. But this time, when they got there, he took out a camera.

She stared at it. He kissed her and then started to unbutton her blouse. It was just that she was so beautiful, he explained rapidly. He wanted a picture of her like this, to always remember, for when they got old.

The idea that he was thinking so far ahead into the future thrilled her. "You know, Yitzie," she cooed, "we really should do something about this if we love each other so much. Why don't we just get married?"

She saw his eyes twitch as he continued to smile and fiddle with her buttons.

Had he not heard her? she wondered, as she suddenly leaned out of his reach.

He sat back. "What's wrong?"

"I asked you a question."

He made a sound like *mmmmhummyeehmm*.

"What does that mean?"

"It means you're interrupting me."

She snatched the camera and threw it against the wall.

"What the . . . ?" Yitzie jumped up. "That's a Canon!"

"I want an answer."

He was on his knees, gathering up the pieces, appalled. He looked at her, his eyes narrowing. "Are you sure?"

"Yes, I'm sure!" she told him hotly, as her heart sank.

He shrugged. "It's been fun, but you've gotten the wrong impression."

Her face paled. "What impression is that, Yitzie?"

"That we're a nice Orthodox Jewish couple from Brooklyn who's just blowing off a little steam until we fall back into the fold."

That's exactly what she'd thought, except for the Brooklyn part. She was, after all, from Queens, a major difference as far as she was concerned. "I know that! Who said I want that?"

He touched her face; his eyes held a sardonic gleam. "Don't you? Aren't you just dying to pick out your colors and move into my family's two-family in Crown Heights where we can live until we have the down payment for our own house in some swanky Jewish neighborhood, walking distance to the local shul?" He sneered.

She shrugged off his hand. "So what if I am? Who do you think you are, Mick Jagger? You're Rabbi Polinsky's son, the one who wears a *streimel* and *kapota* every Saturday, like some Polish nobleman from the Middle Ages. Sooner or later, if you wait around, they'll fix you up with some short rabbi's daughter with thick stockings from Beit Yaakov. She'll make you turn off the lights and put a hole in a sheet."

His hands fumbled around, looking for a cigarette. He lit it and lay down on the bed, exhaling large smoke rings that rose and broke against the dirty white ceiling. The smell of smoke was suffocating. "You know, Delilah, that hole-in-the-sheet thing? It's a myth."

She began to cough. He ran one finger up her arm from wrist to elbow. "I'm going to miss you," he said.

She thought perhaps she hadn't heard him right.

A few weeks later, she missed.

Well, that was putting it pessimistically, she told herself. After all, she didn't always get it on the day it was supposed to come. There were a million reasons. I mean, she wasn't a clock the way some girls were.

But then four more days passed. And a fifth.

She called Yitzie, but all she got was an answering machine. She left ten messages, one every half hour. Then she went knocking on Sharona Gottleib's door.

Sharona opened it. She looked annoyed. "Well, well."

What had she ever done to her? But there was no time for game playing. "Listen, I've got to get in touch with Yitzie. He doesn't answer the phone—"

Sharona pulled her in and shut the door behind her, her fingers painfully tight around her wrist. "Not so loud, you idiot!"

"You don't understand."

She arched her brow. "No, huh? Late, are we?"

Delilah sank down on the bed. "Well, maybe. But I'm not even sure we had . . . that we did . . . What am I going to do, Sharona?"

"I tried to warn you. But you wouldn't listen."

Was that true? Delilah searched her memory and came up with a few snooty remarks thrown in her direction by Sharona when she'd asked for Yitzie's phone number. Something like, "You are making a huge mistake.

He's poison." She'd chalked it up to jealousy. Or to Sharona feeling she wasn't as good as Penina, not worthy of the great Yitzie Polinsky.

"But you were the one who fixed him up with Penina! If you felt that way, why did you do it?"

Sharona's face went rigid. "I had no choice. He's got some photos of me."

This information sank in with horror. "Oh, no! Sharona, what am I going to do?"

Sharona went to the door and opened it. "You'll figure it out."

Oh, God. Oh, God. Oh, God.

She lay back on her bed, the blinds drawn, the sounds of New York City street traffic rolling over her as if she were lying spread-eagled on 42nd Street and Sixth Avenue. Instinctively, she stretched her fingers over her stomach, as she tried to imagine the future. Was it her imagination, or was it already rounder, fuller?

She saw herself waddling through the halls, her sweaters stretched over a basketball-sized lump. She imagined the shocked and horrified stares of her classmates, the good yeshiva girls, the out-of-town rabbis' daughters, as they whispered just behind her. She saw herself summoned into Rebbitzin Craimer's office, the way she would ease her bulky pregnant body into the narrow chair as the old yenta lectured her about being a bad influence, a disgrace to the good name of the institution. What could she answer? She'd even have to agree!

And then they would throw her out of school with no degree, all that tuition and studying about plaque down the toilet, and all her student loans coming due with no way to pay them off! Her father (her mother, she was sure, would not be around, having died of a heart attack the moment she'd heard the news) would grudgingly take her in, and she'd have to listen to his snoring and watch him sit around in those sleeveless undershirts he liked, his skinny chest and hairy arms flailing as he tried to comfort her. She'd have to listen to his advice: Go back to Dallas or Houston. You'll be better off. Sorry I ever came to this city. They've got plenty of rabbis down in Texas. Don't worry. You'll find rabbis.

Or perhaps she'd throw herself on the mercies of the city's welfare system and rent a little apartment, a fourth-floor walk-up where she'd sit terrified behind thrice-bolted doors, hoping crackheads and dope fiends wouldn't break it down and kidnap her and her baby, selling them both into white slavery. A place where for recreation, she'd watch the roaches race each other across the kitchen counter. None of her friends would visit her. She'd be an outcast.

Hot tears dripped into her pillow as she rolled over onto her side.

There was another way. A trip to a clinic—they were clean and efficient, and it wouldn't be worse than going to a dentist—and before you could say Yitzie Polinsky, the little bugger would be an ingredient in some new antiaging cosmetic venture.

Her baby. They'd suck it out of her.

She'd seen that book with the pictures of fetuses inside the womb. Whatever those crazy women's groups told you about freedom over your body, it was a baby. It had a head, and a little tush, and tiny fingers and those tiny closed eyes. And they'd just Hoover it out of her, like some mess that needed cleaning up.

It was then she'd felt the entire true weight of sin crash down on her. Whatever she'd done in her life so far, she hadn't actually done anything hurtful to God. But killing a baby, even the froglike beginnings of a baby, because it was too inconvenient and embarrassing, would be a true sin. The God she seldom thought about, but always believed in, would not be able to forgive that. And for the rest of her life, she would have to live in a world in which she knew she had done this terrible thing, until the day she died, at which point her true punishment would only begin.

According to some woman who'd undergone a near-death experience— a bunch of bricks fell on her head while she was walking in the street— and had explained it all on *Oprah*, when you died you had this moment when you were forced to sit back and watch your life, like a movie. You couldn't close your eyes, because you had no eyelids. God would be watching her watch herself as the film showed her walking to the clinic, filling out the forms, lying down on the table. It would show her letting them, *telling them*, to rid her of this God-given life. A child, hers and Yitzie Polinsky's.

She was more frightened than she had ever been in her life.

"Can I put on the light?"

It was her roommate, Rivkie.

Rivkie Lifschitz was blessed with all things. She was from a respected well-to-do family and already engaged to an acknowledged Torah scholar. Perhaps because life had treated her so gently, she had also become a kind and generous human being. She was the kind of girl who learned the Torah portion of the week and managed to extract some beautiful moral lesson even from those difficult sections that dealt with body sores full of pus and the minutiae of the laws involved in animal sacrifices. "Blind or broken, or maimed, or having a wen or a dry or moist scab, ye shall not bring these near unto God and as an offering made by fire shall ye not bring aught of them unto the Altar." Even in this, Rivkie Lifschitz would manage to find some redeeming little detail, something about the priest's wife, and how the rabbis say that a man's house is his wife. How a woman completely bears the character of the home, and how holy that is. And a woman who is the wife of a temple priest—or his daughter—has a higher degree of holiness. . . . Only Rivkie could ferret out these details.

Once, she'd even had a discussion with Rivkie about *bedikot*, those mandatory self-examinations pious women performed for a week following their menstrual period to check if their vaginal discharges were completely free of blood before immersing in the ritual baths and resuming relations with their husbands. If the inserted cloth came out white, no prob. If it came out red, big prob. But if it came out yellow or brown, a woman had to ask a rabbi to examine it and decide whether she could count it as a clean day, and go on toward the finish line and her husband's arms, or if she had to return to Go, and start counting all over again.

"It really isn't as bad as you think. You can FedEx it to any rabbi in the country. He doesn't even have to know who you are. Or you can give it to the rebbitzin."

"You've got to be kidding!"

Rivkie had looked at her, surprised. "Look, we're all just trying to do God's will because we love Him so much. If He is asking us to separate until we can count seven clean days, we have to do it in the best way possible, because He is so good to us, and asks so little. . . . It would be terrible to separate a couple more than is necessary, and terrible to allow them to be intimate when it's against God's will. It's part of a rabbi's job description to help couples keep their marriage holy in God's eyes. And if I, as the rabbi's helpmate, can help him, or help the women in my congregation feel more comfortable about asking, then it would be a tremendous good deed, no?"

That was Rivkie. The perfect future rabbi's wife, whom no detail of ritual observance, no matter how gross, demeaning, or disgusting, could derail her from her earnest pursuit of true holiness.

No one could dislike Rivkie. It was impossible. She was so giving, so sincere. And even though you might smile behind your hand at her earnestness and the way she bounced around the world with love and enthusiasm, there would be no way you could fault her. There wasn't a mean or selfish bone in her body. Whatever she learned, she put into practice.

They'd been roommates for about six months. They hadn't spoken much. This, Rivkie chalked up to the fact that Delilah was a little older than she was and perhaps from a family of lesser means, which forced her to be extra busy earning money to finance her studies. The few times they had had a conversation, Delilah had wound up borrowing clothes, which Rivkie was only too happy to lend her—overjoyed, in fact.

She felt guilty sometimes for coming from such a wealthy family, being engaged to such a wonderful young man, having her health and her whole future ahead of her. She wanted to thank God every waking minute, and any good deed she managed to do she felt gave God back some pleasure. She felt this way even when her clothes came back to her wrinkled and stained—or failed to come back at all, which she viewed as an even bigger mitzva, because Delilah obviously needed new clothes badly, enough to take someone else's.

Rivkie sat down at her bedside, shocked. "Delilah, what's wrong?"

Her voice, so sweet and kind, filled with true concern, demolished the floodgates. Delilah sat up and sobbed—loud wet sobs full of the breathless sucking up of phlegm.

Rivkie, horrified, put her arms around her and patted her back. "Can't you tell me what's the matter? Maybe I could help you?"

At this, Delilah sobbed even louder.

Rivkie hugged her. "You don't have to tell me. But you should tell God. Talk to Him. Explain it to Him. Ask Him to help you."

Delilah looked up with surprise. Taking the tissue from Rivkie's hand, she considered it. Yes! Yes! This was the answer. Who was compassionate and kind and forgiving? Who, after all, caused new life to be created in the first place?

Most of all, who could perform miracles?

Yes, yes, yes!

She put her arms around Rivkie's slim shoulders, noting through her misty eyes that she was wearing a new blouse, one that had yet to be hung up in the closet, and that it was a very nice material. Silk? And that color, sort of a summer green. She wiped her eyes carefully, not wanting to get water spots on it that might ruin it, because she had a skirt that was the perfect match. . . . "Thank you, Rivkie. You've saved me. That's what I'll do. I'll pray." She saw her roommate's eyes shine through undropped heartfelt tears.

For a moment, Delilah felt her heart pierced by the knowledge that such innocence and sincerity existed in the world. She didn't doubt for a minute that if she poured her heart out and told Rivkie everything— which, of course, she had absolutely no intention of doing; she wasn't a complete idiot—the girl would not sit in judgment.

She suddenly remembered what her teachers had once told them about Judaism being a system in which human beings attempt to imitate God. Until this moment, she had never understood what such a thing could mean. Rivkie, like God Himself, would without question react with sympathy and compassion.

Delilah was suddenly flooded by an aching desire to be a person like that, someone who went through life cleanly, openly, helping others, at one with God and other human beings. Perhaps it was not too late? Jews believed in repentance and clean slates and having your sins wiped away.

She would pray to God. She would ask His forgiveness, ask Him to solve this problem to which she could find no solution that would not lead to even worse problems. She would hand the whole sordid mess over to Him. And if He answered her, she would finally and absolutely know there was a God, and He wasn't just a mythical being, like the tooth fairy or Santa Claus, a concept created by the popular imagination because human beings have to have explanations, and because they want to believe that their lives have some purpose, some meaning. She would bury all her skepticism, her doubts, and be reborn.

She got up.

"Do you want me to go with you?" Rivkie asked.

She shook her head. "No. I need to do this alone."

She took her purse and put on a pair of sunglasses to hide her eyes, since it didn't seem appropriate to begin repairing her makeup. Then she walked slowly around the corner to the synagogue.

Of course, it was locked. For a moment, all her good feelings evaporated. Why was it, she fumed, that churches were always open, always filled with quiet darkness, candles, etc. etc., and synagogues never were? And even if she waited around in the faint hope that some beadle might come by and unlock it for men wanting to say their afternoon prayers, still, she'd be the only woman there, and all of them would stare at her.

So where now? Where could she go that was dark and secret and spiritual? Where she would feel free to express her deepest soul and ponder the mysteries of the universe, God, and faith? She looked up and saw the movie house. They were playing *Star Wars*, which she had been planning on seeing again anyway.

The movie was just starting, but the theater was practically empty. She took a seat in an empty row at the far end of the aisle near the front, where anything she said aloud would be swallowed by the Dolby sound blasters. There was some kind of loud galactic fight going on.

"Please, God, I know I haven't been behaving myself the way You'd want," she whispered, then stopped. It sounded like she was talking to a school principal. She took a deep breath. "Dearest Father in Heaven," she began. But it sounded so phony, so Holy Scroll Press, that religious publishing house that translated Hebrew prayers into unbearable English and published books professing to be compilations of standard Jewish laws but were actually modern reinventions so stringent and reactionary they made Maimonides look like a flaming liberal. She sat back quietly, exhausted, and watched.

Obi-Wan Kenobi and Qui-Gon Jinn, who had only good intentions, who were actually sent to make peace and stop the trade blockade of a perfectly innocent little planet, were about to be killed for no good reason. She felt angry tears drop at the terrible injustice of the world, where innocent people with good intentions—*had she ever had any other kind? Had she not been, at the very moment disaster struck, planning to be a good Jewish wife and mother, taking care of a family in a large and comfortable house?*—were pursued mercilessly by evil.

She put her hand over her stomach. Well, a baby couldn't be called evil. It was a consequence but not an evil consequence. Just very inconvenient and embarrassing.

Her prayer was not going well at all, she realized, taking her eyes off the screen just as they landed on Tatooine and met Anakin Skywalker. . . .

She closed her eyes, gripping the seat in front of her with both hands. "I'm not good at prayer," she whispered. "It's hard for me to concentrate; my mind is always wandering. But I'm scared, God. Really scared. I know I deserve to be punished for all the bad things I've done"—*clothes strewn over the floor, body parts touching intimately*—"but I really, really want children some day. But in the right way. With a visit to the ritual baths, and a marriage canopy, and a marriage contract handwritten by a scribe on vellum, signed by witnesses. Please forgive me for even considering aborting a child, if I am . . . if I am . . ." She hesitated, then stammered the word out loud. "Pregnant!" She looked around, frightened she'd been overheard. But people's eyes were on the screen. She sighed, her heart racing. She put her palm over it. "You are smarter than I am. Please find some way to help me out on this. I don't want to hurt an innocent child, or my future husband, or my parents." She took a deep breath. "But if I have a baby now, I will be thrown out of the Jewish community. I will never be able to marry a decent man, to be a good Jewish wife and mother. And I know that's what You want for me, isn't it?"

So far, she didn't see how God could be impressed, since she was even boring herself. And so God, who must hear this kind of stuff 24/7, must be snoring. She felt a sense of desperation, as if she were watching a delicate operation and the patient was flatlining and the doctors were using those electrodes, or whatever, to zap the heart one last time before calling it a day.

She leaned forward, a new sense of desperation making her body stiff and electric with passion. "Please, God, get me out of this! If You do, I swear on everything holy that I'll change!" She rapidly went down a checklist. "I'll pray every morning. I'll starve myself on all the minor fast days. I'll wear skirts that cover my knees and blouses that cover my"—briefly, she considered saying *wrists*, but there was no way—"that cover two fists above my elbow. I'll marry a good Jewish man and I'll be the best wife, the best religious Jewish wife and mother. You won't be sorry. Please help me!"

She felt a sudden warm flow between her legs. The skirt, she realized, was ruined. But her life was saved. It was a good trade, especially considering it was Rivkie's skirt.

Her life, she knew, was about to undergo a transformation.

That morning, she carefully culled her closet of anything above the knee, anything red, anything too form-fitting. She culled and culled and culled. Finally, she put on the only white long-sleeved blouse she owned along with a skirt that reached mid-calf, which was possibly Rivkie's. It certainly could not be hers; she couldn't even remember ever trying on such a skirt, let alone actually buying it. Combing and twisting her long hair into a bun, she took out her prayer book and sat on the edge of her bed, praying. When she was done, she kissed the prayer book and put it down.

Rivkie looked her over approvingly. "So, you feel better?"

Delilah nodded. "God has answered my prayers. I don't know why. I didn't deserve any special favors."

"You know, when God tells us to imitate Him, that's what He means. He does favors for us not because we've earned or deserve them but out of infinite compassion and mercy. That's why *chesed* is such an important part of being a Jew. Do good deeds because it's the right thing to do and you have the opportunity to imitate God. That's the only way we can ever pay Him back for everything He does for us. He gives us the sun, and He only asks that we light a little candle."

Rivkie's words, although full of every cliché religious teachings had to offer, somehow touched Delilah's wounded soul.

"Rivkie, I have to change my life. I want to be just like you. I want to have your goodness. I want to go out with only good, religious boys. Men with good hearts. I want to reach out to people and help them. I want to get married. Can you help me, Rivkie? Can you?"

them), little Chaim went
ing approval.
At first, he didn'
ruler in the hands o
palm as he walked
soon, Chaim cau
Hebrew vowels
the daily praye
ing attention
book. . . .
Aroun
to give h
palm b
nails
wou
wa
p

{ THREE }

When Chaim Levi was five years old, his grandfather, a Holocaust survivor and the venerated rebbe of a small *shteibel* in Ocean Parkway, enrolled him in a yeshiva in Williamsburg where the rabbis' beards were long and gray and they conversed as if the village in Poland they'd grown up in had been relocated, not wiped off the map.

Chaim's father, an electrical appliance salesman in Canarsie, beardless and dapper, was a man who respected tradition but knew which world he was living in. Still, out of respect and pity and guilt, he bent his will to his father's, hoping the old man might find in his grandson what had been lacking in his son.

Chaim was a handsome little boy, with big dark eyes and a shy, sweet smile. Not particularly bright, but good-natured and pleasant, as only the favored, longed-for man-child of a family starting from scratch could be (*kaddishel*, they called him, someone able to say the prayer for the dead for

to yeshiva with an expectant smile, never doubt-

really understand the meaning of the long, heavy
the bearded little rebbe, who slapped it against his
up and down between the rows of seated boys. But
ght on. *Smack!* For not getting your mouth around the
of the biblical verse fast enough. *Smack!* For not reciting
rs with enough devotion. *Slam! Smack! Crack!* For not pay-
for fidgeting in your seat, for forgetting to kiss the prayer

d the room the little rebbe went, gesturing impatiently for each
m their hand. Once in his possession, he would grip the small
tween his thumb and forefinger, slamming the ruler down on the
s often as it took to bring a howl. That accomplished, the hand
d be released. Then, astonishingly, the rebbe would jut his head for-
d and point to his cheek, indicating where the victim was expected to
ant a grateful kiss to thank him for his instruction.

At recess, when the boys finally escaped into the yard to play baseball,
calling the plays in Yiddish, there never failed to appear another little
rebbeleh, a gnomelike figure in a tallis and tefillin, who would rush into the
yard and insist on reciting his morning prayers at the top of his lungs, demanding that the boys stop playing and respond *Omeyn* in all the right
places. By the time the praying was over, so was the recess.

Chaim complained to his parents, who secretly raised eyebrows and
exchanged worried glances but nevertheless publicly backed the teachers.
He began to wet the bed. He broke out in hives. He bit his nails to the
quick, then let the ragged edges bleed.

He tried to learn, practicing the Hebrew words. He tried to sit still. To
pay attention. But when the rebbe (*wham!*) wished—for Chaim's own
good, of course—to (*WHAM!*) help free him of the unaesthetic and distasteful habit of nail-biting (*wham! Wham! WHAM!*), he felt a little vol-
cano suddenly erupt in his brain. He ran to the window of the classroom
and jumped down to the adjoining fire escape. Looking over his shoulder,
he quickly ran down two flights to the street. Once there, he carefully
spread-eagled himself on the pavement.

Carefully, he opened one eye, just in time to see the rebbe swoon, his
ruler clattering to the ground. The boys, hanging out the window, cheered.

With his parents' and the yeshiva's full agreement, another school was found for Chaim, an Orthodox Hebrew day school, where smooth-cheeked American rabbis cracked jokes, and public school teachers in high heels and red lipstick came in the afternoons to teach them about the Statue of Liberty and the *Mayflower*. A place with a gym and a basketball court and vending machines.

His grandfather was heartbroken.

But when the boy was actually able to recite Talmudic passages in Aramaic and knew the difference between a Rashi and a *tosefot*, he relented. Little Chaim had taken a detour but was nevertheless on an upward path toward taking over his grandfather's congregation. An *illuy*, a Talmudic genius, he wasn't. But when he put his mind to it—or was coerced or bullied into putting his mind to it—he managed to keep up with the class, although he never rose to more than a middling student.

He had little imagination, but he was good at memorizing. He memorized whole passages from the Talmud, which sometimes convinced a certain kind of dreamy and unduly optimistic teacher that he had a special aptitude for it. Truthfully, most of the time, he had no idea what the passage was about that he rattled off with such ease. He couldn't decipher it and wasn't interested in it. The give and take of Talmudic discussions he viewed with trepidation, fearing they would reveal his intellectual deficiencies. Still, he always managed to get A's in Talmud, which thrilled his grandfather.

When Chaim entered high school, his grandfather offered to pay his entire college tuition if he would consider getting *smicha*, rabbinical ordination. It was the old man's fervent hope that, when his time came, his grandson would step into his shoes, shepherding and nurturing the beloved congregation he would leave behind.

It was a generous offer, but Chaim wasn't so sure. To put it mildly, his grandfather's modest synagogue did not reek of enticing possibilities. His mental image of the place conjured up dusty, mostly empty pews and creaky tables laden with anemic sponge cake and plastic cups of cloyingly sweet wine, all set out to fete a congregation transferring with alarming rapidity from rent-controlled Bronx apartments to paid-up plots in Forest Lawn. The demographics of the neighborhood had changed. The building had future Baptist Temple written all over it.

All his friends were interested in careers in computers or accounting, neither of which thrilled him either. Basically, all he wanted was something respectable, where he wouldn't have to work too hard and which would provide him with a reasonable and steady income, enough to afford a two-family house in a better section of New Jersey, a Chevy station wagon, a JC-Penney charge card, and tuition at Hebrew day schools for his children.

What else did he need, really?

When it came to religion, he was not a cynic, like so many of his classmates, who were only in the lifestyle until they could escape their parents' clutches. He was simple in his faith, a sincere, Torah-observant Jew, a person who prayed and practiced, studied and struggled. A person who sometimes succeeded, sometimes failed, repented and tried again. And all through his growing years he eventually developed a trust that his faith would see him through every joy and sorrow. It didn't always make sense to him, the myriad laws, the intricate web of custom and lore that ruled every minute of his life, but it felt comfortable, like an old house that has its creaks and leaks but nevertheless embraces one with its sheltering arms. As for God, He was a comfortable, familiar presence, someone who sat next to him on the couch when he watched television, and who jogged alongside him in the park.

He never understood Maimonides' God, that cold, far-off, unknowable Being, more an intellectual exercise than a Father, who had nothing to do with the heart. He believed in a God Who listened to phone calls, heard prayers and whispers, and was not above lending a helping hand when the occasion required it.

Chaim was comfortable in his own skin, happy with his place in the world, the little niche he'd been born into. A poor imagination is sometimes a blessing. In Chaim's case, it helped him to ward off frightening visions of a future full of fierce ambitions to accomplish outlandish scenarios in which he would be the main character.

The idea of taking over from his venerated grandfather, someone he truly loved and respected and in whom he felt great pride, seemed preposterous. A rabbi? Someone who stood at the front and had all eyes glued to him? Someone others looked to for guidance and wisdom? He didn't see himself as a do-gooder or a leader or even a politician, all of which he understood were invaluable qualities in a pulpit rabbi. He much preferred—and planned for—the simple life of the follower and had no doubt he would eventually discover a leader whose devoutness, charisma, and brilliance would shine out like a lighthouse, leading him in the right direction.

His parents were satisfied. The last thing they wanted was for him to take over his grandfather's annoying and penurious congregation of pensioners, who kept pennies in jars and cooked meals on one burner. His mother, who knew a thing or two, was especially appalled by the idea of such an un-American profession for her one and only son, a job that promised bad pay, no advancement, and plenty of aggravation. She wanted him to be a dentist, which in her mind lacked all such drawbacks. His father wanted him to be happy and, if possible, to sell stereo systems.

At some point during his sophomore year in high school, he realized that math—necessary for both computers and accounting—was not his best subject. As for dentistry, he learned from a distant cousin, who had recently set up an office in Queens, that tuition to dental school rivaled that of medical school—that is, if you could get in, not a small question considering his grades. And even if you passed all the hurdles, you were still left with buying all that expensive equipment, unless you wanted to hire yourself out to an established office and work for someone else "forever for nothing," as his cousin put it to him. The student loans and the bank loans for the machinery would take years to pay off. Besides, people's breath in your face . . . the sound of the drill . . . the smell of those metals and powders and gummy pastes . . . ?

The summer between his junior and senior year, another cousin found him a job up in the Catskills as a busboy at a strictly kosher hotel. He lied about being eighteen, so they hired him. It was a nice enough place for the guests, but the staff lived in ratty, mosquito-filled bungalows and were fed leftovers by hotel owners who took the epithet "cheap bastards" to a new level. The food first went to the adults. A day later, whatever the adults hadn't managed to eat was served up in the children's dining room. Whatever the kids were bright enough to bypass showed up on the staff's plates.

So of course the waiters and busboys never saved anything, effectively ending the leftover problem. In fact, they felt spilling out the day-old milk before it was foisted on the unsuspecting babies (not to mention themselves) was a mitzva. When the owners somehow got wind of the situation, they started going through the trash. They were experts at eagle-eyed discoveries of unsqueezed lemons, which they insisted be washed off and served again.

The guests, however, were decent people, and the tips made the summer stay worthwhile, providing most of them with a good chunk of their college tuition and living expenses. So, Chaim stayed on. It turned out to be a fateful decision, because that summer, he experienced a revelation that changed his life forever.

One weekend, the hotel hosted its annual convention of the Council of American Orthodox Rabbis. Hundreds of Orthodox rabbis and their wives descended upon the resort from all over the country. Chaim had expected dignified men in dark suits, black hats, big skullcaps, and dark beards, men who were shy and retiring, whose weighty conversations would revolve around serious moral issues.

Instead, they arrived in shorts and flowery, big-printed Hawaiian shirts. Rabbis on vacation, he realized, were more or less like everyone else on vacation, with wives in short summer dresses and bikinis by the pool. The hotel was filled with loud laughter and card-playing. He hardly saw one of them crack open a book, let alone a heavy Talmudic tome. And in between, they would saunter into the auditorium and discuss "The Future of American Judaism."

It was then Chaim had his revelation: Rabbis were ordinary human beings. Nothing special. I could do this, he thought. But why would I want to?

One of the old-timers, a professional waiter who'd been around, told him that they used to have the National Council of Synagogue Youth conventions the week before the rabbis' convention, and then treat the most sincere kids to stay over and be inspired. But soon they switched the order, so the rabbis and their bikini-clad wives were gone before the kids got there.

And indeed, a week later, the kids showed up. A few of the rabbis stayed behind to organize seminars on Jewish values and modesty and service to the community. They changed into dark pants and white open-collared shirts. The fresh-faced, wide-eyed kids in their mid-to-upper teens, who had come from all over the country, gathered in small seminars in banqueting halls and on the lawn. The waiters poked one another and made snide remarks about jailbait. But Chaim, who in general didn't have a sense of humor about such things, said nothing. And then one evening, when he had cleaned off his table and eaten his dinner, he wandered into one of the seminars and sat down quietly in the back.

The rabbi giving the lecture was short and youthful, with immense energy that seemed to lift him off the ground as he spoke. "The most important two things in life are renewal and courage. Turn the page and begin again, as if you are starting from scratch; as if the world had never been created, and you are at that moment creating it. I'm not saying this is easy. I'm not telling you that you won't fail sometimes, that you'll never get depressed. Never give in to depression, whatever the reasons! Even if you feel the years have flown by and all your mistakes have just piled up, never despair. This is the greatness of our Creator: His compassion has no end. He will never give up on you, so never give up on yourselves. He knows who we are—He made us, didn't He?—so even the worst person, the biggest crook, the most evil gossip, is God's child, and God looks at him and, like a father, always hopes he'll turn it around. It's never too late.

"To be a Jew is to remember that we are in charge of makeovers. Not the kind with the hair and the nails. Universe makeovers. We take terrible situations where there is only evil—people who are unkind to one another and full of hatred—and we transform lives. We change things. And we start by changing ourselves.

"You, the youth of tomorrow, the leaders and rabbis and doctors and artists, you are going to make over the world you were born into. You are going to give it new hope, new chances to be the beautiful moral place our Creator envisioned when He separated the water from the dry land, when He set down Adam and his wife Eve. In every generation, you are Adam and Eve in Eden, able to start again."

Chaim studied the enthralled, uplifted faces of the young people around him. He too felt uplifted. To be a rabbi like that! To stand in front of a group of people and fill their hearts with hope, their minds with good intentions and proper desires. To lead people forward to a new place where they would be happier, kinder, and more just, making the world that much happier, kinder, and more just. It was a noble thing, was it not?

Could I? he wondered. Was it at all possible? What did it take to become a real rabbi? And did he have it in him?

He didn't know.

But as he looked over college brochures and added up the numbers for tuition and board at places like NYU or Columbia, the realization struck him that Brooklyn or Queens College were in his future, along with some express ticket to nowhere called a BA in education or sociology. So when his grandfather repeated his long-standing offer to underwrite Chaim's tuition at Bernstein Rabbinical College if he was accepted to their Rabbinic Ordination program, it suddenly seemed like a reprieve.

Bernstein expected its rabbinical students to get a secular degree as well. And having *smicha* didn't force one to actually become a practicing rabbi. Many a lawyer, store owner, and insurance salesman on Ocean Parkway had *smicha*.

In addition, at Bernstein he'd be assured of a steady social life, a stream of willing Orthodox girls who attended Stern College or Bernstein Women's College, many of them from well-to-do newly religious families, girls who, unlike those in the fancy Hebrew day school he'd grown up with (who wanted handsome Orthodox future doctors), would be only too thrilled to meet a nice Jewish boy from Brooklyn who came from a rabbinical family. At Bernstein these girls would be thrown in his direction in droves. No senior—however bad his teeth, poor his personality, or ordinary his family—would be permitted to get his diploma without a wife, and preferably a small noisy child, sitting in the audience to applaud him.

And some of these girls, he'd heard, the ones from down South or the Midwest, were real lookers.

He began his studies with the serious, dogged determination that had seen him through high school. He took classes in Talmud, contemporary Jewish law (*halacha*), and Introductory Rabbinic Survey. In addition, the school required him to concomitantly earn a master's degree in either Jewish education and administration, social work, or psychology, which he could opt out of only if he was willing to take six intensive semesters of advanced Talmud study, which was for him not an option, thanks. He opted for social work, which is what he thought being a rabbi was all about anyway.

In his rabbinic studies, he worked diligently, memorizing what he could and avoiding class participation whenever possible. He could repeat what you told him, almost word for word, but when asked to elucidate the law, to leap ahead to original conclusions, he was lost.

His teachers, compassionate men who had seen their share of losers, knew with whom they dealt. Keeping in mind the joys and struggles of their own early scholarship, as well as the apocryphal story of Akiva, the ignorant shepherd who was over forty when by sheer diligence he began a study program that turned him into Rabbi Akiva, one of Judaism's greatest scholars and leaders, they were not without hope. Rabbi Akiva had said that the image that had inspired him to greatness was that of water dripping on a rock until it finally made a hole. When they looked at Chaim, they saw the rock, imagined their words as water, and hoped for the best.

They gave him passing, if not wonderful, grades that would permit him to continue, so that other rabbis would have to deal with the situation and have it on their conscience each Yom Kippur. In this way, he passed from class to class and rabbi to rabbi until his four years were almost over and, except for one semester on a particularly difficult segment of the Talmudical tractate *Yoreh Deah* with a young teacher who graded him objectively and without compassion, he managed, miraculously, not to flunk anything.

In his social work courses he did especially well, finding a real affinity for the course material, which had no apparent discipline, scientific basis, or true information that one couldn't figure out simply by using average common sense. He felt triumphant, and looked ahead to a promising future out in the world, where grades would cease to matter, and no one would be checking his scholarship with a magnifying glass. All they would see was the *klaf smicha*, the traditional ordination certificate handwritten by a scribe on parchment, with his name carefully spelled out in calligraphic letters to prove his worthiness and competency to head an Orthodox congregation.

As his course work wound down and he began to envision his future, his thoughts turned more and more to the subject of marriage. Few and far between (in fact, he had never in his life heard of such a thing) was the congregation whose rabbi had no rebbitzin. Indeed, the interviews took the wife into consideration with almost equal weight. After all, she would be an integral part of his work. She would create the proper atmosphere in the synagogue, a hominess, openness, and warmth. She'd be up there in the front pew, setting an example with her diligent prayers, her friendly smile, her many well-disciplined children, her compassion, her modest clothing, her great hat, wig, and so on. She would set the style for the women, showing the ideal of wife and mother that each needed to aspire to, just as the rabbi set a shining example to the men with his good nature, good deeds, and scholarship.

Yet he never thought about the woman he would marry in terms of a work partner. He wanted, first and foremost, someone he could love and who would love him. He wanted someone he felt attracted to sexually. There had to be some chemistry, hormonal flows, a little tickle in his stomach. He liked nice legs and a shapely body, the same as any other man. He had been going out nonstop for years, date after date. He'd dated the sisters of fellow rabbinical students, the out-of-town rabbis' daughters (he hadn't gotten the lookers), even, desperately, some granddaughters from his grandfather's congregation. But nothing ever came of it. At most, it fizzled after date three.

Almost always, it was he who put an end to it, with blessings and relief.

He tried to analyze why this was so and came to the following conclusion: It was like the plate of roast chicken and mashed potatoes they put in front of you at a decent restaurant—perfectly adequate, probably good for you, but completely disappointing.

Why was it, he bemoaned, that he saw hundreds of beautiful, exciting, luscious girls every, single day—on the subway, in department stores, and on the crowded streets of Manhattan, Brooklyn, and Queens—and one was never tossed his way? How could it be that the laws of chance should have been so slanted against him?

So when his roommate, Josh, told him about his fiancée's roommate, a girl sincerely interested in finding a marriage partner, he didn't exactly leap at the chance.

"I don't know, Josh. I'm so tired of blind dates."

All those days comfortably behind him, Josh laughed sympathetically. "Here," he said generously, whipping out a photograph of his darling Rivkie sitting on the bed of her dorm room with several girls. "It's one of those."

Chaim studied the photograph. He recognized the pale sweet face of Rivkie. His heart sank as his eyes ran over two similar girls—both dark-haired and excellent rebbitzin material, he had no doubt—but then he stopped, zeroing in on a blonde who looked into the camera with no smile at all. She seemed to be staring right at him. And there was no doubt about it: She was definitely a looker.

{ FOUR }

*H*e went to Bernstein Women's College that Saturday night. He shaved closely and, on his roommate's advice, borrowed a nice blue sweater to wear over slacks, instead of his good Sabbath suit, which had a spill of schnaps on his lapel from that morning's kiddush. His hair was combed back and neat, but not greasy. His eyes were eager.

"Chaim Levi for Delilah Goldgrab," he told the housemother, who looked him over with a tentative smile of approval. Obviously, she had seen worse.

He sat on the sofa edge and fidgeted with the gray tweed upholstery beside other fidgeting young men, most of whom looked severe and distinguished in their black suits and homburg hats. Future sages of America, he thought miserably, cursing the little brat who had pushed passed him toward the pretzels and damaged his suit and probably his future.

Graduation and rabbinical ordination were just around the corner. He was eager to try out his skills with a congregation, feeling more and more certain that this was his calling in life. His job applications needed to be filled out; otherwise he'd have no choice but to work in the Bronx for his grandfather. This was not his first choice by any means, but it was something he could fall back on; he felt fortunate to have it. Among his classmates, he knew, there were many eager applicants for the few assistant rabbi and teaching positions available in normal geographical locations around the country, classmates who were smarter, better qualified, and more articulate than he. Leaving the space for Spousal Information blank was a sure way to ruin his chances. Nevertheless, job or no job, he told himself, there were limits to what a man could force himself to do, what he should be expected or required to sacrifice. This certainly included giving up any hope of happiness by marrying a woman for whom he had no passion.

He'd searched diligently through the sacred texts for backup and enlightenment on this score. What he'd come up with was advice that ranged from: *Rise up, my love, my fair one and come away. For, lo, the winter is past and the rain is over and gone. The flowers appear on the earth; and the time of singing is come . . . My beloved is mine and I am his.* To: *And I found more bitter than death the woman.*

It was confusing, Chaim thought, shaking his head, particularly since both sentiments were expressed by the same man, considered moreover to have been the wisest one of all, Solomon himself. Chaim's teachers had sometimes taken pains to explain away the discrepancies by pointing out that Solomon had written these things at different stages in his life. Still, Chaim wondered about taking marriage advice from a man who'd had a thousand wives and hadn't been happy with any of them.

He stared through the partition at the girls emerging from the elevator, all of them bright-eyed, attractive, and modestly dressed. Perky, he thought, depressed. He had been dating their clones for years. The sincere, "deep" conversations about the duties of Jewish parenthood and the sacredness of the home. And all the while, there was this subtle undercurrent of probing remarks designed to dig out how much money his parents had, where he expected to live, and if he would be learning full-time and expect her to be a Woman of Valor—breadwinner, bread baker, and babymaker rolled into one obviously saintly package—or if he would be bringing in some money too and, if so, how much and doing what?

Of course, none of these questions was asked openly and none of the answers was given frankly. All these conversations were always held on the highest moral ground, cloaked in the most impressive and saintly verbal packaging. Words like *tafkid be cha'im* (life's calling), *messirat nefesh* (dedication of one's soul), *gemilut chasadim* (charitable good works) were bandied about like the little hard candies thrown down at a Bar Mitzva boy to celebrate his successful reading of the Torah portion before the congregation, candies that often hit you in the head and accomplished minor concussions.

Then the elevator door opened and there she was. Or at least, he certainly hoped this one was his. He stood up. She was a vision in a slim skirt and green silk blouse, her blond shoulder-length hair tumbling to her shoulders in a mass of golden curls. He swallowed hard, mesmerized, thrilled, and incredulous at his good luck. He couldn't wait for her to give his name to the housemother. When she did, he took a step toward her. "Delilah?"

She looked up. He was taller than she, but only by a few inches, nothing like Yitzie. Nor did he have that sexy, rock-star slenderness around the hips or that certain way of moving—fluid and a bit dangerous—that never failed to give her those little pinpricks of electric shock. She took a deep breath, accepting that there would be no thumping heart, no flowing juices. Instead of that, there would be a perfectly respectable, good-looking young man, with a conventionally handsome face, fine dark eyes, and a square manly chin. Someone who would look good to her family and friends under the marriage canopy. A genuine Orthodox Jewish catch.

She began to imagine herself as a pious rabbi's wife. It's what she had been praying for, the opportunity to reform herself, to wash the slate clean. Besides, she was acutely aware that her shares on the *shidduch* market were in a highly volatile state right now. All that was needed was for some busybody to start a little rumor about her unhappy romance. It was like when people began to question whether butchers were really selling glatt kosher meat. Once there was doubt, prime ribs became chopped meat and it was all you could do to give them away.

She smiled at him. He smiled back, his kind open face guileless, his eyes almost childish in their innocent, unfeigned delight. He hid nothing, she thought, surprised and a bit contemptuous. He was hers. He would be easy to manage, not the touchy type who took offense or held a grudge or got angry—unless you banged him over the head with a hammer. And even then. The hair was too short, and that outfit . . . Still, she had seen much worse.

He watched as her sparkling blue eyes slowly took him in with approval. His sweater, he realized, had been the right choice. She wouldn't have liked a suit.

"Chaim?" she asked, and her white teeth, perfect and small and straight under cushiony lips, peeked out at him in a tiny secret smile. Oh, how he wished he could widen that smile, see those teeth in all their porcelain glory!

Is it necessary to expound upon the process of falling in love? The butterflies that wander through the digestive tract? The sweaty palms, the tickle below the belly button? The eyes that light up the object of desire like car headlights falling into a fog, all smoke and mirrors and nothing quite real? Let's just say it: From that moment on Chaim Levi was smitten. As such, he didn't understand anything that was happening.

They walked out into the New York night of twinkling lights and crowded streets, cars zooming, and couples walking arm in arm, their feet clicking against the pavement. He took her to a kosher delicatessen where religious couples on first dates often came. It was noisy and full of teenagers, and he regretted his choice immediately. He ordered pastrami on rye. She demurely ordered a salad, which she poked at tentatively, saying she had eaten so much all day, she wasn't really hungry. His sandwich smelled really good, she said appreciatively. With a great show of reluctance, she finally agreed to take half, feeding it to herself in greedy little bites. Pressed, she also agreed to order dessert, a gooey pecan pie that disappeared from her plate with surprising swiftness.

"I have a sweet tooth," she murmured, blushing a little with embarrassment.

She was so shy, he thought, entranced. So delicate, he thought in wonder, watching the color deepen on her pale golden skin as he spoke to her of his dreams and plans. She seemed immensely interested in everything he had to say, hanging on his every word as if it resonated with some hidden, kabbalistic meaning.

Basking later in the afterglow of the evening, he realized she hadn't spoken about herself at all. She remained as much a mystery to him as when he'd set out that evening to meet her.

～ ～

"So, *nu*?" Josh asked. When Chaim smiled but didn't answer, Josh tilted his head and nodded. "Oh, I see. But I should warn you—"

Chaim's ears pricked up.

"She's got a bit of a reputation."

"Delilah?"

"Well, just a few things, nothing serious—" Josh squirmed, aware that he should have had this information long before proposing this match.

Chaim interrupted him rather sharply. "Doesn't this fall under the category of evil gossip? Isn't it sinful?"

"When it comes to information about a *shidduch,* we are allowed to tell all. It falls under the category of *Before a blind man, place no obstacle.*"

Chaim, who wished to remain a blind man where Delilah was concerned, tried another tack. "Not all information is reliable."

"Oh, this is. It's from Rivkie."

The paragon of virtue herself. Now his curiosity was piqued. This was no idle gossipmonger, no catty, loose-lipped female out to destroy for the sheer joy of feeling her own power. No. If it came from Rivkie, and if she thought it important enough to send on to Josh, who thought it important enough to share, it would be stupid of him not to listen. And yet . . . the girl's body, her face, her golden hair, her mesmerizing eyes. If the information was compelling enough, it could paralyze him, making it impossible for him to reach out and take her, like the brass ring. And he had been on so many merry-go-rounds, ridden so many painted horses with their short dark sensible hair, bright eyes, and housewifely bodies that would no doubt balloon into a perfectly round *balaboosta's* after the first child was born. He wanted her.

"What?" he asked impatiently, because he had to.

"Well, she has been around the block, if you know what I mean. She had a boyfriend, and I understand the breakup wasn't fun. She was pretty hysterical about it."

"A boyfriend?"

This was unusual. Religious girls didn't have boyfriends. They had dates with prospective marriage partners. After a certain number of such dates—two or three for the extremely pious, maybe a dozen or so for lesser souls—a decision had to be made, a proposal offered that needed either to be accepted or refused.

"Breakup? You mean, she refused his proposal?"

Josh winced. "Not exactly. He never asked her. And they went out for quite some time."

Chaim studied him. This was not good. Protocol demanded that a relationship between a man and a woman be based on investigating the possibility of marriage, getting engaged, arranging the wedding details, then getting married. Anything else was *pritzus*, in other words, screwing around. A girl involved in a longtime relationship that had not resulted in marriage was one of two things: an unfortunate victim of an unscrupulous and non-Godfearing boy who had led her on; or a willing participant in a very unsavory and unacceptable liaison that marked her as nonkosher marriage material.

Chaim nodded, disturbed but not defeated. As he saw it, he now had two choices. Like a rabbi asked to judge whether a chicken was kosher, he could probe and probe its insides, examine its viscera, turning it over and over until he found some reason to call it *treife*. Or he could look at the chicken's owner to see if he was a rich man or a poor man, deciding how much he needed the chicken. Thinking of her, Chaim decided on the latter tack. Under no circumstances was he willing to call this chicken *treife*. That being the case, he thanked Josh for his honesty and his help, broadly hinting that he needed no more information.

"I appreciate what you are trying to do, Josh, really. But I know you and Rivkie would never have arranged for me to meet Delilah in the first place if you'd thought there was something wrong with her behavior."

That, of course, put Josh into a serious bind. What could he say? That he had not been aware of any of this until his Talmud study partner, who knew Yitzie from the neighborhood, had mentioned it in passing? And that only then had he squeezed the information out of Rivkie, who was on close terms with both Penina Gwertzman and Sharona Gottlieb and had reluctantly sought the source of her roommate's heartbreak—with the best of intentions, of course. Josh of course forgave her for not being worldly enough to understand the implications of such behavior. But to admit his error, he realized, would be to jeopardize his own infallible reputation, as well as that of his future wife, who had set this whole *tsimmes* boiling in the first place. Besides, all things considered, Chaim's other marriage prospects were not brilliant, and Delilah Levi seemed to be his heart's desire. Was it not written that *Forty days before conception a heavenly voice cries out, "This man for this woman?"* Who was Josh to argue?

He didn't, nodding in silent acquiescence and hoping for the best.

Two weeks before the wedding, Rivkie bumped into Delilah and Chaim on a street in Manhattan. Delilah, Rivkie thought, looked great. She was wearing a blue cashmere sweater and a slim skirt of supple black leather that ended just above her knees. She had on blue eyeshadow and liner, and fabulous red lipstick that Rivkie admired but would never, ever, have had the guts to wear. Rivkie noticed how Chaim looked at her. His yearning was almost palpable, like that invisible energy field around the body Chinese doctors are always fiddling with.

Delilah, who hardly ever went to class anymore and who hadn't been in the dorm room for weeks, was all smiles and hugs and kisses on the cheek.

"I'm having a beautiful dress made, in that building over there, on the sixth floor," Delilah said, looking up and pointing toward a factory loft on Seventh Avenue. "We got it wholesale. First I tried it on in Saks, and then my mother got our neighbor to get it from the factory. He's a button salesman, so he knows the wholesaler. And all I had to do was invite him to my wedding. It cost me a fraction!"

The skin of her throat was smooth and white as she arched her neck, pointing upward at the factory loft where, even as they spoke, her Queen for a Day dress was being hand-stitched by Guatemalan seamstresses in daily danger of INS raids. Rivkie watched Chaim watching her. And when Delilah turned around and spoke to him, she saw how he bent low and leaned in close with his ear toward her, looking into the distance and smiling vaguely, as if he were listening to music.

Delilah held out her engagement ring, a modest little thing but one that obviously thrilled her. "It's a marquise," she said, stroking it. "Isn't that a nice shape? I mean, for the price of a marquise you can get a round stone twice the size." She shook her head in delight. Only then did she remember Chaim. He didn't seem to mind.

"Rivkie, meet Chaim. He's going to be a rabbi," she said, and Rivkie could see that Delilah expected her to be astonished, and that she herself was astonished no less.

FIVE

*A*h, the wedding. Minor slights that had led to major family feuds and cutting decades-old silences had suddenly been forgiven. Animosities begun over Passover seder invitations and Rosh Hashanah cards and condolence calls withheld or insufficiently appreciated, were set aside. There was hope that all hard feelings would travel the labyrinthine road toward reconciliation, making their final exit via a white envelope containing a generous check. And so, forgotten relatives had been pursued in far away places like Hyattsville and Toronto. New cousins had been discovered. Old friends had been looked up. Addresses and phone numbers had been relentlessly tracked down with archival diligence through phone books and the Internet.

The guests came in alphabet subway trains from Brooklyn and Far Rockaway, in taxis from the Bronx, and in new Chevrolets from far-off Connecticut and Pennsylvania. They arrived early, or late, by Amtrak, Greyhound bus, and El Al flights from Tel Aviv. They poured into the ho-

tel's genteel lobby, gaping at the ceilings, marble floors, and vases of flowers, before crowding the elevators down to the banquet hall. They flooded
through the open doors like salmon swimming against the current in a desperate effort to reach the breeding grounds.

The glatt kosher caterer, who'd recently split with his brother-in-law in
a backstabbing family coup, obviously had something to prove. The room
reeked of gobsmacking culinary art: pirate ships with gangplanks and flags
sticking out of the red flesh of carved-out watermelons; little marzipan
Swiss villages nestled between chocolate mountains covered with whipped-
cream snow that jiggled precariously as overcome children butted their
heads against the table for a better look. And that was just the smorgasbord.

The older women wore long, pious polyester skirts and matching jackets from Boro Park. They wore elaborate gowns shaken out of mothballs
from a child's Bar Mitzva or wedding or Loehmann's back-room bargains
with slashed-off designer labels. They wore hats with feathers and satin
bows. The most religious wore human hair wigs, newly washed and set in
festive big-hair styles.

Some of the younger married women also wore wigs, but they were
long and smooth and sexy, in daring shades of blond and red, bouncing
around their shoulders as they walked or danced. But mostly, unlike their
mothers, they wore fashionable head scarves tied with exotic panache the
way girls out on the settlements do in Israel. They wore flashing engagement rings and matching diamond wedding bands, and intricate gold
necklaces with matching bracelets from H. Stern or Fortunoff.

The singles in their late teens and early twenties, cousins and friends of
the bride and groom, milled around, shooting each other shy, searching
looks. The young men's hair had been cut, their beards trimmed or their
cheeks newly shaved. They wore dark suits and ties like the groom—
except for the Israelis, who came in inappropriate sweaters, or short-
sleeved white shirts with no ties, and pants that didn't really fit. On their
heads they sported dark wide-brimmed hats, or crocheted skullcaps with
geometric designs, or the silly white yarmulkes left in a basket by the door
for those who had come in with nothing at all.

The girls they eyed so optimistically had just been to the beauty salons
or had blow-dried their hair themselves until their arms ached. They'd had
their nails done and their eyebrows tweezed and wore makeup that ranged
from an artistic touch here and there to heavy coats of every conceivable
goo and paste.

They wore long dresses from the post-Christmas reduced racks at Lord & Taylor, Macy's, and Filene's. Or well-cut suits from Ann Taylor or Talbot's petite section, which are hardly ever on sale, and then only in size two or fourteen. They wore gold bangle bracelets and little shiny gold necklaces with five-cornered stars, or Chai or names like Sarah, Rivka, Chana, and Rachel spelled out in golden Hebrew letters made by Israeli jewelers.

And then there were the outcasts, the great unwashed, the children of cousins whom one simply cannot uninvite; who always show up at family celebrations in lesser or greater numbers, dressed in jeans and sneakers and uncombed hair or low-cut dresses with sequins missing; who look like they have just gotten up from the couch after watching a Sunday movie and who never seem to feel underdressed or out of place or even aware of the chagrin and pain their insulting carelessness is causing their hosts. They are the people everyone does their best to pretend aren't there at all, particularly those who invited them.

Toward the back, away from the band, in the best seating area, sat the small cluster of Gentiles: the black woman in a sleeveless Donna Karan dress, looking fabulous; the long-haired programmers; the short red-haired accountant. They smiled with discomfort at one another and the people around them, wide-eyed in the fashion of tourists to Indian reservations, who are anxious to observe the folkways of the natives with stalwart respect.

Teeming hordes of children, looking well-combed and uncomfortable in their shiny, stiff shoes and elaborate outfits, chased one another around the hall, stealing cakes and nuts off plates like locusts, tugging at their parents' legs. The little boys ran wild in white shirts and manly ties, while the little girls wore either miniature versions of whorish fad fashions or old-fashioned picture-book dresses that made them look like dolls.

Up and back they ran, holding sloshing glasses of Coca-Cola, which they refilled at an alarming rate, pushing aside the older men, who waited patiently and diffidently to ask for their glass of scotch and a glass of semi-dry white wine or rum Coke for their wives. The women would drink half a glass and put it down, already feeling themselves growing dizzy and drowsy from the unaccustomed experiment with alcohol that didn't consist of one sip from a communal wineglass Friday night.

There was mixed seating—that is, men and women, husbands and wives and children, all seated at the same tables. But there was also a small section in the rear with a *mechitzah*, so that the more distinguished rabbis wouldn't be forced to sit with their wives. The rebbitzins sat together with their marriageable daughters, all wishing to make a public display of adherence to the most pious stringencies in Jewish law, stringencies invented by the fortunate men who sat all day in study halls and thus had all the time in the world to rescue God from His horrible mistakes in neglecting to include such laws in His Torah and Talmud.

The men's tables included the elderly rabbis and their sons and grandsons, and even some of the more *farchnyokt* friends of the groom, who looked over the elderly scholars the way some men ogle single girls, savoring the possibilities. The thrill of talking to the great Rabbi So-and-so! How they would astonish their friends (and perhaps some unlucky prospective bride on some far-off *shidduch* date) with this tale. How they had brought up some intricate point of law and how the great Rabbi So-and-so had cocked his head and nodded approval as he listened, spellbound, to an explication. Imagine!

Religious men are the worst name-droppers. They will spend half a date regaling you with their exploits in cornering some octogenarian who is—or one day might be—a member of the Council of Sages, whose photos or garish oil portraits appear on posters in Crown Heights, Williamsburg, Geulah, and Bnei Brak like rock stars.

But if a man isn't interested in women before he has a wife, in all likelihood he is bound to be even less interested once he gets one. So any single guy at a wedding who prefers to sit next to bearded sages is not, generally speaking, a good marital prospect.

You see them sometimes, walking four paces in front of their wives and children in parks and zoos during the Intermediate Days of Festivals like Succoth and Passover, barely turning their heads to catch what their wives are saying. They are the ones who take the seat next to the cabdriver, leaving their wives to manage the task of stuffing themselves, a baby, a two-year-old, a carriage, and luggage into the back.

The single girls made their way around the hall, searching for someone who would give them a ride home. That is always the most urgent need when attending a Jewish wedding in Manhattan. You simply do not want to ride out to Brooklyn or Queens on the New York City subway system after 10 P.M. In fact, you do not want to ride anywhere on the New York City subway system at any time, period. The second reason, though, was always more important. You wanted to walk out with your pick from the most eligible single men, ensuring a good hour alone with him. It was considered a party favor, much more urgent and useful than catching the bride's bouquet.

Everyone agreed that the singles crowd at Delilah's wedding was promising, filled with Bernstein and Yeshiva University students, candidates for rabbinical ordination, and third-year dental, law, and medical school students, not to mention the few who already had their degrees in science, engineering, and accounting.

The music began, and Chaim, held at either elbow by his smiling father and chuckling father-in-law, was escorted toward his bride for the bedecking ceremony. He walked clumsily, his legs trembling, his face serious and intent, giving the appearance of one being dragged to his fate, as his friends clapped and sang all around him.

Delilah sat on a throne, flowers strewn around her, her face radiant with triumph. The blond down on her face caught the light, bathing her in a kind of golden shine like those photos of Marilyn Monroe, making her irresistibly beautiful and desirable. You could see the men in that room skip a step and miss a clap as they neared her, breathless.

Chaim too. He seemed mesmerized. The moment when the Jewish groom traditionally avoids Jacob's error by looking carefully into the bride's face to be sure it is really her and not her plain elder sister, before covering her face with the veil, went on almost embarrassingly long. Chaim just kept staring until finally, with an almost imperceptible look of exasperation, the bride finally reached up and pulled the veil down herself.

Delilah's wholesale gown was lovely, a luxurious silk satin, covered with beaded lace, with a long lace-edged train and little puffed lace sleeves tied at her upper arms with a bow. Many religious girls tend to line such sleeves. Obviously, Delilah had opted to skip it, and her flesh shone through the lace like honey. On her head she wore a little hat, like a medieval queen's headdress—very original—covered with the same lace and a double veil of stiff netting.

There were some frowns of disapproval among the older wig- and hat-wearers about the lacy sleeves, but if Delilah noticed she certainly didn't seem to care. She floated down the aisle with the joyous self-congratulation of a Camilla Parker-Bowles while on either side her mother and mother-in-law, carrying candles, made attempts to keep up with her.

Mrs. Goldgrab's face was like an enormous twinkling ornament atop a Christmas tree. Swathed in her sequined rose-colored gown, she threw smiles and waves in all directions. Chaim's mother, on the other hand, walked with her head down, staring at her shoes, an aggravated smile pasted on her lips.

Some of the guests stood or sat attentively through the long ceremony with its many blessings, while others retreated to their places at the tables to examine the first course—a cold dish left waiting on the table so as to hurry the festivities along, ensuring the surly waiters an early exit.

It was a nice ceremony, very traditional, conducted by the groom's venerable grandfather, whose hand shook as he handed the wine-filled silver goblet to the groom, who handed it to his father, who handed it to his mother, who finally lifted the bride's veil and helped her take a sip. Two drops fell slowly, barely noticeable except to the most discerning and those looking for bad omens, staining the white lace.

Escorted by musicians and the dancing, singing friends of the ecstatic bridegroom, the young couple were led off to a private *yichud* room, as was the custom, for their half hour of alone time before rejoining the festivities.

In the meantime, the first course, following the cold plate, was served, a choice of salmon filet or chicken livers in a phyllo dough. And although everyone was already stuffed from the buffet, they opened their mouths wide and devoured this too as everyone waited for the young couple to rejoin the festivities so the dancing could begin.

Rivkie, who had come with a much put-upon and reluctant Josh, was on her way to the bathroom when she noticed Delilah sitting alone on a couch in the lobby, just staring at the tiny wine stain on her dress, rubbing it with her finger. She seemed slightly pale. Chaim was nowhere to be seen.

"Beautiful wedding!" Rivkie called out to her tentatively.

Delilah smiled in vague acknowledgment.

"Where's your new husband?"

Delilah looked up. "Oh, Chaim? He went to talk to a rabbi, some urgent problem—God knows what now. You know, they delayed the ceremony half an hour because one of the letters in the marriage contract wasn't clear enough? Or maybe it was the date. Try to get a roomful of rabbis to agree on anything . . . and nothing moves until they make up their minds." She shrugged. She seemed listless. "Are you having a good time?"

"Wonderful. Everything is beautiful. The food is great. I love the band . . . and your dress is heavenly."

She brightened. "They stained it with the wine, but I'm sure dry cleaning can get it out. Not that I'll be needing it again anytime soon." She laughed, but you could tell she didn't think it was particularly funny.

And then Chaim showed up, a little sweaty and nervous, with a big smile. Behind him were photographers and friends and a man carrying a flute.

Seeing the crowd, a transformation came over Delilah. Like a toy with a new battery, she bounced up, daringly taking Chaim's hand—bride and groom traditionally avoiding physical contact in public—as the cameras clicked away. Color flooded her cheeks. She threw back her head and laughed as the music started up, dancing her way into the banquet hall. Then everyone got up to form circles, the women bearing away the bride, and the men the groom. As they parted Chaim turned, looking back longingly in her direction.

Delilah stared eagerly straight ahead, never looking back at all.

{ SIX }

As the last relatives finally left and the catering staff folded up the soiled linen, Chaim and Delilah made their way upstairs to their hotel room. It was not the bridal suite, but a room specially ordered to suit the needs of the religious bride and groom. So, unlike most wedding suites, it had twin beds, not a double.

They were both a bit awkward, a bit overwhelmed.

Delilah sat down in an armchair in her wedding dress, the bag with the cards and checks in her lap. It was a nice room, even if it was a little cramped, she thought, just a tad disappointed. She stared at the wedding gifts that lay piled up in a corner, all their festive wrappings and bows a bit frayed by being dragged around. Her head swam from glasses of champagne and rum Cokes and even a Bloody Mary, all of which she had managed to order and somehow actually consume.

Chaim approached her shyly, taking the bag from her hands and laying it on top of the table.

ancient Jewish canon. The moment he took her virginity, he would be her
baal in every sense.

He tried to pace himself. He wanted to be considerate, not to frighten
her or—God forbid!—hurt her in any way. All this had been impressed
upon him by mentors provided for him in the yeshiva, kindly rabbis and
older married students who had volunteered for bridegroom consulta-
tions. He tried to control himself, but to his surprise he found himself
clutched and held and pressed and fondled. He was thrilled, even as it
dawned on him that slowly, but surely, he was no longer in control. He
thrust against her, and to his surprise there didn't seem to be anything
standing in the way. But before he could give that another thought, great
paroxysms of uncontrolled feeling and sensation took hold of him, blot-
ting out all rational thought. He felt himself pulled up and up and up and
then suddenly released, allowed to free-fall down the precipice. He lay
back, panting and almost unconscious.

He reached out to touch her, but she was already gone into the bathroom to wash herself off. The towel, too, was gone. Reluctantly, he moved
over to the other bed, as is the custom, the bride and groom separating the
moment that the "red rose" appeared. She would need to count seven clean
days before they could meet again. It was maddening. It was Jewish law.

⌒ ⌒

They had breakfast in bed, a sinful luxury, he thought, a bit embarrassed to
let in room service, who rolled in a serving cart with juice, bread, jam, little
boxes of cereals, silver carafes of milk and coffee, and a basket of fragrant
warm muffins. She wore one of his undershirts, her blond hair tousled and
adorable over her shoulders, her eyes heavy-lidded and satisfied.

"Are you all right, my love?" Chaim asked her, concerned.

"A little sore. There was a lot of blood. Good thing I remembered the
towel," she murmured.

He felt guilty and proud and manly.

She pulled the tray toward her and began to eat.

"Whoa, aren't you forgetting something, my love?" he remonstrated
gently, a bit surprised. She hadn't gone to the bathroom to ritually wash
her hands, spilling water over each lightly held fist three times, to rid her
body of the lingering impurity of nighttime spirits, a ritual followed by
every Orthodox Jew, who believed touching anything with such hands
would not only be sinful but unhealthy.

"I think we should put a towel down first. The hotel staff," she murmured.

"I'm sure they've seen everything." He laughed, touched by his bride's delicacy of feeling. He felt worldly and lusty next to her hesitation. It was just as it should be, he thought. He would be gentle with her, since she was obviously scared. And why not? A religious Jewish bride, so sheltered, so pure! Anything else would have been strange and suspect.

"I brought my own towel, from home," she said. "That way, I can just take it with us. I wouldn't want to steal a hotel towel. Please, just move over, will you?"

He rolled over, watching her outline as she bent over the bed, smoothing down the towel.

"Do you want me to put on a light?"

"No!" she shouted, and once again he felt moved and impressed by the touching urgency of her panic.

He chuckled. "It's okay. Shhhh. I'm sorry, forgive—"

She pulled the nightgown over her head, taking his breath away. By the faint light of the bedside radio and the streetlamps, he examined his bride, absolutely mesmerized, stunned by the outlines of her slim waist and thighs and generous breasts as she got into the bed and sidled up next to him. In a moment, he was lost in the silken feel of her skin, the scent of her warm body, like no other perfume, impossible to bottle. He felt himself transported to another place, a heavenly sphere he had never even dreamed of. Only a poet could have such dreams, he thought as he pulled her close to him, delighting in every new, thrilling adventure that beggared his poor imagination.

He wanted to immerse himself in every aspect of her otherness, to command it, to own it, to make himself part of it. He ran his hands over the taut youthful waist, tracing how it billowed out into her slim hips and softly rounded thighs. Those warm secret thighs!

He was owner and lover and, like a man who has purchased a priceless work of art, he felt both the pride of acquisition and the frustration of knowing this thing was outside him, unknowable. *Baal,* he thought, the ancient Hebrew term for husband which meant *owner.* It was also the name of an ancient Canaanite god. She was his, and she would worship him and adore him as all things male, her first and only man, he comforted himself, thrilled, relying on the sex advice sprinkled with delicacy throughout the

"Plenty of time for that in the morning," he said, deadly earnest, reaching out to squeeze her.

Well, she thought, looking up at him. Well, well.

Gently, she pushed his hands away. "I'll just be a minute, darling," she told him, getting up and escaping into the bathroom with her overnight bag. Inside the bag were two nightgowns. One was a filmy white see-though bridal number with an equally filmy white dressing gown. The other she had noticed when another girl shopping in Macy's had held it up to show her girlfriend, saying, "If I wore this, my boyfriend would kick me out of bed." When they'd both stopped laughing and put it back, Delilah had bought it. It was a long pink number, totally opaque, with a high neck and long sleeves.

Quickly, she stuffed the white gown back into the bag and hung the other up on the door hook. She stepped into the shower, shivering under the stream of hot water. Even as she dried her clean hot skin afterward, she still felt goose bumps as she slid the pink gown over her head. Carefully, she reached into the bag and took out something else she had specially prepared.

"Shut off the lights, Chaim, will you?" she called through the closed door.

"If you want," he answered, without enthusiasm.

She turned off the bathroom lights and then opened the door. The room seemed pitch dark. Chaim was already in bed. He moved over to the edge, reaching out for her.

"You are still dressed!" he said, disappointed, as his hands touched the material.

She reached back. He was totally nude.

"I . . . thought . . ." she stammered. "You're a rabbi!"

"Maimonides says clearly that whatever a man and wife do together in the sanctity of their marriage bed is perfectly fine."

"Whatever?" she said doubtfully.

"Whatever," he repeated decisively. "There is no shame, no bound-aries. Everything is kosher. We are married. You went to the *mikva*. We can just enjoy ourselves. Now, why don't you take that silly thing off? Please, honey?" he wheedled.

"Well, if you're absolutely sure, just . . ."

"What?"

a rabbinic attempt to prevent sin. Now, more than ever, he was painfully aware of the discrepancies. There was nothing wrong with touching her, according to Divine law. It was the rabbis who had come up with this particular prohibition, one of those they considered "building a fence around the law." These were laws meant to create a moat into which men might fall should they even move in the wrong direction. They were a barrier to help men from falling prey to urges that might push them to actually— God forbid!—transgress the Divine will as understood from the Five Books of Moses.

In the eyes of the rabbis who'd created this particular fence, the progression from handing a woman a dish to undressing her and taking her to bed was immediate, inevitable, and forgone. A done deed.

The stringency kings had, as usual, added their own outlandish roadblocks a few hundred miles forward of the rabbinic fence, even forbidding a father and daughter over the age of three from being alone in the house together. But instead of creating a society of saints, their overzealousness and suspicion of human nature was creating a society of perverts, Chaim thought, people who defended and praised such prohibitions, who claimed to understand and agree with such thinking. Ironically, it was these people who were constantly popping up in the headlines for being caught indulging in every perversion known to man. But that was true in all religions. Safe in the privacy of their own homes and secure in the knowledge that their victims will be gagged by the strongly enforced communal code of silence that holds the washing of dirty laundry in public to be a worse sin than actually soiling it in the first place, religious zealots of all stripes find the border between strict religious morality and absolute depravity unguarded and easily crossed.

Chaim was not a stringency king. He believed in moderation in all things, but he was also deeply committed to Jewish law. The avoidance of physical contact was nerve-racking for them both, Chaim assumed. Surely, she must hate it as much as he did. "I'm sorry, my love," he kept whispering to her. "I wish I could . . ." and there he interjected a long series of predicates over which even Delilah found herself blushing.

My, my, she thought. Who would have suspected? She looked at him with a growing fondness.

The successful hurdle of her bridal night complications left Delilah sweet-tempered and unusually congenial. While she was not particularly

pile, to await the garbage trucks of forgetfulness that would hopefully clank along soon, dumping the lot into a landfill soon to be smoothed over and readied for the building of the lovely mansion that she would inhabit for the rest of her life. Soon, she hoped, the whole lot would be incinerated, so that it would all finally seem like a bad dream, as if it had never happened at all.

She had a sudden, wicked thought that her parents, most of all, were on top of that pile, never to hinder or badger or push her again. She'd invite them over a few times a year, she thought, until they were stuck in wheelchairs in old-age homes and she'd be forced to visit them. And she would, if she wasn't too busy.

They took a short trip to the bank to open an account and deposit the loot; then they checked out of the hotel, getting the bellboy to help them load their belongings into a taxi. They tipped him generously, using some of the bills that had been stuffed into the white envelopes, which they decided to stick in their wallets instead of sensibly storing in their new account.

Their first home was a small apartment in the Bronx near his grandfather's synagogue, where Chaim would be employed as assistant rabbi until the next listing of job openings for rabbis was sent to him from his alma mater, which ran an employment service for its graduates. The listings were sent out every six months. Although he had tried to find another position before the wedding, he had had no success. People like Josh, of course, had been snapped up by well-regarded congregations in the suburbs. But for lesser luminaries, the opportunities were less than abundant: an assistant rabbi in Nebraska, a youth leader in Terre Haute. He'd decided to do the sensible thing and wait.

He was a bit deflated when they walked into their first apartment, both of them carrying packages like an old married couple home from their weekly shopping trip. The moment should have been magic; he wanted to carry her over the threshold like something in an old *I Love Lucy* episode, playfully groaning under her delicious weight, her warm body next to his. He felt deprived and resentful, even as he faithfully did his best to adhere to the strictest letter of Jewish law, being careful not to touch her, not even to sit next to her on the couch or hand her a plate.

Unlike most of his coreligionists, who only knew what was allowed and what was forbidden, he possessed the knowledge to make fine distinctions between Divine and rabbinic law: what was really a sin, and what was

She hesitated. "Oh, I did that earlier, my love," she said breezily. "When you were still asleep." She kissed him, even though it was forbidden. He opened his mouth to protest, then shut it. Then she took a knife and spread some jam on a muffin.

"My darling, those muffins . . . they are from the hotel bakery; they don't have any rabbinical *hechsher*, so we can't know if they're kosher."

"But it's just flour, oil, water, and sugar. What could be wrong with it?" she asked him, already feeding herself tiny pieces as she pulled it apart.

"But, really, darling, you shouldn't."

She looked up at him, annoyed.

Should he press her, he wondered, his new bride? Was it worth having a fight over, the morning after their wedding, when no doubt her nerves were frayed? There was such a thing as a pious fool, he told himself, the man who won't rescue a drowning woman because he is too religious to touch a female that isn't his close relative. He wasn't a fool, he told himself. Besides, she was probably right; there wasn't anything forbidden in them. Really, who would make the effort to locate and bake with pig fat in New York City in these cholesterol-conscious days?

He let it go but made a point to wash and dress, feeling he had to set a good example. "I'm going out on the balcony to daven," he told her, taking his prayer book and tefillin with him. When he was finished with his morning prayers, he came back in.

He longed to take off his clothes and get back in with her under the covers. Instead, he sat in a chair across from her, silently eating his certified-kosher Kellogg's breakfast cereal with milk and drinking his coffee and freshly squeezed orange juice, thinking all the while how adorable she looked in his undershirt, her white thighs perfect, her ankles slim, her toenails sparkling with color. According to Jewish law, it would be almost a week before he'd be able to so much as touch her again.

It was maddening.

After breakfast, they ripped open the envelopes and added up their cash and checks, smiling, feeling overwhelmed with happiness and riches. They laughed at the wedding gifts, groaning over the third toaster and fourth blender, exclaiming over the intricately carved silver ritual objects.

With each tearing away of wrappings, Delilah felt the injustices of her deprived childhood recede farther back in memory, their sting softening. Images and memories of middle-income red-brick housing projects, bad haircuts, and dime store shopping trips were tossed onto a mental junk

thrilled to be living in an apartment in the Bronx, she was grateful Chaim would have an immediate income until a suitable position with a lovely home in some leafy, pine-scented suburb came their way.

For the first week, she wandered around the rooms of her little home, touching all her new things. Everything thrilled her: the flatware with their colorful enamel handles, the dinnerware set for twelve with all the matching serving pieces, glasses of all sizes in sets of six, stain-resistant white tablecloths, brand-new no-iron polyester/cotton sheet sets, and dozens of towels. She looked proudly over her new china closet filled with wedding silver and lovely crystal bowls and porcelain. In fact, when they delivered her formal dining room set—something her mother had never been able to afford—she waited for the delivery men to leave and then sat down by the table, rubbing her hand across the sweet-smelling polished wood. She found tears of joy streaming down her cheeks as she contemplated her good fortune and the beautiful life that surely lay ahead of her.

Carefully, she dusted the shelves of their new wooden bookcases, filled with her husband's library: the tricycle-sized volumes of the Talmud and dozens and dozens of other Hebrew tomes: the Pentateuch, books on Jewish law, Jewish history, philosophy, and custom. There were also more popular works, the sound-bite Judaism books that gave you a mitzva a day to do, a Jewish ethic a day to explore, a Jewish value a day to review, and 1001 Jewish jokes for speechmakers. Joining them were Dale Carnegie's *How to Win Friends and Influence People*, Norman Vincent Peale's *The Power of Positive Thinking*, and even some novels left over from various periods in his youth and from various college courses: *Marjorie Morningstar*; *Inside, Outside*; *The Winds of War*; *The Chosen*; *Moby Dick*; *Bleak House*; *The Iliad*; *The Macmillan Handbook of English*; *Eichmann in Jerusalem*.

She brought few belongings of her own: clothes, music disks, her computer, photographs, her high school yearbook, which showed her in a short booster outfit (she never made cheerleader). There were also some of her own favorite books: *Valley of the Dolls*, *Gone with the Wind*, *Jepthe's Daughter*, *Little Women*, and *The Rainbow*—which, along with a few other books by D. H. Lawrence, actually belonged to the public library out in Rockaway.

She had another few months of school to go before she graduated and earned her dental hygienist's license. Her plan was to get a job in some very affluent dental practice and work there for clothes money until she got pregnant. She looked forward to working, trying out her skills, earning her own money. Being married didn't make her feel like an adult. The opposite. She felt as if she'd gone straight from her parents' home to her husband's home, despite the three years of dorming, which never really counted because she'd been obliged to go back home for weekends.

Each morning before leaving for school, she'd prepare Chaim's breakfast, which she'd leave on the table in a covered plate awaiting his return from morning prayers. Chaim would sit down by the table in the empty house, missing her, as he ate his lonely cornflakes and drank his black coffee, before settling himself into the work of assistant rabbi, which consisted of spending long hours in front of open volumes with tiny Hebrew lettering as he laboriously prepared his maiden speech before his grandfather's congregation.

He felt the sweat curl the tiny hairs on his forehead as he delved into the weekly Torah portion, searching for a sentence on which to build a twenty-five-minute talk that would display his erudition, wisdom, and wit. He wanted to enlighten, but also to entertain. When he finished, to his dismay, he found he had twenty minutes of erudition, five of wisdom, and none of entertainment. He closed the books, kissing them and putting them away.

Maybe it wouldn't matter, he told himself. After all, most of these people were used to his grandfather's rambling sermons on the finer points of Talmudic exegesis delivered in an accent that was hard to decipher if you weren't familiar with the speech patterns of American immigrants from that particular corner of the Sudetenland. Besides, most of them didn't hear very well and tended to use speech time to nap, girding themselves for the *mussaf* prayers that were to follow, most of which had to be done on their feet, exhausting for people of that age.

His plan was to win over the congregation not with speeches but with good deeds. By visiting the sick, bringing succor to the bereaved, being friendly and interested in the lives of his grandfather's flock, he knew he could bring them a caring energy that only youth could provide. His grandfather never got around much anymore, his weekly visit to a nearby chiropractor the only outing he continued to make on a regular basis.

Their first Sabbath, Delilah agonized over what to wear to the synagogue. Should she wear a wig, the only one she owned, a long, blond number purchased for exactly such an occasion, or a stylish hat in which most of her own hair would show? Or should she wear one of those horrid hair

And when Chaim finished, closing his book and kissing it, wishing everyone "Good Shabbes," and his grandfather got up to hug him, as if he were a Bar Mitzva boy, the synagogue erupted with interjections of goodwill and praise: *"Yasher koach."* "God bless you." "The apple doesn't fall far." The men's voices rang out, and the women stopped fidgeting. A few came over to Delilah to shake her hand, and their wrinkled arthritic fingers— like old white parchment—were cool against her young warm skin. "You must be so proud!" they told her. "A wonderful job!"

Delilah felt touched and filled with reciprocal warmth.

And then the service was over, and the people filed out as fast as their canes and walkers would allow them, navigating the staircase to the first floor social hall where gray-haired ladies in old-fashioned hats had laid out paper plates with various types of herring and gefilte fish stabbed with toothpicks, plates of dull sponge cake, and stale-looking Stella d'Oro cookies that smelled of anise. No one touched the food until the old rabbi arrived, pouring the red sweet Malaga wine—so thick you could cut it with a knife—into a silver cup, making the kiddush benedictions over it. That taken care of, the ladies brought out steaming platters of brown potato kugel and *cholent*—a dark meat-and-bean stew cooked overnight—which had enough fat in it to clog the last open space in any artery still actually allowing blood to pass through.

Delilah stood by Chaim's side as one by one the members of the congregation filed past, smiling at her and shaking Chaim's hand as the venerable rabbi they adored looked on benevolently. It was lovely, she thought, to be the center of so much positive attention.

She tried to tell herself she was lucky. That she had everything. That she'd been blessed. That it wasn't so bad she hadn't had a honeymoon, some tropical getaway where she could wear a bikini and lie near sparkling pools of turquoise water, lathered with suntan lotion, as sarong-clad men and women plied her with icy smoothies and fresh pineapple speared with festive paper umbrellas. That she could live with the two weeks of physical separation each month; that it would give her private time to read and watch TV in bed when he couldn't lay his hands on her. In fact, secretly, she thought it might be a relief.

In bed, she had noticed, his passion rose quickly and tanked accordingly. He had a self-congratulatory way of smiling afterward that she found irritating. He always rose fastidiously and returned to his own bed, leaving her behind to deal with sticky sheets and rumpled blankets. At first, she

THE SATURDAY WIFE — 65

prayer—steps that separate Orthodox Jews from their well-meaning, but ignorant, Jewish born-again cousins or from curious secular visitors or Gentiles—she could hear the small hiss of relief.

A *shaine maidel*. A beautiful girl.

A *frum* girl. A religious girl.

The rabbi's granddaughter-in-law!

A good match for his brilliant, pious grandson Chaim, their future leader. She could feel their happiness for the good fortune that had befallen their beloved rabbi and his family. It pricked the layers of her heart, making her feel that she didn't want to disappoint them, the way Princess Diana hadn't wanted to disappoint her cheering, devoted subjects, no matter how that Royal thing worked out.

When Chaim got up to speak, she felt herself grip her prayer book as she watched him walk down the aisle and climb up to the podium. He wore a black Sabbath suit and a wide-brimmed hat. He looked like a generic yeshiva boy, she thought, a bit dismayed. The yeshiva day schools disgorged them in colorful crocheted skullcaps, sweatpants, and basketball jackets, and Bernstein got hold of them and turned them into dour, serious, prematurely aged men in dark suits and glasses. There were legions of them, all interchangeable, like those stuffed or plastic effigies mass-produced in the wake of some hit movie. At least he was clean-shaven, she comforted herself. A beard would have been the last straw.

She was anxious for him to do well. She sat back, listening at first. It was about buttons, she realized. Should a button sewn onto a shirt as a spare—the extra button—be considered *muktzeh*, untouchable, on the Sabbath? She stuck with him for a while, listening as he detailed the problem. *Muktzeh* was a rabbinical category in which all things forbidden to use on the Sabbath by Divine decree also became forbidden to touch by rabbinic decree. And if one lived in an area in which one couldn't carry on the Sabbath, because there was no *eruv* (a fictitious boundary which encircled an area making it one and thus permitting one to carry from one place to the next), could one wear a shirt with such a button?

She looked around nervously, wondering if everyone was as excruciatingly bored as she. Discounting the nappers, she realized with relief that the men had their eyes fixed upon her husband with approval and pleasure. And while the women did shift nervously, their chatter rising above the volume and intensity generally to be expected in the women's section of Orthodox synagogues during the rabbi's speeches, it seemed all right.

snoods so popular in Boro Park among the women who took the Woman of Valor song literally (*Charm is a lie, and beauty is worthless; a God-fearing woman brings praise upon herself*). She had one in her closet, purchased to wear to the ritual baths if she wanted to shampoo her hair before she got there, saving time. It was black with little silver sparkles, hugging her head like those towel turbans in the shampoo ads, making her look like an Italian film star in the forties. The wig, on the other hand, made her look like Farah Fawcett when she was plastered on the bedroom walls and lockers of every horny teenage boy in America. She finally chose the hat, which, though it showed most of her long hair, still looked the most respectable, with its cool white straw, band of apricot silk, and large apricot bow.

Choosing the clothes had been less problematic. She took out a lovely apricot silk suit, purchased as part of her trousseau, with a pretty scarf. It was an outfit that covered up everything without looking dowdy.

The women's section was one flight up, a few pews tucked into an alcove like an afterthought. Its front row—the only one from which a glimpse of the men's section and the actual service itself was visible—had a *mechitzah* of wooden shutters and lace curtains so thick it was almost impossible to see anything. Generations of frustrated women, however, had done their best to open it up. Many of the slats were broken, and numerous holes had been poked in the lace.

As she walked down the narrow aisle toward the front, Delilah saw the aged faces turn toward her and toward one another, nodding and smiling with pleasure. She was everybody's just-married granddaughter, she realized. She felt a wave of approval and happiness and love beamed at her from every corner as she heard the whispered word for bride, *kallah*, echo off the walls in all directions.

She smiled with real joy at the old faces shining with love, feeling like a princess graciously accepting the homage of her people. She wondered where to sit. Not wanting to hurt anyone's feelings by rejecting the places they patted hopefully beside them, she chose an empty pew in front. As she sat facing forward, she could feel the buzz moving all around the room, finally landing at a spot on the back of her neck, where dozens of old eyes rested with curiosity and unexpressed friendliness.

When she took out her prayer book, she felt the room shift as the women leaned forward in anticipation, waiting to see if she would turn to the right page. And when she rose to pray, taking the obligatory three steps backward and three steps forward that usher in the Eighteen Benediction

Delilah's mother, Marilyn Meyers Goldgrab, was the middle daughter of American Jews whose Russian grandparents had come over on big immigrant ships during the czars' pogroms. Despite the attempts of the German Jewish immigrants who preceded them to ship them off to Jewless hinterlands where their faithful adherence to the rituals of the Jewish religion would be less embarrassingly visible, and might, hopefully, soon shrivel and die without Jewish communal life, they had stubbornly stayed put in the great Jewish city of New York. They had also stayed strictly Orthodox in practice, raising their sons and daughters to value Jewish custom and Jewish scholarship.

Marilyn's parents—a housewife and an insurance agent—were limited in their means, but nevertheless had high aspirations for their children, for whom they wanted the best of everything. Her mother sewed her clothes and carefully braided her hair. Although they couldn't afford a private parochial school education, and Marilyn had been sent to public school,

a helpmate, opposite him. If the helpmate were another man, that wouldn't help."

Delilah wasn't philosophical, but she was a realist. Jewish men—particularly Orthodox Jewish men—had fashioned the perfect little universe for themselves, and they were not about to give it up no matter how reactionary or unfair it was in this day and age.

To those who met her in the hallways at Bernstein about this time, she seemed reconciled to her new role. In fact, for the first time since they'd known her, she seemed really happy.

It's amazing how fast things change.

had been annoyed about the two-bed thing. "Why can't we just lie side by side on either side of a big bed when I'm a *niddah*?" she'd grumbled. But his response had mollified her. "If I could lie next to you and not sin, I wouldn't be a man."

But later, as time went by, with about half of each month with no physical contact at all between them, she began to feel peeved and insulted and abandoned. She would long for the ritual immersion that would have them resume their physical intimacy, no matter how flawed. In between, she saw him sneaking glances at her naked body like a guilty schoolboy. His yeshiva upbringing had created in him the perennial adolescent where anything concerning sex was involved, a permafrost that would last through all the stages of his life, never ripening into maturity.

She was compartmentalized in his life. Like most religious men, he managed to adore and ignore her simultaneously with breathtaking ease. He congratulated himself on marrying such a pretty, agreeable woman. But it was the idea of her he admired. She was decorative as well as practical, like a good appliance, able to perform many separate functions. He believed in separate "spheres." He believed it was noble and right for him to let her run hers and not to interfere. And vice versa.

He believed in all the old chichés—that women were superior beings, that they were more sensitive than men, on a higher level, blah, blah, blah. But of course, in their own "kingdom," he thought, adopting the language of patriarchal apologists who enthusiastically rationalized why women were entrusted with the tedium of housework and child care and men were fashioned for sitting on their backsides in study halls. Text after text, scholars never tired of trying to compensate for sentencing women to eternal drudgery, which they themselves abhorred, by dreaming up fancy ways of labeling it, easing their consciences and allowing them to view their self-serving little world of men-gods as a fair, nay noble, thing.

Countless rabbis, through hundreds of generations stretching back through time to the Temple itself, had been involved in the conspiracy. The separate-but-equal theory divided man and woman into the masters of their own universes, carefully delineating the realm of his kingdom to include anything but cooking, cleaning, and wiping up the various discharges and sticky liquids of children. As the wonderful German Rabbi Samson Raphael Hirsch put it, "A wife takes over obligations which comprise the great task of mankind, making it possible for her husband to accomplish more perfectly the part that is left to him. That's why it is written:

they made sure she faithfully attended Sunday and after-school Hebrew programs at her Brooklyn Orthodox synagogue.

This was fine with Marilyn. But as she started high school and began to attend Orthodox Jewish youth programs, she became acutely aware of the social disadvantages of her background. Those who had attended the expensive Hebrew day schools and summer camps tended to date each other and to look down on the public school kids, however observant.

For years she tried her best at the Thursday night midtown Manhattan indoor ice skating rink, where young Orthodox singles mingled. But she brought home only sore ankles and bruised pride—not to mention cold sores—for her trouble. Then, when high school had come and gone and she found herself dateless at Brooklyn College, one of her friends suggested investing in a weekend at Grossinger's up in the Catskills, the great, kosher watering hole of mateless Jewish singles on the cusp of morphing from youthful attractiveness into carefully made-up desperation. Marilyn's panic-stricken parents hurriedly laid out the money.

And it was there, on her first try, that she met Joe Goldgrab.

He was her waiter.

Joe had a past that Marilyn liked to call "colorful," at least in front of her family. The child of Jewish parents from Tyler, Texas, he had wanted to be a dress designer, then a sailor, and then a movie producer, and in the middle he had been drafted to Vietnam. After four horrendous years in the military, he had gone back home, only to find he was a piece of a jigsaw but the puzzle had changed. He wound up in New York, where he lived in dives and washed dishes until one of the more sympathetic waiters tipped him off about the big money and big knockers available to him in the Catskills during Jewish holidays.

He had been disappointed on the first count, but not the second.

He had smiled and brought her an extra dessert. She had smiled back. And later that weekend, when the men at her table were busy wooing the skinny straight-haired blondes, graduates of Ramaz and Flatbush Yeshiva, whose parents owned two-family homes and thriving businesses, Marilyn went walking on the grass with Joe. They sat by the pool in cold Adirondack chairs and looked up at the amazing stars. She found his Texas twang charming and his ambitions in fashion design and moviemaking thrilling. His military experience, which under normal circumstances would have anointed him with a huge black X as a marriage prospect, filled her with compassion. As he told it, he had been tricked into joining ROTC by slick on-campus recruiters dangling scholarships and National Guard duty, people who had disappeared along with signed promises not to draft him, replacing his college career with the jungles of Southeast Asia. Sure, he'd been bitter at first, he told her. But there were worse things than serving a country that had taken in his ancestors and protected them from the bullies of the world.

His words touched her.

Soon, he was taking her out weekends, to the theater and to bars, places Orthodox men seldom went. And although he was not what she, or her ambitious mother, had had in mind, both mother and daughter recognized the budding tire that would slowly envelop the youthful slim hips of the younger as it had the elder, realizing it was going to be Joe, or nobody. With her mother's encouragement, she told herself, "I can make him into whatever I want him to be."

Joe, far from home, liked Marilyn's parents, her warm house filled with the smells of chicken soup and *knaidlach*, and her warm, generous, yielding body, which gave a man something to hold on to instead of skin and bones. They got engaged. They got married. It was all a whirl of white— dresses, cake frosting, flowers. They rented a little apartment in Brooklyn near her parents. She dropped out of college, took a course in shorthand and typing, and got a job in an insurance office. He took a course in fashion design at FIT. The other students were a decade younger, savvy New Yorkers. Behind his back, they snickered at his hopelessly dowdy evening dresses, which could be envisioned only on aging, slightly overweight British royalty. He finished the course and got a job pushing around racks of dresses in Seventh Avenue knock-off shops, a job that had come with a nice title and many, many promises, none of which materialized.

She got pregnant. She gained and gained and gained. And with every pound, he lost more and more interest in their marriage and in their life. Big shouting matches ensued. Her parents got involved. The word *divorce* hung in the air like cold smoke from a recent cooking fire.

But when his first child was born, a boy, a new light came into his eyes. The baby was a little blond blue-eyed darling. Joe adored his son with an excess of love that spilled over onto the woman who had given birth to him. He had wanted to create something special in the world: a masterpiece of beauty and charm that was his own vision. With the child, his failures seemed to have been atoned for.

He reconciled with his wife, but insisted they move away from her par-

duce her mother to her new luxuries: the silver and porcelain, the Cuisinart, the Castro convertible with the new curtains to match.

"When," her mother said, taking huge gulps of air, "are you going to be able to move?"

And thus began the relentless campaign of Marilyn Goldgrab to see that her daughter got everything she deserved in life, the kind of things that her snooty classmates and their snooty parents took for granted. Her daughter was as good as any of them and twice as beautiful, she thought. She had had the same expensive education, the same clothes, albeit cleverly obtained at a fraction of the price, but whose business was that? And she therefore had every right to claim the same good life that was the deserved consequence of such faithful adherence to the rules. And Chaim, by hook or by crook, was going to give it to her.

Several times a week, her mother called Delilah, conversations that were full of unsolicited advice, hurtful and insulting admonitions, and dire prophecies. In short, Mrs. Goldgrab was driving her daughter crazy.

"Just don't talk to her," Chaim would say. "Keep it short. Tell her you're busy, that you'll call her back."

Delilah, who could really never stand her mother's pushy, demanding nature, wanted to do much more. And so, inevitably, there was a blowup. Hurtful, unforgivable truths were revealed in great, screaming arguments, and a soothing but troubled silence followed that lasted several weeks, until holidays and family celebrations intruded, necessitating a quick reconciliation. Marilyn called again, less frequently and more cautiously, nevertheless managing to preserve the needling subtext that was clear from everything she said.

"Your friend Adina is moving to Teaneck. I hear the houses are really beautiful there. I think her mother said it was a two-story colonial with a finished basement. . . . And your cousin Myra's husband—the one who went to work for your uncle Sam in his import business?—well, he just bought some license from Diesel to make watches, and now he's designing watches and selling them by the thousands, and soon they are moving to Great Neck . . . a house with a swimming pool!"

Like the centipede that enters the ears of people in horror movies, slowly taking over their brains and driving them insane, she felt her mother's words seep into her thoughts.

And then Chaim's mother began to visit her new daughter-in-law on

by landing on your nose, she swatted them away with a determined murderous hand.

No, with Chaim, all their dreams would come true. A beautiful house connected to a magnificent synagogue, where her son-in-law would stand in front of the Ark of the Torah, distinguished and revered. Her daughter would sit in the front pew, endlessly admired, envied, and imitated. And she, the rabbi's mother-in-law, would sit next to her in a stunning hat. And when she got up, everyone would get up. And when she sat down, everyone would sit down. And the children—her grandchildren!—would be the sons and daughters of the rabbi and the rebbitzin. And her daughter, aside from giving a few parties at her lovely home, which would be catered by staff, would have the leisure to improve her mind and do countless good deeds, all the while shopping in Lord & Taylor for beautiful modest clothes, because, as the rabbi's wife, she'd need to set an example. And her son-in-law would have plenty of time to spend with his family, not like men who work nine to five. A few sermons, some back-patting, shmoozing, nice words at funerals that could be endlessly recycled, a few blessings under marriage canopies for which he would receive a generous check (and a full free catered dinner to follow, not to mention the smorgasbord that preceded). Actual working days would be limited to Friday night and Saturdays, with the rest of the week practically a paid vacation.

With this in mind, she slowly relinquished the cherished visions of the successful diamond importer, the high-paid lawyer, and the brain surgeon, destined to put her charming blond daughter into a mansion in Short Hills, New Jersey. She had made the engagement and wedding plans with joy, borrowing freely and expansively to usher her child into the long-awaited, triumphant future.

Her first visit to her daughter's first home, a few weeks after the wedding, sent her into a tailspin. Her vision of the Bronx had been upscale Riverdale with the million-dollar mansions. Her vision of her daughter's first home had been a three-bedroom condo. For several moments, she stood stock-still, staring at the recently whitewashed graffiti on the front of the building in the crumbling neighborhood. In shock, she labored up the dark stairwell to the second story, a slow fury building inside her as she entered and took in the tiny rooms, the small kitchen with its old appliances. She sat down on the couch and wondered how she could have been so misled.

"Isn't it nice?" Delilah said, smiling, waving her hand as if to intro-

ents. And so they found a place out in the Rockaways, near the ocean. He had always been clever with his hands. He got a full-time job in a car repair shop and took up part-time alcoholism. He tried to be a good father to make up for being a disinterested husband.

By the time Delilah was born, her parents had settled into their private Cold War, their dreams exploded into rubble. Like the inhabitants of Dresden, they built a new life on top of the debris. Using their dead hopes as fertilizer to help raise a new generation, they would never cease to burden their children with the task of fulfilling their own unfulfilled desires and expectations from life, all the while insisting "they only wanted the best" for them.

Delilah's brother, Arnie, was totally uncooperative, finding meaning in the dangerous, poverty-stricken idealism of kibbutz life. He left for Israel as soon as he was legally able, married a kibbutznik, and limited his connections to his parents to holiday phone calls and thank-you notes for care packages containing American coffee, tunafish, Entenmann's donuts, and children's clothes.

Delilah had been Marilyn's last hope.

The engagement of her daughter to Chaim Levi, future rabbi, and the grandson of a distinguished, if little-known, leader of a synagogue, initially filled Delilah's mother with a heady sense of victory. While she had never envisioned her future son-in-law as a religious leader, scion of a rabbinical family, she was nothing if not flexible, willing to unhitch her dreams from one wagon and hitch them to another, as long as there was a horse.

Marilyn's rosy vision of her daughter's future prospects were based on those rabbis she'd met who were the principals and administrators in her daughter's school—dapper little men who wore suits and smelled of aftershave, who knew how to squeeze the last dime of tuition out of pretension-filled parents—and the fathers of some of her daughter's classmates who lived in the Five Towns, one of the most affluent Orthodox areas in America.

In her mind, she conveniently edited out all the rabbis stuck teaching Bible and Prophets to fourth-graders—men struggling with mortgages on small frame houses in deteriorating neighborhoods—as well as her own rabbi, who worked in a tiny dwindling congregation in an expanding ghetto; a congregation that could barely afford to keep the synagogue in plastic cups, let alone pay their rabbi a decent wage. When these things intruded on her vision, like the pesky insects that ruin a lovely photograph

derful old house, a place that had been meticulously redecorated and enlarged with enough basement and attic space to house several more families their size without the least discomfort. It would be a house they'd bought from anti-Semitic WASPs who'd simply died out or frittered away their money or retired to an adults-only golf community in Phoenix or Florida, a place where guards kept out the grasping poor and sticky-fingered, noisy grandchildren had strictly enforced visiting hours.

They were in love, she imagined, or, at least, content with each other and the life they'd built: walking-distance-to-synagogue communities, Ivy-prep yeshiva day schools, holiday trips to Israel on the New Year and Succoth, and Kosher Club jaunts to Acapulco or Grand Cayman on Passover.

And they deserved it all because they were good people, generous people.

Oh, my, yes.

They gave and gave and gave and gave. To Israel. To the handicapped. To political parties that supported Israel. To their synagogue. They were the most hounded and solicited beings in America and their checkbooks always stayed open. And in due time, they would grace fund-raising dinners for this or that as the honorees. She would look fabulous in a custom-made dress that was deceptively simple yet beautifully made and cost a fortune.

But they were not adventurers. They would not risk some idealistic move to the barren, fractious, terror-filled Middle East, no matter how their hearts swelled and tear ducts worked overtime each time they sang Israel's national anthem, "Hatikvah," meaning the hope:

Deep in my heart a Jewish soul yearns.
Our eyes to Zion look forward.

Right.

They were like their parents before them, like her parents—sensible. America was a gift one held on to for dear life.

It was everything she wanted in life, Delilah realized, her eyes shining.

On that same plane, just behind her, was yet another Orthodox family. They too had been on vacation and had also enjoyed their trip, except they had most probably not slept in hotels with stars of any kind but on mattresses on the floors of various Israeli relatives.

The woman was about the same age as the woman who sat in front, ex-

sive. But even those parents who couldn't really afford it felt ashamed not to let their kids participate. So, along with many others, Delilah's parents took out loans, packed her suitcase, and sent her off.

Everyone had a great time wandering through the ancient ruins and the modern malls, riding up to Masada and standing teary-eyed by the Wailing Wall. On the flight back, sitting just two rows ahead of her, Delilah encountered her vision of the New York Orthodox Jewish couple who had it all.

She couldn't take her eyes off them.

She imagined they were coming back from a lovely vacation at five-star hotels, no doubt returning to Cedarhurst or Woodmere or another of those Long Island enclaves where mansions vie with each other on park-like lots nestled behind high stone fences, everything dappled by huge shady trees. New York's Orthodox Beverly Hills. They were both tall and slim and were traveling with two children, surprisingly advanced in age, considering the parents still looked like recent yeshiva high school gradu-ates. The daughter was about fourteen, the son maybe nine.

The mother was a smoky blonde with long hair. Even after ten hours of being squashed on El Al, her hair still framed her face in perfect ellipses. You could still detect in her the yeshiva girl cheerleader that the disgrun-tled rabbis kept exhorting—to no avail—to lengthen her skirt. Now she wore a white cashmere sweatshirt with a hood and a pleated gray tweed skirt and black textured stockings that only legs like Angelina Jolie's could pull off. Her face was WASP princess: upturned nose, deep blue eyes. Delilah wondered if she'd had plastic surgery or if it was the same genetic magic that had Jews from Uzbekistan looking Mongolian and Jews from Great Britain like Margaret Thatcher.

Delilah drank her in like a free airline Diet Coke.

The husband, too, was gorgeous in his Banana Republic khakis and a blue striped shirt—Hugo Boss?—which had probably not been bought at discount at Century Twenty-One but at full price at Lord & Taylor's or Bar-ney's during a busy lunch hour. He could no doubt well afford it. He was doing very well, thank you very much, Delilah thought, conjecturing if it was venture capital, heart surgery, or law, practiced from some office with ten-foot-high windows that looked over New York City like a personal backyard. He wore a discreet crocheted skullcap in no-nonsense black.

She imagined how they would gather their Louis Vuitton luggage and load it into their SUV. How they would drive and park in front of a won-

a regular basis. She brought cookies and fattening but delicious kreplach and *knaidlach* and *rogelach* in large plastic containers meant for catering halls. And she never left before leaving behind a piece of her mind as well.

Like Emma Bovary, Delilah "accepted her wisdom; her mother-in-law was extravagant with it." They spoke to each other like people in a documentary about family life: with exaggerated consideration. But when Chaim's mother began a sentence with "I have to be honest with you," Delilah cringed, knowing that something disagreeable and insulting was on its way like a projectile, a Kassam rocket catapulted with reckless abandon into the soft flesh of populated areas.

The woman was relentless. Her criticism ranged from the kind of floor wax Delilah bought (too expensive) to the way she washed her dishes. "That set I bought you is porcelain, it should be hand-washed or the gold trim will turn dull."

Chaim, caught in the middle, tried to mediate and wound up getting himself exiled to his own bed even during the precious days when he could finally move into hers. Finally, there was the inevitable explosion, and his mother stopped bringing her plastic-covered caloric masterpieces. Instead, they went less frequently to her house to eat them.

Delilah, kept busy with classes and synagogue functions, didn't have too much time to brood. But eventually, she got bored. This was no fun, she thought. She tried doing more. She began preparing elaborate Friday night meals, inviting the synagogue president, the cantor, and his wife. But they were both in their seventies, on strict diets that precluded salt, sugar, fats, red meat, and just about anything else worth eating. Besides, she realized, what was the point of buttering them up? Her husband would be rabbi of this synagogue anyway; it was his by inheritance. And this life was going to be her life, until further notice.

She looked out her windows at the treeless streets and old brick buildings. She examined her apartment, whose novelty had already worn off and whose deficiencies showed through with devastating clarity.

She brooded, suddenly hearing her mother's voice without a phone.

And so the snake of discontent entered the garden of Delilah and Chaim's newlywed bliss through gates as wide as barnyard doors. In fact, it was inevitable, even without Marilyn.

The summer of Delilah's sophomore year in high school, the school's Hebrew department had arranged a class trip to Israel. It was very expen-

cept that she looked it. She wore a pious hair covering of crocheted nylon that hung down her back, covering all her hair. Her husband wore a dark suit and a white open-collared shirt that seemed a bit yellowed from too many machine bleachings. He spent the flight pouring over religious texts with tiny Hebrew lettering. There were twice as many children, of all ages, who needed constant care. The husband helped, cheerfully and so ineffectually that the wife soon took over, sighing, freeing him to stroke his beard and read on.

Delilah imagined their many heavy, torn, unmatched suitcases, which relatives who came to take them home would manage to stuff into banged-up Fords. Some of the children would sit, unseat-belted, on top of them, until they drove to their cramped rented apartment in Kew Gardens or Boro Park, a place with many bookcases, bunk beds, a large dining room table, and convertible couches.

They would talk about this trip until their next one—perhaps a decade away. And their next vacation would be a ride to Hershey, Pennsylvania, and one night in a Comfort Inn.

Each time Delilah passed them in the aisle on the way to the lavatory, she cringed. Only if she were already dead and it was part of some afterlife punishment cooked up especially by God to make her pay for all her sins would she ever agree to be part of that scenario, she told herself.

She tried to anazlyze why. After all, they looked perfectly happy.

It was then she had her revelation: Heaven and Hell, she realized, were the same place. It was, for example, a room with a long table, and all people did all day was sit around and study. For the saints, it was Heaven. For the sinners, it was Hell.

She glanced over her shoulder as the poor woman in the polyester snood stood up, trying to rescue her baby from her two-year-old, who was poking the infant in the eye with his El Al–supplied crayons. This, she thought, was her vision of Hell.

And so, when Delilah woke up one morning, five months after her wedding, drenched in sweat from the realization that—without major intervention—this was exactly the life that loomed ahead of her, she must have been desperate. Which, of course, always explains many sins, but does not necessarily excuse them.

{ EIGHT }

*A*nd so, a little over five months after Chaim's shirt-button sermon, as they were walking home after yet another shiva call (they'd been averaging one or two a month), Delilah turned to her new husband and said, "I can't stand this anymore."

Chaim looked at his new bride, astonished. "What's wrong?"

She turned her ring around her finger nervously. "What's *right*? This shul is falling apart, and the people are going with it. It's going to bury us alive. And this crumby apartment in this old building. The Bronx! And the polluted air. I want my own house. A backyard for the children. . . ."

He stopped dead in his tracks, focusing only on her last words. Was she trying to tell him some happy news? Oh, wouldn't that be wonderful! His face lit up.

"Uff, don't be an idiot! I'm not pregnant, and there is no way I'm getting pregnant in this neighborhood, in this apartment. A child in this shul would be like one of those wonders in Believe It or Not museums. I'm

said was absolutely true. When faced with this reality, there was only one
thing for her to do, one thing every wife can and must do when forced into
such a corner: *change the subject.* The more irrelevant and unrelated the
topic, the better, especially if it allows one to hurl hurtful truths that are
sure to make one's husband blow his top, saying things he'd never believe
himself capable of, things that will appall him when he calms down, making him forget what the argument was about in the first place, and forcing
him to beg forgiveness, eat dust, and crawl for a very long time.

"If he wasn't your grandfather, they would have fired you already!
Those sermons. . . . Buttons! Who wants to hear about buttons? The
world is going up in smoke, terrorist attacks, natural disasters left and
right, and you? You talk about buttons. Don't you see how you put them
all to sleep, even the ones who try to stay awake? You get away with it because they don't dare fire you. You are just afraid to go to a place that will
judge you like anybody else, a place where you'll have to stand on your
own two feet!"

Chaim turned white and sat down. "Is that what you really think? Is
that really true?"

She was braced for insults, not immediate surrender. It was their first
fight and his quick capitulation filled her with equal parts of regret and
contempt. She calmed down, afraid she'd overplayed her hand. After all,
the last thing she wanted was to undermine his confidence. How would
that help her get on the fast track? "Oh, it was just that one sermon.
You've been getting better, really, like last week—when you talked about
the ten tribes. . . ." She only vaguely remembered that, since she automatically tuned him out whenever he got up to speak now.

He looked devastated, but it couldn't be helped. She was entitled to
the life she wanted. And it couldn't be lived in a Bronx apartment as the
wife of a rabbi who spent his time at funerals. "You have so much to give.
You could change lives. The people here . . . their lives are behind them.
You need to be in a place with young people, young families. You could do
so much good."

"They slept through it? Is that true?" he repeated, his eyes glassy, not
hearing a word. Perhaps she was right. He *was* a dismal failure. He knew
he wasn't all that bright, but he had worked so hard. This was his first congregation, and they were used to his brilliant, pious grandfather. Still, he
had thought he was holding his own. At least he hadn't heard any complaints. But maybe they just didn't want to hurt his grandfather's feelings.

synagogue. Why, it would break his heart. Besides, when he retires, I'm in line to take over. I have no competition."

"If they keep losing members at the rate they're going, when *he* goes, there won't be a congregation!"

"But I could attract new people, young people! Don't you see? It's a wonderful opportunity, Delilah! Besides, I've heard stories about how the boards of some synagogues treat their rabbis. You are constantly under their thumbs or they'll cut off your head and cancel your contract. If you try to do your job, actually teach them something, deepen their obser-vance, get them actively involved in supporting Israel, they get tired of you, and then they get annoyed, and then they get vengeful. And out you go, back on the unemployment line. At least here, we have Grandfather to stand buffer. They wouldn't dare fire Reb Abraham's grandson. We're safe here, darling."

"So, what are you telling me? That for the rest of my life all I have to look forward to is another roach-infested apartment in yet another Bronx walk-up? Is that it?"

What could he say to that? As long as he was connected to this syna-gogue, they would always have to live in a neighborhood within easy walking distance, because Orthodox Jews don't drive on the Sabbath. "I'm sure we could find something nicer. Maybe not Riverdale, but some-thing—"

"Riverdale is the only place in the Bronx worth living, and this syna-gogue is nowhere near Riverdale and never will be, and you know it! It's in the Bronx. THE BRONX!" She raised her voice, causing passersby to pause a moment and look their way. They hurried forward in silence, wait-ing to continue in the privacy of their own home.

They drew the curtains and closed the windows.

"I didn't marry you to live in some dusty slum! I have my own plans, my own dreams, and if you really loved me, you'd want me to be happy!"

"Of course I want you to be happy. But what in all of this didn't you expect? I told you everything: about my grandfather and his synagogue and the offer he'd made me. We picked out this apartment together. I don't understand you, Delilah! None of this was forced on you; you agreed to everything!"

Delilah was quiet, trying to think of a reply that wouldn't make her the bad one, the selfish materialistic one. But she couldn't. Everything Chaim

tired of going to funerals! I'm tired of being nice to talkative old biddies who have nothing to do all day but crochet you sweaters that don't fit and bake me cakes that would turn me into a fat old cow, just like them, if I ate a fraction of them!"

He looked crushed. Could this really be coming out of the mouth of his dear, delicate young wife? Such cruelty, such ungenerous words, about people who had done nothing but shower them with kindness? People who listened appreciatively to his sermons? Who treated Delilah like a favorite granddaughter? He stared down at the pavement, slowly putting one foot in front of the other.

Everything had been going so well, he'd thought. He'd been incredibly lucky to have a job so quickly. Most of his fellow classmates were still scrounging around for some teaching job in a yeshiva day school, which—if they were lucky—could be finessed into an assistant rabbi job five years down the line. He was already there, with a synagogue primed for him to take over.

And the apartment, what was wrong with the apartment? It was big enough for the two of them, after all. How much room did two people need? They even had an extra bedroom they were hardly using, a place for guests. . . . He glanced over at his wife, annoyed, then noticed two big tears snaking down her cheeks. He was alarmed, confused, his heart melting.

"Please, Delilah. Don't." He handed her a crumpled tissue. "What is it you want me to do?" he asked her helplessly.

"Find another job! Somewhere out of the city, in some nice little community with lots of pretty houses and trees."

Chaim, who only a few months before had wanted nothing more than to do just that, was suddenly loath to consider the idea. Despite his earlier fears, he now found himself almost addicted to the easy adoration of this congregation. Their warmth and praise were a balm for his jittery fears of inadequacy, fears that had plagued him all during his rabbinical studies. Like a child cuddled in the bosomy warmth of maternal approval, the longer he stayed, the more reluctant he became even to consider wrenching himself away by sending out his résumé.

He was succeeding. He had as much money as he thought he needed. Why take chances? Besides, it was by no means certain there really was any other place out there that would be eager to take him in.

"I can't believe you want me to give up my place in my grandfather's

Torah as it was paraded around the men's section, barely visible to the women behind the partition.

The rabbi, who had tried a number of times to talk to this group, now refused to go back, as did the other two teachers hired for the Sunday school and Bar Mitzva program. As assistant rabbi and newcomer, the task had fallen to him. Just the thought of facing them filled him with aggravation. And now this.

"Why are they so desperate for our company all of a sudden? They haven't been in touch for months."

She shrugged. "I can't answer that. But Josh, my dear, I think we need to be generous. We are, after all, so blessed." He clasped his hands in front of him and looked at them. "And I think"—she paused delicately—"they might be going through a bit of a transition. You know, being married isn't so easy for everyone, like it is for us." She smiled at her husband, who took her hand and kissed it.

He had endless admiration for his wife's good heart and patience. He told himself that—like the patriarch Abraham—he should heed everything his wife tried to tell him. But this was too much. A whole weekend with those two!

"Can't we put it off?" he begged.

"It won't be so bad. You'll be in the synagogue most of the time anyway. It's just Friday night and Shabbes afternoon. I can invite some other guests. You won't even notice them," she promised, kissing him on the top of his head. "It's a real mitzva. And we can use all the blessings we can earn right now."

He put his hand on her growing stomach, and gave in.

~ ° ~

Delilah was thrilled. Here was a chance to socialize with another rabbi's wife. To check out what life was like out in the suburbs with a different kind of congregation, one where little kids ran around, babies cried, and pretty young mothers whispered secrets to one another, showing off their latest new hats and stylish suits. A chance to show off her own latest hat and stylish suit. And most of all, a chance to network.

Chaim, too, was pleased. He liked and admired Josh, despite the unfortunate little incident before his wedding. Josh was considered an *illuyi*, destined for greatness. He was also a good person, who kept to the strict

ers, Rivkie would have been able to beg off by truthfully claiming she didn't listen to gossip. But as it was, Delilah was talking about herself. Her latest purchases. Her sex life. Her brilliant innovations in the wonderful classic old synagogue where her husband, Chaim, would soon take over as rabbi. And always, she had ended the calls by saying how much she missed Rivkie. How she was dying to come out and spend some time with her. This had been going on for weeks. Until finally, her facade of giddy success and self-congratulatory pride gone, replaced by raw misery, Delilah had said point-blank, "Chaim has next Shabbes off; can we come to you? If I spend one more weekend with these old folks, I'm going to get bunions and grow a mustache."

"I can't just blow her off. After all, we were their matchmakers."

He shifted uncomfortably.

Chaim had never been a close friend, just an acquaintance for whom he—and most of his classmates—had felt a sort of undefined pity: he tried so hard, and achieved so little, always hanging on by his fingernails. Now he had married a girl with a checkered reputation, blond hair, and a pretty face, a girl whom no one—except Chaim—thought a suitable wife. It was like being forced to eat a dish full of bad ingredients prepared by a lousy chef simply because you'd lent someone a cookbook.

"Chaim is a fine person," Josh said carefully.

"Apparently, he's very unhappy with his job. It seems to be mostly with seniors."

"Seniors are wonderful. I'll take ten seniors for every teenager," he grumbled.

He was sitting at the dining room table perusing a lengthy Talmudic discussion from which he planned to prepare a program for his teenage Saturday afternoon discussion group. They were a difficult bunch, full of questions, doubts, and heresies, especially the girls, who were a hard sell on anything to do with the place of women in the traditional Orthodox synagogue service. You couldn't really blame them, since women had no place at all in the traditional Orthodox synagogue service, except as ob- servers behind bars, lacy curtains, pretty wooden screens, or other inven- tive methods of keeping them at bay. Go explain that to intelligent teenage girls, many of whom were fluent in Hebrew from their expensive day school educations. Explain why they couldn't read the Torah, couldn't be called up for any of the shul honors, couldn't even kiss the cover of the

Perhaps all this time they too had been laughing at him behind his back, just like his wife.

Delilah and Chaim didn't speak for the next few days, except for business.

"Pick up the challahs."

"Don't forget the dry cleaning."

"Mrs. Farbish called and wants you to visit her husband in the hospital."

The pangs of regret began to hit Delilah about the third day. She wasn't sorry for what she'd done. She was sorry that this had been the result. Only one thing was worse than being stuck in this dump with Chaim; being stuck in it with a Chaim who wasn't speaking to her.

She wanted things to go back to normal. She wanted things to change completely. What she needed, she thought, was a plan.

Rivkie and Josh, she thought.

She'd last seen them three months before at their wedding, which was held at a posh country club in Westchester. Josh was now assistant rabbi in a beautiful synagogue there, a place with seven hundred young families, all of them professionals who lived within walking distance of the synagogue. She was dying to see Rivkie's house. And Josh had connections in the rabbinic and yeshiva world. He was from a rich prominent family. He might know which one of the jobs listed on Bernstein's Rabbinic Alumnus Employment Bulletin would be willing to take Chaim, with the proper references, which clearly, as a friend, he would be able to supply. It wouldn't be asking much. Just a little help. After all, Josh already had a job in some leafy suburb. Why would he begrudge the same to a dear, close friend like Chaim?

It wasn't being needy and pushy, she told herself as she dialed Rivkie's number. It was networking.

~⁀~ ⁀~

"I think we have no choice but to invite them," Rivkie told Josh.

He put down his pen and looked up from his book. "Rivkie, you are such a wonderful, kind person, but really, *is* this necessary?"

Rivkie nodded. "Yes, I think it is."

Delilah, who had made no effort to stay in touch since her wedding, had suddenly begun a relentless campaign to become her best friend. She called three times a week, long, rambling, intimate conversations about things Rivkie didn't want to know. If the information had been about oth-

letter of the law in anything having to do with his ethical and social behavior. He was from a wealthy family but never made a big deal about it, even though it was well known that he had turned his back on taking over his father's multimillion-dollar diet-drink company to become a struggling rabbi. Josh had never shown him anything but kindness. But the discrepancies in their prospects, backgrounds, and personalities were not conducive to friendship. Josh was royalty. Chaim was one of the peasants. Chaim had always acknowledged this fact without resentment or jealousy, as a given.

The invitation was unexpected.

"But why have they invited us? Why now?" he asked, puzzled.

"She's been after me for months. I guess she's lonely. You know she's always considered me her best friend. And I'm just so busy during the week, I don't even have time to pick up the phone and talk to her. We never get a chance to see each other. I invited them here, but you know, he can never get away. He's assistant rabbi, or something," Delilah said casually, deciding between two outfits. The skirt on one was longer but hugged her behind, as opposed to the one with a looser skirt that hit right above her knees.

"I'm also assistant rabbi. What makes you think *I* can get away?"

"But your grandfather . . . he wouldn't stop you. You've—we've—been here every Saturday for months." Her voice rose petulantly.

Seeing where this was going, and considering that it really wasn't too much to ask—he should be flattered and might even enjoy it—Chaim gave in.

They put their suitcases into their little Ford Escort, and drove off.

Delilah looked out the window at the ugly red bricks, the billboards, the housing projects, and the few bedraggled trees on the Drive. She took in the graffiti on the sides of the buildings, the rusting fire escapes, the self-storage units, the eyesore of old bricks painted an appalling red, white, and blue. They passed the White Castle on Bruckner Boulevard; the pawn, cash, and loan stores; the horrid rusting cars raised on pedestals in front of used car dealerships and muffler shops. They passed Co-op City, a housing project that rose like some set in a futuristic horror movie, where a hapless mankind is imprisoned and forced to live like ants in gargantuan prison complexes. And then, suddenly, it was all behind them.

Highway signs flashed by indicating Mount Vernon, one quarter mile; Scarsdale; Mamaroneck. Lakes of mirrorlike water held reflections of beautiful fall colors from overhanging trees. Bridges reached over the road like filigreed bowers. And all along there were glimpses of huge, wondrous homes, larger than any family could ever need, deserve, or use, nestled on huge private lots. Homes with pumpkins on front lawns, and yellow, red, and green forest trees in backyards. The cars that passed them on the highway were gleaming and rich, with suit jackets hung on backseat hooks, driven by men heading home from upscale Manhattan offices who would park in front of trendy updated farmhouses painted maroon, or renovated Colonials with white siding, trimmed in black shutters: places with manicured bushes and huge artistically placed poinsettia, their red leaves like torches leading up to the front gate.

It was all out there, Delilah thought. Prosperity and peace and success all tied up with a big red bow and a mortgage.

"Are you sure this is it?" Delilah asked Chaim, as they pulled into the driveway. She looked out, disappointed. She'd been hoping for more, while at the same time prepared to feel horribly jealous and put upon if it met her expectations. As it was, it turned out to be a relatively simple and modest brick house on a generous plot of tree-filled property on a quiet cul-de-sac.

It was much nicer inside, Delilah saw immediately. The living room had a fireplace surrounded by rough-hewn stones, with built-in holders for logs. There were oak bookcases, comfortable couches, and a whole separate room just for dining room furniture. "Wow," Delilah said, when she walked in.

"We didn't have much choice. We needed something within walking distance to the synagogue, and they didn't have much on the market. It's really more than we wanted to spend," Rivkie said in a rush, almost apologetically.

"You mean you bought it? I thought the synagogue—?"

"No, they only provide a house for the rabbi. Assistant rabbis are on their own. And mostly the bank owns it." She smiled uncomfortably, already feeling the weekend stretch out ahead of her in endless tedious blocks of time, through which she would have to be on constant guard. She didn't want Delilah's envy, or her friendship, or her confidences. She wanted to do the right thing, to offer loving kindness to another human being who seemed troubled and wanted (insisted?) on her intervention and help.

Delilah dressed carefully for dinner, deciding to wear a wig because Rivkie was wearing a wig. She put on her most pious suit, the one with the ankle-grazing skirt, then went downstairs to light Sabbath candles. Rivkie had already set up two candles for her on the tray next to her own elaborate silver candelabra, the traditional gift of a mother-in-law to her daughter-in-law before the wedding. It was gorgeous, and held at least eight candles. Rivkie only lit three. "I'll add another with each child," she explained, blushing.

Delilah dutifully lit her candles, waving her hands over the flames, covering her eyes as tradition required. When she finished, she saw that Rivkie was still deep in prayer, her eyes shut, as she silently mouthed heartfelt requests for good health, happiness, and good fortune for everyone she knew, an addendum to the candle-lighting blessing that pious women created for themselves over the centuries, convinced that the heavenly gates of mercy were open wide at that moment in time to the prayers of Jewish women.

Delilah studied her tranquillity, her sincerity, her really, really nice engagement ring, wondering why the words always felt like overchewed gum in her own mouth, a tasteless, meaningless exercise you were only too happy to spit out and be done with. She envied Rivkie her peace of mind, her convictions, the easy way in which things always seemed to work out for the Rivkies of the world. She felt bitter that her own life had been one panting uphill struggle.

It was so unfair. Which is why, she thought, the Rivkies and Joshes of the world were not being generous when they helped people like her, but simply being just. This was the very least they could do. And so when you asked a favor of them, you were simply giving them an opportunity to behave in a way that was required of them, after all. Excessive gratitude was not only unnecessary, it was counterproductive, the heavenly reward for good deeds being inversely proportional to how much praise and fawning gratitude they netted you from the recipients of your largesse. By not falling all over herself to thank them, she'd be doing them a favor, Delilah told herself, getting ready to pursue her latest goal.

But just when the coast seemed clear, someone knocked on the door. It turned out to be the wives of the Talmud Torah teacher and the beadle, both of whom had been invited to dinner, Delilah realized to her chagrin.

She smiled her way through helping to set the table, as the women chattered on about their most recent experiences in their charity work (visiting the sick, helping new mothers, collecting clothes for the poor). When they turned to her and asked in a friendly way what she was involved in, she said, with great conviction, "Old-age homes."

Dinner was lively, with lots of singing around the table and many learned discussions among the men, while the women automatically jumped up to clear and serve, without resentment. The women seemed to know each other well and were constantly referring to study groups, exercise classes, and book clubs they were part of. They all lived within a few blocks, no doubt in similar homes, she thought enviously, with big yards and leaves to rake and the smell of burning wood.

～ ～

Saturday morning they rose early to the singing of birds. Josh and Chaim left for synagogue together, while Rivkie and Delilah had a leisurely breakfast. Delilah tried to be chummy and familiar. Rivkie did her best not to offend her but had no intention of paying for unwanted intimacies by supplying similar information of her own. This annoyed Delilah, but she chalked it up to Rivkie's boring piety.

The synagogue was packed with young families, baby carriages, toddlers. The other young women greeted Rivkie with warmth, hugging her. They were gracious to Delilah as Rivkie's guest. It was like being back in school again, Delilah thought, except, being the rabbi's wife, you would never get left behind on the punchball fields without being chosen. They'd have to pick you. In fact, you'd be the captain, and you'd pick them, your attention and affection a prize to bestow on the fortunate. You were important, because the rabbi was important. And holy. Don't forget holy. If he was holy, so was she, she thought, smoothing her hair beneath her hat and pulling down her skirt. Yes, this is what it would be like to be the rabbi's wife in a real congregation, one that was filled with potential celebrations instead of tragic losses.

Kiddush after the service was catered in a large and airy social hall. In honor of the day's Bar Mitzva boy, there were trays of piping hot potato, noodle, and spinach kugels; individual quiches; platters of vegetables with dips; and fresh salmon on beds of parsley. The dessert table held giant fruit displays, chocolate-dipped strawberries, and beautiful little petits fours.

They were so full by the time they reached home, they couldn't even imagine lunch. But there it was, a beautiful buffet laid out in all Rivkie's best Mikasa wedding china. Thankfully, there were no other guests. She felt happy and sleepy and content, unwilling to pressure her hosts or disrupt the pleasant atmosphere. There'd be time for that later, she told herself.

And as they lay down for the traditional Saturday-afternoon nap in the comfortable guest room, which smelled of lavender and newly ironed sheets, she realized just how lonely she'd been the last few months. And just how much she really hated the Bronx, her apartment, and the synagogue full of old people.

She reached across the bed, taking Chaim's hand. "Are you having a good time, Chaim?"

Half asleep, he murmured, "I suppose so. But I prefer the city."

She drew back, scowling. In the dappled shadows of the afternoon, his figure in the bed suddenly didn't seem human anymore. He seemed like a bottle wrapped in cloth. And his head was the bottleneck, she realized, something she would have to pull herself through, kicking and screaming, to get where she wanted to go.

❦

Delilah chose the quiet private third meal of the day to make her move. Seated across from her hosts at a table filled with coffee and cake and various salads, Delilah said, "We had such a lovely time. This is such a great congregation. So many young people! Chaim is always saying if he had a young congregation, he could do so much. You know that image of writing on blank paper, rather than paper that's got writing all over it?"

Chaim, who had never expressed—or felt—any such thing, just stared at her.

"Really, Chaim? Would you prefer youth work?" Josh asked him.

"Well, I can't say I wouldn't like it. I just don't have much experi—"

Delilah laid her hand on his arm. "You know Chaim, he makes modesty into a fault. He has so much experience! The NCSY youth groups. Yavneh. Hillel House," she said, smiling, winking, and waving her arms in all directions.

Chaim, who had never worked with any of those groups, coughed until Rivkie brought him a glass of water.

"He is wonderful with the seniors. But he is wasted in the Bronx. Wasted. You wouldn't know of another congregation that has an opening, would you, Josh? In some small, pretty place like this? A young congregation?"

"Well, usually you need about four or five years as assistant rabbi before you can even apply for a position as rabbi," Josh explained.

"Usually, but not always," she said cryptically, with a secret smile.

"I suppose, theoretically, that's true." Josh nodded, wondering how long they would be held captive before the Sabbath was out and they smiled their goodbyes and the Ford disappeared down the road.

"I don't think an ad in the Rabbi's Forum of *Bernstein's Bulletin* is theoretical. It looked pretty practical to me," she said, pulling out the paper. "Especially if someone with your connections and reputation could pull a few strings—"

"Really, Delilah," Chaim murmured, mortified.

"Oh, I'm sorry." She looked around, innocent and bewildered. "Did I say something I shouldn't?"

"What congregation is it?" Josh asked, his curiosity getting the better of him.

She smoothed the *Bulletin* down and licked her finger, turning the pages. She jabbed at it, the way one would spear a particularly delicious hors d'oeuvre. "There!"

Josh took the paper and read. "You aren't talking about the ad for that synagogue by the lake, are you?" His look was incredulous.

"*Young, affluent community, interested in open-minded spiritual leader,*" Delilah read. "How can you tell where it is?"

"They've been running that ad for months," Chaim informed her.

"Congregation Ohel Aaron. In Connecticut," Rivkie said quietly, raising her eyebrows at her husband and quietly taking Delilah's hand in solidarity. "She couldn't possibly have known that," she admonished him.

"Well, maybe not," Josh conceded. "But Chaim, surely, you've heard the story."

"What story?" Delilah demanded, turning to her husband.

"The story of why Congregation Ohel Aaron of Swallow Lake, Connecticut, will never get a rabbi," Chaim said quietly. "Isn't it time we got back to the synagogue for the evening prayers?" Josh nodded gratefully, and the men started the song that ushers in Grace After Meals, putting an abrupt end to the discussion.

Later that evening, when they finally stood at the door to say their goodbyes, Josh put his arm around Chaim's shoulder. "It's an honor for you to follow in your grandfather's footsteps. He has quite a reputation. I envy you."

"Thank you, Josh. They are enormous shoes to fill," Chaim said gratefully.

Delilah felt all her dreams slowly stop, the way the bubbles of Coke stop when the bottleneck slows them down and the cap puts an end to their escape.

She kissed Rivkie. "I'll call you," she murmured, clutching her a little more tightly than was appropriate.

Rivkie nodded uncomfortably. "I'm sure you will."

The moment they were in the car on the open road that led inexorably back to the Bronx, Delilah turned to her husband and said stiffly, "Tell me, Chaim. Why is it that Congregation Ohel Aaron in Swallow Lake, Connecticut, will never get a rabbi?"

{ NINE }

*I*n the 1950s, the Orthodox Jews of Connecticut joined the national movement out of the inner cities into the suburbs. Jews began showing up in places they were hardly ever seen or wanted. By then, the offspring of Eastern European Jews were already college educated, working in their families' businesses, or successfully developing their own. They sought an area outside of Hartford or New Haven, where they could build and enjoy their prosperity. And so they found their way to beautiful Swallow Lake. They built a large, imposing synagogue and called it Ohel Aaron, after a major donor. They built large, imposing homes with lake views and private boat docks.

Studies in the 1980s revealing that 52 percent of Jews in America were intermarrying sent shock waves through the American Jewish community. Jews began to rethink their values, the education they were giving their children, and the dilution of religious rituals in their synagogues and in their lives. Many decided to send their children to religious day schools.

When a decade later the dot-com bubble provided new wealth to many, yeshiva high school graduates bought into the Swallow Lake community at an unprecedented rate. One of them was a stock market trader who later wound up serving ten to fifteen in a federal penitentiary. To atone for his sins, he built an elaborate Orthodox Jewish day school on part of his Swallow Lake estate, naming it after his parents, who had both died of heart attacks.

The school was soon attracting the offspring of Orthodox Harvard Law and Business School alumni, Orthodox heart surgeons and cancer specialists, and Orthodox venture capitalists. Joining them were Jewish immigrants from South Africa, Iran, and the former Soviet Union, people who, while not Orthodox themselves, were not put off by the Orthodox way of life and were hopeful the day school would prove a bastion to keep their children from the drugs and sex that were rampant in other schools. They were also attracted to the school's reputation for getting kids into the Ivy Leagues. And most of all they wished to join other Jews who could afford homes in the high six- to seven-figure category.

When the aging rabbi of Ohel Aaron had a heart attack, they searched high and low for an Orthodox rabbi who would meet all of the community's needs. The problem, as usual, was that no one could agree on what, exactly, those needs were.

The day school graduates wanted the kind of rabbi they were familiar with from the synagogues of their youth, places with oversized barriers separating men and women; a rushed, rather melancholy, songless service; the words read in Hebrew so fast they sounded like watermelonwatermelonwatermelon. They wanted a rabbi they could look up to, an éminence grise with an iron will, who would be uncompromising and didactic in anything related to law or ritual. Someone who, when you pointed to a phrase in the Talmud, could complete it by heart and tell you the rest of the page for good measure. Preferably, they wanted the scion of a rabbinic family, or at least someone who had served a prestigious congregation and had earned a reputation for honesty, piety, warmth, and leadership.

The immigrants, however, had quite a different view of the situation. They saw Saturday as their day off. While they were willing to join the synagogue service in order to network, and didn't mind putting their wives where they could be neither seen nor heard for a few hours, what they absolutely didn't want—and would not tolerate—was being subjected to weekly exhortations about what they ate, how they lived, or anything else connected to the Ten Commandments, five of which couldn't possibly fit into their lifestyles. They wanted a rabbi who would look the part, but would be friendly and understanding. Someone who would kid around and take things easy. Someone who knew not only how to tell a good joke, but how to listen to one (even if it was just a little off-color). In exchange, they were prepared to let him pick their pockets for whatever cause he wanted.

Enter Rabbi Hershel Metzenbaum and his wife, Shira.

Rabbi Metzenbaum was in his mid-forties, a charismatic and distinguished scholar who had made a name for himself as a prominent member of the Council of American Orthodox Rabbis. He was also down-to-earth and friendly, a hands-on person who truly loved being a rabbi. Young people, particularly, were drawn to him, as he had an easy and respectful attitude toward them. He could play basketball and discuss the latest Star Wars movie. As a result, he headed numerous boards of numerous Orthodox Jewish youth groups.

As the rabbi of a small congregation in the Midwest for ten years, Metzenbaum had done wonders in gathering together unaffiliated Jews, reformed Reform Jews, and local Jewish college students from nonreligious backgrounds, not to mention the youth of his synagogue, helping to build a community dynamic that saw his synagogue grow and prosper, as new families bought houses in the vicinity simply to be able to be part of his congregation. He was adored.

The president of Ohel Aaron had heard about him from his brother, a prominent plastic surgeon in Ohio, who had attended one of Rabbi Metzenbaum's many weekly classes. The Synagogue Search Committee, impressed, put his name at the top of their list.

Rabbi Metzenbaum was used to receiving offers from search committees looking for rabbis. Until now, he had fended them off. But at this particular moment in time, many factors contributed to his reconsidering his commitment to stay put. The salary situation in the Midwest was going nowhere. His house was really too small for his growing family, but a larger mortgage was out of the question. And the kids—all five of them—were attending private Hebrew day schools. The two who were in high school had been forced to board in New Jersey, because there was no local Orthodox high school. Even with a rabbinic discount, the tuition for his five kids was sending him to the poorhouse.

Sensing his vulnerability, the board told him the job in Swallow Lake came not only with a large beautiful house which would be his—rent and mortgage free—for as long as he was rabbi, but also with free tuition for all his children in the elite local Orthodox day school, which included an excellent high school as well. But what tempted Rabbi Metzenbaum most of all was his perception that here was a rare opportunity, the kind most rabbis look for all their lives: a young, growing community, a place full of affluent, prominent people who would form an important stop on the fund-raising tours of every major Jewish organization. As rabbi, he could easily parlay his local popularity into national prominence, which would ensure him prestigious board memberships and thus an opportunity to influence the direction of Jewish education and community life all over the country. Moreover, it was a place where, when he chose to retire, he would be called Rabbi Emeritus and showered with compliments and a comfortable pension that would leave him the rest of his days to learn Talmud and write popular works of condensed Torah wisdom for busy Jews with short attention spans.

And thus, despite his long and revered position in the community, Rabbi Metzenbaum accepted the invitation of the Swallow Lake board to fly down with his family, all expenses paid, for a long weekend to explore the position. They put him and his wife and children up at the lovely home of the synagogue president, with its private swimming pool and tennis courts. They fed him lavish meals. They introduced the children to their peers and the rebbitzin to the sisterhood.

Sizing up his hosts, Rabbi Metzenbaum prepared his maiden sermon with meticulous care. He began with two good jokes, followed by an editorial from *The New York Times*, worked in a few minutes' worth of Talmud, and a few more minutes of light reminiscences of his childhood and memories of his grandparents, ending with a moral punch line, followed by another good joke. And he did it all in under twenty minutes. It was an enormous success.

He spent the Sabbath shaking hands and smiling at everyone, bending his head to listen intently to stories, compliments, jokes, and various normal and abnormal requests. He was friendly. He exuded modesty and compassion. Everybody loved him, except for those few misfits that exist in every congregation who never go along with the majority as a matter of principle; they warned that he was insincere, too religious, or not religious enough.

Shira Metzenbaum also made a favorable impression. She seemed attractive but in a dowdy religious way, which gave her a certain asexuality that relaxed the sisterhood. She smiled and was sincerely interested in the community, making an effort to learn everyone's names. She seemed willing—no, eager—to participate in the sisterhood activities. And the kids were bright and attractive, an asset to the community.

Both the Orthodox faction and the new immigrant faction were happy, and the Search Committee made Rabbi Metzenbaum an offer he couldn't refuse. Soon the Metzenbaums were making tearful announcements, being hugged and kissed and embraced at kiddush functions full of home-baked cakes and plastic cutlery. Far from being resentful or angry, his congregation sincerely wished their beloved rabbi and rebbitzin every happiness and success. Like proud parents seeing off a successful son, as much as they mourned for themselves, they rejoiced in his good fortune, accepting that it was the inevitable step he deserved to take to better his life.

The Metzenbaums attended a lavish going-away party, where there were many toasts, many tears, and many sincere testimonials. They sold their house, packed up their furniture and kids, and moved cross-country to begin their new life.

The rabbi poured himself into his work, getting to know all the movers and shakers, especially the members of the board: Solange and Arthur Malin, who owned a media empire; Amber and Stuart Grodin, who together had designed floppy novelty bears filled with a crunchy fragrant stuffing that became wildly collectible and dominated the aisles in every drugstore; Dr. Joseph Rolland, the world-famous heart surgeon, and his fashionable wife, Mariette; and the Borenbergs, Felice—a savvy businesswoman who had made a killing in her center aisle pushcarts at malls all over America, and Ari, her third husband and former employee.

The rabbi and his wife were a bit overwhelmed by the lavishness of the community, but the rabbi warned the rebbitzin she'd better stop sucking in her cheeks in contempt and disapproval when they showed her their game rooms, their home movie theaters, and their indoor pools with the retractable roofs. She had better remember not to remark with amazement on the self-cleaning wireless remote toilets, whose covers automatically lifted when you entered, and closed and flushed when you left. And she had better stop staring like a hick in Manhattan at the twenty-foot-high limestone fireplaces and the octagonal libraries made of Brazilian mahogany. He reminded her that they were there to focus on the community's spiritual requirements, and that even the most materially blessed could be very poor and needy when it came to their religious lives.

He told himself that this was an important group that could be led in a direction that would cause them to cherish their heritage, and to use their power, influence, and money to benefit the Jewish people. It was a group that was asking his help to go in a new direction.

He did what had worked so well in the Midwest: he began offering weekly classes for the men and boys. Attendance was poor, at first, but grew. Surprisingly, it grew most significantly among the high school boys, who found in the rabbi's sincere love for the Torah—particularly its ethics and morality—a spiritually viable alternative to rock music and Indian mysticism. Most of all, the rabbi was willing and able to give these youngsters what they needed most, something that their wealthy parents simply could not: time. He played basketball with them. He invited them over for little *melave malka* parties Saturday night. He knew what books they were reading. He was willing to counsel them on any subject and offer them help with any problem. He was willing to call their teachers and intervene on their behalf with their parents. He was tireless. And the kids loved him.

Shira Metzenbaum worked right alongside him. For if any woman since the beginning of time could be said to embody those true qualities needed to be a rabbi's wife, his partner in leading a congregation, it was Rebbitzin Shira Metzenbaum.

She not only cooked and baked and cleaned, she infused these tasks with holiness by constantly reminding herself that she was employing these womanly arts to bring misguided congregants closer to God. She was happy to have people join her on the Sabbath and on holidays; she loved a full house. There was never a Sabbath meal that did not include either board members she needed to impress, synagogue misfits she was attempting to remold, or complete strangers she was herding into her little flock. There was never a new mother to whom she did not take a casserole, investigating her mothering skills, or a sick person she failed to comfort by reading Psalms to counteract their obvious sins. There was no funeral or unveiling she didn't attend, no shiva call she failed to make, sitting silently in the house of mourning or offering tactful words of consolation: "It's a blessing you have other children."

As the rabbi tended to the young men, she drew around her the young girls, giving classes in modesty, chastity, Torah, and the Prophets. Soon, the girls were having long talks with their mothers. Gone were clothes that showed too much cleavage, too much knee. Soon, the rebbitzin and her followers began demanding a *mechitzah* that was taller, denser, and blocked the view completely. Certain women stopped using makeup on the Sabbath, surprising the men, who had never seen their wives look that bad. They insisted on trading in their king-sized beds for twin beds, slapping their husbands' hands away if they tried to so much as embrace them or kiss them during two weeks out of the month.

Words like *ruchnius* and *gashmiyus*, spirituality and materialism, began to pepper the speeches of teenagers, who looked around at their parents' lavish lifestyles with new eyes and new contempt. And then a few of the teenagers to whom the rabbi had been particularly close decided to attend yeshiva programs in Israel for the summer. When the summer ended, two of them called their parents to say they'd decided to stay there and join the Israeli army instead of making use of their early admission acceptances to Harvard and the University of Pennsylvania. Later that year, another one of the boys dropped out of Yale and went to live on the Lower East Side, enrolling in a yeshiva. He began wearing a black velvet skullcap, then a black hat and a long black coat. He grew long side locks and an unkempt beard. Soon, he refused to eat anything in his parents' home because he didn't think it was kosher enough. He adamantly refused to even consider returning to finish college, although he had only a year to go and the tuition had already been paid.

The final straw came when the daughter of Solange and Arthur Malin dropped out of Barnard and disappeared. She surfaced in Jerusalem at Michlalat Devorah, announcing she was engaged to a yeshiva student with whom she was planning to have ten kids and whom she would be working to support (presumably with her parents' generous help) for the rest of his life so he could sit and learn. The next day, the synagogue board of Ohel Aaron convened an emergency meeting.

Voices were raised. Hands slammed down on the table. A few punches were thrown. But in the end, when a vote was taken, it was overwhelmingly decided that the rabbi and his wife had to go. Given that the rabbi's contract had four more years to run, and the clause for early termination was going to cost the synagogue most of the funds they'd set aside to redo the catering hall so it could hold six hundred instead of only three hundred, the matter was turned over to Joshua Alterman, a Park Avenue lawyer known for defending white-collar criminals, some of whom were now his neighbors on Swallow Lake. It was Joshua who carefully reread the contract, finding the clause that hinted no penalty had to be paid if the rabbi—or his family—could be found liable for the termination. Brainwashing children into joining harmful cults, he suggested, would fit the bill nicely.

They gave Rabbi Metzenbaum two weeks' notice.

The rabbi and rebbitzin debated hiring a lawyer, but before they could do anything the synagogue sent a van to pack up their belongings and changed the locks on their house. The children were thrown out of the day school.

The scandalous treatment of the Metzenbaums in Swallow Lake soon became a cause célèbre, hotly debated among America's Orthodox Jewish communities and beyond. Soon, long articles appeared in *The Jewish Observer*, denouncing the Ohel Aaron congregation as a disgrace, and their treatment of Rabbi Metzenbaum and his lovely pious wife as tantamount to murder. As the very learned author and main stringency king of Boro Park explained—naming all the Ohel Aaron board members—embarrassing someone in public is considered akin to murdering them. *Midstream* hosted a written debate: "The Case of Swallow Lake: Has Orthodoxy Reached Its Nadir?" Even the religion editor of *The New York Times* decided to put in his oar, explaining to *Times* readers why an Orthodox congregation would fire a dynamic leader for encouraging young people to study in a yeshiva in Israel, or marry a yeshiva student, an article that made Orthodox rabbis and congregations everywhere cringe, made Conservative congregations giggle, and was pinned up on the bulletin boards of Reform synagogues throughout the country.

Soon JORA (Jewish Orthodox Rabbis Association) and RAOR (Rabbinical Association of Orthodox Rabbis) issued a call to boycott the congregation, telling their memberships that no rabbi should accept the now-vacant post of rabbi of Ohel Aaron until the poor Metzenbaums—jobless, living in the cramped basement of her parents' Canarsie home—received both an apology and monetary compensation. Rabbinic organizations refused to run the congregation's want ads for a new rabbi until informed by caustic letters from the Park Avenue law firm of Deal, Deal, Alterman and Goodstein that they were opening themselves up to lawsuits. While they immediately backed down and ran the ads, the word was out that Swallow Lake was a congregation to which no self-respecting rabbi should agree to go.

And that is why Congregation Ohel Aaron of Swallow Lake has been without a rabbi for two years, Chaim explained to Delilah, parking the car in front of their dusty apartment house late that Saturday night.

Delilah sat in the dark. Her eyes gleamed.

{ TEN }

*A*ll that winter, she pleaded with him to answer the ad. "What can it hurt?"

He looked at her, amazed and appalled. "You can't be serious. Don't you understand? They are being blackballed! Anyone who took the job would be a pariah! It would ruin his reputation, maybe get him thrown out of the Council of Orthodox Rabbis of America altogether! I've already told you how it would hurt my grandfather. And just think how offended this congregation would be. Why, they've been so kind to us, Delilah! It would be like spitting in their faces!"

Delilah, who didn't have much patience with other people's emotions, being caught up so passionately most of the time with her own, looked at him coldly, her eyes narrowing. "Do you know what your problem is, Chaim? You have no ambition. You are willing to rot away here in this dive because you are afraid to spread your wings and fly." She said this with a measure of accuracy that made her words doubly painful. "So, Ohel Aaron fired its rabbi. So what? Plenty of congregations fire rabbis! So it wasn't justified, at least according to all the busybodies out there writing articles. But think of this: Out of all those people who want to boycott Swallow Lake, is there even one who actually belonged to that congregation? Even one that had to sit through one of Metzenbaum's sermons or eat his wife's cooking on a Friday night? Josh is just so narrow-minded. There are two sides to every story. Isn't that what you always say? That we shouldn't judge someone until we are in their shoes? Huh?"

He saw she was furious and wished he could do something about it. But applying for the job in Swallow Lake was so beyond the pale, it never seriously entered his mind. His rabbinical life would be over; he'd be attacked by his fellow rabbis. People he respected and wanted to befriend, like Josh, would shrug their shoulders when his name was mentioned. No one would accept his rabbinical decisions. They wouldn't allow him to officiate at weddings. He would never be able to join a rabbinical court and arrange divorces. His career path would be blocked forever.

"Please, Delilah, be reasonable," he begged her helplessly. "Besides, even if I applied, there is no reason they should consider hiring me. Rabbi Metzenbaum was a respected rabbi for ten years. He's published books. He was elected president of all kinds of organizations. I haven't even been an assistant rabbi for one year! We would gain nothing and lose so much. Please, my love, try to understand."

She wanted to smash him over the head for his mild reasonableness, as the fury of thwarted hopes rose up from her bowels. In her mind, she saw the lovely house on the lake in Connecticut fade from view, replaced by used-car lots, smokestacks, and graffiti-smeared brick buildings. In the background, far off but clearly discernible, she heard the lilt of her mother's aggravated nagging, which would now follow her through eternity, reminding her how she could have done—oh, so much better.

Tears of misery tracked her face.

He stared at her, completely at a loss. When he tried to embrace her, she impatiently elbowed him out of her way.

Spring showed up. The bedraggled trees in the Bronx streets and alleyways sent forth a few anemic leaves. There was a drive-by shooting just down the block. And before they knew it, the season changed, transforming into the unbearably hot summer.

Delilah graduated in June with a license to practice dental hygiene. But instead of looking for a job, she did nothing. The idea of scrapping off bicuspids in the mouths of strangers suddenly nauseated her. She sat in her kitchen, swatting the flies, looking listlessly out the window into the street. She made no effort to get dressed, wearing her nightclothes into the late afternoon. Then she'd eat lunch and go back to sleep for the afternoon without washing the dishes from the morning or the previous evening.

One morning, her mother-in-law, who had the skill of a military cryptologist when it came to her son's laconic phone calls, turned up unannounced. She rang and rang the doorbell until Delilah finally heaved herself out of bed. Half asleep, she carelessly threw a short robe over her babydoll pajamas and opened the door.

Mrs. Levi took one look at her daughter-in-law, and one look at the house, before her face turned beet red. "What is the matter with you, Delilah? Look at yourself. Look at this place. You are a rabbi's wife! What if the president of the sisterhood should come to visit you?"

"She's ninety years old and would have congestive heart failure by the time she reached the second landing," Delilah murmured, groping for the coffeepot, which lay hidden under a mountain of unwashed dishes.

"Are you . . . you're not . . . pregnant? Is that it?" Chaim's mother offered hopefully, sending forth the only possible reason she could think of that might in any way excuse this behavior and allow her to feel charity or compassion for this girl, whom she had never liked and never wanted her son to marry.

"Absolutely not, thank God!"

Mrs. Levi turned purple, and began to choke. "Well, I never . . . had no idea . . . a religious woman, to feel that way . . . God just shouldn't punish you!"

"Don't worry. He already has. Look around you, Mama Levi." Delilah swept her arms expansively around the room. "This is what I've got to look forward to for the next fifty years, if Chaim and his grandfather have anything to say about it."

"You picked this apartment out! I distinctly remember the day you signed the lease! You said it had nice, big rooms." The older woman clutched the wall, feeling faint and alarmed. She could never have imagined her daughter-in-law behaving this way. While there had never been much love lost between them, Delilah had always made an effort to keep up appearances, to act the part of the good, religious daughter-in-law, not that she hadn't seen right through it. Still, on those too rare occasions she and her husband had been invited over, Delilah had always been well dressed and made up—even if it was with that horrid red "Hey, sailor" lipstick. The house had always been neat, if not exactly clean, with all the wedding gifts displayed, a few of them even shined and dusted.

"Yes," Delilah agreed. "I really know how to pick 'em, don't I?" she drawled, lighting up a cigarette and blowing smoke rings at the ceiling.

"When did you start smoking? It's a filthy habit." Mrs. Levi coughed, waving the smoke away frantically. She opened a window.

"That's right, Mama. The fresh air of the Bronx. So much better than Lucky Strikes," Delilah said, inhaling deeply as she sat down. The truth was, she'd bought her first pack just the day before. Although she thought the look was right for her present state of mind, she hated what smoking did to her well-cared-for teeth and pristine breath. But at the moment, the sacrifice was worth it. She crossed her legs and rested the side of her head on her hand, passively observing her mother-in-law's meltdown.

"So the real you has finally come out!" Mrs. Levi shouted. "I want you to know you never fooled me! I had your number from day one. I gave you a prince and you turned him into a *shmatte*!" she screamed.

"Excuse me, but that was the condition I got him in!" Delilah shouted back. "A *shmatte*. That's Chaim. A real, bona fide *shmatte*! Now get out of my house. I've had all I'm going to take from you and your precious son! Leave!"

Chaim's mother felt suddenly ill. She sat down heavily in the nearest chair.

Delilah got up. "Are you . . . all right, Mama?" she asked nervously, envisioning the call to 911, the paramedics, the flashing lights, the neighbors on the stoops, a frantic Chaim asking her all kinds of difficult questions, and—if they managed to revive the old crow—getting all kinds of contradictory answers. "Look. Don't get upset. I'm sorry. I'm just not myself."

The older woman stared at her coldly. "You've never, ever, been more yourself, Delilah. You are just like your mother. A pushy, materialistic, social climber. Except you have a better complexion, and haven't gained all that weight. Yet."

Delilah took two steps toward her, her fists clenched.

Mrs. Levi got up stiffly. She went over to the china closet and took out the lovely silver candlesticks that had been her wedding gift to her son's bride. She found a plastic bag on the floor—there were plenty to choose from—and put them inside. And then, wrapping her wounded dignity around her like a pashmina, she walked stiffly out the door, slamming it behind her.

Chaim, who had taken a teaching position in a local yeshiva to supplement their income, came home at five. He found his wife asleep. He also found they had new neighbors: a family of roaches had moved into one of the soup pots that had been lying around since the previous Sabbath. There was nothing to eat. No one had done the shopping. The refrigerator was empty.

He had gotten a frantic, completely incoherent phone call from his mother, calling him a *shmatte* and claiming his wife was a floozy. Even for his mother, it was a bit much. He had tried to calm her.

He loved his mother and respected her, as the Torah required. But from the beginning she had had a problem with his wife. She complained about her blond hair, calling her a "bottle blonde." But she had also told him, many times, that he didn't have what it took to be a rabbi. Now that he had incontrovertible proof that neither of these statements was true, he felt fully justified in ignoring her. Besides, an aging mother is never a match for a luscious new bride, a truth that mothers-in-law all over the world would do well to remember before they commence firing, even in self-defense.

He sat down in the living room and wondered, for the first time, if his marriage, upon which he had placed so many hopes, was falling apart. How had he failed this woman, whom he loved so much? he wondered. And what could he do to make her happy?

He cleaned up the kitchen, then went out and bought some take-out food and a bunch of yellow roses. He set the table, took the food out of the boxes, and warmed it up. Then he tiptoed into the bedroom and sat by her side at the edge of the bed, even though she was in the unclean part of the month. He felt reckless and a bit desperate. He smoothed back her lovely golden hair, breathing in the intoxicating scent of her warm, womanly body.

"Delilah," he whispered.

She opened her eyes, saw him sitting there, and felt a sense of alarm. "Get off, you know you're not allowed!"

He didn't budge. She stared at him.

"I love you," he whispered. "I'd do anything for you. I just want you to be happy."

"You don't care about me at all, Chaim." She shook her head, wondering what he could possibly be thinking if he was willing to sin. It was the first time she'd glimpsed an indication that he was capable of such a thing. The sight of it filled her with both a malicious satisfaction that she had gotten through to him, as well as a strange contempt. The lure of his religious piety during her short-lived repentance had been the bait that had hooked her, she realized. It was the one thing she'd really admired about him.

"Don't you see, I care more about you than I care about all the rabbinical prohibitions, all the fences around the Torah. I've broken them down, trampled on them, for you."

She failed to see what possible good this did her. "So your religion is a fake, the same way your love is?" she asked, annoyed, trying to move away from him.

He took a deep breath, keeping his temper in check. What good would it do to tell her off? She'd just be even angrier, if that was possible. "At least, come have something to eat. I've made dinner, cleaned up."

She sniffed the air. Chinese. All that grease, and you felt twice as hungry when you finished. But so what? She relented, feeling famished. If she got hungry, she'd eat again. What difference did it make if she got fat and ugly? Considering the eyesight of the people she was being forced to spend her time with, no one would notice anyway. She sat opposite him, eating silently and hungrily, filling her plate with noodles and rice and sweet-and-sour tofu made to look like pork. She ate and ate.

"Please, tell me how I can make things better."

She looked across at him. His face was the epitome of longing and misery and helpless yearning, the face of a dumb creature caught in a trap. She felt pity, but nothing else. He, after all, had willingly put his foot into the vice, while she had been lured there with decoys and false promises, she told herself.

The patent unfairness of this as a description of their courtship and marriage did not intrude upon her self-pity. Her equal responsibility for having chosen Chaim as a husband, and this apartment and neighborhood as a home, seemed to her less blameworthy than his having actually married her and dumped her in the Bronx with no hope in sight. Ever since the weekend at Josh and Rivkie's, she'd scanned the horizon like a shipwrecked sailor, hoping for some glimpse of a seaworthy vessel that might land in port and carry her off to the land of her dreams. But there was nothing, nothing. For this, too, she blamed him.

Life was not supposed to be like this. The man you married was supposed to make you happy. He was supposed to know your needs, without being told, and to do everything he could to fulfill them. Like Michael Douglas and Catherine Zeta-Jones. Like Tarzan and Jane. Like Superman and Lois Lane. Like Prince Charming and Cinderella. And it wasn't just a fairy tale. All you had to do was go to any synagogue in Scarsdale, and you'd see pews and pews full of Orthodox women who lived in mansions, wore designer clothes, and had vacations in Acapulco, live-in maids, and jewelry straight out of the ads in *Town and Country*. Why couldn't fate have arranged that for her? Found her a man who'd have whisked her off to Scarsdale, or Short Hills, or Beverly Hills? Why was she, who was so pretty, so blond, with such voluptuous curves, now stuck in three rooms, maidless, wearing rayon and polyester blends and tiny cubic-zirconium studs? All her treasures were wasted, thrown out, given away for pennies, to a man who took her to live in a Bronx apartment and fed her Chinese food out of boxes!

And then, she noticed the roses. A dozen of them. Such pretty flowers. Such a romantic gesture. She buried her nose in them, and the heavenly scent enveloped her like something out of a good dream. She looked at her husband, and then over his shoulder at the kitchen sink. All the dishes had been done, even the greasy pots with the burned-on fat that she had no intention of cleaning, ever. It was all sparkling. In a sudden impulse, she reached out to him. He clasped her hand to his heart, then brought it up to his lips, kissing her fingers one by one.

As their fingers intertwined, the wicked joy of transgressing a particularly annoying rabbinical precept made them feel young and bold and carefree and reckless. It wasn't such a terrible sin, to touch a woman when she was unclean, he told himself, looking at her sparkling eyes, trying to quiet his growing sense of unease. It wasn't like taking her to bed, God forbid! It was just a teeny, tiny step over the fence. He had absolutely no intention of wandering around in minefields.

"So, Chaim, does this mean . . . ?"

"What, my love?"

"That you'll look for another job?"

He looked into her eyes, losing himself in a calm blue sea of ravishing possibilities. What did she want to hear? What should he tell her? he thought, trying his best to navigate toward a safe shore. "If you are really so unhappy, I will, my love. But in order for me to find a job, I will have to keep this one a little while longer."

She took her hand back and placed it in her lap. "How long?" she demanded, her eyes narrowing.

He thought rapidly. "Another year?"

She got up and twirled around, heading for the bedroom.

He got up and went after her. "Well, nine months then. If I can write on my résumé that I've been assistant rabbi for over a year, we'll have a chance of actually getting some offers."

She stopped and turned around. "And then you'll write to Swallow Lake?" She smiled.

Such a beautiful smile, Chaim thought. Such lovely white teeth. Of course, she was a dental hygienist. She knew how to take care of them. Her mouth was a temple of order and cleanliness and plaqueless good smells. And her body. . . .

"Chaim?" she repeated impatiently, her lovely smile shutting down like an unplugged computer.

He thought about it. Nine months was a long time. Perhaps the boycott would be lifted by then. Or they'd become a Conservative or Reform synagogue, in which case they'd have plenty of candidates, no doubt better qualified, flooding them with résumés. Why fight about it now? "Well, if the job is still open, yes. I'll do that too."

"Do you promise?" That smile, that delicious smile, was back.

"I give you my word, *b'li neder*," he said, using the rabbinical formulation for swearing without actually promising anything that you couldn't take back.

Delilah, who understood the formula, also knew that there were many, many exquisite methods of torture that could be employed if he even thought about going back on his word. Moreover, since she could piously refuse to go to bed with him now, it wasn't as if this almost-promise was actually going to cost her anything. All around, it was a good deal. It was the tip of white sail in the distance she'd been looking for. It might take a while for the ship to arrive, but at least, she told herself, it was on its way.

{ ELEVEN }

The very next day, she jumped out of bed, deciding that life was worth living after all. She cleaned up the house, using rubber gloves and putting on her Walkman. She played Donna Summers' "She Works Hard for the Money" (*Some people seem to have everything!*); the Weather Girls' version of "Big Girls Don't Cry"; and Sade's "Mr. Wrong." When she got to Bruce Springsteen's "Janey, Don't You Lose Heart" (*you say you don't have no new dreams to touch*), she sang along, feeling tears come to her eyes. That Bruce, he really, really understood her. More than her parents, this husband of hers, or any of her friends.

She was full of love, passion, hope, youth, longing. She loved life. She wanted to do right by God, her parents, her in-laws, even Chaim and his grandfather and this synagogue full of doddering old folks. But she also wanted to squeeze some fun out of the planet before she got old and fat, like her mother, who'd spent her life stuffing her dreams down her children's throats, making everyone around her miserable.

She thought of her mother coming to the door of those beautiful houses that belonged to her classmates, pathetic in her fake pearls and discount high heels, waiting patiently to be invited in and how she never was; her mother at the wedding in that custom-made dress with the sequins, her hair done just so, waiting for people to look at her and think. "Well, isn't she something? Aren't her children something?" And how all anyone had noticed was her bad complexion and her fat stomach. And now, her daughter, the rabbi's wife, was living in a roach-infested apartment building in the Bronx, from which she couldn't move, because according to the rules of God she had to be within walking distance from the synagogue, the only synagogue in the world where her husband was willing and able to get a job because he had family connections. A synagogue where there was not a single woman that couldn't be her grandmother.

She put the radio on with a pounding full bass and sang along with Britney Spears ("Oops, I Did It Again!"), deciding that she might as well get a job. At least it would get her out of the house for the next nine months, and she'd be able to earn some money toward the wardrobe she'd need when she moved to Swallow Lake.

Through Bernstein's placement service, she found a dentist in Riverdale in an absolutely beautiful home on Goodridge Avenue in Fieldston. You couldn't believe this was the Bronx. It was like using the word *woman* to describe both Uma Thurman and Marilyn Goldgrab. The clients were all professionals or academics associated with nearby Columbia or Barnard, or they were people who lived in Riverdale. She found herself happy to be getting dressed in the morning and going out. And very soon she had a regular clientele, mostly middle-aged men who came in monthly for a cleaning, even though it really wasn't necessary. They flirted with her and complimented her, but as soon as they found out she was a rabbi's wife, they disappeared.

But then, one Friday night, Chaim showed up with a young man. He was respectable, not one of those homeless people who sometimes wandered in off the street during the cold winter months, looking for shelter and a little Saturday-morning booze. He was Jewish, and not a Hare Krishna or a confused Methodist out-of-towner, which also sometimes happened. He had wandered into the old synagogue simply out of curiosity, the way people sometimes step into churches to view the stained glass. He was unfamiliar with the Orthodox service and uncomfortable among all the old men. He'd had your basic American Bar Mitzva education, which succeeds so beautifully in leaving the student with a lifelong ignorance and lack of curiosity about anything related to the Jewish religion. Ascertaining all this, Chaim, thrilled, invited him home on the spot for Friday-night dinner.

"This is Benjamin Eckstein," Chaim said nervously, recalling her reaction the last time he'd brought home an unexpected Sabbath guest. ("So what if Abraham sat outside his tent and dragged in every passing camel? Does that mean I'm running a soup kitchen?" she'd shouted at him. The guest, an elderly shut-in who'd twitched all evening, had luckily been hard of hearing.) "He's new in the neighborhood and is thinking of joining our synagogue," he added quickly.

But Delilah didn't need any convincing. She just smiled demurely and set another plate at the table.

All through dinner, she studied him.

He was about twenty-eight, twenty-nine, she guessed, taller than Chaim but not tall. He looked like a clean-cut rock star, his face covered with a fashionable dusting of light blond stubble. He had a strong jaw, a sensuous mouth. His blond hair had been cut short but combed straight up with gel by a very hip hairstylist. He wore a corduroy jacket with leather patches on the elbows and a long wool scarf that was very Parisian-Left-Bank-starving-student. He had pale furtive blue eyes and pale lashes.

He was recently divorced and his wife had gotten the Manhattan condo, he told them with a certain air of melancholy, implying an unfairness on which he was too decent to dwell, although the truth was it had been hers to begin with. He described a job at a small advertising agency in Manhattan that sounded like creative director, when he was actually a freelancer. There were no kids. He made it sound as if the choice of an apartment in the Bronx had been an existential, almost spiritual choice, rather than a financial necessity. "I think the area has something really interesting going on," he told them, pouring the last of the wine into his glass and finishing it. He told long rambling stories about advertising rates and the cola wars. Chaim listened appreciatively. He loved hearing people's stories, and he enjoyed not having to entertain anyone, since he was "on" all weekend.

Delilah found him intensely interesting, despite the fact that she couldn't have cared less about anything he had to say. She made a special effort to sparkle and twinkle in his direction, speaking at length about her favorite commercials and how an infomercial on the shopping channel had once convinced her to buy a brush that spun around automatically, but it had broken down after three months and they wouldn't give her the money back.

He, too, tuned her out.

Yet all the while, voices inside them kept up a continuous murmuring communication that had nothing at all to do with what inanities their lips were forming. Secret knowledge passed between them through furtive, hidden glances; through eyes that narrowed and flashed, and did everything but outright wink. Like a promo for a new movie, these voices hinted at all the highlights and delights that awaited them if only they bought tickets to the show.

He began showing up at the synagogue regularly, secretly searching the pews for Delilah. It took him awhile to realize that almost no women showed up for services Friday night. So he started attending Saturday-morning services as well.

He was lonely and bored. The only women he met were blowzy middle-aged secretaries and jailbait from some of the modeling agencies. He didn't like models, he decided, after numerous attempts, one of them serious enough to have landed him in divorce court. They were women who liked to talk but didn't know how to listen, and for whom you functioned mainly as a mirror. While it was thrilling to wear one as an accessory out in public, where people could envy you, they soon became more trouble than they were worth, like stunning new shoes that killed your feet.

Delilah, on the other hand, was real, he told himself. He caught tantalizing glimpses of her through the lace curtains that hung along the wooden latticework that separated the men from the women, her face suffused in radiant light. The old, blazing chandeliers, the silver chalice covering the sacred Torah scrolls, the elderly rabbi's long, white beard, the patina of heavy golden-hued wood—all of it together seemed to create an aura of saintliness that rubbed off on her the way a cat leaves its scent on its owners.

He focused on her prayer-murmuring, lipstick-less mouth, her charming retro hats, her modest but well-fitted suits. And that blond hair! And those big blue eyes! And the white skin! And the unbridgeable moat between them! It was deliciously tempting in all its contradictory allure. He felt elated by the possibilities and at the same time challenged, depressed, safe, and hopeless at the improbability of breaking down the walls that surrounded her.

Delilah, equally bored, was flattered and amused by him and eager to play the game. She made sure to pull back the little lace curtain, pretending to want a better view of her husband, or the elderly rabbi, all the while aware of Benjamin's head turning in her direction. At kiddush, she felt his shadow move across her plate as she filled it with kiddush junk food: cookies, various oversalted or oversweetened morsels from cellophane bags. She looked up and smiled into his eyes just a fraction of a second too long. It was he who lowered his gaze first, shuffling off to the other end of the room to speak to the rabbi.

"Why don't we invite Benjamin for lunch?" Chaim suggested.

"Who?" she answered innocently.

"Benjamin. You know. The art director. The divorced one. He's all alone."

"Oh, I don't know," she said reluctantly, a small thrill hiding at the pit of her stomach.

"Don't you like him?" Chaim asked her, surprised.

"It's not that, it's . . ." She shrugged, trying to look annoyed. "But if you want. If you think—"

"No, no, it's not important . . ."

"But if *you* want," she continued, with a new insistence in her voice that thoroughly confused him.

Chaim, by now, was used to being confused. In fact, he considered it whimsical and charming that he could never understand a single, solitary thing when it came to his wife's motives, moods, interests, or desires. "Are you sure you don't mind?"

"No. Why should I? If I've cooked already for four guests, what's one more?"

He opened his eyes wide, but didn't say anything.

Benjamin was delighted to accept the invitation. He wore a dark suit that fitted him well, she thought, and a blue striped shirt with a tie that was knotted a little too tightly. She saw the red streaks of a too-close shave on the delicate skin of his neck just above his collar and how his light skin reddened in the winter wind. It filled her with tenderness.

He brought them a bottle of rare kosher wine for which he'd traveled all the way to lower Manhattan in the hope of future invitations. He'd run home after services to fetch it, looking forward to the opportunity of handing it to her, acutely aware that it would be their first physical contact.

"Oh, look, Chaim, French kosher wine!" Delilah said, delighted, delaying the transfer of the bottle from Benjamin's hands to hers a little longer than absolutely necessary. Her touch went through him like an electric shock. He moved his hand so quickly that the bottle almost fell.

She pressed her lips together, hiding a smile as she dipped to rescue it.

"Ah, a true *Oneg Shabbat*." Chaim nodded. "But it looks very expensive. You shouldn't have. I'll be afraid to invite you if it forces so much trouble on you!"

"No trouble at all," he lied.

Two of the shul's board members and their wives—kind, aristocractic, German Jews who spoke with a thick accent—had also been invited. Benjamin sat at the end of the table, casting sidelong glances at Delilah as she passed up and back, serving the food, conscious of how her shoulder arched beneath her dress as she brought in the trays and set them down. The first course was some kind of mushy-looking whitish thing covered with horseradish. "It's gefilte fish," she murmured, breathing softly in his ear as she put the plate in front of him. Her fingernails were well trimmed and painted a delicate shade of clear pink that made them look shiny and clean, like a newly washed child's, he thought. And her cheeks, pink and hot from the steaming kitchen, gave her a moist youthful glow. She smelled like vanilla.

There was a sudden knock at the door.

"Zaydie!"

Chaim's grandfather walked in with a gracious smile. He hardly ever visited and then only during weekday holidays, like Chanukah and the Intermediate Days of the Festivals, when taking a car was permissible and Chaim's parents could drive him over. That he had made the effort to walk several blocks and climb up two flights of stairs was remarkable and a bit disturbing. Chaim, touched and concerned, ushered him in with great reverence, giving up his own seat at the head of the table. "This is such a long walk for you. Why did you strain yourself, Zaydie?"

The old rabbi coughed and looked down at the table. "I spoke to your mother. She's . . . well . . . she thought it would be a good idea if I came to see you a little more often. I hope you don't mind. Please, go on with your meal."

"I was just about to serve the chulent, Zaydie," Delilah said, laying a plate for him, not looking into his eyes. She hurried into the kitchen, leaning heavily against the sink for a moment. What could Chaim's mother, that *klafta*, have told the old man? She could just imagine. She shrugged. Well, what of it? What could she do?

She served Chaim's grandfather first and then went over to Benjamin.

"Would you like meat or potatoes?" she asked him, and for some reason it sounded intimate, like a separate, secret conversation that involved only the two of them. Her eyes glanced at him sideways, a small smile on her pursed lips.

The old rabbi's eyes glanced up, studying them.

Benjamin caught the end of the heavy platters, helping her support them. They gave each other a quick but meaningful glance as their fingers touched. "Oh, whatever you give me will be fine," he said softly.

The old man suddenly pushed his chair back from the table. "I'll go now," he said, getting up abruptly.

"But why, Zaydie?" Chaim begged him, upset and confused. "You just got here! Please don't go!"

But the old man was already at the door.

People began to leave after that, a sense of impropriety and discomfort suddenly poisoning the atmosphere like someone rudely exhaling from a big cigar as all around people choked on the smoke. They quickly said the Grace After Meals, and were gone.

"Why don't I bring some tea and cake?" Delilah said brightly when only Benjamin was left. She, Benjamin, and Chaim sat together around the table, drinking tea, speaking casually, as Chaim, trying to be hospitable despite his sense of lingering discomfort, talked in a friendly way about his adventures with various shul committees about upcoming synagogue functions.

Always, the topic returned to the morning prayer service. They needed at least ten men—a minyan—to hold a prayer service. It was a disgrace, a disgrace!—that in a community of this size they had trouble finding ten men. Every morning! The absence of mourners required to say Kaddish for the departed souls of parents—the mainstay of Orthodox morning prayer services everywhere—left them at a distinct disadvantage, most of their congregants having lost their parents decades ago. Benjamin, who felt he should now offer to get up at five every morning to attend, shifted uncomfortably in his seat. There was no point in offering if he had absolutely no intention of keeping his word. And yet—

"I'd be happy to join," he found himself saying, aware of her eyes on him and the small nod and smile with which his words were acknowledged.

"That would be great!" Chaim rubbed his hands together appreciatively, already feeling better, fully rewarded for his efforts to integrate this stray. "Really wonderful."

"More tea? Or coffee?" Delilah murmured to Benjamin. Their eyes held.

Chaim, already busy pouring over the Torah reading of the week, smiled but didn't look up. "Thanks, my dear. Coffee."

As the liquid cooled in their cups, Delilah and Benjamin sat across from each other in the living room, she on the sofa, he in the armchair, reading magazines. "I think this is a beautiful ad," Delilah said as she thumbed through a women's magazine, trying to find in it something that would connect them. She wanted to sound sophisticated.

He took the magazine from her, pretending to study it. It was a silly ad, he thought, predictable and corny: a family in white shirts sitting on the grass. It could be selling anything from detergent to perfume to milk of magnesia. "I see what you mean." He nodded seriously. What lovely eyes she had! That color, like a jewel, with tiny gold flecks. "It takes special eyes to notice this kind of thing."

She found herself blushing.

"Well." Chaim yawned, oblivious, stretching.

Benjamin, who had only his lonely apartment with its unmade bed waiting for him, reluctantly began to realize that he too was expected to leave. At the door, she handed him a package.

"Here, another piece of cake. I know how single men are. They have empty refrigerators," she scolded him, her hands touching his. His fingers pulled back as if scorched. When he got home, he unwrapped the package, eating the cake greedily, crumb by delicious crumb.

He took to jogging past her house Sunday mornings.

Delilah, her hands encased in rubber gloves as she scrubbed the grime of the city from her neglected windows, felt herself start when she saw him run by. How slim he was, she thought. His shoulders and stomach were like a college student's in his running outfit, his hair still adolescent in its thick golden shine. She gazed at her reflection in the glass, studying her face: still young, still sexy. She pouted at herself until she heard Chaim open the door as he returned from the morning minyan.

"Could have sworn that was Benjamin . . . strange guy. He hopped over to the other side of the street when he saw me coming."

"Maybe he's embarrassed he didn't show up for minyan," she said, her eyes lowered.

"Yeah, that's probably it. But, then, what is he doing hanging around here?"

"He's jogging!"

"But he's got a park right across the street from his house."

She didn't answer him. Why should she? He didn't expect her to know anything. Besides, she wasn't sure she did. It could be a coincidence. He had plenty of women in that ad agency, all those *Sex and the City* wannabes breathing down his neck.

Be realistic, Delilah.

But it was so much fun to think about. Much more fun than thinking about her next scrape and polish. Or her next *chesed* project.

If you were the rabbi's wife, you always had to have a *chesed* project. Feed the hungry, visit the sick. The more time-consuming and distasteful, the more worthy the project. So far, she had resisted anything with hospitals. Chaim got stuck with all the sick calls; considering that the entire congregation practically took weekly vacations in Mount Sinai the way other people went to Florida, he spent endless time in sickrooms.

They had been after her to do the old-age homes, the openmouthed snorers sitting in their diapers in wheelchairs. The mumbling, insistent ones who grabbed you and made you their slaves. Get me this. Pick up that. Wheel me there.

She wasn't going back to the Moscowitz Hebrew Geriatric Center. Only one afternoon, and it had taken her three shampoos to get the smell out of her hair. She liked kids well enough. She offered to find some Jewish ones and do something with them.

"That doesn't actually sound like much of a plan," Chaim said mildly.

"So you think of a better one!"

"I don't know," he said, exasperated. "Maybe you could help some of the shul members with their shopping. Or take them to their medical appointments—so they won't wind up in the hospital."

"Old people," she griped.

"Well, it's their pensions that are putting food on our table and paying our credit card bills, my love. Show a little compassion. We'll be old one day too."

She looked up at him, suddenly stricken with conscience pangs. He really was a good person, she realized, ashamed of herself. He really did care about other human beings. And she, in taking on the job of being his partner, had to be a better person in spite of herself.

"All right. I'll take them shopping. I'll even do makeovers."

"Honey . . ." he cautioned.

"Just kidding."

She began by making a few phone calls, asking for advice from the president of the sisterhood, who liked her. She got a list of names and went about calling them, asking if they'd like her to join them the next time they went shopping. But that's not what they wanted. What they wanted was for her to pick up their shopping lists and do their shopping for them.

So, after work, she hurried to make dinner, then ran down to pick up their lists. Then she took the car and drove from store to store, buying farina and canned green beans and Metamucil, standing in lines and carrying heavy brown bags to the car. And, of course, she bought the *wrong green beans*, the ones with salt. They all had salt, except for one brand, sold in a little health food store where it was impossible to find parking. In the end, the old biddy even refused to pay for it. "I'll just have to throw it out. All that salt could increase my Lenny's blood pressure. Is that what you're trying to do, give him a heart attack?! What kind of help is this, anyway?"

Without telling anyone, she stopped picking up the shopping lists. Chaim was deluged with phone calls from outraged congregants who had immediately gotten used to the idea of having a personal shopper and were now furious at having their old lives back.

"You work for the shul, not me. I quit," she told him when he protested. "You go search all over town for low-sodium vegetables."

Being left with no choice, he came to a compromise, offering to drive them around to their stores. But this meant he needed the car and Delilah would have to take the subway to work. She was furious.

"Why is it I'm always the last person on the list, the last one you worry about being nice to?" she fumed. "Why does every stranger in this place, people who hardly say hello to you, who don't care about you at all, always have to come before me, your own wife?"

He shrugged helplessly. "I'll try to work something out. Please, Delilah, just be patient!"

But as she entered the subway station, there was Benjamin, waiting on the platform. They approached each other a little awkwardly at first. But then, meeting every morning, he got more talkative. He told her about his childhood, the inevitable grandmother who lit Sabbath candles, the grandfather who was "very religious," which Delilah knew could mean anything from eating chicken soup to wearing a *streimel and kapota*. You never knew what people meant by it. What Benjamin meant was that his grandfather wouldn't eat pork in the house, only in restaurants.

What had brought him to their synagogue? Delilah asked.

"I don't know. I was feeling kind of lonely, maybe. At loose ends, with the divorce and all. I was thinking about families and rituals, and I just happened to pass your synagogue. It was dark outside and the building was all lit up. I just walked in. Your husband was so friendly. He seemed really glad to see me."

"He is glad. The synagogue needs new blood."

"The old people seem to love him. To love both of you," he hurriedly corrected himself.

"Sure," she said wearily. "But let's not talk about the synagogue. Let's talk about you and your relationships. What kind of woman are you looking for?"

He swallowed hard.

"Don't be shy. This is what rabbis and their wives in Orthodox congregations often do for members of their congregations," she assured him. That was it! A *chesed* project! He was obviously unhappy. Perhaps she could help him? "Tell me about your ex-wife."

He spoke at length, in intimate whispers, making up things as he went along, editing out his penchant for short-lived affairs, creating a persona that was similar to his but deeper, more steadfast, more moral.

She listened with deep concentration, offering Dr. Phil–type clichés that made her feel both virtuous and wise and salved her conscience.

He looked at her, taking in the pious high collar, the demure covered knees, the silky blond hair beneath the charming beret. How does one seduce such a woman? He entertained the idea idly, not so much making plans as daydreaming. He pondered her, and his predicament. She was, after all, the rabbi's wife, like Caesar's, above reproach. But he could tell she was fed up with her husband and her life, even if she couldn't. A woman like that could be dangerous, he knew. And he certainly wasn't ready for anything sticky or complicated—not after having just extricated himself from a mess of lawyers and court appearances and fights over CDs and dishes.

But there is a certain unmatchable allure religious women have for a certain kind of secular man. In a world filled with licentiousness—women who wore practically nothing and wrapped their legs around the backs of chairs to sell everything from computer chips to chocolate chips in once-respectable magazines—a woman who covered her body had an infinite charm. Then, too, the constant threat of deadly sexually transmitted diseases made the virtues of sexual chastity as secretly appealing to the sex-glutted psyche of the modern man as short skirts and sexual availability were to his father and grandfather.

He knew that in her code of ethics adultery was as bad as murder, a commandment etched in Moses' tablets by God's own finger, brought down amid fire and brimstone. And yet, the thrill of trying! Imagine winning over such a woman! And truthfully, he admired her for all the qualities he imagined religious women have, bestowing them all upon her in his imagination, never once dealing with the fact that, if she yielded to him, she would no longer possess that which had attracted him to her in the first place.

But then, who among us can think clearly when our brains are awash in hormones?

After weeks of subway rides, the furtive stretching of hands along the back of her seat, the moving of thighs just an iota closer so that their coats touched, he decided he would declare himself. Then he decided not to. Then he gave himself ultimatums, deadlines, only to forget about them, or extend them or rethink them. He was terrified to move too quickly, afraid she would take flight.

Delilah began to dress more carefully for work, to try out different shades of lipstick, different hair clips. She'd adjust her hat at new angles, eyeing herself seriously in the mirror, turning her head first to the left and then to the right, smiling seductively at her image. Sometimes, as she lay in bed in the mornings before getting dressed, she thought of how she had asked him about his beard and how he had leaned toward her intimately and said, "I thought religious women liked men with beards."

"Maybe they do," she'd answered boldly, "but I don't."

The next day, he had shown up clean-shaven.

It had thrilled her. She began to daydream. What if Chaim should be rushing across the street, and a bus should come along! Oh, the horror of the ambulance, the blood, the hospital! But then it would eventually all be over. A coffin. A funeral. And she would mourn him. She could already see her eyes unattractively red, in great need of drops. But she'd also heard that widows lost weight because all they did was smoke and drink coffee. And then she would be allowed to stop mourning. And she would have a little condo in Manhattan, and a husband who wrote advertising copy for expensive magazines. A man who had weekends off, and had no congregants swarming around him that needed to be fed like pigeons in the park, who, the more you gave them, the more they left their droppings all over you . . .

And then, one morning, as she and Benjamin were sitting cozily on the subway, laughing, his arm draped across the back of her seat, she looked up and saw Mrs. Schreiberman, vice president of the sisterhood, who reached into her bag and took off her reading glasses, replacing them with her distance glasses. As Delilah saw it, she had two choices: one, to lean back on Benjamin's arm and ignore the woman completely; or, two, to wave casually, like this was normal. As forest rangers will tell those traipsing through national parks who might run into an eight-hundred-pound grizzly bear, the worst thing she could do was jump up and run.

She waved. But the little smile on her lips faded as she stared into Mrs. Schreiberman's shocked and outraged face. She had apparently decided not to play games. Delilah stiffened, giving Benjamin a quick nudge with her elbow. He looked up, realizing what was happening. If he had had the presence of mind to wave also, Delilah just might have pulled it off. But as it was, he looked as conscience-stricken as if he had been found in bed with the rabbi's wife, instead of just sitting next to her, fully clothed, in a public subway car.

Mrs. Schreiberman pressed her lips together and nodded to them both, a quick pained nod acknowledging that people like them existed in the world, and Delilah thought: uh-oh.

She considered going over to speak to her, but since she had no doubt been inundated with phone calls from disgruntled former *chesed* recipients who had gotten the wrong green beans and then been abandoned altogether, she thought better of it. What were the chances the woman would spill the beans and talk to Chaim? And even if she did, what could she possibly say? That his wife had taken the same train as a synagogue member? Sat next to him? Shared a laugh? Was it her fault the old bag got her jollies from imagining wicked scenarios?

When Chaim got home that night, the warm scent of baking and the wafting hot odor of soup greeted him at the door. To his shock, the house had been tidied, and the piles of women's magazines that usually covered the sofa and coffee table had disappeared into neat piles on well-dusted shelves. There was music coming from the stereo—some Hasidic boy's choir from one of the few CDs that actually came from his collection. Delilah, who was usually busy watching television when he got home, or soaking in the tub, was actually dressed. She looked very pretty, her smooth blond hair sliding over her shoulders like liquid honey, her lipstick freshly applied.

"Dinner will be ready in a minute, Chaim. Why don't you go wash? I have some rolls hot out of the oven."

"Everything is all right, isn't it? I mean, it's not a birthday or anniversary or celebration, is it?" he asked her anxiously.

She stood there, busy stirring something in a pot, not looking up at him. "No, nothing like that. Why would you even say something like that? What, I never make you dinner? I never clean up the house? It's got to be some special occasion?" Her voice trembled a little.

Now, he'd insulted her, he thought, slapping his palm against his forehead. She finally acts the way a wife is supposed to, and all he can do is be suspicious of her motives. Didn't Jewish ethics demand that one "weight the judgment of every man toward the good"? Was it not written, "Do not cause your wife to cry, as God counts each one of her tears"?

"A pleasant home, a pleasant wife, and pleasant furnishings enlarge a man's mind!" Chaim blurted out joyfully.

Delilah turned to look at him. She studied his rosy cheeks, like a schoolboy's, his wide, unfurrowed forehead, his innocent dark eyes, the sweetness of his untroubled smile of happiness. She smiled back. "Here, Chaim. Come sit down. You look hungry."

They sat across from each other at the table, in companionable silence.

"So, how did your day go?" he asked her, slurping the good vegetable soup with gusto. The sound of it sloshing around in his mouth made her a bit nauseous. She wrinkled her nose.

"Oh, nothing special. I met Benjamin on the train to work. He was telling me some funny stories about one of the models. . . . And right across the aisle, I saw Mrs. Schreiberman. So Benjamin and I wave to her, and she looks at us as if she's caught us making out. These old biddies live a rich fantasy life, let me tell you."

Chaim put his spoon down and wiped his mouth with his napkin, the implications of this conversation slowly breaking on him the way an egg oozes out of a broken shell, turning everything in its path into a sticky, gooey mess.

"Delilah, is there something you aren't telling me?"

She thought about that. What was she hiding? That she had been going to work with Benjamin every morning? That she had been leaning into his arm, which more and more found its way across the back of her seat? That she had been discussing with him the most personal aspects of his sex life? Does a woman have to share everything with her husband?

"Listen, Chaim, we go to work about the same time every morning. That's just the way it worked out since you started taking the car. And yes, we do talk about intimate topics because . . . because I'm trying to counsel him! He's lonely. He needs a *shidduch*. And so he speaks to me about his life. Isn't that what a rebbitzin is supposed to do? Listen and try to help?"

The picture clarified in his mind. His mouth formed an O. His mind formed an *Ah!* And his heart formed an *Oy.*

What now? If Mrs. Schreiberman spread this around the synagogue, and it got back to his grandfather . . . The congregants were very loyal to their old rabbi and very fond of his grandson. But Delilah had made it clear she found them boring, a burden, even a source of jokes. She flaunted her youth in their faces. And while they would have been willing to forgive her many lapses with the tolerance that comes with the wisdom of age, he wasn't sure she would ever be forgiven if the matter wound up public knowledge that would in any way taint or hurt his grandfather.

"Maybe I should speak to her," Chaim murmured, "before it gets out of hand. Explain to her about the—about your . . . counseling." He swallowed, and his voice dribbled off, melting into silence, taking with it his determination and conviction. What if he brought the subject up with her and she'd already forgotten all about it? He chewed his nails.

"Chaim, have your steak. It's fresh from the oven."

He looked up at Delilah, her pretty face, her eyes—blue as a mountain lake in summer—the tiny waist, and the voluptuous breasts. *A pretty woman means a happy husband. The count of his days is doubled*, the Talmud wrote. Then again, it also wrote, *A wicked wife is like leprosy to her husband.* The great rabbis in the Talmud were also clueless when it came to women, he thought. Why did he expect to be any smarter?

He picked up his knife and fork and cut into the tender juicy meat that melted like butter on his tongue. He took a large helping of creamy mashed potatoes and salad, dressed with a wonderful vinaigrette.

Whatever was going to happen tomorrow was going to happen. Tomorrow.

"Why don't we have a nice, relaxed evening, my love? I'll help you with the dishes, and then—" He glanced toward the bedroom. They were in their lucky two weeks out of the month. Like sailors who were gone from home six months out of the year, no matter what kind of a marriage they had, at least half the time they were happy.

{ T W E L V E }

When things that should bring one's walls tumbling down do not, the unexpected reprieve sometimes brings about the exact opposite one would anticipate: not relief and gratitude and rehab, but the idea that one can take even greater risks and get away with it.

Delilah, having weathered the discovery of her delicious little secret without suffering any of the dire consequences, instead of being penitent and taking her undeserved opportunity to redouble her caution, learned the opposite: having escaped she became more, not less, daring.

The morning train rides stopped, Chaim deciding to give her back the car and discontinue the shopping trips. The old people were remarkably understanding—or else they knew something. Or perhaps it was the common idea that while it was perfectly fine to burden the rabbi's wife with their errands, it was unseemly to bother the rabbi himself.

Delilah, far from viewing the car as the opportunity to safeguard her reputation, envisioned it opening the door to even more exciting possibilities. She decided to buy theater tickets. She would invite Benjamin to join her at a matinee on Broadway. It was a sudden impulse, one that came to her because she happened to hear "Cell Block Tango" from the musical *Chicago* playing on the radio at the dentist's office. Something in the wording ("He had it coming all along") struck a responsive chord. And suddenly she remembered a conversation she'd had with Chaim about the theater very soon after their wedding.

Modern Orthodox Jews, unlike their black-coated black-velvet-skullcap-and-oversized-fedora-wearing Ultra Orthodox brethren, do, for the most part, participate in the modern world. They have television sets, are sometimes *Seinfeld* and *Star Trek* fanatics, and will watch—if not admit to enjoying—*Sex and the City*. (Caveat: This is not to say that there are not many, many secret *Sex and the City* fans among Ultra Orthodox Jews, who simply hide their TVs in the closet.) However, the wearing of a religious symbol on one's head *does* build in a shame factor that makes the public viewing and enjoyment of barely dressed women and raucous scenes of a sexual nature difficult and embarrassing for modern Orthodox Jews, let alone rabbis. If you add to that the glorification of murder, adultery, and the liberal use of the kind of profanity that would have made pimps blush not long ago, most Hollywood movies and Broadway plays had become off limits to the skullcap-wearing community, velvet or crocheted.

"I just don't feel comfortable," Chaim explained. "You never know what you are going to see. Or hear! All those disgusting four-letter words. . . . Remember that movie *It's a Wonderful Life*? When beautiful little Bedford Falls turns into sleazy Pottersville? Well, the whole world has become Pottersville. The old black-and-white movies are all right. But movies and the theater these days? No rabbi can be seen in such places."

She understood him. But the idea that her entire life was now subject to a hidden committee who would be judging the appropriateness of all her actions, including anything she chose to see or hear on her own free time, was simply infuriating. And unlike her husband, she wasn't stuck with a big neon light on her head that flashed I'M A HOLY MORAL PERSON, AN ORTHODOX JEW. She viewed herself as free, even if Chaim wasn't. The fear of God, still firmly planted in some little corner of her heart, making her tremble during the closing prayers on Yom Kippur (*who will live, and who will die; who in his time and who before his time*) did not extend to weekday entertainment choices. The God she loved and believed in was a very busy, preoccupied, and long-suffering Deity, who couldn't possibly be checking the titles of the videos she borrowed. Her God was saving His time and energy to track all the really horrible acts being committed in the world: men who slept with their daughters; corporation heads who used up pension funds for million-dollar birthday parties; Muslims who slit the throats of their sisters; rabbis and priests who buggered small children. She figured, when He finished with all of them, He might have time to deal with her movie choices, which gave her plenty of time.

She took the train to Manhattan, took out money from the ATM, and bought orchestra seats to *Chicago* for a matinee the following Wednesday. Then she called up Benjamin and offered him a ticket. He said he had something at work that day, but he'd try to get out of it.

The truth was, he was confused. This was taking it a step further. Why he wasn't absolutely thrilled, he wasn't sure. Could it be because she had preempted him, thus wounding his male pride? Or had he started the process of rethinking the whole situation? He was feeling restless lately, with his go-nowhere job, his cramped Bronx walk-up, his sexless affair. The idea that he was now going to have to fit into her designs, fulfilling her impulses on demand, further eroded any sense of congratulation he might have felt in this proof of the progress he was making in pursuing the untouchable woman who was the rabbi's wife.

Nevertheless, he agreed. He wanted to see *Chicago*, and the tickets were very expensive.

Even though it was a matinee and she expected to be home in plenty of time, a sudden urge prompted her not only to hide her trip to the theater from Chaim but also to tell him her boss might ask her to work an extra shift at the clinic that day, so she might be home really late. She didn't explain this to herself, having found it was better not to tell herself everything.

Wednesday morning, she got up early and prepared Chaim a big breakfast: hot cereal with cinnamon and crushed walnuts, toasted whole wheat English muffins, a tomato-and-feta-cheese frittata. He sat there, pleased, slowly chewing, talking about some shul member who wanted to donate his house to the synagogue because he was a Holocaust survivor and had no one to leave it to. He had asked Chaim's advice.

"But I don't know. Maybe I should tell him to leave it to Israel or to shelters for abused women. I don't know what to tell him."

Something about his confusion, and the sincerity of his struggle with something that would have presented no moral dilemma for most people, touched her.

"Chaim, maybe you'd like to go to the theater with me today? A friend of mine has two tickets for a matinee—"

"But I thought you said you had to work late?"

"I could call in sick. We could go together. Come on, it'll be fun!"

He smiled and kissed her hand. "I don't go to the theater. You know that. What play is it, anyway?"

"*Chicago.*"

"Whew. That's definitely off limits. Those costumes. And murder and adultery. Religious Jews shouldn't be watching that," he said, shaking his head.

The primness of his dismissal made her jaw tighten.

"Maybe we could go to see *Golda's Balcony*. Or *Fiddler.*"

She ignored that. "So, you don't want to?"

He stared at her, shaking his head. "Why would I?"

That was certainly true, she thought, relieved. So taking Benjamin wasn't actually taking anything away from Chaim.

She parked the car and met Benjamin in front of the theater. He wore a long camel-hair coat that looked handsome, if a bit worn. He had his fingers in the pockets and his thumbs beat a nervous tattoo against his thighs. She didn't approach him right away, standing on the side to watch him, wanting to examine him a little more closely, to decide what exactly it was that attracted her.

But the more she stared, the more confused she became. He was good-looking, true, in a very Gentile kind of way that had never before attracted her. But it wasn't his looks, not really. When they were together, a little voice inside always whispered with irritation, "So what?"

Truthfully, she liked him better when he wasn't around. She liked the idea of him, the daydreams she wove around him, with herself in the center and him fluttering like a moth, irresistibly drawn to her charms. His attraction to her was his strongest, sexiest quality.

He, on the other hand, felt the opposite. As much as he occupied her thoughts when they were apart, she disappeared from his. He actually managed to forget what she looked like from encounter to encounter. But when he saw her, he always felt a little thrill.

She looked so pretty, her complexion a lovely, rosy color from the cold and her body unfashionably shapely and soft, with real breasts and real hips. It was the way a women's body should be and had been, until designers and ad men decided to turn women into hipless, flat-chested, coltish adolescent boys, he thought.

For the first time, he offered her his arm. She decided not, hanging back. Then she decided—why not?—slipping her arm through his as they went off in search of their seats. What did it matter, after all, if their fully clothed bodies politely touched?

The show was wild. The costumes—if you could call those little bits of torn string a costume—draped provocatively over those perfect bodies; all that bumping and grinding. The music and dancing, the clever irony of plot, involving corrupt politicians, lawyers, and journalists, combined to make it a great show. Chaim might have enjoyed it too, whatever he said. But his public persona—the pious rabbi with the dignified public stature—would have insisted on coming along too, sitting between them, crushing both their joy with the weight of scandalized disapproval. If only her husband had been able to leave his public persona behind every now and then, she mused, inside the same Borsalino hat box that held his black Sabbath hat.

As an Orthodox woman, she understood the public need to defend modest dress and condemn loose women. She herself would not have wanted to actually wear any of those outfits she saw on stage. Still, she couldn't go along with Chaim's ban on Broadway, because that would be a slippery slope. First came Broadway shows, next was bathing beaches with bikini-clad women, then in-flight entertainment. And then where would she be? Stuck in a colorless Oz with no ruby slippers; inexorably hemmed in, trapped, by all those fences around the Torah that Chaim was always talking about.

Everyone had to decide on his own fence, Delilah thought. And some blessed creatures should always be allowed to roam the range with no barriers at all. Fences, after all, just gave certain people the urge to climb over or crawl under. In her personal experience, the only barriers that stopped someone from going where he shouldn't were the ones that did severe tire damage, putting you and your vehicle out of commission. FORBIDDEN. KEEP OUT! was like waving a red flag in front of a bull. If you thought you might get away with it, including tiptoeing successfully through a minefield, then fences simply became a welcome challenge, a way to show you knew better than the fence makers what was, and was not, good for you.

After the show, they exited into the snowy city streets, his blond head bare of any covering. It was the first time she'd ever gone somewhere accompanied by a bareheaded man. She found it strange yet liberating. When you walked in the city accompanied by a mate possessing unmistakable religious symbols on his person, people tended to draw in their chests tensely, as if your mere existence demanded that they make some kind of decision, choosing one thing over the other. Now, if people stared, it was simply because they were such a handsome couple, both young, both blond.

The out-of-towners especially, in their inappropriate-for-every-occasion clothing and obscure sports-team caps, looked at them with envy, she thought, instead of the veiled, vague hostility that came her way whenever she ventured out into Manhattan tourist spots with Chaim.

"Let me take you out for dinner," Benjamin offered. He liked her. She made him laugh, but she was never coarse. He like the innocent pleasures she fought with herself over enjoying, the way her clothes always left so much to the imagination. She thought she was daring and yet, she was at heart such an innocent. He began to remember why he had been drawn to her in the first place. There was something devastatingly attractive in a woman who struggles with her better instincts all the time and loses.

She turned to him, blushing. How much fun that would be! A proper dinner out. But it would have to be in a kosher restaurant, she realized. No matter in which fenceless fields she roamed, she was not about to trespass into anything clearly, black-and-white sinful, like eating unkosher food. But in a kosher restaurant, someone she knew was sure to spot them.

"Too public?" he surmised. She nodded. "So, why don't I go into Broadway Deli and buy lots of takeout, and we can put it in the car and take it to my place and eat in peace."

He wanted her to go up to his apartment. That was all she heard.

She hesitated.

"Listen, maybe I was out of line. But let me go in and buy you some food for dinner, just to thank you, and then you can just drop me off on your way home."

That seemed reasonable, she told herself, already disappointed, as if he'd rescinded the invitation.

They drove along the busy Manhattan intersections, not saying much, because they both knew they were entering a no-turning-back zone. When they got to the Bronx and neared his building, he turned to her, putting his hand on her arm.

"Please, Delilah. Come up with me."

Her thoughts jumped around in her head, doing back flips and somer-saults, running forward, banging into brick walls, then going around and around until finally stopping with exhaustion. The idea of returning early to her staid married life in the drab apartment she hated, to the placid hus-band who bored her with his goodness, made her feel like an insect caught in amber. She felt sleepy and unwilling to resist any temptation that came her way.

"Just for a minute," she told him, parking the car a block away, in a neighborhood she was sure was out of the radius of walking distance to their synagogue. She looked around her furtively as she walked with him toward his apartment. Only when they got inside did she concentrate on what she was seeing. His building was even worse than hers, with graffiti all over the walls and run-down hallways perfumed by cheap cooking oil. Only a brass door plate announcing DR. AVRAM MENDES, SECOND FLOOR gave the building its solitary touch of respectability.

"You have a doctor in this building?"

"A chiropractor who is at least one hundred and fifty years old, they say. I've never actually seen him come out of his apartment. He might have died ten years ago, for all anyone knows, and be lying there, rotting."

She looked up at him, surprised. What did she know about him, really? He could be one of those serial ax murderers, the ones that have a signature. Maybe he was the kind that wandered into synagogues and wound up strangling rabbis' wives. Maybe there was a whole file on him that would become another episode on *Law and Order*.

"Delilah?"

He was smiling at her, his feet on the stairs. She smelled the pastrami and sour pickles in the brown bags from the deli. She loved pastrami. She followed him up. His apartment was larger than hers—or maybe it just looked that way because it was so sparsely furnished. There was an old white couch with some colorful Indian pillows. An exotic animal-print throw rug on the floor. Framed prints of what looked like advertising posters on the wall. "Are those your ads?" she asked, hoping to be im-pressed.

"Some of them," he said, waving vaguely in their general direction.

"Wow, they're beautiful!" She was overwhelmed by talent of any sort, people who actually created something from nothing. She wandered into the kitchen. He was already taking the food out of the containers, putting them into plates and bowls.

"Um, is this your meat set or your milk set of dishes?"

"Huh?"

"You have two sets of dishes, don't you? Meat and milk?"

He shrugged. "Sorry. Just the one."

She stared at the food. If it was cold, she'd be able to eat it. But not if it was hot and had been put into a dish that had once held ice cream. The biblical prohibition of not cooking a calf in its mother's milk had, through the centuries, turned into one of the most exacting and wide-ranging set of laws separating meat from milk, to the extent that religious Jews waited up to six hours to allow milk to enter their mouths again after they'd eaten the flesh of cows, chickens, turkeys, ducks, bison, and any other living creature except fish, just in case some meat might still be caught between their teeth.

"Listen, why don't you let me do that?"

She searched through his barely filled cupboards for paper or plastic plates, or maybe just some glass bowls, which the rabbis had decided were nonporous and thus could be used for both meat and milk dishes, if thoroughly washed in between. Luckily, the deli had packed plastic flatware. She carefully transferred the cole slaw and potato salad.

He sat down, watching her, amused. Here she was, back in rabbi's-wife mode, making sure she had a perfectly kosher meal in the most unkosher of settings.

"Finding everything you need, dear?"

She looked up at him. *Dear?* Such a husbandly term, she thought. It made her feel strange. She unwrapped the sandwiches and placed them on paper plates. He sat down across from her at the all-purpose table he used for dining in his living room, reaching out for some food. A sudden, heavy silence fell on them both. Delilah looked around her. She was alone with another man, a man who adored her. A man who was probably expecting something more than a sour pickle.

And would she give it to him? Would she pole-vault over the fence and land straight into the quagmire of unforgivable commandment breaking, where she would be transformed for all time from a creature that tiptoed close to the edge of volcanoes to one who had actually fallen right inside, all her convictions, what she told herself about herself, going up in smoke, singed and blackened and unrecognizable?

And would it be worth it?

She thought back to the dates she had had with Yitzie Polinsky, the thrill that had filled her body at his touch, the sense of release and satisfaction she had felt in his arms. How he had made her laugh. . . .

Yitzie.

The bum.

Was Benjamin another Yitzie? Would she again be reduced to begging God for a miracle to save her from ruin? And, more importantly, was the risk worth taking? Were the rewards worth desiring? She looked at him: his fair skin, his long fingers. Then she looked around the house. He lived like a tramp, she realized. And the posters that he had hung on the walls were, she realized, famous ads for vodka or cosmetics she had seen hundreds of times in many magazines, absolutely nothing original.

"Let me get you something to drink, Delilah. Rum Coke? Bloody Mary?"

"Sure," she said, suddenly needing less clarity.

All she wanted was a little excitement in life. Something to break the routine. To take her out of herself and give her a glimpse of the possible, a future where the sun rose and set by a new horizon. But the more she looked around—the broken floorboards, the scratches on the Plexiglas coffee table, the missing knob on the kitchen cabinet door—the more she felt she had taken a step backward, not forward.

She drained the glass he put in front of her and felt the soothing flow of alcohol loosen the tight knot of dismay pulling ever tighter in her chest. Her body felt warmer, calmer. Her mind was less judgmental, more open to suggestion.

"Why don't I put on some music?" Benjamin suggested.

He was now on familiar turf, his role in this scenario a comfortable fit for his talents. He wrote advertising copy, created ad campaigns to convince people to do and think all kinds of things for all the wrong reasons. He seduced them to smoke by convincing them it would make them appear smart and muscularly independent and daring to the opposite sex; to eat high-cholesterol sweets because it would make them part of a crowd of youthful, healthy, beautiful people; to purchase cars that would put them in endless debt because it would show how successful and rich they were. And now he was busy creating an ad campaign that would convince the rabbi's pretty wife that sleeping with him would make her life easier and more enjoyable.

He shut off the overhead lighting and lit a few lamps, an amazingly simple gesture that instantly created an atmosphere of intimacy and romance. He put a music disk into the stereo.

"Frank Sinatra!" Delilah exclaimed, finishing her second drink and reaching for a pickle. She started to hum along, then sing outright, finally getting up. "I did it my waaaaaaay!" she sang, sudden tears filling her eyes.

Uh-oh, Benjamin thought.

She put her arms around him and sobbed. "I'm such a bad person. Such a bad, bad, awful person!" He felt the shoulder of his new Ralph Lauren shirt dampen and wondered if she was wearing waterproof mascara. He put his arms around her and kissed her on the temple, smoothing back her soft shiny hair. It smelled like almonds and honey, he thought, wondering what kind of shampoo she used and who wrote the ads. They stood in the middle of the living room, clinging to each other as the music played. He patted her softly, then let his hands run smoothly up and down her back. She arched toward him like a cat.

She was tired, tired of everything, of the hypocrisy of it all, of straining toward a happiness that never seemed to get any closer, of craving money and a nice house and a passionate love life. She was tired of playing the dutiful little rabbi's wife in her modest hats and wigs and long-sleeved over-the-knee clothing; tired of cleaning out people's neglected, debris-filled mouths, flirting with elderly men, and kowtowing to their judgmental wives.

She wanted to smash something. To hit Chaim over the head for his consistency, his placid acceptance, his calm ability to wake up every morning and get through the day. Why not, then, just smash her life?

She felt the arms of the man around her. He was a cipher. Not important at all. She didn't care about him, not really. She didn't even know who he was, with his *treife* kitchen and no mezuzah on the door. He might as well be a goy, a Gentile prince. He didn't even have money. And, she finally realized, he probably didn't have a very good job either, if he was living in some run-down Bronx walk-up decorated with cliché posters produced by other, really successful ad men.

But what did any of this matter? She needed someone to fall in love with, someone who would destroy the channels through which her life flowed, allowing her to irrevocably change direction. He was at the moment the only one available. It would be good, she thought, her hands reaching up to caress the back of his head.

It would be good enough.

She felt his hands harden their grip around her, leading her into the bedroom.

She followed, almost in a daze, allowing herself to be led. He bent over her, kissing her full on the lips. She tasted the pastrami. She pushed him back.

"What?"

"I—I've got to *bentsch*," she told him.

"You've got to . . . *what*?"

"*Bentsch*. To say Grace After Meals."

He sat down on the bed, flabbergasted. "By all means." He waved her off.

She sat down by the table, trembling, wiping his kiss off her mouth. She took a little Grace After Meals book out of her purse, the souvenir of some cousin's wedding.

"Blessed art thou, O God, King of the Universe, who feeds and sustains the whole world with grace, compassion, and pity."

She felt the flush of shame crawl up her throat, turning her face hot.

"Fear God, you who are sanctified to Him, for there is no want for them that fear Him. Young lions have always become poor and suffered hunger, but they who seek God shall never want for any good thing. Avow it to God that He is good, and His love endures forever. You open Your hand and satisfy the desire of every living thing. . . ."

She finished, wiping her full eyes. And there was Benjamin, leaning on the doorpost to the bedroom, completely naked. She stood up, grabbed her purse, and ran out the front door and down the staircase.

Just as she neared the last landing, the door to the doctor's office opened and someone stepped out into the dark hallway. She veered to the side, nearly knocking him over.

"Delilah?"

She stopped and turned around. Horror washed over her. *Oh, no!* she thought. *No, no, no!*

There stood Chaim's grandfather, coming out of his weekly visit to the chiropractor. She stared at the old rabbi, her cheeks burning. Then she looked over the old man's shoulder. There, just above, running down the steps after her, was Benjamin, wearing a half-opened bathrobe. She motioned to him in hysteria.

"Delilah! Wait, don't go! I'll put my clothes back on!"

She watched helplessly as the old rabbi slowly pivoted, looking up the stairs behind him.

She turned and ran, down the steps and out into the street, not looking back. She sprinted to her car, her heart pounding as she rummaged frantically through her purse, searching for the car keys. Her hands trembled. She felt faint and breathless as a slow panic rose in her chest. In what seemed like an hour, she finally managed to open the car door, start the engine, and drive off.

When she got home, Chaim was already there.

"So, quite a day, no? You must be exhausted."

She stared at him.

"Your double shift at the clinic? All those patients?" he repeated, puzzled.

She didn't hear him. It was as if he were one of her patients, his mouth stuffed with dental cotton and instruments, trying to make himself understood.

He came to the bedroom. His forehead was wrinkled. He was moving his lips.

"I'm not feeling very well, Chaim. I think I'm—" She barely made it to the bathroom before throwing up her entire dinner.

He was immediately concerned. "Do you want me to call a doctor? Do you have fever?"

She wished he would just shut up; his solicitations and good-natured concern were making her feel even sicker. She put on the shower, blocking him out, waiting for the inevitable and terrible ringing of the phone, which would usher in the apocalypse.

I have to think, think, she told herself. It's not so bad. What does he know, the old man? Then she remembered that look he had given her and Benjamin at lunch and his abrupt leave-taking. In slow motion, her brain did a retake of the slow turn of his head toward the stairs.

She was lost. This was the end. He was old but nobody's fool. And if he had heard the rumors from Mrs. Schreiberman, he would feel it his religious obligation to tell his grandson of his suspicions, because a man was not allowed to live with a woman suspected of committing adultery. The fact that nothing had happened wouldn't matter.

Once Chaim threw her out, who would take her? Damaged goods. A divorced woman. A rabbi's wife thrown out of the community. They wouldn't even allow her to pray in an Orthodox synagogue. They'd whisper behind her back for the rest of her life. And all those girls from high school who had considered her a bleached blonde from a poor family, a girl who would never be their social equal, would gleefully tell one another, 'Did you hear what happened to Delilah? Didn't we all know it?"

She heard the phone ring. She heard Chaim gasp. And then she heard him pound on the bathroom door.

"Delilah!"

She took a deep breath and wrapped herself in a towel as attractively as possible, giving herself a quick once-over in the mirror before opening the door.

His eyes were wild. Her heart sank.

"It's my grandfather. They've taken him to the hospital! He's had a stroke!"

Delilah stood absolutely still, her brain computing all the possibilities. Finally, she moved toward her heartbroken husband, laying a hand on his shoulder and looking deeply into his anguished eyes.

"Major or minor?" she asked him.

{ THIRTEEN }

Reb Abraham hung on for several days. The family held vigil next to his bedside. Attached to an intubation tube that went down his throat, he looked at them silently with open eyes that seemed to yearn for a method of communication. Everyone tried to talk to him, but he gave no response until Delilah, very reluctantly, entered the room. The transformation was remarkable. Color rushed into his white cheeks.

"Look, he's so happy to see you!" Chaim exulted. "He looks better already!"

Mrs. Levi pursed her lips sourly, amazed and chagrined.

Then the old man tried to sit up, his hand shaking uncontrollably. He snatched at the intubation tube, trying to pull it out of his mouth. Delilah froze. The family, alarmed, rang for the nurse, who injected some kind of sedative into his intravenous tube, and he sank back into oblivion. And then, on the morning of the fourth day, Chaim's phone rang. It was his father, telling him it was all over.

Chaim was distraught. He blamed himself. If only he had taken the time to accompany the old man on his weekly appointments, to help him climb the stairs. If only he had checked more thoroughly the treatments the old chiropractor was foisting off on him as therapy. Obviously, that quack had to be responsible; after all, his grandfather had collapsed right outside his door.

His grandfather's sudden, precipitous demise was horrifying. Despite his extensive grief-counseling experiences, there was a fundamental and inescapable horror tinged with guilt in seeing someone he loved lose his grip on life. Age didn't matter. Seeing the upright body—always so dignified and tall—suddenly reduced to pale flabby flesh, bloated from excess fluids, expanding and contracting with the mechanical whir and sob of the intubation machine, was traumatic. The hospital visits, in which the doctors assured the family that all manner of medical tortures were absolutely necessary and unavoidable and might possibly result in a cure, were brutal. He felt intuitively that his grandfather was in pain and that all the medical establishment was really doing was making it impossible for him to leave this world with some peace and dignity. So that when, finally, the struggle ended, it came almost as a blessing.

But loss is loss, a tearing apart that is wretchedly wounding. Chaim mourned the loss of the old rabbi with all his heart. He leaned on Delilah, who behaved with such exemplary consideration that even her mother-in-law, who had spent the entire week sending guilt-inducing waves of hostility in her direction, finally relented. And when, soon after, Delilah made the announcement that she was expecting, even Chaim's mother smiled and hugged her, putting aside her suspicions and holding her tongue, realizing she had been upstaged. Besides, there had been enough grief in the family. A baby was exactly what everybody needed.

Chaim behaved as if his wife had been touched by a miracle. New life, just when he was in the depths of despair over death. Delilah's pregnancy blessed him, filling his mind and soul with new hope. He prayed it would be a boy, someone who could be named after his grandfather, a man he had loved and admired his entire life, as it was considered a special merit to the deceased if he had a namesake within the first anniversary of his death.

And then, before he had caught his breath, the congregation began to fall apart. In rapid succession, the membership began to scatter, moving to nursing homes and retirement communities. He just couldn't understand how it had all happened so quickly.

The first inkling that something was amiss had come during shiva. He had tried to talk to the congregants who came to pay their respects, but they were silent, stiff and uncomfortable, anxious to leave. All except for Mrs. Schreiberman. She showed up every day, full of venom, spouting incoherently cryptic sentences like "You can fool an earthly judge but not the heavenly court!" and "Poor man! Poor man! He died of a broken heart!"—looking straight at Delilah. And then one day she tried to attack the rabbi's young wife, charging at her with a rolled-up newspaper. "You little bitch. You know what you did. You killed him, you floozy!"

Delilah had had to run to her bedroom, barricading herself inside, while Chaim called the medics. The old woman had been ushered out, taken home, and heavily sedated until her daughter showed up, and, not knowing what else to do, placed her in the mentally challenged wing of an excellent nursing home. Chaim had chalked it up to grief, but rumors and interpretations of the incident ran through the congregation like wildfire. Within six months, the congregation was down to thirteen members, and the board voted to sell the synagogue building, the proceeds of which were donated to Israeli terror victims.

Chaim was shell-shocked. Confused, bereft, and financially vulnerable, just at a time when a baby was on the way, he clung to Delilah. Finally succumbing to her tearful entreaties to apply for the job in Swallow Lake, he very reluctantly, and despite his better judgment, decided to try his luck.

To his surprise, they put him on a waiting list. Despite the ban, the search committee had, apparently, still found plenty of candidates. But when they finally invited him and Delilah down for the weekend, things went amazingly fast.

{ FOURTEEN }

Swallow Lake in May: the mirrored, calm surface. The large oaks leaf-ing out. The dogwoods and crab apples in full bloom. The yellow flowering buttercups. The forests of oak and hickory. The smell of lilacs so thick and heady every breath makes you feel as if you are swallowing large glasses of perfumed alcohol. Intoxicating.

"Delilah, isn't this unbelievably beautiful?" Chaim gasped, thinking that, whatever happened, it was a joy simply to visit such a place.

It was like a picture postcard from the most WASP-y dream imagina-ble, Delilah thought. In fact, it made Woodmere and Cedarhurst look like middle-class Jewish suburbs.

The scenery was great, she agreed. But it was the houses that really interested her. Those homes, those fabulous homes, Delilah thought in wonder. The Colonials, the farmhouses, the Arts and Crafts cottages, the Tudors, the brick Georgians. They were straight out of some E Holly-wood *Houses of the Stars* program. Houses so large, on plots of land so enormous, it didn't seem quite possible for anything smaller than a municipality to actually own and inhabit them. And the maintenance. Talk about attention to detail: the perfectly painted shutters, the newly painted clapboard siding. The bluestone walkways, the gleaming monolithic glass windows overlooking infinity pools, lakes, sunsets. And the landscaping: shrubbery, flowers, and trees in perfect harmony and design.

"Wow, wow, wow!" Delilah repeated, overcome. This, she thought, is heaven.

She felt a tinge of sudden irrational anger. Why, she asked herself, couldn't she have been born into one of these houses? Better yet, why couldn't she have married a man who inherited one, or had a sibling who was a dot-com genius who'd bought one for her, or won the lottery herself and built one? Why had she been condemned to live out her days in little 600-square-foot boxes? But then the anger passed and she was filled with joy.

"I can't wait to see the inside of one of them." She squeezed Chaim's hand. He looked at her. Her face was shining like a child's presented with a large gift-wrapped box. He tried to remember the last time he'd seen her looking like that. It was that moment, just before they'd walked down the aisle, when he couldn't bear to pull the veil over her face. And now she was carrying his child, he thought. This woman he loved so much and had been trying, with no success, to make happy.

Until this moment, he hadn't been nervous about this job interview, because he really didn't want this job, so fraught with complications and controversy. But now, looking at Delilah's happy face, he exhaled, returning her squeeze, touched by a new determination to do everything in his power to get her what she wanted.

"We're here."

They pulled up to the entrance of a lakefront estate. The gates were ornate grillwork edged in gold leaf. And they were firmly shut. Not a living soul was visible anywhere.

"Now what?" Delilah asked Chaim, who shrugged, as mystified as she at the ways of the extremely rich. "Maybe there is a button to push somewhere? Go out and look, Chaim."

There was, indeed. Chaim found it and pushed. A disembodied and suspicious voice asked them who they were and what they wanted. Soon the gates magically slid to one side, allowing them to drive through.

The house was fronted by a circular driveway, at whose center was an island of exotic plants.

"Please don't say *wow* every five minutes," Chaim begged her.

Delilah, who was about to say *wow*, closed her mouth.

The front door was answered by the lady of the house, a tall, blond-haired stick of a woman who could not possibly have been any thinner without an IV attached to her arm and round-the-clock medical supervision. Her face was a battleground in which formal hospitality, suspicion, and sincere dismay struggled for prominence.

"I'm Solange Malin," she said, with faint traces of a British accent, a mask of politeness finally winning out, which was fine with Deliliah, who preferred phony good cheer over frank nastiness any day. Their hostess extended her hand in welcome. Chaim stared at it uncomfortably, wondering if he should overcome his pious scruples about touching a woman or risk offending the wife of the president of the synagogue's board from the word *go*. Delilah saw him hesitate. She hurriedly reached over him, pumping the bony fingers while secretly kicking him in the ankle. He shook the woman's hand.

"An honor to meet you, Mrs. Malin. I've heard so much about you and your husband. Your charitableness and good deeds are well known to everyone in the Jewish world."

Delilah's heart swelled like a mother watching her child get the lines right in a school play.

Solange's eyes crinkled in pleasure at the compliment. She smiled. "Not at all! Everyone on the board is dying to meet you. And please accept our condolences on the loss of your grandfather. I understand he was a very important rabbi, leader of a well-known New York synagogue? We read all about him in the *New York Times* obituary. They called him 'One of the last great European scholars,' and they called the synagogue a landmark. And you, I understand, are his successor?"

Chaim, to whom this was news, nodded, surprised. "He was a wonderful man. And yes, I'm his only grandson."

"Such a privilege! Please, let me get someone to help you with your luggage. Anna-Maria?" she called over her shoulder.

"No, please. It's not necessary. All we have are these overnight bags," Chaim protested.

"Oh, well. That's fine then. Please, let me show you to your room."

The entrance hall was truly breathtaking, with a winding staircase leading to a square upstairs gallery on which large, magnificent canvases of bold modern art caught your eye from every corner. Off the entrance hall was a huge dining room, which seemed to be undergoing a massive upheaval.

"Excuse the mess. I'm redecorating. Please—" she gestured up the stairs, as if anxious to have them settled and out of the way.

When she showed them to their room, Delilah tried very, very hard, not to say *wow*! It was twice the size of their Bronx apartment, with a huge double bed, French doors leading to an open balcony, a huge dressing room, and an enormous private bathroom with a Jacuzzi, sauna, and heaven knows what else. Only one thing seemed odd: There were about ten heavy dining-room chairs scattered around the place. But the room was so large, Delilah hardly noticed them.

"Oh, my!" Solange Malin gasped. "No, this is not right! I'm so dreadfully sorry!" She pressed an intercom and said, very firmly, "Anna-Maria, would you come up here, please?" They all stood around uncomfortably, shifting from leg to leg, waiting to see the reason for this sudden fall in the friendliness barometer.

"What, in heaven's name, are the chairs doing here?" she asked the squat, brown woman who walked in, her brows already lowered in bull-like defiance.

"You tol' me, get dining room ready. I take out chairs," the maid said sullenly.

"But I didn't tell you to put them in here!"

"We put in here, always," she said stubbornly.

"Well, take them out immediately. Don't you see we have guests?" The maid didn't budge.

"Anna-Maria?" Solange Malin demanded, an octave higher.

"They heavy."

It was a standoff. After a moment of silence, the mistress of the house got on the intercom again. "José, can you come up here, please, and help Anna-Maria."

Soon the chairs were marching out of the room under the straining torsos of two huffing servants, who were exchanging choice phrases in Spanish under their breath, glancing at Chaim and Delilah and their employer with barely contained malevolence.

"Well, I hope you'll both be comfortable here now." She smiled.

"Oh, this is more than comfortable. We can't thank you enough,"

Chaim said sincerely, feeling a sense of vague discomfort as he looked at the straining backs of the two employees.

"I don't know about you, but I'm ready to dive into that Jacuzzi. Wheee!" Delilah said with glee as soon as Solange Malin took her leave. She began unbuttoning her blouse.

"Delilah!"

"What? We've got plenty of time. Why don't you take off your clothes and join me. It looked awfully roomy." She giggled, only to turn around and find the two servants gaping at her.

"Mis. Us. Shee. U. kam. U. moo," Anna-Maria said urgently.

She clutched her blouse together, raising her eyebrows at Chaim, who stared back helplessly. They went through this about four times until Delilah finally realized the woman was here to usher them out of paradise into yet another bedroom. Delilah could see the hatred just behind the woman's eyes as she helped them gather their things together. She wondered why Solange Malin put up with this kind of live-in enmity. If she ever got enough money to hire servants, she thought, she'd fire them faster than they could say *Adios!*

The new bedroom was more magnificent still. And it had twin beds.

"I thought you'd be more comfortable in here," Solange said, suddenly reappearing. The two Mexicans stared impassively at the floor, no doubt wondering—as were Chaim and Delilah—why she hadn't just moved them here in the first place, since they were mobile and the chairs were not.

The new room was black and white and red. On the walls were framed photographs, everything rather blurry in shades of red.

"Chaim used to take pictures like that until he went digital. They come out perfect now," Delilah said.

"They're Desmond McClintocks," Solange said stiffly.

Delilah looked at her blankly.

"The abstract photographer? The one who just had a retrospective at MoMA? Do you like them, Rabbi?" she said, pointedly ignoring Delilah.

"Oh, they're wonderful," Chaim said hesitantly. "So . . . so . . ."

Red, Delilah thought, her face burning with embarrassment.

". . . evocative," he finally said.

"Oh, what a charming photo," Delilah said, trying to recoup, suddenly picking up a small framed photograph on the nightstand. It was of two little girls in plain dresses that seemed way too big for them, covering them up from neck to ankle. Their hair fell over their shoulders in long tight braids. "They look just like those little Hasidic girls in Jerusalem! Don't they, Chaim? Is this also by the same famous photographer?"

Solange grabbed it out of her hands in a tight-lipped silence that left Delilah breathless, wondering what rule of the very rich she'd broken now.

"I didn't remember I'd put it in here," Solange murmured. "As a matter of fact, my son-in-law took it. They're my granddaughters. And they live in Jerusalem."

There was a big period at the end of that sentence. Chaim and Delilah heard it clearly and asked no more.

"This is our best guest bedroom." Solange nodded, making them wonder what had transpired to get them an upgrade so soon. "I thought twin beds would be more comfortable," she added, as if reading their thoughts.

"It's very kind of you to take so much trouble," Chaim said.

"Not at all! We are very excited about having you both here. Our community has suffered a great deal with this whole, scandalous Metzenbaum business. We are hoping for some new leadership. Not fanatics out to brainwash people and alienate them from their children"—she picked up the photograph and stared at it in silence—"or busybodies out to condemn our customs and practices. We need team players who are warm and responsive, who will join actively in our community and our way of life." She turned her head, looking at Delilah carefully. "Some rabbi's wives these days refuse even to join the sisterhood. They think it's beneath them because they have high-powered jobs, law or medical practices, or they're VPs of some computer company. Career women," she said with a sniff, as if the air had suddenly been fouled. "That's not who we're looking for here."

Chaim shifted uncomfortably.

"Oh, I know what you mean. It's terrible." Delilah jumped in eagerly. "I know quite a few rabbi's wives who are always thinking about themselves. But I have always believed that being the wife of a rabbi is the highest calling any Jewish woman could possibly have. It's an opportunity and a privilege to serve a community."

"Well." Solange's nose unwrinkled, the air suddenly fragrant again. "I'm so glad you think so. Perhaps if you have some time before dinner, you'll allow me to show you around?"

"That would be wonderful," Delilah assured her, thrilled. She couldn't wait.

"I'd better go now. If you need anything, I'll just be downstairs. Otherwise, I'll see you in time for candlelighting." She nodded, forcing a smile on her lips and taking the photo with her.

Two wonderful Tibetan wooden lion carvings stood on either side of a low carved ebony wood table. Chaim tried hard to tiptoe around them, terrified he might bump into one and knock it over. It was like being given a bed in the Metropolitan Museum, he thought uncomfortably.

The furniture was beautiful, even if the decorations were a bit weird. But this bedroom had no Jacuzzi, Delilah noted with disappointment. What it did have, she discovered to her joy, was a magnificent porch with two rocking chairs overlooking the lake and a bookcase full of magazines. Big, fluffy robes were hanging in the bathroom, along with the softest, thickest towels she'd ever seen. Delilah took a long soak, using the French bubble bath and the Italian shampoo, then curled up in a white wicker rocker. She could see the turquoise blue of the swimming pool sparkling down below and hear the gentle whack of tennis balls bouncing off the red clay courts visible over the hill.

She was supremely happy, all her angst suddenly melting, all her worries, anxieties, bravado, defenses, and heartbreak over things she'd never be able to solve magically evaporating.

She couldn't understand Solange Malin, who was obviously nursing some heartbreak, despite her palace. All the conventional wisdom about how money isn't everything, how a house is just a shell was just baloney, Delilah thought. There was no human need that owning this house and land couldn't fill, as far as she was concerned. Anyone who couldn't be deliriously happy here might as well join Osama bin Laden's merry men in their caves.

"Chaim"—she caressed his face, looking deeply into his eyes—"I've finally found all the answers."

"What were the questions?" He laughed, caressing her back.

They sat next to each other quietly, each thinking their own thoughts. This was the way their relationship should be, Delilah thought, like two potted plants, next to each other but not in each other's space, each of them growing and blooming at their own pace, enjoying each other's foliage without insisting on sending out spores that would colonize and take over. They were both so different, but in a good way, she told herself.

Both of them had been taught that a person's goal in life should be to serve God. But the older she got, the more complicated that became. It seemed that at every given moment, there was some other extremely complicated and usually inconvenient and difficult thing that needed to be performed *in exactly the precise right way* or it—and you—were worthless.

For example, Grace After Meals. There was an entire little book of things you had to say to thank God for your food after every meal. But on holidays, you had to add a special paragraph. On Chanukah and Purim, another one. And on the new moon, still another. And even if you said the whole book, if you forgot to add precisely the appropriate paragraph, then your prayer was worthless and you needed to say the *entire thing all over again*.

She sighed.

Someone once said that if the Jews celebrated Christmas, there would have been at least three, four-hundred-page volumes of Jewish law—with commentaries—describing exactly how tall the tree had to be, what color, how long it needed to be in the house, and when and how you were allowed to throw it out. There would be a long list of commandments and prohibitions concerning the decorations and the exact angle that they had to be hung, with commentaries on the different rabbinical schools of thought—both stringent and lenient—concerning candy canes.

She glanced at her husband. Chaim never seemed to have any doubts or hang-ups. Often, Delilah admitted to herself, she envied him this. She took his hand and kissed it. "Chaim, please get this job. It would be so good for both of us. And I promise you, this time I'll do better. I'll make you proud of me."

Chaim put his arm around her, squeezing her shoulders. "I'll do my best, my love."

~ ~

That evening, just after lighting the Sabbath candles, Chaim and Delilah were given the grand tour of the house and grounds. There were many impressive works of art and many beautiful pieces of furniture. Solange, acting as docent, pointed out the big expressionist canvases by Gregory Armenoff, a Roger Shinomura woodblock, a fantastic Romare Bearden collage, as well as wonderful Israeli works by Lea Nikel, Dorit Feldman, and Menashe Kadishman. One entire room had been given over to dreamlike glass masterpieces by Dale Chihuly.

But when the tour was over, Chaim admitted to himself that the thing he envied most were the views from the back porch over Swallow Lake just as the sun was setting. Good thing the Tenth Commandment talked about coveting one's neighbor's house, not his scenery, he thought with a smile. As far as he knew, that wasn't a sin. As for Delilah, she felt her entire being awash in an almost hypnotic sense of longing. Oh, to acquire and own and use and take for granted such riches! Even to live nearby. It would be everything she ever dreamed of.

They waited in the entrance hall for Arthur Malin, who was chairman of the synagogue board, who was going to walk with them to the synagogue. Chaim realized his hands were sweating. He felt as if he were about to meet Donald Trump, not sure he wouldn't point a finger and yell, *You're fired!*

What kind of man owned this palace, he wondered? A person who was not only rich, but cultured and intelligent, with amazing good taste. And what kind of rabbi was he looking for?

They waited and waited, until, suddenly, a voice called out, "Shaindel, where's the apple cider?"

Solange blanched. "He likes to call me that. It's my Hebrew name. He's the only one," she explained, flustered. Chaim and Delilah kept their faces passive, but reached out to pinch each other when she wasn't looking.

Arthur Malin walked into the hallway, glass in hand. "A refrigerator the size of Milwaukee and no juice." He shrugged. He seemed amused. When he saw them he stopped, his face lighting up with a kind smile.

"Hello, hello. Welcome. Good Shabbes." He greeted them warmly, in a heavy Brooklyn accent.

Delilah gulped. He looked like one of her favorite high school *chumash* teachers. "We were just admiring your collections, Mr. Malin."

A maid they hadn't seen before came over hurriedly, pouring him some apple juice. He took it from her gratefully, his eyes lighting up. "*Gracias,* kid," he said, gulping it down and giving her the glass since she seemed to be waiting for it. Then he turned to Delilah. "You like? Good. I don't know much about it. We have a guy that helps us pick things out. He goes for the bright colors, and all the little pieces of material and wood glued on with the *shvartzas*—by what's-his-face—Reardumb?"

"Avrom!" Solange said sharply, her British accent suddenly gone with the wind. Then she seemed to remember herself, glancing at them nervously. "I mean, Arthur," she corrected herself, the Queen's English suddenly making a reappearance. "Please! You know that you and I are the ones who make the final decisions." She turned, smiling. "We just love Bearden."

"Yeah, we decide everything, especially what color ink to use on the checks!" He laughed uproariously, slapping his knee. "Oy, that was good. What do you want, Shaindel? They should think we're big art mavens? I embarrassed her, right? I always embarrass her, my darling wife. He put his arm around Chaim's shoulder. "So, Rabbi, *vus macht du*?"

"We are both doing great. Such a beautiful place. I'm ready to pitch a tent and squat," Chaim said jovially, liking Arthur more with every word he said.

"Rabbi, you don't have to pitch a tent. We already have one, a big one."

"Arthur . . ." Solange raised her brows in warning.

"It's our synagogue!" He roared.

Delilah blanched. "You don't mean the rabbi and his family live in the synagogue?"

"Well, what do the two of you live in now?"

"We have a very nice apartment," Delilah began, wondering if they were already in negotiations.

"All six hundred square feet of it." Chaim laughed.

"Do they come that small? I'd forgotten." He smiled, shaking his head. "I grew up in Bensonhurst, Brooklyn. My parents' apartment was bigger than that, but not much. Here, even the cars get more room to themselves."

"My husband has a very special sense of humor," Solange broke in. "Of course, the rabbi's house is very nice. A two-story Colonial, about two thousand square feet, with a full finished basement. It's very comfortable."

"They'll see it, Shaindel. I promise."

Delilah exhaled. Two thousand fricking feet, she thought, exulting. And a finished basement!

The plan was to walk to the synagogue, where Chaim would give his first speech, and afterward join the board members at the home of the Rollands for Friday-night dinner, where they could all get to know one another.

The walk took them past the Swallow Lake Country Club. It had a 13,000-square-foot fitness center, sandy beaches, eight tennis courts, and an Olympic-sized pool and marina, Arthur Malin informed them. He was a founding member, he said. He believed in physical fitness. All those days sitting in yeshiva on his *tuchas* had convinced him that body and soul needed to be nurtured simultaneously. He seemed in excellent shape, despite creeping baldness and a challah-eating paunch.

All the way there, he regaled them with stories about his yeshiva days in Brooklyn and how the rabbis told his parents he'd wind up in jail. "The rabbis were always trying to convince us not to go to college but instead to sit and learn Talmud the rest of our lives and have the community and our rich fathers-in-law support us. Once, Rabbi Pupik gets up and says, 'You know what happens to boys who go to college? They wind up becoming organic chemists. And do you know what organic chemists do? All day they spend with their hands in what comes out of behinds. People behinds, animal behinds.' Then he'd roll up his sleeves and pantomime it, holding it up to his nose, licking it with his tongue. We were all adolescents, we were rolling around on the floor going, *Uch, uch, uch!*" He laughed. "I'll tell you what. Maybe we didn't become Talmud scholars, but not one of us became an organic chemist!"

Instead, he'd gotten into real estate, learning the business from his mother's uncle. And then, just on a fluke, he'd started purchasing radio stations one at a time when nobody wanted them. Delilah found the whole story a little hard to follow but understood he now headed a media conglomerate that supplied news and entertainment to a vast number of people in the United States and elsewhere.

And while he didn't say so, Chaim already knew that he was also one of the most giving and generous men in the world, involved with a vast number of charities, both Jewish and non-Jewish, with a particular interest in the handicapped. He was one of those people who earn your respect and overcome your prejudices, Chaim thought. As much as those with no money would hope to at least be able to boast of a superior moral edge over their very wealthy counterparts, the truth was that it is equally possible, and far more likely, he believed, for a rich man to be a good person than a poor one—tightfisted grasping hands, let's face it, being more of a problem among those who have grabbed little than those who have grabbed much.

"Oh, my goodness!" Delilah gasped, when she saw Ohel Aaron.

Huge vertical columns of concrete, interspersed with thin ribbons of stained glass, rose into the air, meeting at a point in the center that looked as if it had been tied with some kind of gigantic leather belt.

Arthur Malin shrugged. "I know, I know. It's supposed to be an Indian tepee. The first Jews in Swallow Lake wanted to do something that fit into the environment and would be respectful of local traditions. *Ich vast?*"

It looked, Chaim thought, like a huge ice-cream cone that had been turned upside down and smashed into the pavement by a vengeful three-year-old. "Well, it's the inside that's important," Chaim said.

"That's even worse," Arthur Malin admitted, opening the doors.

He was right. It was vast and rather gloomy, lit by massive wooden chandeliers straight out of the Ahawaneechee Lodge. All that was missing were the antlers and other dead hunting trophies. The bimah, which stood at the center, seemed to be made out of bark-covered log cabin blocks. The Ark of the Torah, hewn out of a massive redwood trunk, seemed to be covered—could that actually be?—in leather. On either side, huge electrical fixtures in the shape of flickering torches finished the effect of a Comanche tribunal gathered to do a war dance.

It took every ounce of self-discipline Chaim could muster not to ask, Are you sure this is Tent of Aaron, and not Pocahontas?

"Let me guess. The *mechitzah* is made of feathers?" Chaim whispered to Delilah.

"He'll hear you!" she hissed.

As it turned out, feathers would have been more traditionally acceptable according to Jewish law than what he found: solid panels of beaten bronze, each one in the shape of a different wild bird, placed at widely spaced intervals that allowed men and women to see each other clearly. He gulped in panic. According to Jewish tradition, the birds were for the birds. There was no question in his mind that any Orthodox rabbi worth his salt must absolutely refuse to officiate over a synagogue service in such a place. He glanced at Delilah, who sat in the front row looking at him hopefully, her face beaming in excitement and expectation. He walked in heavily. This wasn't his pulpit—yet. There would be time to make changes, if and when he got the job, he told himself.

Delilah looked around her, delighted. There were many women of all ages, and at a Friday-night service, which was traditionally almost entirely male. Usually, this meant either that the congregation was young and sassy and used the synagogue as a social watering hole or that the women were in love with their rabbi. In this case, she had no doubt they'd come to gather early impressions by inspecting them both. She smiled until her mouth ached, her entire body tensed and ready.

There is always a little break in the Friday-evening service, when afternoon prayers are over and evening prayers cannot yet begin. In most synagogues, this time slot is filled by the rabbi giving a short learned discussion on some obscure point in Jewish law, saving, as rabbis do, the major heart banger for the larger gathering on Saturday morning.

Chaim stood up and walked to the podium. The place was packed, he realized with pleasure. Quite an achievement in a relatively small place like Swallow Lake, when, all over the country, synagogues—and churches—were empty 363 days a year; and Bar and Bat Mitzva kids disappeared faster than free champagne the minute they'd unwrapped their presents and recovered from their hangovers.

Delilah sat tensely at the edge of her seat. Chaim hadn't discussed his sermon with her. *Please, please,* she thought, her heart clenching, *don't blow this! Just get this job and I'll be the best wife, the best rebbitzin, I promise.*

"The rabbi and his wife were cleaning house," Chaim began, with no introduction, "when the rabbi came across a box. 'What's in it?' he asked the rebbitzin. She said, 'Leave it alone. It's private.' Well, what can you do? A rabbi is also a person; he was curious. So one day, when she was out shopping, he ran to find it and opened it.

"Inside were three eggs and two thousand dollars. He waited patiently for her to come home, and then he demanded to know what it meant. 'Every time you give a bad sermon, I put an egg in the box.' "

" 'Twenty years, and only three eggs! Not bad! But what about the money?'

" 'Every time I get a dozen eggs, I sell them to the poor for a dollar.' "

He waited for the laughter to die down before raising his hand. "I hope I don't get an egg for this one. But before I start, I'd like to tell you another story.

"A young Talmud scholar was invited to become rabbi in a small old community in Chicago. On his very first Sabbath, a violent debate erupted as to whether one should or should not stand during the reading of the Ten Commandments. They asked the new rabbi to decide. 'What's your custom here?' he asked them. But no one could tell him. So the next day, the rabbi visited the synagogue's oldest member in the nursing home. 'Mr. Fine, I'm asking you, as one of the oldest members of the community, what is our synagogue's custom during the reading of the Ten Commandments?'

" 'Why do you ask?' asked Mr. Fine.

" 'Yesterday, we read the Ten Commandments. Some people stood, some people sat. The ones standing started screaming at the ones sitting, telling them to stand up. The ones sitting started screaming at the ones standing, telling them to sit down. They insulted each other, threw chairs, slammed doors, threatened to leave the synagogue, and called me an idiot—'

" 'That,' said the old man, 'is our custom.' "

Chaim followed his jokes with a short speech that discussed the Torah portion of the week, combining it with a good-natured attempt to inspire more ethical behavior among neighbors when it came to borrowing and returning things, which everyone found equally amusing and useful and not overly flat-handed or judgmental.

Not everyone was happy. Some thought the speech was too lightweight, while others thought it was too preachy. But that is normal in all congregations.

Watching a new rabbi approach a congregation is like watching an acrobat on the high wire. Not content to just watch him rush across the abyss to safety, we demand that he stop in the middle, open an umbrella, and sit down on a chair that totters this way and that, while down below we judge his skill and daring and entertainment value. Most of us hold our breath wishing for the rabbi's success, although—admit it—disaster is much more fun to watch, and there is always another rabbi waiting in the wings just in case, ready to take over as soon as the body of the old one is removed.

But there was something so sincere and naive—and pathetic?—about Chaim Levi that even those with the most cynical hearts rooted for him to succeed.

The women were very nice to Delilah. They were gratified and flattered at her absolute unfeigned enthusiasm and delight with everything she had seen in the community. She was a yeshiva graduate. And although she was blond and young and pretty she was also obviously pregnant, wearing one of those "good girl" pregnancy dresses with the high collars and little bows. And a wig. The more they probed, the more they realized she was nothing like their last rebbitzin, and they—and their husbands—need not fear aggressive classes in family purity or campaigns to import the ethos of the stringency kings and their revisionary attitudes toward keeping women in their place. She seemed like a friendly open girl who liked a good manicure and colorist and yet would be willing to play the role of community organizer when asked. She seemed, in short, like a good team player.

The men who interviewed Chaim were satisfied that he knew how to learn Talmud and had a fundamental grasp of religious law. He smiled a lot. But when they asked him about his vision for the congregation, his mind went completely blank. After a long awkward silence, he answered, rather sheepishly, "I think a rabbi should try to serve the congregation's needs. I think he should listen more than he talks."

To his surprise, they hired him on the spot.

{ FIFTEEN }

*D*elirious with joy, Delilah moved into her new home, leaving urban decay, suspicious glances, and a checkered past behind her. The home she moved into had a lovely living room with a bay window, a formal dining room, and an imposing wood-paneled study for Chaim. It had a huge master bedroom with a working fireplace and three smaller bedrooms. In the backyard, there was a well-kept lawn with some nice shrubs and a picnic table. For days, she wandered around, feeling as if she was an intruder who would soon be caught and evicted. She touched the walls, wiggled her toes in the carpets, drank lemonade in the garden. She was sweet and good-natured to Chaim, preparing good dinners and giving him little hugs and kisses as she rapturously unpacked her belongings and set them up around the house. There was so much room! She slid across the parquet in stocking feet like a ten-year-old blissfully home alone.

She was so happy, she felt grateful to God, her stars, and every other

power over the universe and her personal destiny. This was a new beginning, she told herself, assuaging the waves of regret that sometimes enveloped her. For the first time in her life she began to appreciate her
religious instruction. For if there was one thing you learned in yeshiva, it
was how to deal with sin and guilt. No matter how awful you were, there
was no thread so scarlet that it could not be bleached as white as snow.

Unlike Catholics—who made a group project out of it—Judaism was
strictly do-it-yourself in the repentance department. You started by admitting your terrible deeds, regretting them, and making yourself a promise
never to do them again. Only when that was done could you hope to approach God and ask Him to wipe the slate clean. Unlike Catholics, however, Jews never got that comforting *Say ten Hail Marys* that ended the
matter. Barring a burning bush, you were more or less in a state of perpet-
ual doubt as to whether you'd been forgiven. Which is why the words *Jewish* and *guilt* are so often found in close proximity.

Delilah had been shocked and horrified at the turn of events in the
Bronx, particularly her part in what had befallen Reb Abraham. But working on herself, she had learned to live with it. After all, he had had to go
sometime. No one lasted forever. And she hadn't really done anything
wrong, it was simply appearances that had been incriminating. Furthermore, if the old man had been as sincere in practicing moral restraint as he
had been in preaching it, he would have given her and Benjamin the benefit
of the doubt, despite the admittedly unfortunate and weighty circumstantial
evidence. And while she certainly wasn't happy he had taken it all so hard
and had wound up giving himself a stroke, she had to admit the timing, in
any event, had been perfect. It had proved the magic bullet needed to make
the Bronx congregation disappear, and her husband soften up.

Chaim, it was true, had suffered. But look where he was today! The
rabbi of a rich and important and thriving congregation in such a beautiful
spot, a place that loved him and treated him so well. Why, just the other
day Mariette Rolland had told her that her husband was a "blessing" to
Swallow Lake! And Felice Borenberg had mentioned how much she loved
to listen to him speak.

One day, she knew, he would thank her.

Full of gratitude, having put the past behind her, she was determined
not only to become a good rabbi's wife but the *best* rabbi's wife. Chaim,
having landed this position, was suddenly the focal point of her admira-

tion. She wanted to help him, to become queen to his king over the moral lives of the people around them.

She smiled and said hello to everyone, even those who treated her coolly. She made weekly sit-down dinners for twelve. She agreed to open her house to monthly sisterhood meetings. She stayed on the phone for hours listening to problems and offering solutions. She even prepared and gave a *shiur* for women on the Torah portion of the week.

And then, one morning, she found she simply couldn't get out of bed. Her limbs felt like lead and her head swam. She felt hot, thirsty, depressed, confused.

"You are doing too much! I tried to tell you to slow down. Darling, don't forget you're pregnant."

"I'm fine. Pregnancy isn't a disease," she told him curtly, quoting Mariette Rolland, who'd recently told her all about how she'd canceled only one day of work appointments to give birth to her last daughter.

She suffered strange cravings, waking Chaim at 2 A.M. to search for passionfruit sorbet and peanut-butter brownies. She fell prey to bouts of depression: "I look like a cow! My mother has nicer ankles! And just look at my stomach, my boobs. . . ."

Chaim stared at her, shocked and dumbfounded. The truth was that pregnancy had brought a blush of radiant health to Delilah that made her body softer and rounder, her skin gleam with a luscious dewy softness. She looked sexier than ever. And if everyone was looking at her, he had no doubt as to why.

"Delilah, darling, you're more beautiful than ever, really" he did his best to assure her.

"Don't lie to me, Chaim! I know everyone's staring at me, thinking how ugly I look! And I'm sick of these goody-goody dresses with the Peter Pan collars and bows! I'm sick of these sensible low-heeled old-lady shoes. I want my body back! I want this *thing* out of me!"

He couldn't reason with her. And then, one morning, he overslept, missing the morning minyan. That same week, he found his eyes closing and his head nodding when he tried to prepare his sermon. He awoke with a start several hours later with nothing accomplished.

He didn't know what to do. He had zero experience with pregnant women, viewing Delilah as a delicate piece of china carrying a soft-boiled egg, imagining that the slightest jarring motion would do irreparable damage to both. With a touch of desperation, he sought out someone who could advise him. The only person who came to mind was Josh, who had been through this only recently himself.

Josh was surprised to hear from him. Once Chaim had gone against the ban and accepted the job at Swallow Lake, they'd lost contact completely, much to Josh's delight. "Well, this is really not such a good time for me."

"Please, Josh, I'm in trouble," Chaim confessed.

"What's wrong?"

"My wife—that is, I—*we* are expecting our first child. Delilah is very worried—depressed—and frankly I'm not getting any sleep. This is a new job. I'm afraid the congregation will begin to grumble."

Josh put his hand over the phone and hissed to his wife, "It's Chaim Levi. Delilah's pregnant and driving him crazy." She shook her head, backing away. "Please . . ." He made a begging face.

Rivkie took the phone. "Hi, mazal tov, Chaim! How wonderful. . . . Hmm, hmmm. . . . Yes, some women have harder times than others. Why don't I call her? . . . No, no bother at all, I'm happy to help. I apologize we haven't been in touch. You know what it's like, or you will, a new baby—"

Delilah was not particularly happy to hear Rivkie's voice, the voice of judgment. She hadn't forgiven their silence when Chaim got the job at Swallow Lake. But Rivkie was very sympathetic and supportive, and Delilah found herself actually enjoying discussing her feelings with someone who wasn't a member of the congregation with an ax to grind, someone with whom she could be completely honest.

"I'm frightened, Rivkie, and I feel like hell. I'm throwing up. Even the smell of Sabbath food makes me want to puke my guts out, let alone preparing these meals for guests. And I can't stand all these needy phone calls, all this meaningless shul chitchat, when all I want to do is just go to sleep! If I only had the weekends off, but that's when we're most *on*."

"I know. It's hard. But people will understand if you're honest and give them a chance. Tell them how you feel. Drop out for a while. It's OK. You are in for such an exciting, wonderful experience! Start focusing on the fun aspects of having a baby. Have you planned your nursery and layette yet? Why don't you go shopping? And most of all, you've got to get yourself a doula."

"A what?"

"It's a Greek word that means—well, helper, servant—slave, anyhow, not really sure. They are women who help you through the birth. I had one. She was wonderful, *baruch Hashem*.

"You mean, a midwife? I already have a doctor."

"No, no. She doesn't have any actual medical training at all. She doesn't deliver the baby."

"Then what *does* she do?"

"Well, before the birth she gives lessons to the couple so the husband can share and participate in the birthing experience. She gives massages with aromatic oils. She sings and dances and says special prayers to ease your spirit and comfort you. And once you're in the delivery room, she—"

"She comes to the delivery room? What does she do there? I mean, if she has no medical training. All you need is an epidural, right?"

There was silence on the other end of the line. "We don't believe in epidurals. Giving birth is a sacred experience, a gift from God. When you get all drugged up, you cut yourself off from the connection to God, and your body—"

Delilah's heart missed a beat. "You mean to tell me you went through labor and delivery cold turkey?"

"It was a fabulous experience, believe me! Extremely spiritual. Never have I felt closer to God, more like His holy vessel. I'm not saying it wasn't hard. I mean, they call it labor, right?" She chuckled. "And of course there was some pain," she admitted dismissively, "but that just made it more real. Believe me, I wouldn't have missed it. And my doula was wonderful."

Where did she get this stuff? Delilah thought enviously. She could just see herself repeating those words in a lofty and pious tone when the young women of Ohel Aaron came to her for advice. In general, anything she could lift from Rivkie would be wise, she told herself. She didn't actually want the doula—it sounded pretty grim—but what she did want was to impress people on how she had breezed through her pregnancy and childbirth on spirituality alone. Besides, you could always get rid of the woman and have an epidural if things didn't work out.

She took down the woman's name and phone number and then refocused the discussion in a more useful direction. "Where did you go to shop?" she asked.

Rivkie was full of useful information. "But you know, Deliliah, the Jewish custom is not to make any preparations at all and only buy baby things once the baby is born."

"Not even diapers?"

"Nothing. But you can take down ordering information."

So, one afternoon, she got Chaim to drop her off at a mall with a Pottery Barn for Kids. There, Delilah made a remarkable discovery: A baby was made to be accessorized! She imagined herself standing over a white French-provincial baby crib, smiling with maternal joy at her designer-dressed infant angelically asleep in its color-coordinated sheets, bumper, and blanket, a matching rug at her feet and matching wallpaper all around. She took a catalog and furiously wrote down numbers.

She looked around at the other pregnant women who wandered with shining eyes among the treasures. They too were lumpy and thickened. But among the women carrying small babies or wheeling toddlers in carriages, a fair number were already back to being thin and young, she noticed, cheering up, imaging herself back to normal too, the only remnant of her pregnancy a double-D bra cup and glowing hormone-enriched skin.

She went on a cancellation spree, telling everyone she needed her rest so the dinners and sisterhood meetings and long phone calls and the *shiur* were all off until further notice. When a panicked Chaim mildly suggested she might try to stay a little more involved, she said, "Rivkie did the same thing when she was pregnant. She says it's perfectly all right. People will understand."

To Chaim's surprise, everyone did. They were extremely understanding, even sympathetic. Besides, no one had the stomach to start interviewing new candidates all over again, and word had gotten around that the new rebbitzin wasn't the world's best cook and her attempt at a *shiur* had been basically to steal a whole chapter straight out of one of those books by Nechama Leibowitz, the Bible scholar, which most people had read already long ago. So they were only too happy to forgo her dinners and lectures.

Remarkably, the less Chaim and Delilah did, the more their popularity rose. The women loved how the rabbi was taking care of his pregnant wife, and the men deeply sympathized with his plight. The fact that his sermons seemed to go from lightweight to featherweight was not only accepted but appreciated. Who wanted moral discomfort and inspiration disrupting their otherwise relaxed and pleasant weekend anyhow?

Within a few weeks, Delilah underwent a remarkable transition: She seemed to blossom. Her nausea lifted, and she began eating like someone just coming off a five-month stint on Weight Watchers, wolfing down food in alarming amounts. She sank back into her new role as baby maker like a pasha into his pillows

Chaim, stretched to the limit from doing laundry, shopping, cooking, and cleaning, in addition to his work as rabbi, often wondered what she did all day. Every time he saw her, she was sitting around with her hand on her stomach, rifling though yet another baby catalog, adding more numbers to her list. She insisted on hiring a local doula, recommended by Rivkie's doula.

"I don't know. She's very expensive. Do you really need her?"

"Don't you want this to be a spiritual experience for me, Chaim? After all, it's God that is forming this child in my womb. I want to feel God during my labor. And if I'm all doped up, how can I do that? Besides, Rivkie said it was fabulous."

He dragged along with her to private coaching lessons, where the doula—a petite dreamy yoga instructor with prematurely gray hair covered by a pious snood—lectured him on understanding his wife's emotional needs and helping to ease her physical pains. He learned to coach her through contractions, to remind her of breathing techniques. He was taught to dab her lips with ice, to support her back, to adjust her pillows. Chaim, surrounded by demanding women, did everything that was asked of him, reluctant to say a word. He was simply grateful that now both he and Delilah were sleeping through the night.

They had begun to think their lives would go on this way forever, when one night, while they were in a movie theater and she was halfway through a box of popcorn, Delilah leaned over and gave the box to Chaim, complaining, "My stomach is killing me."

He was immediately alarmed "Maybe we should go home."

"No, I want to see how this movie ends."

By the time the closing credits were flashing on the screen and they got into the car, she had the worst stomachache she had ever had in her life.

"I'm swearing off popcorn forever," she said.

By the time they got home, she was in agony, barely making it to the bathroom. It was there she saw the tiny blood-tinged mucus and understood that her labor had begun.

"Call the doula! Get my bag!"

In the midst of a maelstrom of horrible physical pain that filled her with panic, she heard Chaim's calm voice. "Relax, darling. Everything is under control. Just take a shower if you feel up to it. Do you need help getting dressed? Remember to breathe. Do you want me to massage your back?"

She grabbed his cheeks like pincers, squeezing and shaking him back and forth.

"*Get me to the hospital, you idiot!*" she screamed.

The ride took forty minutes. Her contractions were coming sixty seconds apart, with peaks that lasted close to two minutes. The pain was intense, disabling, paralyzing. Chaim, his cheeks still stinging, was afraid to open his mouth. He was actually happy to see the doula, who arrived with a small bag and a large Zen smile.

"I know you are in pain, Delilah. But try to remember, your pain has a wonderful purpose. It's actually a gift. It's a blessing, this pain. It's preparing your body. Just think, if your body wouldn't be prepared, how would your baby be released into the world? Thank God for the pain, Delilah. Say a prayer, thanking God for it, for His kindness. Appreciate and give thanks for every contraction—"

"Get that woman out of here before I kill her!"

The doula's smile faded. "Perhaps you'd like a Shiatzu massage?"

"If she lays a hand on me, she's a dead woman!"

"Oh, dear." The doula sighed. "This is a difficult situation. Let's try some visualization techniques . . . or maybe you'd like me to sing? I've got a tambourine with me. Here, let's try. Think of your womb opening, allowing the sacred passage of this blessed new soul into the world: *Pisku li, shaare tzedek, avoh bam, Odey yah.* Open for me the gates of mercy, I will enter and bless You," the doula sang, shaking her tambourine.

"I want my doctor! I want an epidural!"

"Now, now, you know how we feel about epidurals. . . . Here, let me try some aromatherapy. Let me see." She rummaged through her bag. "I've got some lovely lavender, some sage. . . ." She opened some bottles, spilling the liquid into her palms, rubbing her hands together to warm them. "Now, just a touch of this on your forehead and behind your ears—"

Delilah grabbed her hand and bit down on her fingers.

The doula screamed. "Oh, my God, oh, my God, there's blood!"

"Say a prayer for *that* pain, you incompetent piece of garbage!! I should have known. I'm going to kill Rivkie!"

"Nurse!" The doula wept.

"Oooh, that looks nasty," the nurse agreed. "You'd better get yourself down to emergency." Weeping in pain, the woman fled.

"Please, Chaim, get me a doctor, get me an epidural. Please, I'm begging you!"

"Delilah, the doctor's on his way. He'll be here any minute," he explained helplessly. "Maybe she wants me to adjust her pillows?" he asked the nurse, frightened.

"I'll adjust your head, you imbecile!"

Finally the doctor arrived.

"Thank God! Please, doctor, give me an epidural, Demerol, anything!"

"Well, let's just take a look, shall we?" the doctor said calmly, poking around familiarly in her private parts. "Oh, my."

"What? Is something wrong, doctor?" Chaim asked, terrified.

"No, not at all. But she's too far along for an epidural, I'm afraid."

"*What do you mean!*" Delilah screamed.

"Well, you said on your form you were planning on bringing a doula, so we assumed you wanted a natural childbirth, which is why we didn't offer you an epidural when you first came in. Also, either you waited too long to come in or the birth is going very fast. In either case, it's impossible to give you one now. It's much too close to the birth. It might injure the baby."

"*No. Please!*"

"Delilah, be brave! Remember, God is with you! It can be a true spiritual exper—" Chaim tried.

"I'M GOING TO REDO YOUR CIRCUMCISION WHEN I GET OUT OF HERE, YOU MORON!"

Delilah closed her eyes. The pain was worse than anything she had ever in her life imagined possible, except when she fantasized about what they did to you in Auschwitz. *This was Auschwitz!* Why hadn't anyone told her it was going to be this bad? That Rivkie, that doula—they had all had children, they knew! *Liars.* And God? Where was God? And then it dawned on her: The curse of Eve! "In horrible pain will you deliver children" or something like that. This *was* God's will. His plan. But what about the curse of Adam? "In the sweat of your brow you'll bring forth bread." When was the last time she saw her husband—any man—sweat? Men had gotten a reprieve. But the curse against women went on and on and on and on. . . .

From the corner of her eye she saw Chaim sitting, small and exhausted, in the corner of the room with his face in his hands. A rabbi. God's little helper, she thought malevolently. They were all in it together. A conspiracy. God and her husband and that doctor and brainwashed religious women! And she had fallen for it like a dope. As she figured it, in the sin department, whatever she had done was nowhere near what had been done to her. If anyone had to repent for doing horrible things, she wasn't at the top of the list. From now on, all bets were off.

As she looked at her husband, he seemed to grow smaller and smaller, until finally she had the sensation that he wasn't a man at all, not even a person, just an insect, a fly on the wall, whom she hoped someone would swat away.

She started to scream and wouldn't stop until they finally wheeled her into the delivery room. Her son was delivered, with shocking speed, after only three pushes, the strength of which made her experienced obstetrician open his eyes in wonder. Never had a child been expelled faster or with more determination from a mother's womb.

"It's a boy!"

"Figures," she muttered.

"Do you want to hold him?" the nurse asked her.

"I'll catch him later." Delilah grunted, turning over and falling into a dead sleep.

{ SIXTEEN }

*D*eli, where should I put the flowers?" Mrs. Goldgrab asked her daughter.

"Don't touch them, and don't call me Deli. I'm not a pastrami sandwich," Delilah growled.

It was bad enough she had roped herself into this sit-down dinner a week after giving birth, but to have her mother not only in the house but trying to rearrange things according to her taste was quickly sending Delilah over the edge. Now, awaiting her guests, the baby all washed and dressed in a lovely baby sailor suit, blessedly asleep in his beautiful new carriage, she tried to take a deep breath and remember why, over Chaim's objections, she was overtaxing herself, insisting on doing it this way.

"Look, Chaim, I've never had the whole board over. Now I've got household help, which I won't have in a few weeks. And everyone will ooh and aah over the baby, and even if I screw up they'll say, 'Oh, she just gave birth.' So, let me do it now."

She'd also decided to invite some friends, feeling she not only needed some allies but some messengers who would spread the news of her triumph to all her old schoolmates. Who knew that the only person who would accept would be Tzippy, a school friend she was never overly fond of, whose greatest asset was that she always seemed to accept Delilah's invitations and actually show up? She was not only coming but bringing a friend, someone Delilah had never met. The Malins had agreed to host the two for the weekend after Delilah explained that Tzippy was her "best and closest friend." That way, they could attend the Saturday-morning circumcision ceremony in the synagogue,

"So, how can I help you, darling?" Mrs. Goldgrab said, peeved.

"Just stay out of my way! Don't rearrange anything, and don't talk to anyone!"

The older woman, insulted but not surprised, took a large brownie off a plate and went out to sit on the back porch to feed herself chocolate comfort and nurse her grievances.

Having her mother and father in the house was just about the last straw. She had readily come up with a number of imaginative and convincing reasons to explain their absence, but Chaim had been scandalized. "We can't very well hold a bris without inviting our parents. It's wrong to deny that respect to them. Besides, what will people think, that we're orphans? Or black sheep?"

The thought of her mother sitting down next to Solange Malin and striking up a conversation about any subject of interest to her mother was breathtaking in its possibilities for disaster. Oddly, while she disliked her mother-in-law intensely, she was less concerned about Mrs. Levi proving an embarrassment. Like it or not, she had grudging respect for Chaim's mother, who could certainly hold her own in any company.

In fact, Chaim's mother had so far proved extremely helpful. After dressing the baby, she had skillfully set the table and helped arrange the catered food on the platters. Since Delilah's pregnancy, there had been an undeclared truce between them. As in so many cases of this kind, once a daughter-in-law becomes a grandchild factory, all bets are off and grandmothers eat crow, a fact it would do well for mothers of the groom to bear in mind before beginning any sentence to the bride with "I'll tell you very frankly."

You might be able to live without your daughter-in-law. You might even be able to manage without your precious son. But no one in her right mind is going to forgo a relationship with that soft little last-chance package of big eyes and baby fat you've waited so long to cuddle to your milkless breasts.

All this, Delilah knew well. But being shrewd if not wise, she discerned that good behavior on her part at this moment in time would yield rewards far richer than simply seeing Chaim's mother grovel. And as she looked at her little boy, so beautifully groomed and ready for inspection, she saw that she'd been right.

Delilah wandered around her home, inspecting.

During the months that had gone by, she'd developed a different set of eyes. After her first visit to the Malins, she had thrown out her globe lamp and the collection of ceramic cats with pink fur. After the Grodins, the little glass vases filled with plastic flowers and the plastic refrigerator magnets had gone. And after the Rollands and Borenbergs, Chaim had had to argue with the truck driver from Goodwill, who had knocked on the door ready to move out their entire bedroom set, his parents' wedding gift. The problem with it, she tried to explain to him, and with their Mikasa china pattern (which she was secretly and deliberately breaking piece by piece), was that everything matched. Matched sets—furniture, china, silverware—were embarrassingly middle class, she had learned from her visits to Felice Borenberg and Mariette Rolland. She wanted to start over, mixing patterns, filling her bedroom and living room with antiques, no two pieces the same, but all polished to a high shine.

Her taste was changing. Unfortunately, her finances were not keeping up.

Now—as Delilah was well aware—no one wants a rabbi or his wife to live better than the average congregant. A rabbi is supposed to represent contempt for material things. He is supposed, by his very being, to point the way toward a happiness that is not measured by what you have, but who you are. On the other hand, a congregant does not want to feel like Scrooge visiting Bob Cratchit.

What Delilah was planning to do—and really it was the right and commendable thing for her to do—was to convince the board that the rabbi's wife was hardworking and had excellent taste, and that the only thing standing between her and the exploitation of her potential as premiere hostess to the Swallow Lake community was cold, hard cash.

She looked forward to plunging back into the role suspended by her pregnancy of wonderful rabbi's wife. It would be nothing like it was in the

Bronx, she convinced herself, because the needs of the rich were altogether different.

First of all, they didn't treat you like slaves, because they actually had slaves, people they paid to insult and order about; people who had to pick up their groceries and tend to them when they broke an ankle or simply felt bored. And you weren't constantly in hospitals, because if there was one thing rich people knew how to do, it was take care of themselves.

They exercised and ate blueberries and strawberries and oatmeal and brown rice and fresh salmon and green tea. They went to spas, slathered themselves with expensive mud from the Dead Sea, had Norwegian gods who massaged away their tensions and cellulite, and yoga teachers who kept them supple. They avoided pneumonia by wintering in Hawaii and avoided assorted melanomas by applying extremely expensive sunblocks that left them looking like pale toast rather than pumpernickel. They used hypnotists to convince their subconscious they didn't like smoking, so lung cancer was out. They remembered flu shots and vitamin supplements and practiced meditation. And most of all, they didn't have infusions of industrial sewage to pollute their water or belching factories to destroy their air quality.

It was easy to stay out of hospitals if you were rich and cautious.

Since they had their physical well-being pretty much under control, Delilah imagined she'd try to win her place in the community by showing them how to develop their spiritual side. She asked Chaim for his advice. As usual, he had been no help at all.

"Just be yourself. You're fine. You do plenty." He tried to comfort her. "You don't have to please anyone but yourself."

Right.

What she needed was a *chesed* project, she decided. Some series of good deeds that would occupy her time and prove to the community that she deserved their respect for being their proxy in all kinds of worthwhile and unpleasant tasks that needed doing. Soup kitchens would have been perfect, if only there was anyone in Connecticut who was hungry.

She remembered the famous story of the rabbi of the Reform temple in the next town, who decided that on Thanksgiving the community should prepare turkeys and pies and all the trimmings "for less fortunate members of the community." He and his wife and several members of the congregation loaded the food into a van and started looking for the poor. Problem was, they turned the car in the wrong direction. The houses just kept getting more and more palatial, with not a poor person—Jewish or otherwise—anywhere in sight. So, finally, they made some phone calls, turned the car around and drove three hours until they finally, wearily, unloaded the feast on a bunch of startled Baptists, who were pretty much full from their own meal.

Then she thought: fund-raising.

That had all kinds of fun possibilities. Dressing up in fabulous new clothes and having your hair professionally colored and styled in order to hit the malls for free "favors," getting jewelry and nice clothes and vacations donated for raffle tickets. There was only one main problem. You had to have something to raise money for.

Well, Israel, of course. There was always someone over there who was recovering from some horrible outrage, physical or emotional. Poor kids. Better: poor Black Jewish kids. Hospitals. Terror victims. Better: poor terror victims just out of hospitals who were unemployed, divorced, or widowed with children (two terror victims!) with empty refrigerators. Victims of left-wing government atrocities who'd had their homes bulldozed, the same homes that previous left-wing governments had built with other charity money.

Whatever. Israel was a gold mine.

But then, like any gold mine, you had many miners: The six-figure salaried professionals in expensive suits from United Jewish Communities and Israel Bonds, people whose expense accounts and cushy business-class trips and overnight stays at fancy hotels were on the line. People with motivation. Or the powerhouse women volunteers from Hadassah. People who knew what they were doing, who had experience and connections.

A rank amateur couldn't very well compete with them and win. Besides, when she dropped the idea casually on Solange Malin, her reaction had been pointed and hostile: Perhaps if the rebbitzin had time on her hands, she might consider fund-raising for the shul. Yeah, to raise the rabbi's salary. Talk about worthy causes! But you couldn't very well consider that a *chesed* project, now could you?

"Too tacky, even for us." Chaim shook his head.

So, there she was, with no acceptable *chesed* project. And she the rabbi's wife, the community role model for sainthood.

It bore down on her, the weight of unmet expectations, of disappointed desires, of unearned admiration. She wanted desperately to make a good impression.

She knew that Chaim had not been their first choice. That they'd wanted the grandson of the legendary European rabbi who had founded the famous Yeshiva. As it turned out, the community who'd won him, had gotten much more—or much less—than they'd bargained for. He'd wound up embroiling them in a major scandal involving after-hours rabbinical "counseling" to widows, divorcees, and, yes, married women in good standing. He would have gone on his merry way if one hadn't become obsessed, stalking him wherever he went, so that even his wife, Rebbitzin Clueless, finally had to wake up and say, Whoa. Now lawyers and lawsuits were pelting them like hail.

So, as she saw it, Chaim had been quite a bargain. For aside from not being particularly bright, and not really having all that much to contribute to his congregation's spiritual life, he was basically harmless. He told some good jokes and didn't make enemies by pushing unpleasant agendas, like forcefully denouncing intermarriages or scolding people for not sending their kids to Israeli summer programs. He was happy to give eulogies and make short speeches at Bar and Bat Mitzvas—in which he invented Nobel Prize–winning accomplishments and character traits for twelve- and thirteen-year-olds. As far as she could tell, he was well liked by most everyone except the chronic complainers, who exist in every shul filled with unreasonable expectations, who wanted a rabbi who is a mentor, a leader, blah, blah.

As if. Congregations didn't want leaders; they wanted shleppers, rabbis who were always scurrying to catch up with their fickle needs. Today, they wanted the women called up to the Torah. Tomorrow, they'd want sushi at shul events. The next day they'd want armed guards with Uzis to roam the shul complex . . . and the rabbi was expected to fall in and support the powers that be. Except that those powers were always shifting.

Their lives, she realized, were built on beach sand. And she, no less than he, was responsible for keeping the powers that be from washing them out to sea.

The unexpected situation she had fallen into by becoming the wife of a rabbi had dawned on Delilah in stages. Stage one, she had been filled with the romantic illusions carefully nurtured in the classrooms of her youth, places where rabbis and rabbis' wives held sway. Life, they'd explained, was to be lived in order to earn great rewards that could only be cashed in after you died, in the "next life." A woman, unable to earn much spiritual change on her own with the measly religious duties that fell her way—drops from the great ocean that washed over the men—could nevertheless increase her bottom line by supporting her husband's myriad religious duties. And the greater the husband, the more credit the wife earned. The wife of a rabbi who was a scholar, head of a great congregation, a leader of men, never had to worry about her spot in the World to Come. It would be an orchestra seat, center stage.

For this, sacrifices had to be made. Like not being able to express yourself freely, having to dress and behave like a dowdy pious matron. Most of all, you had to defer to your husband, helping to feed the myth that every word that fell from his mouth was a pearl of wisdom.

And then came stage two, the realization that a rabbi was just a man, a husband, who had his moments, good and bad, all that Talmud study notwithstanding. That when he pronounced "too much salt in the kugel" or "that dress seems a little too tight around the hips," it was not the word of God. That he was capable of locking himself in his study for hours to compose a sermon about the virtues of compassion, kindness, and peacemaking, only to emerge and threaten the rowdy kids next door with bodily harm if they didn't shut up.

But, then, there were also the times when she saw him secretly donate money from his own pocket to help out divorced moms, or send kids to summer camp, or pull strings to get teens into rehab centers. Times when she felt she might actually be earning World-to-Come credits by supporting him and being part of his work.

And then came the last stage in which the shocking realization dawned that, like it or not, she had no choice: being married to the rabbi, she, too, was an employee of the shul. It was two for the price of one. A package deal. The salary he was paid, and the good life they enjoyed, devolved on her shoulders as well.

She looked out to the back porch where her mother was sitting, with its view of the forests and backyard swings. At first, just the idea of a backyard and front yard, of your own trees and plants, had made her so happy, she'd find herself just sitting outside, tearing up over her good fortune. But now, she was already beginning to feel the small ping of discontent. The beautiful lake view was blocked. The backyard was adequate but small. There was no swimming pool. No Jacuzzi. No sauna.

And while the bedroom was three times the size of the one they'd had in the city, their bathroom had one sink, not two, and it was tiled with plain-colored tiles, nothing imported from Spain or Mexico or Portugal. The refrigerator was a Westinghouse, not a Sub-Zero.

Despite the twinges of discontent, Delilah was still telling herself that she was happy. And in many ways, she was.

Why, just that morning she had lain in bed examining the cards and gifts that had not stopped pouring in. There was a gorgeous sequined diaper bag by Isabella Fiore from Mariette Rolland, who had exquisite taste in everything. The Malins had sent over a classic pram, navy and white patent leather with an adjustable backrest, an air flow adjustment device, and a genuine porcelain medallion, a gift of the congregation. The Grodins had sent over their novelty bears, about ninety-five different models, while the Borenbergs had sent clothing by Minimun, which, someone had explained to Delilah, looked ordinary but cost a fortune.

Despite her sore body, she'd leaned back, sighing with satisfaction and happiness. Even though she was married to a man who catered to the needs of endless strangers, people who claimed and received his time, energy, worry, and interest twenty-four hours a day, seven days a week, she felt she could make her marriage, and her life, work in a place like Swallow Lake.

"Why don't you ask some of the women tonight about a suitable *chesed* project? Maybe they'll have an idea," Chaim had suggested that morning. She'd stared at him, stunned. Finally, her husband had a good idea. This alone, she thought, was worth a celebratory dinner.

{ SEVENTEEN }

*T*he Grodins arrived first, bearing a bottle of expensive wine. Amber was a large woman who wore custom-made clothes that seemed to float over her body benignly, giving away no secrets. Like many heavy women, she had a strikingly lovely face that people bemoaned, as if it were a tragedy. "Such a shame!" they'd say. "Such a beautiful face! If only she could lose a little weight, she'd be such a knockout." Since Amber had been overweight from the age of thirteen months, she had been waiting her entire life for someone to call her beautiful without an addendum.

Her husband, Stuart, was equally heavy and gave the impression of being a laid-back guy with a killer sense of humor. Nothing could have been further from the truth. Far from being easygoing and self-satisfied, he was the opposite: a kind of fat Richard Dreyfuss in *The Apprenticeship of Duddy Kravitz*, constantly looking for a new angle to exploit, seeing in every social relationship the hidden opportunity for scoring.

Whenever he was together with the rich birds in his neighborhood, he never ceased hoping they'd molt when he was around, leaving behind some golden feather he could scavenge and cash in. Sometimes it was a stock tip, but often it was just the small talk that went on between very wealthy men, about investment advisers and commodities and real estate opportunities. He lunged for the information like a Venus flytrap, before anyone could catch on.

He was always a little nervous around people like the Malins, feeling that he was a fake, a one-trick pony, who had had some luck that could always peter out. He and Amber had been in the novelty business for years—producing instantly breakable and forgettable objects—until they hit the jackpot with the bears.

"Delilah, sweetheart, mazel tov! Let me see the baby. . . . Oh, Stuart, look at this baby!" Amber cooed, looking him over. They had one grown son who lived in Miami whom no one had ever seen. There didn't seem to be a daughter-in-law in the offing or a grandchild on the horizon.

"Cute," Stuart agreed, giving the baby a quick little look over, then nervously canvassing the room. "Are we the first?"

Delilah nodded. "But they'll be home from shul soon. Please, sit down."

She didn't offer them anything, because traditionally one didn't eat or drink Friday nights before hearing kiddush over the wine, which would only take place when the rabbi walked in and the meal began.

The Borenbergs came next. Felice was in her late forties, but you would never have guessed it. She was tiny and wore her hair down her back almost to her waist, like a fairy princess. The cost of dye necessary to keep it that shade of platinum could have put a deserving student through medical school, Amber once snickered to Solange, who was only too happy to join in, resenting the woman's overt sexiness along with everything else about Felice.

Women of a certain age, Amber and Solange were in whispered agreement, should cut their hair to a sensible length instead of running around like Venus on the half shell. Whenever Felice walked into the women's section, the two of them—and many many others—seethed at the way the head of every man in the synagogue turned to look at her. Men never realized how tacky that kind of behavior was, Solange and Amber agreed. But they never said any of these things to her face because Felice was constantly throwing the most wonderful parties in her exquisite home. She always had the best cook, the most wonderful gardener and florist, the most efficient and pleasant household help that stayed with her for years. Amber and Solange would have been devastated to be cut from her guest list.

Felice was also a terror on the StairMaster and never skipped her private pilates and yoga sessions, giving her the figure of a junior high school cheerleader. That was bad enough. But what was truly unforgivable was that she had actually founded the multimillion-dollar company that allowed her to maintain her lifestyle at Swallow Lake, rather than having married the man who did.

A rabbi's daughter who had wound up at Harvard Business School, she had come up with the brilliant idea of putting pushcarts along the center aisles of malls, in which she sold everything from back massagers to pearl jewelry, amassing countless millions. She had actually been written up in *Fortune* as one of America's foremost entrepreneurs. There had been three husbands, the first two long gone and forgotten. She had a number of children away at college, leaving behind only her baby, now a pimply sixteen-year-old sophomore in the local yeshiva high school. She had sold half her shares in her thirties and had been pursuing a life of leisure ever since. Her current spouse, Ari, was the son of Israelis who had left the country when Ari was ten in search of the American dream. And although Ari had been back only twice in the last twenty years to visit his grandmother and relatives, he considered himself the resident expert on anything to do with Israeli politics, culture, or economics, insisting on having the last word on Middle East history and politics. He was at least fifteen years younger than Felice, the only man on the board who still had all his hair in its original color.

"I hope I'm not too late to help," Mariette Rolland said briskly, as she walked in alone. Her husband, Joseph, the heart specialist, was a man whom no one ever actually saw, although his existence was a well-established rumor. Mariette was cover-girl beautiful, with strawberry-blond hair cut into a shoulder-length bob.

A clinical psychologist with a thriving practice, she was also the mother of four children—a fifteen-year-old son and three very beautiful daughters aged sixteen through twenty-three, the oldest of whom was already married and the mother of two babies.

She was also very kind. She never gossiped. She contributed generously to every imaginable charity, as well as baking cakes for them, and opening her home for countless fund-raisers. She gave dinner parties for her husband's medical colleagues. She ran support groups for women with osteoporosis. She volunteered at battered women's shelters, taught quilting, and took gourmet cooking classes. All this, she managed single-handedly as her husband jet-setted all over the globe, attending medical conferences and tending to an international roster of patients, including a member of the Saudi royal family, making him one of the few Jews to have gone in and out of that country alive.

Mariette did it all with aplomb, patience, good nature, and good cheer. She was also one of the few women who insisted on a token head covering for her hair, out of respect for the rabbinical injunction. She always found the perfect hat to match every single one of her perfect outfits, which was in itself enough to make you want her dead.

"Delilah, how are you? Tell me how I can help. Oh, look at the baby! Such a little darling. How was the birth?"

"Oh, it was an amazing spiritual experience. You know, I didn't have any drugs. I had this doula. And I never felt closer to God, believe me. I felt He was directly responsible for everything that was happening to me."

"How inspiring! Usually a first birth is pretty difficult," Mariette said, impressed.

"It all depends on your spiritual strength." Delilah nodded. "*Baruch Hashem.* It's an experience I'll never forget. In fact, I'm thinking about giving a *shiur* about it."

"Mariette, that's such a lovely suit! Wherever did you find it?" Amber asked enviously.

"I got it in this little shop in passy the last time I was in Paris." She sighed mournfully.

Mariette's married daughter lived in Paris, so she had a perfect, morally iron-clad reason to travel there often. In between her shopping trips to the Galeries Lafayette, there were often side jaunts to Provence and the French Riviera. But she made it a point to disavow any enjoyment from her travels. "I am counting the days until my family finds their way back to America, or even to Israel, believe me!" she'd say fervently, shaking her head as she fingered the exquisite rose-shaped sequined buttons on her suit jacket—such as can only be found in Paris. "Such anti-Semites," she'd murmur, shrugging helplessly, steadying her upper lip. "But what can I do? She's my daughter." In answer to any question that broached the subject of when her daughter was actually planning on leaving France, she'd exhale slowly, explaining for the umpteenth time that there was a business that needed to be sold, some big factory her son-in-law had inherited, was now in charge of, and was unfortunately unable to sell. "Everyone has their burdens." She'd smile bravely, planning her next trip.

There was the obligatory oohing and aahing over the sleeping infant, who slept under the watchful eye of the au pair, who stood by ready to whisk him out of sight and hearing range the moment he showed any actual signs of life.

{ EIGHTEEN }

*D*elilah, look who I've brought," Chaim said cheerfully as he walked
in from shul, accompanied by the Malins and two women. Delilah
walked over to him, a big smile on her face. She gave the strangers—whom
she assumed were shul strays—the barest of smiles and an offhand nod,
before turning her attention fully to the Malins.

"Solange, Arthur, thanks so much for the beautiful carriage! And for
hosting my dearest friend! I can't wait to see her!"

A strange look came over Solange. "You're very welcome, Delilah.
Your *friends* also couldn't wait to see you!" she said, gesturing pointedly
toward the strangers.

"Don't you recognize me, Delilah? It's me, Tzippy."

Delilah took in the woman's gelled black hair that stood up in spikes,
the ends tinted blond, the low-cut vintage dress, the chains with numerous
symbols. For a split second, the rather overweight, studious girl with
glasses she remembered from high school peeked out at her.

"Tzippy? Is that really you?" she said in a tiny, hoarse voice. She felt breathless, as if she'd swallowed a fish bone and was afraid of inhaling it into her lungs.

"Yes, it's really me. And this is Fréderique." She reached out, threading her fingers lovingly through the hand of a petite blonde in a red pantsuit and bringing it to her lips.

Delilah froze in horror.

A gay person in the Orthodox community is like a beer-guzzling Muslim in a mosque: totally impossible for the faithful to publicly embrace. While the rest of the world might have moved on, and even certain Reform and Conservative Jewish congregations in New York, Los Angeles, San Francisco, and Boston might have graciously finessed their way around it, most people in the religious Jewish world continued to view homosexuality in biblical terms, i.e., as an abomination worthy of, if not currently punishable by, stoning. The more widespread its acceptance, the more Orthodox religious leaders pointed to it as proof of the current decadence of modern life, and to themselves as guardians of the last bastion left standing against it. The depth of one's horrified rejection was often the yardstick to one's piety.

"It's so good to see you! Mazel tov on the baby!" Tzippy went on cheerfully, oblivious, hugging her. "I don't know if this is the right time to announce it—I know you're not supposed to mix one *simcha* with another—but I just can't resist: I also have a mazel tov coming to me!" she looked lovingly at Fréderique. "We're engaged!" she announced. "We hope to have a commitment ceremony as soon as our rabbi gives birth. We'd be honored if you'd be one of our chuppah holders."

People standing within hearing range turned astonished faces in their direction. Delilah shrank.

"I was really surprised you called. Frankly, I'm not in touch with most of the girls we grew up with anymore. Nothing personal, just, you know, nothing in common. And even my family—well, you can imagine. Intermarriage is bad enough. But intermarriage with a same-sex partner who's Catholic and French—which is almost as bad as being German these days—was too much for them. So we thought it was a pretty important statement, didn't we, Fréderique? I mean, you being the rabbi's wife and all of an Orthodox congregation and still being willing to invite us and introduce us to your community as your friends."

"*Best* friends," Solange said slowly. "Isn't that what you said, Delilah?"

"She told you that?" Tzippy beamed at Fréderique, who beamed back. "I had a pretty big crush on her too."

Delilah stepped back, dizzy, rapidly reevaluating all those times she'd worn her bikini and shared a beach blanket with Tzippy during the summer of her sophomore year.

"*Bon soir*, I've heard a lot about you," Fréderique said, looking her up and down. "And it was all true."

Delilah touched her sweating forehead.

"Is that French I'm hearing?" Mariette called from the other side of the room. "*Ça va?*" she ventured, moving toward them, smiling. Having used up her entire French vocabulary except for *How much? My size is the American size eight*, and *Give me a low-calorie soft drink*, Mariette returned to English. "I'm afraid my French is pretty bad," she said. It was not. It was nonexistent. "So, are you two roommates? I remember how much fun it was when I was in college to bunk with a roommate—"

"Yes, we live together, but not as roommates," Tzippy began instructively, as if she were about to deliver the main address at the Gay Pride parade.

Delilah suddenly plucked her peacefully sleeping infant unceremoniously out of his carriage. He howled.

"Oh, what do you know? He's hungry again. And I just fed him! What an appetite!" Delilah said in a booming voice over the baby's screams, putting an end to all conversation. "Chaim, why don't you seat everyone? I'll just feed him and be back in a jiffy." She ran up the stairs to the bedroom.

Felice arched a brow, while Solange and Amber went silent, staring at their feet. The lesbians and the disappearing act were bad enough, but nothing compared to not having provided place cards and having left the responsibility for seating in the hands of a husband at the last minute. That could only be characterized by one hyphenated word: low-class.

Chaim looked anxiously around at the knots of people, wondering how to untie them and where they were supposed to go.

"What a wonderful idea!" Mariette declared brightly. "So much better than boring place cards. This way, we can all decide. You don't mind, Rabbi Chaim, if we take it out of your hands? Now, let's see, I am dying to sit right next to Arthur—you don't mind, Solange, do you? And why don't you and Stuart sit over here. And Felice, you and Amber can be here, next to Chaim's mother and father. And Mrs. Goldgrab, what about here?" Mariette kindly and charmingly filled in for her AWOL hostess, making it all seem like great fun, instead of a major screw-up. "Tzippy, Fréderique, why don't you sit together over *here*," she said, placing them firmly in one corner with smiling efficiency so no one would be forced to speak to them.

Delilah leaned up against the bedroom door. The baby flailed, moist and angry, getting justifiably redder and more furious by the minute. She undid her bra and compressed her generous nipple into its tiny mouth, effectively shutting him up.

A dyke, she thought with horror. Tzippy Rosenfeld, who'd sat next to her in *chumash* class learning all about the Temple offerings! Quiet, unattractive, frizzy-haired Tzippy, full of sardonic humor no one got! And she'd been introduced to the Swallow Lake board *as the rebbitzin's dearest friend!*

Delilah sat down, her nipple aching from all the unaccustomed tugging. Perhaps it wasn't as bad as she thought. Perhaps not everyone had overheard them. As for the hand-holding, after all, good women friends often held hands as a sign of innocent affection, didn't they? And lots of people dressed strangely these days. It was Britney Spears pollution. Chaim certainly didn't seem as if he'd noticed anything strange. But she got scant comfort from that. First, because he never noticed anything, and second, because even if he had he'd still be incapable of snubbing someone, anyone, even if his life—or, more importantly, his job—depended on it.

And then, finally, another realization dawned on her: They'd be staying overnight at the Malins! Although she was fuzzy on the details—what, in heaven's name, was there for two women to do with each other, after all?—a cold shudder of terror crawled up her spine. What if they woke Solange or Arthur's mother, who would discover them in flagrante delicto?

She sat on her bed filling with despair, imagining how the information would spread like wildfire all over the community Delilah so wanted to impress with her goodness and piety. She could see with clarity how all the eyes in the women's section would turn to stare at her, people whispering in shocked low tones behind her back how the rebbetzin's friend, *her very, very best friend in all the world, the only one she'd invited to her son's bris out of all her many, many friends*, had performed acts of lesbian lewdness under the roof the president of Ohel Aaron.

People were shifting nervously, beginning to wonder if she was ever coming back, when all of a sudden, Delilah suddenly reappeared. Her eyes looked slightly red, and she had a sweet, sad smile on her wan face, like someone who has witnessed the last act of a Shakespearean tragedy and emerged purified and uplifted by the cathartic horror of it all.

She sat down at the other end of the table, facing her husband, and managed to avoid looking at or speaking to either Tzippy or Fréderique the entire evening. Even though Chaim tried to be hospitable, including them in the conversation whenever he could, they began to shift uncomfortably, exchanging meaningful glances. Finally, just before dessert, Tzippy suddenly answered her cell phone, even though no one had heard it ring. It was urgent family business, she apologized, rising from the table together with Fréderique, which necessitated their immediate departure.

They said their goodbyes. Delilah walked them to the door.

"So sorry you've got to go!" Delilah said brightly. "But thanks for coming!"

"You mean thanks for leaving, don't you?" Tzippy said, looking at her for what she knew would probably be the last time.

"You always did have a strange sense of humor."

"Relax, Delilah. There's no need to pretend. We get the picture."

Delilah's smile faded. "And don't you pretend you don't know what's going on here. You went to yeshiva. Our jobs are on the line here." She sighed. "Look, I'm really sorry. I just never imagined. . . . It's nothing personal. Goodbye. I wish you both luck."

"So long to you too, Delilah," Tzippy answered, looking at her steadily. "I wish you luck too. Take it from me you'll need it. A person can only pretend to be something they're not for just so long."

"What is that supposed to mean?" She bristled.

"Oh, I think you know, *Rebbitzin*," Tzippy murmured meaningfully. "But hey, to each his own closet." They closed the door behind them.

She came back to the table and sat down, smoothing her skirt beneath her.

"Lovely girls," Solange murmured.

Delilah nodded. "I know what you are all thinking. But if it hadn't been for the accident—"

"What happened?" Amber asked.

Delilah shook her head. "A tragedy. Such a solid, religious girl. She won second prize in the Bible quiz! She was engaged to an accountant from Boro Park and studying to be a—a librarian. At Brooklyn College." Delilah stared at her hands. "She's been my *chesed* project now for years."

"Head trauma?" Mariette asked sympathetically. "You get all kinds of personality changes," she told the others.

Delilah nodded sadly. "She was praying so hard one Yom Kippur she actually tipped right over from the women's balcony into the men's section. Head first into the bimah. It was terrifying."

"Well, I'll be damned!" Delilah's father boomed

Solange's mouth dropped open. Mariette and Felice exchanged wondering stares.

"Most unfortunate." Arthur shrugged. "How kind of you, Rebbitzin, to be so loyal. Poor thing."

"Yes." Mariette nodded. "Emotional support is so important to trauma victims. It's a really worthy *chesed* project."

"That's the way I brought her up, to do good. It's our way of life," Mrs. Goldgrab piped up, poised to elaborate until she caught a glimpse of Delilah's half-lidded, sidelong glance, which reminded her of a crocodile just about to have lunch.

Chaim, who had been listening to all this in dumbfounded wonder, suddenly cleared his throat. "Speaking of *chesed* projects," he interjected quickly. "Delilah has been searching for a new one for our community. I told her she should ask all of you."

"A *chesed* project! Why, you are going to have your hands full with your new baby, my dear. That is the biggest *chesed* project any woman can take on," Solange said loftily.

"Be real, Solange!" Felice waved her hand dismissively. "You can go crazy in the house all day with a screaming kid. First of all, get a babysitter, so you'll have a few hours a day for yourself. And whatever you do, don't get involved in hospitals. All those germs!"

"And you don't want to get involved in fund-raising either, believe me. It's too time-consuming," Mariette pointed out. "And the competition is cutthroat."

"I've got an idea! What about collecting clothes for Israeli terror victims?" Amber said.

"Oh, clothing drives are so passé. Besides, why would old clothes do anything for terror victims?" Solange asked.

"But what about handbags!" Delilah burst in suddenly. "Designer handbags!"

"Designer Handbags for Terror Victims," Felice mused, rolling the phrase over on her tongue.

Delilah leaned back, pleased. "Well, I was looking at some of those horrible pictures of bus explosions, you know? And on the sidewalk was this handbag, just lying there. And I began to think of all those Israeli women who had lost their handbags . . . and you know, if you give victims money, they'll just spend it on the house or on food. They would never go out and buy themselves a really, really beautiful handbag. They wouldn't allow themselves that pleasure, and as we all know, a special handbag can do so much for a woman's feeling about herself."

"That," Ari said slowly, shoving yet another slice of kugel onto his already overcrowded plate, "has got to be the dumbest idea I ever heard."

"What do you mean!"

"How can you say that?"

"Spoken like a man!"

Each of the women jumped on him, causing his fork to pause in midair before it could deposit its next unnecessary load. He looked at them, astonished. "You can't be serious. Come on! I'm Israeli, I know what I'm saying. Israelis have stubborn pride. They hate charity."

"Has anyone ever mentioned this to the UJC?" Stuart murmured

"All right, all right. Explain the logic of it to me," Arthur said calmly, raising his palms upward, ever reasonable and wanting to spare his hostess further humiliation.

"Well," Delilah began eagerly, "let's say you were depressed over your appearance, as I imagine some terror victims are—all that stress, not to mention physical injuries." She shuddered.

"And maybe no matter what clothes you wear, you still feel fat or you can't find your size," Amber joined in.

"But a beautiful handbag never has to fit, and it makes every woman feel special," Felice concluded.

"Exactly," Delilah agreed triumphantly.

"What do *you* think, Rabbi Chaim?" Ari said, suddenly turning to him.

Chaim looked from the disbelieving eyes of the men to the agitated and defensive eyes of the women, finally staring straight into those of his wife, who looked back at him, expressionless, waiting.

"Well." He gulped. "Let me tell you a story. Ninety-year-old Moishe is dying. There he is, in his bed, getting ready for his last hour on earth, when suddenly the smell of newly baked fudge brownies comes wafting up the stairs from the kitchen. This was his favorite. There was nothing he loved to eat more than fudge brownies. So, with his last ounce of strength, he lifts himself up off the bed, clutches the wall, and slowly makes his way out of his bedroom and down the steps, gripping the railings with both hands. Finally, his strength almost gone, his heart beating with his last breaths, he leans against the kitchen door frame and stares in.

"There, in front of him, is a wondrous sight: hundreds and hundreds of fudge brownies. 'Oh, my God, maybe I'm already in heaven!' he thinks. 'But if I'm still alive, then this is the greatest act of *chesed* from my wonderful wife, who knows me so well and has been at my side for over sixty-five years. My darling wife who wants to make sure I leave this world a happy man. I cannot disappoint her.' With one final superhuman effort, Moishe lunges toward the brownies but ends up on his knees near the table. His old hand trembling, he reaches up to take one, his mind already beginning to imagine the explosion of chocolate in his mouth, the thick fudgy taste that will soon fill him with final joy, when all of a sudden— *wham*—his wife whacks his hand away with her mixing spoon.

" 'What are you doing!' he cries out to her.

" 'They're for the shiva.' "

No one said a word, the women looking aghast while the men tried out tentative little smiles.

"With all due respect, Rabbi," Ari finally broke the silence. "What's that supposed to teach us?"

Chaim looked up, surprised, his forehead suddenly glistening with moisture.

"Isn't it obvious, Ari?" Arthur Malin broke in, raising his eyebrows. "No matter what state a person is in, there is always something that can bring him joy. Is that what you meant, Rabbi?"

Chaim nodded his head gratefully.

"Amber is right. Clothes have to fit. Different people like different syles. And I'll tell you something else, trying on clothes is depressing. It's not fun. But a beautiful handbag. It's a wonderful, original idea. Like brownies for the dying," Arthur concluded, smiling encouragingly at Chaim.

So he wasn't the brightest star in the sky, and his wife was even dimmer, Arthur Malin thought to himself. But he would rather have the community collecting pocketbooks than brainwashing their young people to join the black hats. He thought of his grandchildren in their broken-down apartment on a poor Jerusalem side street, their father jobless and probably going to stay that way, living on handouts from America. At least Rabbi Chaim would do no harm.

"I can give you a few handbags, and I know some other women who will be happy to contribute, Delilah." Felice offered.

∼ ∽

After services the next day, they held the bris. They named their son after his great-grandfather, Abraham. It was a very moving ceremony in which the entire community participated. Afterward, there was a sit-down luncheon in the catering hall served on china plates that were a far cry from the plastic forks and paper shnaps cups of the Bronx.

{ NINETEEN }

Delilah's dreams of spending her time searching for designer handbags to cheer Israeli sufferers of posttraumatic shock were not exactly working out as she had planned. In fact, being a rabbi's wife in Swallow Lake wasn't turning out as she had planned.

She realized this the morning of the sisterhood meeting. She was in the kitchen, preparing the evening's food, which Solange had suggested be a dessert buffet in a baby shower theme, because one of the sisterhood members had just found out she was pregnant. So there were going to be baby bottles holding little tulips, and diaper-pin napkin holders, a large stuffed animal in a diaper holding the silverware. There would be parchment paper cones of peanut brittle held in ice-cream-cone holders and tall martini glasses with little silver scoopers holding jellybeans. There would be a blueberry-lemon crème brûlé tart, chocolate peanut-butter diamonds, fudge-covered brownie cheesecake, chocolate-dipped almond horns, cupcakes, plum crumble cake, fresh fruit cut up to look like lollipops, and a peach and berry crisp.

The baby was screaming, so she picked him up and balanced him on her hip, as she creamed the confectioner's sugar into the butter. The phone was ringing.

"Chaim, can you get that? *Chaim?*"

It kept ringing.

"Hello?"

"Rebbitzin Levi?"

"Yes, who is this? Shhhh. . . . No I'm not shushing you, it's my baby. How can I . . . ? Oh, Mrs. Stein. You really should discuss that with my husband. . . . I'm sorry he's so hard to catch, but he's. . . . Yes, I realize that it's important. . . . Of course, I'll remind the cleaning staff to wash off the plants in the synagogue lobby before your son's Bar Mitzva. . . . No, I don't think it's petty, not at all. You have out-of-town guests; of course you should feel comfortable. *Sssssssshhhhhh!* No, no, really, it's the baby—"

Was that the damn doorbell ringing?

"CHAIM!" Where was he?

"Sorry, I've got to go. 'Bye."

She hung up the phone and ran to the door.

"Oh, Mrs. Cooperman. How are you?" She smiled as best she could at the young woman on her doorstep, who wordlessly handed her a white envelope, turned her back, and fled. Delilah held it in her fingertips gingerly, imagining the piece of cloth tinged with vaginal secretion inside, releasing it over the pile of mail on the dining room table meant for Chaim.

The baby was not going back to sleep, she realized, sitting down and pulling out her breast. She sat down on the couch and closed her eyes as the infant nursed, pulling on her nipple, which was sore and cracked. She put him over her shoulder to burp. He let loose a large wad of goo, which, as usual, managed to miss the diaper and run down her shoulder, thus destroying yet another blouse.

No, things were not going as she'd imagined. For starters, there she was sitting in the front pew in the synagogue, a sitting duck, listening to all the whispers as Chaim was speaking, wondering if they were laughing at him or angry at him or just ignoring him and discussing where to buy shoes, as he gave his weekly sermon. At first, she had concentrated on his every word, tense and defensive, cringing when she heard him say anything the least bit controversial that might wind up with some incensed synagogue member accosting them at kiddush to bawl him out. But as hard as she listened, it was impossible to predict. Once, he told a touching story about the daughter of a friend who had celebrated her twenty-first birthday in Jerusalem by preparing a Sabbath dinner for friends. He compared that to the twenty-one-year-olds who celebrate by getting drunk in bars with friends. Who could have predicted that this would lead to a half-crazed congregant cornering him over the potato kugel, shouting, "Not every American kid gets plastered on his birthday! What are you trying to do, talk all of us into sending our kids to Israel where they'll be blown up by suicide bombers?"

After that, she'd tune out his speeches completely. It was bad enough she had to show up at the synagogue every Saturday morning, baby or no baby, rain or shine. And it wasn't enough just to come, she had to show up in the best possible outfit, with a matching hat or wig that covered all or most of her hair.

Never in her wildest dreams had Delilah ever imagined she'd wind up covering her hair. The custom, as far as she knew, had started with the biblical phrase in Leviticus that described the *sotah* ordeal that a woman had to undergo if her husband suspected her of committing adultery but didn't have any actual proof. The poor floozy was taken to the temple where, the Bible says, "The priest shall present the woman . . . before God and uncover the head of the woman." How that had morphed into every married woman being obliged to shave her head—or wear a wig, or tuck every last strand of her hair inside some dorky-looking snood—was beyond her. But there it was. Her own theory, adopted from a talkative and rebellious classmate who had wound up marrying a Gentile, was historical: Given the fact that only prostitutes had not worn a hat in the Middle Ages, medieval rabbis had found some way to update biblical Judaism to be in tune with the times. Unfortunately, Orthodoxy's innovations sort of froze in the fourteen hundreds. So when women all over the world stopped covering their hair, Orthodox rabbis forgot to update. Now, women were stuck with two impossible-to-explain ideas: that a wig was more modest than your own hair and that being the only woman in the entire city to wear a hat—thus calling undue attention to yourself wherever you went—was a source of modesty.

As a girl, she'd only seen the most pious rabbis' wives and her Torah teachers wear wigs. Other religious women teachers had worn hats, although with visible reluctance, and the hats kept getting smaller and smaller as time went by.

Strangely, although her mother's generation and even her grandmother's had neatly done away with the hair-covering custom altogether, it was her generation that had set themselves the reactionary goal of bringing it back, something like Iranian girls making a revolution to put themselves into veils and under the thumb of the mullahs and imams.

How many discussions had she had with her Bernstein Seminary classmates on whether or not they would cover their hair when they got married? How many hours had been wasted describing the merits, exploring the major moral significance, and plumbing the religious joy of buying either a hat to match every outfit or a fantastically expensive custom-made wig usually reserved for chemo patients who had lost all their hair? Whatever the conclusion they came to, most agreed that—outdated custom or no—it was a religious obligation you simply couldn't wiggle out of. Some girls even claimed it had nothing to do with modesty; that it was one of those unfathomable Divine decrees, like the red heifer, whose sprinkled ashes somehow had the mystical power to cleanse the nation of sins and impurities.

But as far as Delilah could see, forcing women to cover their hair was no red heifer; it was simply a gimmick—one of many—that rabbis had dreamed up just to make married women uglier than unmarried women, so that men could easily tell them apart, ostensibly for the purpose of encouraging them to keep their hands off the married ones.

Wig wearing wasn't helpful in the least to this endeavor, which is why the stringency kings wanted to outlaw wigs. For many years they had waged a guerrilla war against the wig stores and *shaitel* makers, coming up with ever more imaginative ways of doing battle. Their ultimate coup was achieved by spreading the rumor that wigs contained hair donated by women as part of the idolatrous worship of Hindu deities. The resulting wig burnings that took place all over the religious world—reducing many a panicked matron to ugly head scarves and wig store owners to bankruptcy—filled them with rapturous satisfaction. But the rumor was eventually quashed, and the sale of wigs shot back up to normal. This time, though, wigs had to carry a rabbinical stamp of approval ascertaining no Hindu deities had been deprived of their due.

Many of Delilah's friends viewed the prewedding wig-and-hat-buying spree as just one more lovely, religiously sanctioned prenuptial extravagance. They would no more have dreamed of forgoing it than they would have given up the sterling silver candelabra they had coming to them from their mothers-in-law.

But as married life rolled on and all that wig wearing gave them headaches, ruining their natural hair; and the effort to find a hat that would match every single outfit began to drain their ingenuity—not to mention their cash—they began to realize what a fine mess they'd gotten themselves into. By then, of course, it was much too late. If a bride never covered her hair, that was one thing. But if she covered it and then decided as a married woman to uncover it, that was a major religious statement that needed to be accounted for among friends, family, and community, a monumental showdown that most religious women didn't have the stomach for, even when their husbands backed them up.

Not that many husbands did. Given that their own religious status would be vulnerable to a staggering blow should their wives suddenly feel the joy of having the wind blow through their hair, such a man was rare. Except for the singular man of moral courage who sympathized with his wife's frustration or had the intellectual honesty to admit the silliness of the prohibition, most men were perfectly thrilled to maintain religiously sanctioned control over their wives' femininity.

Delilah had also bought into the hats and the wigs but had become disillusioned rather sooner than most. She immediately discarded her head covering while in the privacy of her home, ignoring the example quoted in the Talmud of the sanctimonious and insufferable matron who declared the secret to her success in mothering some outrageous number of priests in the Holy Temple had been entirely due to the fact that "the walls of her house had never seen a strand of her hair." But that was just an opinion, not Jewish law. All rabbis agreed that you only had to cover your hair outside the house. If any man came over, she threw on a scarf, of course.

However much she longed to go back to wearing her hair the way she had as a single girl, she was painfully reconciled to the fact that it would be tricky if not impossible now that she was the wife of a congregational rabbi and all eyes were upon her, grading her saintliness. How could people rely on a rabbi who couldn't maintain strict adherence to Jewish law even in his own home?

While she chafed under the prohibition, she made do by constantly wearing an exquisite blond wig, custom-made at enormous expense to fit her perfectly. She looked so stunning in it, she left Chaim alone. Unfortunately, constant wear and many washings and blow dryings had taken their toll; the wig, alas, had lost its appeal. In fact, it was actually beginning to look like a wig, which is the last thing any religious woman wants. Equally unfortunately, the thousands of dollars necessary to replace it were simply not available. What she was left with was buying the kind of out-of-the-box human hair/polyester weave worn by Hasidic women, Halloween revelers, and call girls, styling and length being the key differences.

She tried turbans. She tried snoods. She tried berets. She tried baseball caps worn frontward and backward. While all these things were workable, if not beautiful, adequate to run errands and wash the floors, they simply would not do when she made her slow triumphant walk down the center aisle to the front of the women's section to the seat marked with a brass plaque: RESERVED FOR THE RABBI'S WIFE.

Hats, at least the kind worn by the women in her congregation, cost a fortune. And clothes like theirs an even bigger fortune. But what could she do? Living among the very wealthy, being invited to another Bar and Bat Mitzva or wedding almost every month, she needed something respectable and festive to wear. And since everyone she knew in the community came to these affairs, she couldn't very well wear the same outfit each time, now, could she? Besides, it would wear out eventually, unless it was made of iron. Couple that with the constant gifts that she and Chaim had to come up with, the extra quantity and quality of food she had to buy for the unending stream of guests, the high heat and electric bills for the large house, not to mention the babysitters needed when she had to accompany her husband to unveilings, evening events, shiva calls, and many other duties that necessitated leaving little Abraham behind, and they were effectively broke most of the time.

She considered going back to work, but when you took child care into account it wouldn't have left her that much. And somehow the business of being the rabbi's wife, while unpaid, was slowly encroaching on more and more of her time.

She once sat down and calculated where her week went. The weekends of course were shot. Not just Saturday, but all day Friday and much of Wednesday and Thursday had to be spent shopping for food and cleaning up the house and cooking for a steady stream of weekend guests who came expecting to be served three opulent sit-down dinners, beginning Friday night and ending late Saturday night when they all cleared out.

And even shopping for food was not a simple thing if you were a rabbi's wife. There was that time, after a sleepless night with a colicky baby, she'd rolled out of bed and shlepped to the supermarket, only to be hailed from across the aisles by a "Yoo-hoo! Hello, Rebbitzin! My goodness, you look awful! Have you been showering?" Or the time she was accosted in the frozen food section by a woman who stared into her shopping cart, examining each item's *hechsher* to see if it was kosher enough. "I'm surprised you are buying things marked with a star-K instead of an OU, not to mention the half circle-K." She sniffed, scandalized. "My husband says the rabbis supervising aren't reliable. He won't touch a crumb, not a crumb, if it's not stamped with an OU. Do your guests know what they're eating?" Or the time she was a second away from her turn on the checkout line when a shul member grabbed her by the shoulders and insisted on regaling her with an half-hour's worth of disgustingly graphic medical details, hinting broadly that she needed someone to drive her to her appointments and hold her hand during treatments. Or the stranger in a polyester jogging suit wearing a large cross, who—seeing her head covering—barred her from picking up nail polish remover, insisting on knowing if she was Jewish and, if so, why she didn't believe in Jesus.

Sundays were spent going to unveilings or funerals or condolence calls. Mondays were when the week began again with obligations and other synagogue-related work that she had never had to worry about in the Bronx among the aged.

For example, women started showing up at her doorstep, demanding her attention and wordlessly handing her white unmarked envelopes. The first time it happened, Delilah opened the envelope, thinking it might be a donation to the synagogue, but all she found was a bit of stained white cloth. Slowly, it dawned on her where this material had been and where the stain had come from.

She confronted Chaim, fuming. "Read my lips. No-way-José am I going to examine some woman's vaginal fluids and tell her if she can or can't have sex with her husband. I am not touching these disgusting things. Tell them to leave me alone!"

"Listen, Delilah," Chaim had answerered reasonably, "most rabbis' wives are happy to do it. It's a woman's thing. And women feel more comfortable talking to another woman. But if you can't, you can't. Just give them to me."

She was only too happy to do so. But she was still stuck with being the go-between, giving them back to the women, telling them the results, and explaining the consequences. In the worst case, it could mean another two weeks of sexual abstinence and dealing with a frustrated husband—girl, you don't want to know . . . While Delilah sympathized, no way was she interested in becoming privy to whether or not each one of them would or would not be having sex with their husbands, thus becoming a living repository of the entire community's sex life. Nor did she particularly want the entire community to keep tabs on hers.

This was not as easy as it sounds in a community with only one *mikva*. Although efforts were made to hide the entrance to the ritual bath from the street, still, once inside, everyone she met there knew exactly when she'd be having sex with her husband, the rabbi. In addition to that, they had the opportunity to inspect how short her nails were (the very pious cut them to the quick on *mikva* night, making long nails and manicures impossible) and how she looked without her hair and absolutely no makeup of any kind.

Moreover, the "*mikva* lady," that stalwart institution of religious life, chosen from the ranks of the needy and overly pious but not overly bright, made privy to information of the most personal nature, could not always be relied upon to be discreet. "Hello, Mrs. Goldberg, I haven't seen you in months," said at full volume in the supermarket, for example, announced a pregnancy to the community like an engraved invitation to participate in the most intimate details of someone's private life.

Then, of course, there was the monthly sisterhood meeting. During the intensive Metzenbaum era, it had been moved from the synagogue to the rabbi's house, because Shira Metzenbaum didn't have enough to do, and now no one saw fit to move it back. And it was not just a meeting, she was led to understand; it was an event.

The food that she had to prepare had to be as imaginative as the way she served it. Each meeting had to have a "theme," to help keep the women interested in coming back, she was advised. Last month it had been a Ladies Who Lunch theme, with flower-filled shopping bags from Nordstrom's and Lord & Taylor, and wigs and hats on Styrofoam heads, elaborately decorated to look like some of the synagogue members. She'd prepared white carrot and sweet potato soup, persimmon tuna salad, and little chocolates she had to make in special plastic molds that turned out dreidels and menorahs and other symbols of the season. Often, Delilah cursed her hyper Martha-Stewart-in-a-wig-on-uppers predecessor, feeling *schadenfreude* for the woman's present life in Canarsie.

It wasn't just the preparations that were driving her crazy. During one sisterhood meeting, she'd found two women in her bathroom discussing the hair dye and prescription medication they'd found in her medicine cabinet. At another, a woman she hardly knew told her that her baby was looking "much better" than when he was born, when he'd been "like the puppy in the litter you throw away." After another, she'd found a silver cake server missing, and then a whole Wedgwood plate. And then there was the woman who had asked all kinds of personal questions about Chaim, finally admitting that her first rabbi had been touchy-feely Moishe from New Jersey, who had had his wife killed by a hit man, and her second, a rabbi in Florida, who had been arrested as a pedophile, so she was just trying to make sure it wasn't her fault the third time around.

And in between, day and night, there were the phone calls—*brring, brrring, brrrring!*—day in and day out. The woman who called them at 1 A.M. to complain that her little Lenny had been traumatized by getting a doughnut with pink icing at the *Oneg Shabbat* party. The man who was incensed that the Lion of Judah giving category in the latest United Jewish fund-raising campaign was between twenty and forty thousand dollars, leaving "those who are just as pious but not as rich" out in the embarrassing cold. Could the rabbi deal with that? Can you give the rabbi a message? Can you remind him? Can you talk to him about it? Could you possibly mention that in his last sermon he spoke too long, too short, about a topic we don't care about, do care about, but not to that extent, in that way? Can he talk about twelve-year-old girls getting nose jobs in time for their Bat Mitzvas? Can he talk less about Israel; more about Israel? Can he stop supporting the right-wing fanatics, who won't compromise, and who will get the Jewish people wiped off the planet? Can he stop supporting left-wing fanatics, Israeli peace nuts, who are giving in to our enemies and are going to get us wiped off the planet? Can he stop putting so much pressure on our young people, who are going to wind up with black hats and beards, unemployed and with ten kids? Can he put more pressure on our young people, who are going to be drug addicts and get lost in rave parties in India?

Blah, blah, blah, like she actually had nothing better to do than to consult with Chaim on his boring sermons.

And then there were the phone calls that were actually for her. A cousin of a synagogue member, a very nice thirty-two-year-old girl with a good job as an editor at a big New York publishing firm, was looking for a very attractive lawyer or doctor who was also Orthodox but open-minded. Would she know of somebody suitable? Could she set it up?

Gee, honey, if I knew anybody suitable who matched that description, why would I give him to you? I'd take him myself, she thought. "Not right now, but let me write down the information," she'd answer sweetly, making no effort to get a pencil. Why bother? Go find a modern Orthodox man in his thirties who wasn't holding out for a girl who would think as highly of him as his mother, looked like Kate Winslet, was as saintly as the matriarch Sarah, and had the domestic skills of Martha Stewart. Listen, she wanted to shout at these men, the girls are all five-foot-two dark-haired teachers or social workers who will never cook you a kreplach or kiss your feet the way your mother did. Get over it!

And then there were the men who couldn't wait to get married, who would marry anyone: the divorced men. The stingy, over- or undersexed grouches with bad tempers, body odors, and hanging bellies full of brisket and donuts who had already made one woman miserable but were anxious to make it two. They too were on the phone, seeking her help.

Even the mothers and fathers of college students, who should, for Pete's sake, have been able to fend for themselves, were calling her, demanding she find suitable matches for their offspring so they wouldn't bring home a *sheygets* or a shiksa from their ivy-covered campuses, along with their 3.9 grade-point averages and wildly expensive degrees. Some of these callers were super-religious, people who insisted on knowing the color of the girl's mother's Sabbath tablecloth. Was it white—acceptable, conservative—or any other color? And did the family have two or three sit-down meals on the Sabbath? (The third meal—which no one could possibly fit into an average stomach—being considered a sign of extra piety.) And was the boy actually going to use his law, accounting, or computer degree or put it aside and let his wife support him forever while he twiddled his thumbs and spoke on his cell phone from Talmudic study halls?

And then there were those people who saw her as the representative of the entire Jewish religion, people who would read the newspaper and then call her up to ask indignantly how a rabbi could run off with a former Russian Orthodox nun who had once been a flamenco dancer, shack up with her in a Miami condo, and leave his wife and congregation behind? "He said it was because his wife sometimes ate shrimp, but I'm not buying it!" they'd shout.

And all this, mind you, she was supposed to deal with on top of her newborn.

The baby. Little Abe.

That was a whole other story in itself. She looked down at the infant in her arms, sucking away like a leech. It had taken Delilah only several weeks to realize that, among her many interests and talents, mothering was not among them. She was as surprised to learn this as the next one.

Like most of us, she had always assumed that the ability to mother was a raw, animal instinct, hormonally supplied by the same chemicals and brain synapses that came along with the birth of a child. The truth was that the insistent, desperate cry of a newborn, added to the insistent, desperate cries of members of her congregation, was just about driving her over the edge.

"He hates me!" she yelled at Chaim, bursting into his study when he was putting the final touches on his weekly sermon on how husbands should be compassionate and unselfishness and helpful. "Just look at his eyes. Look!"

"Delilah, I can't concentrate with all that crying. Could you possibly take him outside for a while?" he'd say, not looking up until she shoved the baby into his arms and disappeared.

After these outbursts, she'd be overcome with guilt. She'd sit in her bedroom, listening to her albums and weeping until she had no more tears left. Then she'd go into the bathroom, wipe her eyes, and examine the sad state of her skin and the tire around her middle that simply refused to vanish. She'd return to Chaim, retrieve her son, and cuddle him tenderly in her arms, crooning lullabies and whispering to him.

She would never, ever, she told herself, do anything that would remotely harm the baby. Why, just the idea that a single hair on his little head might be pulled filled her with horror and pity. In fact, every time the child went to sleep, she remembered that she was deeply in love with him. She'd sit for hours, examining him, every minute detail. But she had to admit, he disappointed her. He had his grandfather's little eyes, which seemed to stare at her accusingly, her mother's big nose, her mother-in-law's thin dissatisfied lips, and her husband's dark hair. She would have preferred a girl with a beautiful little face, big blue eyes, and darling blond curls. A little doll she could buy adorable baby J-Lo dresses for with matching hair bows.

But she took some pride in having created a son. Little Abraham was a credit to her. She had produced him, after all, when she could just as easily have produced a girl as first-born. Orthodox Jews, no matter their well-concealed disappointment and shocked denials, were no different than the members of most other religions and cultures on this point. Let's face it, girls are not considered much to celebrate. There's no ceremony. No gathering of rabbis and friends to welcome her into the tribe. And even though politically correct modern Orthodoxy has been embarrassed into sanctioning the *mesibat bat*, or girl party, and the Bat Mitzva, everyone is in on the fact that it is just a pale-flaccid little consolation prize.

He was her pride and joy, she reminded herself. If only he wasn't so much work. If only she had more time. . . .

"Normal people look forward to weekends! What do I get on weekends? I get to be inspected, to serve armies of house guests, to visit cemeteries. I'm a prisoner here. Getting away for the weekend, or for holidays, is always impossible!"

Chaim, used to Delilah's tantrums, had learned to tune them out.

However, later that evening, after she'd said goodbye to the last of the sisterhood members and loaded the dishwasher and vacuumed the carpet, she leaned against the doorpost of his office and said, very calmly, "Did you know that Andrea Yates was class valedictorian? Captain of the swim team? In the National Honor Society? A nurse in the cancer ward?"

He'd stared at her in horror. Then he picked up the phone and made immediate arrangements for a private meeting with Arthur Malin.

Soon after, the synagogue board voted to provide the rabbi and his wife with some weekly hours of child care and housekeeping and to give Delilah a free yearly membership in the Swallow Lake Country Club.

As with many kind gestures, this move also proved the wisdom of the saying that no good deed ever goes unpunished.

{ TWENTY }

*D*elilah Levi walked through the doors of the Swallow Lake Country Club with the exact opposite feeling with which she walked through the doors of Ohel Aaron: the delicious sensation of being invisible, instead of a walking poster for Virtue of the Week. With her brand-new skin-hugging Lycra shorts and tank top, her brand-new New Balance cross trainers, and a headband that made her look like a Jane Fonda video backup girl, she joined the aerobics classes, letting herself go, shimmying and grapevining across the floor as she admired herself in the mirror-lined room. She loved the way she looked, her blond hair loose or up in a ponytail, her figure rapidly going back to its prepregnancy youthfulness, the stomach and waist melting away. There, among other women her age who didn't know who she was, she felt released from the burdens of her fishbowl existence.

It was a great revelation to learn that she was as lonely in the Swallow Lake congregation as she had been in the Bronx. Here too, the movers and shakers on the board were grandmothers. As for befriending the younger women, it was complicated. She wasn't their equal. She was supposed to be their superior, or at least to maintain that myth. A synagogue hired a rabbinical family to put on a pedestal, to be looked up to and imitated. To breach the distance, to become chummy, exposing the reality behind the perfect picture, could jeopardize that illusion and, she worried, her family's position in the community.

While she couldn't avoid every single woman in her congregation, she quickly learned to steer clear of the country club in the very early hours when Mariette came in; and the one afternoon a week Solange used it. Felice, who had a private trainer and a home gym, never showed up, nor did Amber, who wasn't into exercise.

Relaxed and temporarily unburdened of the plethora of rabbinical prohibitions concerning her body, dress, voice, and flesh, which only had force when men were around to stare and listen, she left her anxieties behind in the bubbles of the Jacuzzi and the pool of sweat in the sauna. Soon she was striking up conversations with strangers her age, gossiping about clothes and movie stars and men, sending caution to the wind in her hunger for companionship, telling herself it was good enough if they didn't look too familiar.

One woman in particular caught her attention. She was about the same height and body build as herself, a sexy blonde she had never seen before. Her hair had been colored by a genius; it was the most delicate shade of ash blond with marvelous natural highlights. Her body was tight, like a dancer's, and as voluptuous as Pamela Anderson's. There had no doubt been a boob job. Nobody with the possible exception of Barbie had boobs that big and hips that slim. And the nose? That too had been surgically snipped to shiksa perfection. And boy, was this woman in shape! When the rest of the class was groaning from the stomach crunches, she was still crunching away even more effortlessly than the instructor. Delilah often followed her around the gym like a groupie. One day, she managed to meet her at the lockers.

"You are in such wonderful condition. What's your secret?"

The woman threw her exercise bag over her shoulder, turned, and looked at Delilah curiously, her eyes flicking up and down, leaving no part unregistered. "You are?"

Delilah wiped her sweaty hand on her tank top and held it out. "Delilah. Delilah Levi."

The woman smiled and shrugged, declining to take it. "I've got a thing about germs. Nothing personal. Joie Shammanov."

A bell, low and resonant, clanged in Delilah's head.

Shammanov.

For months she had been hearing about the fabulously wealthy Russian businessman who had bought the biggest estate in Swallow Lake and had been building on it ever since. Shammanov, it was said, would be in court for a hundred years battling the county's municipal authorities for having broken every single zoning law to build what was rumored to be Xanadu on uppers. But no one knew for sure because, to the chagrin of Swallow Lake's leading citizens, who were dying of curiosity, no one had been invited to the house, despite numerous overtures. The Shammanovs were Jewish but had no intention of becoming part of the community, spokespeople who answered the phone said firmly.

Like his estate, Shammanov himself was also shrouded in mystery. Although he had been featured on the cover of *Fortune* magazine, the article had revealed very little, calling him secretive, a shunner of limelight. According to *Fortune*, his wealth had come from his near monopoly on shares of the privatized oil fields in his native Turdistan, following the fall of the Soviet Union. He was said to own banks, real estate, airlines, hotel chains, and innumerable corporations. His wealth, Amber had whispered, was equal to the gross national product of certain small countries.

Delilah whistled in nervousness. "Wow, interesting name!"

"So is yours."

"Please, let's not get into it. It's been a pain my whole life. It was my grandmother's name and my father insisted—"

"Parents." Joie pursed her lips in disgust. "I really sympathize. I've got the same kind. Never happy unless they are making you miserable."

Delilah, who wasn't prepared to go that far, decided nevertheless not to blow this bonding opportunity. "I guess we just have to live our lives and put up with them," she agreed. "Love what you've done with your abs. You've got such . . . definition."

"Really?" Joie looked at her arms, pleased. "You think? You also look great. I envy those stomach muscles."

Coming from the crunch queen, that was high praise indeed. "Oh, thanks!" Delilah gushed, thrilled. "I just had a baby, and I'm dying to get rid of these extra pounds. They are so stuck on."

Joie stared at her. "Oh, I also just had a baby! I thought I'd never lose them."

"You look fantastic!"

"Thanks. I have to get ready for my son's Bar Mitzvah."

"You have a son who's thirteen years old? You look like twenty yourself." Delilah said, truly amazed and not a little envious.

The woman turned to her, put down her bag, and smiled. "Oh, he's not mine. He's my husband's, from his first marriage. You are so nice! Not like most of the snobs I've met here. They are so full of themselves. And most of them go to that synagogue with the men on one side and the women on the other. I never saw such a thing."

Delilah shifted uncomfortably. "Actually, it's not so bad."

The woman's face dropped. "Oh. Do you go there too?"

Delilah nodded. "I'm the rabbi's wife."

Joie slapped her forehead. "Oh, so sorry! I'm just such a blabbermouth. My husband always tells me. He's Russian and very outgoing, and I'm always saying the wrong thing, screwing up his multibillion-dollar deals left and right." She held out her hand. "Please, forgive me?"

Delilah took it gratefully. "There's nothing to forgive. Believe me, I know it seems weird to outsiders: the separate seating, the hair covering, the no phones, no cars, no cooking on the Sabbath."

"It's not weird, it's just that I'm so ignorant and prejudiced. I think you have to grow up in a family that has respect for religion, for traditions. And I didn't. My parents weren't at all respectful. And I think I lost out a lot because of it."

"Well, it's never too late to learn." Delilah couldn't believe she heard herself say this, in perfect imitation of a rebbitzin on the make for lost souls. "Oh, no, forget I said that!"

"Why?"

"Because this is the one place on the planet where I don't have to do this."

"Do what?"

"Convert people to the true faith. I can just forget I'm hemmed in by all these weirdo rules, by all these rabbis, and just wiggle and crunch and grapevine and boogie. I know I could put on a tape and do it in my bedroom, but I find if I have people to compete with, it keeps me going. It gets so lonely, you know, with a new baby, and my husband is never around."

The woman's face softened. "I know exactly what you mean." She hesitated. "Look, I was just heading home. If you've got a few minutes, why don't you come over to the house for a cup of coffee? I've also got this home movie theater, and we just got a preview copy of this year's Oscar nominees. . . ."

The idea of making a friend of the elusive Joie Shammanov, who incidentally had a home movie theater and movies not yet available even in DVD and whose husband was making multibillion-dollar deals, intrigued Delilah. Besides, she was always happy to inspect and then eat her heart out over the glories of yet one more Swallow Lake estate.

A blue Bentley was waiting at the entrance for Joie Shammanov. A chauffeur got out and opened the door for her. Delilah followed behind in her beat-up Ford.

When Delilah Levi drove past the polished bronze gates, under beautiful scrollwork that spelled out USPEKHOV, she began to feel a little like Dorothy at the end of the yellow brick road. Rising to her right on a low hill stood a breathtaking Romanesque-style castle straight out of Fantasyland in Orlando, Florida. To her surprise, the Bentley drove right past it, turning off and continuing down the road toward the lake.

She couldn't believe her eyes when the car pulled up to a huge lakefront mansion.

"Joie, what does *Uspekhov* mean?"

"It means success." She smiled.

They'd built a brand-new second house on the property. Talk about excess. It was mind-boggling. But she reminded herself not to go around saying *omigod* and to make believe she saw this kind of thing all the time, so as not to put off her new friend with any hick behavior.

She needn't have worried. As it turned out, Joie was only too happy to discuss her wealth. Over lattes served on a deck overlooking the lake and an infinity pool, Delilah learned that the Shammanovs' purchase of forty acres of lakefront property had included a 7,500-square-foot French château that neither of them really liked. But instead of tearing it down and rebuilding, they'd decided to simply put up a second house, nearer the lake. They had been building for over a year, but the place still wasn't quite finished, although Joie was happy to report that the 45,000-square-foot home was already estimated to be worth well over $90 million. They had a screening room, a Japanese garden with 500 rare species of trees flown in from Japan, office facilities, a gym, and a library. The living room alone was over 3,000 square feet, with an adjoining reception hall large enough to seat 150 people for dinner or hold 200 people for a cocktail party. There was a 70-foot pool with an underwater sound system, as well as a trampoline room, an Art Deco theater, and goodness knows what else. Joie said even she didn't really know.

"This is my husband's thing. He loves to build. He's never going to finish this house. Every time I think we're almost done, he finds something he doesn't like, or he gets a better idea and tears everything out and starts over. We ordered Brazilian rosewood for the library? After it was all built, he decides it's too dark, so he throws the whole thing out and orders a different wood. And the tiles in the kitchen, handmade in Mexico? He saw something similar somewhere, which made him mad, so he had them all taken out and ordered tiles from this tiny factory in Portugal." She laughed, her eyes grim. "So many of them broke on the way over, he had to order them fifteen times before he had enough."

After coffee and a few delectable scones, Delilah said delicately, "Love to see this place sometime."

"Would you? Oh, sure. If you've got time, come now."

Oh, the marble floors! she thought in rapture. What had they done to get rid of those pesky grouted lines? How did they get it to shine seamlessly, like glass? And how did they get those designs, the red and cream and white marble laid out in an intricate pattern like some handwoven rug? And how did they get the walls to look like some Chinese lacquer box? And where did they find those chandeliers, and that furniture, all oversized like a scene out of some forties Hollywood movie? It was extremely costly and yet, overwhelmed as she was, even Delilah recognized everything was a just a tiny bit off. A little too much, a little bit old-fashioned. A little bit Arab or Eastern European in its decadence, where huge sums had been poured into projects that, instead of showing off the owners' impeccable good taste, did quite the opposite. It was like those sultans known as boobs of the rain forest, who give solid gold watches custom-made to hold tacky nude photos and then throw in CDs, some cheesecake, shortbread cookies, and a candle. The Queer Eyed folk would have wrung their hands.

Nevertheless, the sheer enormity of the place, and its mind-boggling expense, rolled over Delilah like a large vehicle going full speed. It was simply on a scale too grand to envy, the way no one actually envies Queen Elizabeth her Buckingham Palace. It wasn't a place anyone could actually aspire to own or even if they did, would really want to live in, the way no one would actually want to live in Grand Central Station, even if it could be remodeled as a private residence. Unlike the homes of the Malins, the Grodins, the Rollands, and the Borenbergs, fabulous estates that one nevertheless felt were possible to get your greedy little hands around—given the right luck—this house was quite a different story. It was a place only a person with unheard-of appetites and a truly fabulous imagination, matched by an equally bottomless pot of money, could have envisioned, let alone build.

"It's like the castle in that old black-and-white movie," Joie said.

Delilah looked at her blankly.

"*Citizen Kane.*"

"Oh, of course." She smiled. Who in heaven's name watched black-and-white movies? She resolved to take it out of the video library next chance she got. Hopefully, Ted Turner had gotten around to colorizing it.

"Want to see the baby?" her hostess said suddenly, apparently bored with the tour.

Delilah, who would have much preferred to continue opening doors and prowling hallways, nodded. They took an elevator lined in mirrors and marble up a few flights.

The nursery was done up exquisitely in pastel nursery-rhyme themes. An enormous pink dollhouse you could actually walk into was filled with stuffed animals and lovely dolls. There were rocking chairs and window seats and soft carpeting that matched the walls and curtains. In the center of this fairyland sat an old woman with enormous breasts holding an infant swathed in clothing more suitable for a little Eskimo in an igloo than for a child in a heated nursery. The baby was cute: blond, with large blue eyes. She was about six months old. She looked up at her mother in wonder.

"Here she is, my little Natasha," Joie said, smiling at the baby, her arms outstretched. The woman, unsmiling, grasped the child closer.

"Let me have her, Yelena," Joie demanded.

There was a volcanic storm of Russian, whirling up a notch in belligerence with each passing moment. The old woman shook her head and then her fist, shooing them both away.

Joie turned on her heel and walked out, slamming the door behind her.

"Gee, you're a saint! If *my* babysitter pulled that, I'd fire her on the spot."

Joie looked up. "That," she said slowly, "is my mother-in-law."

"Oops. Sorry."

"Don't be. I wish I could fire her. She makes my life a living hell."

"You know, Joie," Delilah said thoughtfully, "the Jewish religion is very clear about a man leaving his father and mother and clinging to his wife. There is actually a phrase in the Bible that says exactly that. And our rabbis teach us that a man mustn't let his mother get between him and his wife. His wife comes first."

Joie looked at her, transfixed. "A verse? In the Bible? Really?"

Delilah nodded. "I could show it to you."

"That would be fantastic. Viktor had a very religious Jewish grandfather. He was a rabbi, Viktor says. Viktor has a lot of respect for religion—but you know, brought up in the Soviet Union, he had no one to teach him. His father was an atheist. But Viktor loved the old man, who died when he was just a little kid. He talks about him all the time."

"You know, my husband would be really happy to learn with your husband."

"Learn?"

"Oh, that's just the way we Orthodox Jews put it, when we talk about religious instruction. It's considered a joint effort. Teacher and student learn together."

"Really? You think your husband would be willing to teach Viktor that verse in the Bible, about the clinging and about the mothers-in-law?"

"Joie, I don't think it, I know it. My husband has a heart of gold. He's always telling me we should be encouraging more people to join our synagogue."

"Well, if your husband can get my husband to part with his mother, I would be grateful to you for the rest of my life."

That was the moment when Delilah Levi and Joie Shammanov became instant best friends.

A week later, Chaim began learning with Viktor Shammanov. And two weeks after that, the elderly Mrs. Shammanov found herself with a one-way ticket on a plane to Miami.

{ TWENTY-ONE }

Great unhappiness can only come about when one has known great happiness. This is the irony that people refuse to understand when the wheel of Fate turns and gives them their heart's desire. The cocktail waitress who bets a few dollars in Vegas and winds up with the jackpot. The nebbish who asks the girl of his dreams to marry him and gets a yes. The plain girl with the glasses who lands the captain of the basketball team (a common occurence, by the way; just look around you). All these people, God bless them, are primed for the worst of disasters, while the rest of us—who shlep along with average luck and average successes and failures—are immune.

That is not to say one should not rejoice in one's good fortune. As Henry James taught us in the most frightening of horror stories ever written, "The Beast in the Jungle," the anticipation of disaster can, in itself, become the disaster. To paraphrase King Solomon in Ecclesiastes, rejoice in your good times, because time and chance happen to all.

This was Delilah's good time, the best time in her life. There were picnics and pool parties at the Shammanovs. There were shopping trips to New York and stays in private hotel suites. There were manicures and pedicures and private masseuses who came to the Swallow Lake mansion and were just as happy to do two women as one. There were daily outings and private confessions. The good times were limited only by Delilah's child-care arrangements; Joie had no such restrictions. Once she packed her mother-in-law off to Florida, she hired a daytime au pair and a nighttime au pair and even an au pair for her dog. "He is very jealous of the baby as it is. We don't want to make it worse."

Far from judging her friend or even envying her, Delilah rejoiced in her good fortune. While she knew that the average person would have been appalled at the meager amount of time Joie spent with her daughter, Delilah tended to agree with Joie that the time she did spend with Natasha—usually when the child was fresh from being bathed and diapered and fed—was "quality" time.

Delilah wondered what it would be like to foist her son off on somebody else whenever he was dirty and hungry and cranky, and to get him back clean, fed, and smiling. Why, they would only see each other at their best! And while she knew there were those who would condemn her for being a bad mother, she wondered if in the best of all possible worlds all children wouldn't be better off bonding with their parents under such ideal circumstances. Imagine a world full of adults who had only known smiling, relaxed mothers! Why, they could close down the UN—that humongous waste of time and money whose only useful function, as far as she could tell, was to provide freedom from parking tickets and assorted felonies to Third World bureaucrats. And they could forget about nuclear nonproliferation treaties, because why would calm, smiling, satisfied adults want to build bombs to murder other calm, smiling, satisfied adults and their perfect offspring?

Every woman, Delilah, thought, should have a Joie Shammanov. She never ceased to rejoice over this unexpected relationship. She had a best friend. A shopping partner. Someone who made her feel smart and good and didn't judge her.

Joie, for her part, seemed very happy to have Delilah's constant companionship. Her marriage to a Russian Jew and her relocation to the very Jewish Swallow Lake had left her like a fish out of water.

Because the fact was that Joie Shammanov, until very very recently, wasn't Jewish.

Born Jill O'Donnell in Lodi, New Jersey, to a housewife and a construction worker with a bit of a drinking problem, she ran away from home when she reached sixteen. It wasn't a horror story. She wasn't abused; she didn't have a drug problem or an unwanted pregnancy; she was simply bored. The life of a New Jersey teenager—stupid parties, backseat romantics, cramming for exams, worry about SAT scores—just weren't enough for her.

She wound up working in a clothing store in Manhattan, living with the owner and two other girls whom he put up in his Manhattan apartment. He took turns with each of them, which was fine with Jill, because it was better than putting up with the owner all by herself and it was a very nice apartment after all.

When she was eighteen, she moved out and decided to try her hand at modeling. But she wasn't tall enough and, truth be told, wasn't pretty enough, given the raving beauties from all over the world who were her competition in New York City. Her nose was a bit thick and her eyes rather narrow. But she had a beautiful figure and stunning hair, so every once in a while the agency found her work as a hair or figure model, where they needed just parts of her instead of the whole thing.

It wasn't enough to live on, so she moonlighted in a bar in one of the downtown hotels. And it was there, one night, that she happened to serve a bunch of Russians. They were all overweight and absolutely interchangeable. But when the evening was over, one of them handed her a $500 tip and his card.

"Call me," he said.

She didn't, having no interest in expanding her already sizable knowledge of heavy drinkers. The next night, he showed up again, this time alone. He sat in a corner, nursing one drink until closing time. He then gave her a $1,000 tip and another card.

Still, she didn't do anything. He was too muscular, she thought. Too foreign. Too old. He came in every single night, and each night he upped his tip. After a week, when she still hadn't called, he disappeared.

She took the money and went on the mother of all spending sprees. She paid off her credit card debts. Then she bought a coat at Bendel's for $2,000. A pair of boots for $1,500. She had her hair and nails done and used some to have her teeth whitened.

By the end of the second week, she was broke again.

The following month, a car pulled up to the bar and a chauffeur came in with a box with her name on it. He left it with her boss, who called her into the back. It was Russian sable. Stunned, she slipped it on, sliding her hand down the heavenly softness, into the silk-lined pockets. Inside was a velvet box holding a diamond and emerald bracelet. There was also a note that said he would pick her up after work.

She didn't wait until after work. She grabbed her purse and walked out of the bar and never looked back. She went straight to her apartment and packed a suitcase with all her new things, then went straight to the Greyhound station, and bought a ticket on a bus to San Diego that was leaving in three hours.

After the first hour, she got hungry, so she bought herself a hamburger. As a blonde in a sable eating a hamburger at a Greyhound bus station, she attracted quite a bit of attention, which she rather enjoyed. She finished the food. She found a comfortable seat away from any weirdos and thought about San Diego: the beaches, Marine World, the year-round sunshine. And then she thought, I probably won't need a fur coat in San Diego. Which was just as well, because she'd probably need to sell it so she'd have money to rent an apartment. She didn't really have enough for more than a few days in a good hotel. And the more Jill O'Donnell thought about life on her own in San Diego, the more she thought about the man who had given her the coat and the bracelet and who seemed to have money coming out of his pores. She compared him in her imagination to other men, the kind she'd meet in San Diego; young, blond, and flat-stomached who spoke nonaccented English. They would all basically want the same thing from her, which she would or wouldn't want to give them to a lesser or greater degree. And none would be as generous.

She sat there, trying to remember what he looked like, trying to imagine what would happen when he came to pick her up and she wasn't there. First, she felt sad for him, imagining his disappointment. And then, suddenly, she felt frightened. She had, after all, walked off with tens of thousands of his dollars and had given him nothing in return. Then, suddenly, she looked up and saw them. The terminal was suddenly packed with them, like some scene from *Angels in America*, except instead of angels it was full of fat Russians who seemed to have appeared out of nowhere. Or maybe it was just her imagination. She began to sweat. She took off her coat and tucked her bracelet inside her sleeve. Then she picked up her suitcase and hailed a taxi back to the bar.

She stood outside, waiting for the car to show up. When it did, she got in.

{ TWENTY-TWO }

*D*elilah, the phone has been ringing off the hook. I have had at least twelve different people in the synagogue call me up, furious. You aren't returning phone calls! You aren't giving me their messages! You aren't taking their envelopes, or answering their questions, or discussing their matchmaking needs! They say you are rude. That you've stopped inviting people over, that you aren't going out into the community enough, making enough of an effort to attract new members to join the synagogue."

Delilah listened, her face impassive. When he was finished, she looked up calmly. "I'm really, really sorry to hear that, Chaim. I have some suggestions for them. Why don't you tell them all that they can just kiss my mezuzah!"

"Delilah!"

She leaned back indifferently, taking out a pack of cigarettes, lighting one up, and blowing large smoke rings toward the ceiling. She'd taken up smoking again. She was trying to imitate Joie, how she held a cigarette, the way she tilted her head back *just so,* exhaling with world-weary ennui.

Chaim's arms waved frantically, dispersing the smoke in all directions. "And what is this with the smoking already? If you don't care about yourself, think about me, about the baby, for goodness' sake. You're filling *our* lungs with tar and nicotine deposits too."

"So, I'll smoke outside."

"Please, Delilah. What's gotten into you? The shul has been so generous. They've paid for household help, a babysitter, and time off. Is this how you show your appreciation? Be fair!"

"Fair? You want *me* to be fair? Tell me this, Chaim, while we're talking about being fair. How fair is it that some women get husbands who buy them Harry Winston diamond bracelets and some get men who grit their teeth when they shell out fifty-nine ninety-nine for gold earrings at Macy's during the Presidents' Day sales? How fair is it that some wives have cooks and chauffeurs, and—oh, four or five maids, and some have to beg and be grateful for four hours of housecleaning a week, if that much? That some women get their hair colored in Frederic Fekkai, and some do it themselves over the bathroom sink?"

She threw back her head, took another deep puff, and exhaled, studying Chaim through the haze of smoke, watching as his body and face faded, becoming blurry and indistinct, like some screen saver disappearing from a computer screen. Who was this guy, she thought, surprised, this person she was tied to for the rest of her life, who didn't provide her with a single thing she really wanted?

"Delilah, what's gotten into you?" Chaim shouted, astonished.

She didn't want to be a rabbi's wife, she suddenly realized. She wanted to be the wife of a rich man who would spoil her, the way all the women in her congregation were spoiled. The way Joie Shammanov was spoiled. Why did she have to be the good one, the moral one, the kind one, the generous one, the hard worker, the woman of virtue? Had she ever pretended to have *any* of these qualities, ever valued them, or aspired toward them, like the goody-goodies in Cedar Heights, the ones with the calf-length skirts who stayed after school for extra brainwashing in *mussar* and how to improve your judgmental skills and guilt quotient? No, it was all just a big accident, a big celestial joke—and it was on her, she realized.

"They are complaining that you are spending all your time with Mrs. Shammanov—who isn't even a member of our congregation—doing who knows what: neglecting the congregation, not to mention your family. That you are acting like some airhead high school girl. It's got to stop!"

Finally, miraculously, she was having a little fun, enjoying the pleasures she would only get to have in this life vicariously if at all, and there was a conspiracy afoot to deprive her even of that! She stubbed out the cigarette viciously into the carpet. "Look, get this through your skullcap. Joie Shammanov is the best thing that has ever happened to me. Why should I give her up—give any of it up? So that you can keep on playing social worker, psychiatrist, and Catskills entertainer to a bunch of self-indulgent whining *machers* and their wives who treat us both like low-level employees? They may own you, but they don't own me."

Just then, the phone rang. Chaim picked it up.

"Hello, Solange, how are you? . . . Good, good. Yes, well *now* is really *not* a good . . . Of course, of course. I understand. She's right here. I'll put her on." Apprehensively, he handed Delilah the phone. *Please,* his eyes implored.

"Solange, Delilah here. . . . Well, let me just interrupt you, Solange, to tell you what *I* was thinking. I was thinking that the sisterhood meeting should really go back to being at the synagogue where it belongs. . . . Oh, you like it better in someone's house? Well, then, Solange, maybe you can have it at yours. And while you're at it, you can get your chef and five slaves to decide the menu and the theme, and cook it and serve it and clean up afterward. And then the sisterhood can check out *your* hair dye and steal *your* plates!" She slammed down the phone.

Chaim went white.

They didn't speak for three days. And then Chaim came home early. He brought a bottle of wine, some flowers, lit some candles, brought in take-out someone had picked up for him especially from the Broadway Deli in Manhattan: Delilah's favorite restaurant, he remembered. He arranged for a babysitter. "Come, let's have a quiet dinner and talk, Delilah," he coaxed her.

He sat down across from her. They ate in silence. "Delilah, I've straightened it out. I called Arthur Malin. He is such a mensch. And he knows Solange can be a bit of a character—"

"She's a *klafta.*"

He took a deep breath. "Now, now, don't be unkind, dear."

Chaim groveled. He apologized. He explained. He was as nice and understanding as he could possibly be. He even apologized for not having thought himself of moving the sisterhood meetings back to the shul or somewhere else. He even, in the end, agreed, that Solange Malin was, and had always been, a *klafta*.

Delilah listened wordlessly, amazed. "Well, I have to say this for you: you're trying."

He certainly was. After an emergency call from Arthur, the two men had sat together and decided the best course to take. He was now taking it.

"I have an idea, my dear."

OK, she thought, putting down her pastrami on rye, which brought back some mixed memories. She swallowed and tapped her mouth with a napkin, all the better to open it good and wide if circumstances should so require.

"Maybe you could influence the Shammanovs to join our synagogue. The board would be thrilled. Everyone has been dying to meet them. And then, perhaps, if the Shammanovs became more active, in a little while I could ask for a raise, and all the other things. . . . We would be able to afford more household help, child care—"

"You want me to talk them into coming to our synagogue?!"

"Yes, why not? Didn't you tell me there is a boy who is almost Bar Mitzva age?"

"But they're not religious at all! She's a convert!"

"Think about it, Delilah. I know you've become her friend. Now, as her friend, wouldn't you be helping her by bringing her and her family closer to their roots, their heritage? The Jewish people are strengthened every time another family joins a synagogue and becomes part of the community. And of course, I admit it, this would be such a good thing for us—for the synagogue, of course—but not just that. Even rich people can be lonely. Why don't you invite them over for Friday-night dinner? We'll invite the board. You can even have it catered if it's too much for you to manage."

Somewhere inside she understood that all this was perfectly reasonable. But the truth was, she felt stingy about sharing her friend, about destroying the special relationship they shared. Most of all, she didn't want to introduce Joie Shammanov to Rebbitzin Levi; she wanted to keep the two worlds separate.

"Please, Delilah?"

She narrowed her eyes and looked at him squarely. "Chaim, I also have an idea. How would you feel about not being a rabbi?"

He looked at her blankly. "Not be a rabbi? What would I be then?"

"Well, you could be many things. A businessman, for example."

"I don't know anything about business."

"What's there to know? Do these people look like such geniuses to you? Listen to this business: You go to some clothing line, you know, some jeans manufacturer, Diesel."

"Diesel?"

"Or another one, whatever," she said irritably. Was it Joie or her mother who had told her all about this? Never mind, she told herself. Even Marilyn knew something some of the time. "It doesn't matter. And you buy the rights to the name. And then you get some cheap belts or watches from some factory in China, and get them to put Diesel on it, or any other name, and you sell it in all the big department stores. You just have to tell them how to make the watch or the belt look. And that's easy. I could do that myself."

"You want me to be a watchmaker?" He shrugged helplessly.

"You are totally missing the point! What I'm saying is that these business ideas are a dime a dozen. They are easy. You just have to understand how to do it. You need a friend in the business world to help you get started. I'm sure Mr. Shammanov—" She had never actually met the elusive husband of her friend, but Chaim didn't have to know that.

"But I don't want to be a businessman, Delilah, I want to be a rabbi. It's all I've ever wanted to be. I wouldn't be good at anything else." He cradled his head in his hands, his shoulders round with defeat. "Delilah, what do you want me to do?"

This simple question, asked in all innocence, which should have touched her heart and filled her with remorse and pity, alas, did just the opposite.

"*To do*? What do I want you *to do*? Well, I'll tell you. For starters, I want you to put up office hours and unlist our home phone. I want you to get a day off every two weeks so we can go somewhere together. I want you to arrange for more than a measly one-week vacation during the summer. I want you to demand they get a junior rabbi to take over the youth minyan and the Bar Mitzva program!"

He lifted his head and stared at her. "Are you deliberately trying to get me fired? Is that it? Because if you are, you'd better think about it. I took this job because you wanted me to. And when I did, I became a pariah. If I need another job, I've got the mark of Cain on my forehead. We'll wind up in some tiny community with no Jewish school and a twenty-member congregation that meets in our basement. You'll be baking all the cakes and making *cholent* for the entire congregation every Saturday. And everyone will have to stay with us until the Sabbath is over because it will be too cold and too far for them to walk home. Heck, they might sleep over Friday nights too, with their entire families."

She listened to him in horror, her heart skipping a beat. "No one is going to fire you. I mean"—she hesitated—"what makes you think that? You are doing well, aren't you? I mean, I haven't heard anything—"

"Delilah, you aren't listening. There is a whole group that wants to get rid of me. They never wanted me in the first place. Some say I'm not serious enough. Not enough of a scholar. Not bright enough. And the others are complaining I'm too serious. They are furious I closed down the kiddush Club, that custom they had of going out before the Torah reading and finishing off a few bottles of Scotch and then staggering back in."

"Why did you close it down?"

"Well, remember that Shabbes when I said 'How are you?' to Selwyn Goldbart and he said, 'F— you?' Whereupon I reminded him that the traditional greeting was Good Shabbes?"

She nodded.

"That's when I decided the drinking had to stop."

"I don't see why that means *I* have to do things differently."

"Because"—he paused ominously—"I'm not the only one they're complaining about."

There was silence, the information sinking in with a large thud.

"You mean to say—after all I've been doing—that they've still been . . . someone has been complaining . . . about me?"

"I kept defending you, but I can't anymore. You haven't offered to teach any classes for the women, your dresses are too short, and your wigs are too long. And you aren't setting a good example to the other wives and mothers because of all the time you are spending having fun. Be realistic. All they need is a good excuse, and you are giving it to them."

"So, after all I've put up with! And this is what they say about me?" A little plume of red smoke wafted in front of her eyes that wasn't coming from her cigarette. "Who, exactly, did you hear this from?"

He shook his head and shrugged.

She grabbed him by the shirtfront. "Tell me!"

"Well, the Grodins."

"Amber and Stuart? What's their problem?"

"You aren't taking an active enough role socially, to bring people together."

"So he can pick their brains and empty their pockets. Who else?"

"Mariette."

She was wounded. "Mariette?"

"Well, you never did follow through with the designer handbag thing—"

"I've been busy!"

"And Felice Borenberg mentioned something to her husband about your wardrobe being inappropriate for the rabbi's wife. And Solange said the same thing to Arthur."

"They're just jealous because I look so good," she said, with no small measure of truth. Nevertheless, she felt a stab of panic. The entire board was complaining about her! What would she do if they fired Chaim? If she had to leave Swallow Lake, just now, when everything was going so well? Where would they go?

She studied her perfect manicure.

Why, those little shits, she thought. Who did they think they were dealing with, *mikva*-pure Shira Metzenbaum? Maybe one day she and Chaim would walk off into the sunset into something far more lucrative and less intrusive. But no one was going to send them packing, not if she could help it.

She thought of the dinner party she would arrange and the phone call to Solange Malin she would have to make. She considered how she would introduce the board to Viktor and Joie, and how on a visit to their home she would give the women of Swallow Lake something to drool over that would fill their hearts with discontent and their minds with greedy visions of what was possible, if only their husbands could approach the wealth of the Shammanovs. They would never again be happy with their 3,000 square feet once they saw the Shammanov's 45,000 square feet, their acres of lakefront property, their Japanese gardens. If she never accomplished another thing, that was an experience she felt sure would do their souls good (she knew it would do *her* soul good). And if Joie and Viktor really did become active members of the synagogue, they would no doubt be invited to join the board, replacing some of the others. And then no one would dare to criticize her or even suggest firing Chaim.

And in the end, they would all agree that she, Delilah, was a wonderful rabbi's wife and that the congregation was lucky to have her and her special skills.

{ TWENTY-THREE }

Solange was chilly but correct. And Joie Shammanov was unaccountably delighted and grateful to get the invitation. In fact, she seemed thrilled.

"Viktor has been after me to make some friends, to get us more involved socially. Who will be coming?"

Delilah described the board members, and Joie seemed extremely interested. "But I have to warn you, Joie, they are all twice our age."

"I don't think that matters, do you? Have you seen their homes? How do they dress? What cars do they drive?"

Delilah was only too happy to tell her everything she wanted to know. And in the end, Joie even offered to send over her own chef to help Delilah plan the menu and do the cooking.

"That would be fantastic!"

The chef was a fairly new French import. He had fabulous ideas. "What about ze Peking duck and ze green papaya salad in a rich ginger and cardamom sauce, and zen ze pan-roasted squab stuffed wiz truffle and soft polenta, wiz per'aps an Armagnac-scented *jus*. Charlotte *aux fruits de saison* profiteroles *au chocolat*?"

She discussed it with Chaim.

"I don't know, Delilah. Is this guy Jewish? Does he know anything about preparing a kosher dinner?"

"What difference does that make? We'll buy all the ingredients. He'll use our utensils. I'll be in the kitchen to supervise him. What in this menu sounds problematic?"

"No, nothing—well, truffles."

"I thought they were like mushrooms?"

"They are not *like* mushrooms. They *are* mushrooms. But it's an interesting halachic problem. What blessing do you say over them? The Talmud in Berachos 40b states that even though mushrooms grow on the ground, they don't get their nourishment from the soil. But the *Aruch Hashulchan*, among others, hold that if one made a mistake and recited the blessing over vegetables on mushrooms, it's nevertheless acceptable—"

She rolled her eyes. "Chaim?"

"Oh, yes, what were we talking about?"

"So they are kosher, right? You can eat them?"

"Yes, of course."

"And Joie's chef can do the cooking?"

"Delilah, I'm really *not* comfortable about a non-Jew doing the cooking. I'm sure he wouldn't do anything deliberately, but there is always something he might not understand."

She stood still and lowered her head. "Well, if you really think so."

Chaim, who had expected a huge argument, was taken aback. She was, after all, doing this for him, and it was going to be an enormous amount of work. Why shouldn't he try to make things easier for her? "Look, I don't want to take a stringent view for no reason. As the great Reb Yechiel Halevi Epstein used to say, 'To say *forbidden, forbidden, forbidden* doesn't take a great scholar. But it takes talent, wisdom, and understanding to take a lenient view and say *permitted*.' I suppose it would be all right. Do you promise to supervise him carefully and not let him bring in any food or utensils?"

"I promise! Thanks so much!" She hugged him.

"And please, Delilah. Don't make yourself crazy. The people who don't like us now, won't like us even after they've eaten a wonderful dinner," he said with a shrug.

She bought all the ingredients, which cost a fortune. She hired a serving girl to help her for the evening, and even rented a uniform for her. She bought a lovely toile tablecloth and matching napkins and had a professional service draw up place cards using hand calligraphy. Joie's florist sent over the flower arrangements, and the whole house smelled of lavender and roses and lilacs and peonies. Joie's dressmaker made Delilah a fantastic wraparound dress the color of her eyes, copied from the latest styles seen on the runways in Milan and Paris, from which Joie had recently returned with the real thing.

"Are they here already?" Stuart Grodin asked, his eyes staking out the territory, while Delilah and Amber kissed the air outside each other's ears.

"Who?" Delilah asked innocently.

"Why, the Shammanovs," Stuart said, rubbing his hands together, like a baseball player getting ready to hold the bat and hit the ball out of the park. "I understand you know them well, Delilah?"

She smiled mysteriously. "Yes, we've become dear friends."

"What are they like? What's the house like?" Amber pressed her.

Delilah smiled, ignoring the question. "Would you excuse me, Amber? I need to be in the kitchen."

The chef was working his magic. Everything smelled wonderful, and he seemed to be managing just fine. "Go, go." He shooed her out the door.

She heard the door opening and closing, Chaim greeting more guests.

It was the Malins, the Rollands, and the Borenbergs. Mariette came around and kissed her. She had a tall handsome stranger with her, who turned out to be the elusive Dr. Rolland.

He had thick, salt-and-pepper hair, perfectly and recently cut, an aquiline nose, a strong jaw, and firm, young skin, except for a few distinguished creases on his forehead. He was really tall and broad-shouldered and athletic, Delilah thought, as his heavy-lidded blue eyes peered at her beneath thick, dark lashes. In short, a ladies' man with all the qualities needed to fulfill his potential. He gave Delilah a hug, his hand dipping just a bit too low.

"Good to finally meet you." He smiled.

"Yes, finally. You certainly do wander," she said, firmly moving his hand off its target.

Mariette's eyes were suddenly cool.

"Wherever did you find that dress, Delilah?" Felice Borenberg demanded.

"Why, yes, dear. It looks as if it were made for you!" Solange said enviously, as Amber looked on, her lips pursed in disapproval.

"It was. Made for me," she said nonchalantly.

"Well, I had no idea you were getting your clothes custom-made these days. It must cost a fortune," Felice said, raising her eyebrows at Solange.

"Joie Shammanov has the best little dressmaker. She did it for me practically as a favor. Please, come in. Let me take your coats."

"Everything all right in the kitchen, Delilah?" Chaim whispered.

"Everything is fine. I was just in there a minute ago!"

"Please, you promised!"

"I can't be everywhere, Chaim!"

She rushed back into the kitchen. The first course was already being plated: a fantastic mixture of duck and papaya salad. The chef stood at the stove stirring the ginger sauce. The scent alone made Delilah's mouth water. They smiled at each other.

"*Fantastique, non?*"

She nodded, smiling. "Fantastic." The bell rang again. She heard Joie's high-pitched laughter, and then a deep, unfamiliar bass. She rushed into the hall.

"Joie! So good to see you!" Delilah hugged her. "They are all dying to meet you! So, how does it look so far?" she whispered.

"Everything looks fab," Joie whispered back. "Delilah, my husband, Viktor."

Viktor Shammanov was a bear of a man, with the back and shoulders of a body builder, the kind that are so pumped up they seemed to be constantly leaning forward in a Mr. Universe see-my-muscles pose. He had to be at least six foot three. His hair—spread over the top and back of his head in thinning, unnaturally black waves—swept over his forehead from a strange side part. His face was part pit bull, part Khrushchev. And although he wore a suit of impeccable cut, a silk tie, and shiny black shoes, still he resembled one of those guys on *The Sopranos*. He took Chaim into his arms and hugged him, kissing him vigorously on both cheeks. "Viktor Shammanov. Good to meet you, Rabbi! My vife, she spends the day now with your vife. Is good!"

"Yes, it's great. They've become great friends. Mr. Shammanov, let me introduce my wife, Delilah."

Delilah waited in apprehension for the grizzly to pounce. He didn't. He didn't even hold out his hand to her.

"Am grandson of big rabbi, Ukrainian rabbi. I know not to touch rabbi's vife." He bellowed with laughter, his voice bouncing off the walls like a sonic boom.

"Very good, very good!" Chaim rubbed his hands together nervously. He suddenly noticed another couple standing by the door. He'd never seen them before.

"Please, come in, won't you? I'm sorry. You are?"

"Khe doesn't speak English." Viktor unleashed a flood of Russian. "Khe is cousin, bodyguard. And khis vife. Also cousin."

The man took off, prowling around the house, looking for assassins. Delilah quickly added two more settings to the table.

"Let me introduce you to our synagogue board, Viktor," Chaim said, making the introductions. He went through the names, and each person then stepped up like a petitioner at the court of some Oriental potentate, almost curtsying as they shook his hand and nodded to his wife. Only Joseph Rolland took Joie's hand and kissed it, causing Viktor Shammanov to stop what he was saying and stare. Dr. Rolland soon stepped back.

"In Russia, you take khand of another's man's vife to your lips, and you die," he said casually. There was a sudden silence. Then he bellowed with laughter. "Kidding, just kidding," he boomed.

Everyone exhaled.

"Please, everyone, why don't we just wash and then sit down to dinner?" Delilah said, with perfect poise.

"Vash? Am I dirty I need to vash?" Viktor asked, looking around him with mock shock like a Catskills comedian.

"I know it sounds strange, but it's a religious custom. We wash before saying grace over the bread, the way the priests in the Holy Temple washed before preparing sacrifices on the altar," Chaim explained companionably, taking Viktor's arm and leading him off to the special basin built into an alcove of the dining room for exactly this purpose. Everyone followed. Delilah then helped them find their place cards and be seated. Chaim said blessings over the bread, then tore off some pieces and dipped them in salt, handing a piece to each guest, as was the custom.

Delilah rushed back into the kitchen. "Is everything all right?"

"Of course, madame," the chef said, taking a large swig from a very expensive bottle of wine bought especially for the evening. It was, she noted, already half gone.

"We've got two extra guests. Maria, you can start serving now," she told the help.

The girl lifted the plates up to the chef, who ladled generous amounts of sauce on top of each. She carried them to the table and began to serve.

Viktor handed his plate to his bodyguard, who tasted it. Everyone stared, wondering how long Viktor would watch him not dying before agreeing to eat. He didn't wait very long. "Food vonderful!" Viktor announced. "I loff good food."

"Yes, I have quite a few business contacts in Russia, and they all know how to eat," Stuart Grodin said obsequiously.

"You khav bizness, in Russia? What kind bizness?" Viktor asked.

Stuart was thrilled. He started discussing the subcontractors for his bears, who were going to manufacture them under license and distribute them all over Eastern Europe.

"Bears? You sell bears to Russians? Like snow to Eskimos!" Viktor roared. "You vant bizness in Russia, is only vun bizness. Only vun bizness in vorld."

Everyone leaned forward a little in their seats, placing their utensils down so as not to make a single sound that might obscure the answer.

"Oil! Oil bizness. You heard of Turdistan? You khear what happen to oil after communists? All people get certificates, oil certificates in Turdistan. Every family have certificate. But don't need certificate. Need—" He rubbed his thumb and forefinger together. "So me and brother, ve buy certificates. Ve get friends to buy certificates. Now ve own oil company. Now ve drill, make oil company bigger. Ve sell certificates. Our friends, all very rich. Like Sultan of Brunei!"

"Can others buy these oil certificates? Is it like stocks and bonds?" Stuart asked eagerly.

He tilted his head, then shook it. "Is very difficult. Need to organize. Only Russian peoples who lives in Turdistan can buy. Is almost impossible for people like you to buy. You buy bears!" He looked around the table, smiling. No one smiled back. "Vhy so serious, you Americans? Ah, yes, I know vhy." He looked around the table expectantly.

"Viktor, are you looking for something?" Chaim asked.

"Vodka! Ve make toast!"

Delilah ran to get the bottle out of the liquor cabinet, together with the shot glasses.

"Varm vodka?" Viktor bellowed. "In Russia, vodka cold, like Kremlin in vinter!" He filled his shot glass and raised it aloft. "Ten years ago I go to Moscow on buziness. Vladimir vent, also Yuri." He turned to his wife. "You remember Yuri? The vun vit daughter Galina, who haff trouble vit kidneys from eating bad pork, vun vit small face, vun who married police captain? . . . In Russia, very important to have relative police captain, very khelpful to many buzinesses; also bear buziness, also oil buziness. Ve did vell, so ve vent into restaurant to celebrate. They don't know how to fix kebab, but bread and soup and pirochki vas excellent. Ve make big buziness. Ve sign big contract. Ve become very, very rich. And ve move here, to America. I find vife in America. I have my beautiful daughter Natasha in America. Ve build house in America. In America, you can be Jew. I bring my son to live in America. I vant Bar Mitzva. I don't know khow to make Bar Mitzva. And now I meet Rabbi Chaim, and khe vill khelp me make Bar Mitzva for my son. And all you my friends, my American friends, you vill come to my son's Bar Mitzva. I velcome you to my khome, as you velcome me to your khome in America. I raise glass to Rabbi Chaim." He poured everyone a drink. Then he threw back his head and downed it, wiping his lips across his sleeves. "And now, raise glasses, drink to Svallo Lake, to friendship!" He poured another round.

Delilah signaled to the serving girl to start clearing off the table and to bring the next course. Her head was already swimming from the pure alcohol now coursing through her veins. She walked into the kitchen to supervise.

And then she spied something. It was a little container. She lifted it. CRÈME FRAÎCHE, it said. "Hello? Where did this come from?" she asked the chef.

"I bring it *avec moi* from Paris, Madame." He gave her a superior and knowing smile. "*C'est impossible* to find decent crème fraîche in America."

"You were told specifically not to bring in any food!" Her head swam. "What's in it?"

His lips thinned with insult. He looked down his nose. "Just ze cultured cream. It make ze sauces very smooth, very *riche*."

"Cream? Cream! In all the sauces? Don't tell me you put this in the duck salad sauce, and the sauce that went over the squab, and into the profiteroles!"

He drained his glass of wine and poured himself another, finishing off the bottle. "But of course!" His brow wrinkled in displeasure. "In France, zis is well known." He shrugged, that go-to-hell French shrug of nasty waiters and impatient shopowners.

She clenched her fists. "But none of the recipes you showed me even called for cream!"

"Recipes!" he mocked. "Who writes zis? Ze little cook, ze *New York Times*. Ze great chef? We do not read zeez silly instructions."

"You nincompoop! I told you, I'm a rabbi's wife! We are Orthodox Jews! All our guests are Orthodox Jews, you French nitwit. We don't mix meat and milk. I told you that!"

His whole body stiffened with offense. He bowed. His hand waved over the kitchen dramatically. "Pardon, madame, but I do not see ze meat here. Only ze duck and ze chicken!"

"I'm going to kill you!" She lunged at him. He picked up the carving knife and moved back, waving it at her. Delilah grabbed the hired girl and hid behind her. He started swearing very rapidly under his breath in French, the word *Juifs* appearing again and again, in what was apparently not a paen of praise to David Ben-Gurion or Moses. Then he threw down his apron and walked out the kitchen door, slamming it behind him.

She leaned against the wall, trembling.

She thought of the religious men and women sitting around her table, the synagogue-owned table in the house of the community's spiritual leader, its rabbi. And she was his helpmate, the person who sat by his side, who was supposed to help the congregants keep God's commandments.

She had, it seemed to her, a clear choice. She could go in and tell them what had happened, insulting Joie and Viktor, whose chef, after all, had managed to screw up, sending everyone home early with nothing to eat. Chaim would make her throw out all her dishes, after he berated her with a million *I told you so*s. Solange and Mariette would arch their brows and nod at each other at the debacle. And who knew what the decision would be, the next time the board took a vote?

Or, she could . . .

She looked at the delectable squab already arranged on the plates, covered in sauce. She searched the pans to find a piece that had not yet been plated and doused. There was only one left. She took out a clean plate and placed the squab on it, adding the vegetables. "I'll take in this one. You take in the rest," she told the girl.

Then she reached for the almost empty container of crème fraîche, opened the garbage can, and buried it deep inside, covering it with debris. She picked up the plate and carried it into the dining room, placing it in front of her husband.

"Ah, I get special service. A true woman of valor!" Chaim said, kissing her hand.

"You see, little voman, this is vay vife treat husband," Viktor boomed, squeezing Joie's knee.

Delilah smiled at him and sat down, looking down into her own plate. Slowly, she scraped the sauce off the squab with her knife, eating tiny, relatively sauceless pieces as best she could.

"Umm, this is just scrumptious!" Solange exclaimed, putting a sauce-drenched morsel on her tongue.

"Yes, divine. The sauce is so creamy and rich. I've never tasted anything like it," Mariette said, savoring each piece. "You must get us the recipe, Delilah."

Delilah nodded silently, not looking up.

"Come. Ve toast some more!" Viktor called out.

Chaim downed his fourth glass. He staggered to his feet, shakily holding up his shot glass. "Now—now it's my turn. Shhhh, shaa." He waved at everyone. "Sit down! To all my wonderful friends in Swallow Lake, who have entrusted me with their spiritual growth and who have allowed me to become a part of their lives and the lives of their families, so that we might be true to our heritage and our holy Torah, fulfilling all the commandments of our God."

My God, were those tears in his eyes? Delilah thought, horrified.

"And to my wonderful wife who has made this fabulous evening possible, bringing together old friends and new, nourishing us with a gourmet kosher"—Delilah started to cough—"meal." She coughed louder and louder.

"She's choking!"

"Somebody do a Heimlich maneuver!"

"I vill do it!" Viktor sprang up.

"No, I'm fine—don't," Delilah protested, terrified as she watched Viktor Shammanov lumbering drunkenly toward her, getting ready to squeeze her in half. "I'm fine. Something must have just gone down the wrong pipe, that's all." She smiled, wiping her eyes. "See?"

Viktor smiled and sat down. "Finish toast!"

"Ah, yes." Chaim nodded. "To my wonderful wife, who has been a true helpmate, like Sarah to Abraham, like Rivkah to Isaac, like Rachel to Jacob. . . ."

Like Eve to Adam, Delilah thought.

"May God bless her! It's not easy to be a rabbi . . . so many things I'd like to do, and it's impossible . . . to please everyone . . . and some people are jerks, you can never please them, and some are just drunks, like the kiddush Club members, and the ones who tell me they go for lap dances because it helps them fulfill their God-given duty to pleasure their wives . . ."

Felice turned sharply to her husband, Ari, who stared down at a fork he was digging into the tablecloth. Joseph Rolland cleared his throat.

"Chaim!" Delilah said sharply, pulling him back down into his seat.

"Er . . . I think maybe it's time for dessert?" Arthur pointed out.

"What did you say, time to desert?" Stuart Grodin laughed.

"Is that a true story?" Mariette turned to Delilah. "About the lap—"

"Wait, wait, I'm not finished," Chaim muttered, struggling back up to his feet. "And to the women who want to know if they should tell their husbands one of the kids isn't theirs or if it would be a mitzva to keep the information to themselves . . ."

"Oh, ho!" Viktor roared.

"And of course, to my beautiful, difficult wife . . ."

She elbowed him. "You already did me!" she hissed. "Sit down!"

He ignored her. ". . . whom I love, and who makes my life miser—"

"Chaim!"

"To Delilah. I raise my glass to her and to all of you!"

"To Delilah!" The men roared, while the women studiously avoided looking at each other.

Delilah drank another shot of vodka. The room was swimming in front of her. Solange looked suddenly fat. And Mariette looked like she was wearing devil's horns. Or maybe that wasn't Mariette; maybe it was just her own reflection in the glass of the china closet.

TWENTY-FOUR

People remember what they want to remember. And while everyone had had a great time at the rabbi's house meeting Viktor and Joie Shammanov, they soon forgot the circumstances of their initial meeting, remembering only that they were now dear friends of the fabulous Shammanovs. In fact, soon it felt as if they had known them forever.

Joie made an effort to invite the women over to her home at least once a week, preparing fabulous meals. After some coaching from Delilah, she got rid of her French chef and hired one who had once worked in the Catskills at a kosher hotel. She had Chaim over to supervise making her kitchen kosher. And even when he went a bit mad with a blowtorch, effectively ruining the inside of their $6,000 Gaggenau oven, she told him not to worry about it, and just replaced it. The silverware and glasses could all be made kosher by plunging one into boiling water and by just soaking the other. The dishes, of course, were a bit of a problem; there is no way to make porcelain dishes kosher if they have held milk and meat or pork or shellfish. But even Joie, caught up as she was in fitting into her new community, balked at throwing out an entire set of $200-a-plate Hermes Toucans dinnerware, with its $1,500 soup tureen. What they did was order additional plates to use when the synagogue came over.

Sightings of Viktor Shammanov in earnest conference with the board members and others from among the most prominent citizens of Swallow Lake became more and more frequent. Meanwhile, the women of the synagogue board had taken it upon themselves to advise Joie Shammanov on how to make a Bar Mitzva.

"I once went to a Bar Mitzva where they turned the entire synagogue into a circus tent, and the Bar Mitzva boy greeted the guests on an elephant. . . . They had flame eaters, clowns, and jugglers," Amber told her excitedly.

"And I was at one where they turned the place into an African jungle, with grass floors and tribal dancers flown in from South Africa. All the food was African too. It was something to remember," Solange remarked.

"That's nothing. I was at one where they flew everyone to a safari game park in Kenya. But we wound up waiting on line for hours to get in. It turned out there were two other Bar Mitzvas in front of us," said Felice.

"You don't want to go to Africa," Mariette counseled authoritatively. "Joseph and I were there once, for some conference. The minute we finished breakfast, the monkeys descended on the tables and ate all the packets of sugar! They were all over the place! It was disgusting. And that's not the worst of it." She lowered her voice conspiratorially. "I was reading their local fashion magazine, and they had a full-page advertisement for *rape insurance*! They promised to bring you AIDS medication first thing the next morning," she whispered, shuddering.

Joie's eyes widened.

"Then again," Solange said brightly, breaking the stunned silence, "you could always rent a fabulous place right here. Like Radio City Music Hall. Or Madison Square Garden. Then you could put the name of the family up on the marquee. It's great fun!"

"Been done." Felice shook her head. "They even hired the Rockettes to dance with the Bar Mitzva boy. The police had to rope off half of Manhattan."

"That's peanuts! Did you read about that music producer who built an entire synagogue in the south of France just for his son's Bar Mitzva and afterward just took it apart? He flew in Beyoncé Knowles and Justin Timberlake!" Delilah said delightedly. "I read all about it in *People* magazine at my last gynecologist's appointment."

Joie lifted her head. "Oh," she said, "that does sound like fun!"

"But does it sound to you like a *religious* occasion?" Solange tilted her head.

"Doesn't it?" Joie looked at Delilah, who was already deep in daydreams, envisioning herself in a pink bikini lolling about on the beaches of Cannes. She looked up, suddenly realizing that everyone was staring at her, waiting for an answer.

"I can't see anything wrong with it," Delilah said.

Solange looked puzzled. "But didn't Rabbi Chaim say he was against this kind of thing?"

"Why do you say that?" Delilah felt her underarms break out in sweat.

"Well, he gave a whole sermon about it about a month ago. Were you there, Amber?"

"Oh, yes, *that* sermon." She arched her brow.

"Oh, sure!" Delilah nodded. "I know what you are talking about now," she said, her mind a complete blank. "But I don't think he was talking about the same thing."

"No? Then what did he mean when he said that these kids end up spending two years going to multiple parties every weekend, that they get used to drinking and eating too much and getting all these party favors, so that afterward when the parties stop, they are just so blasé about everything they wind up taking drugs and getting into all kinds of trouble just to keep themselves amused?"

"Yes, that's exactly what he said," Mariette agreed. "I remember, because a lot of people were complaining about it afterward. People who'd had Bar and Bat Mitzvas. They were very hurt!"

"Well, you see, I'm sure you misunderstood, because there is *no way* Rabbi Chaim would *ever* say anything controversial that would hurt people's feelings," Delilah pointed out, relieved. "He probably meant they shouldn't attend too many every weekend. But one would be all right."

"So you are saying that your husband is in favor of a Bar Mitzva party like the one in France, the one that cost millions?"

"I think I can safely say that my husband would never condemn anyone because of how much money they have, or if they wanted to spend it on fulfilling one of God's commandments. You know, there is this concept of . . . of"—she thought back to her yeshiva days, desperately searching for solid ground—"of *hedoor mitzva*."

The women tilted their heads quizzically.

"It's the idea that you should go a little overboard when you're doing God's commandments. Like . . . let me see—you know, like choosing an *etrog* for Succoth."

Joie looked at her blankly. "Succoth? *Etrog*?"

"Oh, it's the Feast of Tabernacles, a seven-day holiday in which we are supposed to 'dwell in booths.' So we make this little hut, a sukkah, outside our homes, and we let the sun bake our heads, the rain and snow fall in our soup," Delilah went on.

"Whatever for?" Joie shook her head.

"Oh, uhm. Well," Delilah racked her brain. "It's . . . it's supposed to teach us to have faith in God. And that a home, no matter how solid and expensive, can't really save you from the rain or the sun. . . ."

Joie blinked, looking back at her house. "That's exactly what a home *can* do."

"Yes, I know. But—"

"What she means, my dear, is that living in a flimsy hut for a week is supposed to make us understand that we need His help and protection, because, you know, a house can be gone in an instant. Hurricanes, floods, tornadoes," Mariette told her, nodding sagely. "Isn't that what you were going to say, Delilah?"

"For sure. Now, where was I? Oh, the *etrog*—that's a citron. It looks just like a lemon, except it doesn't have any juice, and not much taste, but it smells heavenly. For some reason, the Bible chooses the citron, and a few other things, to symbolize the holiday. You are supposed to hold them in your hands and shake them in all directions."

Joie blinked.

"Well, anyhow, God says to take a citron, any old citron. But people decided it would honor God more if we made an effort to find the *perfect* citron, the one with no spots or blemishes. One perfectly shaped, not too big or too small. And sometimes, people go around with magnifying glasses when they shop for their citron. They can spend thousands of dollars on one. They think it's a way of honoring God. You could say the same thing about going over the top in a Bar Mitzva."

Solange and Felice looked at each other, their mouths falling open.

Mariette shook her head. "You can't be serious! I was once at this Bat Mitzva in the Plaza Hotel. To enter the reception, you had to pass through a corridor lined with eight-by-ten-foot photos of this twelve-year-old girl doing various dance and acrobatic moves. I mean, I applaud the concept in theory. But a twelve-year-old girl really shouldn't be blown up to eight by ten feet. She had braces and acne. And when we got into the reception, there were all these well-known chefs standing at different serving stations, preparing food. There were fountains of champagne. And when we were finally stuffed to the gills and sat down, the lights were lowered. And there comes this litter, supported by six-foot "slaves" in loincloths, and on top is the Bat Mitzva girl dressed like Cleopatra. And then it *really* got ostentatious," Mariette said. "That can't possibly be a good thing spiritually. You didn't mean that seriously, did you, Delilah dear?"

"Well," Delilah swallowed, feeling herself challenged, "at least it's something that little girl will remember, isn't it? Maybe she'll remember what fun she had and want her own daughter to have a Bat Mitzva!"

"That's good enough for me!" Joie nodded. "You know, I have to be honest with you all, this wasn't something I was looking forward to, but now I can truthfully say it's going to be great fun! The only question is where to do it." She chewed softly on the nail of her forefinger, deep in thought.

"What about Israel?" Solange suggested.

"Oh, I . . . don't. . . ." Joie shook her head.

"Why not?"

"Well, for one thing, you can't get prime ribs in Israel," Felice pointed out. "Ask my husband. He goes on and on about how skinny the cows are there."

"And if you forget something, there's no Lord and Taylor or Nordstrom's," Amber said. "You're stuck."

"I had a different kind of place in mind. Something spiritual, with lots of sea and sand and sky," Joie explained.

Solange cleared her throat. "You know, Joie, Israel is on the Mediterranean coast. There are miles and miles of beaches there."

"Is that true? I had no idea!"

"It's also a very spiritual place. It's a holy place to three major world religions," Solange went on, heating up.

"But Joie doesn't mean *that* kind of spiritual!" Delilah stood up.

Solange looked at her, shocked. "Don't you think Israel is the most appropriate place for a Bar Mitzva, Delilah?"

"Well, sure, if you want to go that way."

"What other 'way' is there?"

"I just mean, that different people get spiritually worked up about different things. Now, you might feel spiritual about Jerusalem. But Joie might feel spiritual about a beach in Barbados, or the Dominican Republic, or the Cayman Islands."

"Ooh, that's a great idea, Delilah! We could fly everyone down and rent a whole wing at a resort. Put up a tent on the beach!"

"That does sound nice," Amber agreed.

"It sounds fabulous, Joie. Just fabulous." Felice nodded.

In the end, everyone agreed, even Solange, who was as sick as everyone else of the icy Connecticut winter and needed a tan. You couldn't, after all, wear a bathing suit at the Wailing Wall.

"Oh, this is going to be so much fun! Thanks everybody so much for your help!" Joie kissed them on both cheeks and gave Delilah's hand a special secret squeeze.

Delilah gratefully squeezed her back.

*I*n the beginning, Delilah had been panic-stricken that Joie's newfound acceptance into the community would water down, or destroy, their own special relationship. But that hadn't happened. In fact, Joie seemed to want to be even closer to Delilah, taking her shopping and buying her extravagant gifts—like a Louis Vuitton handbag, the famous monogram in striking colors on a white background, with tan leather handles and little gold zippers and locks that didn't actually lock anything. It was fabulous.

"Chaim, look at this!" she said, overcome with joy, caressing it.

He took his head out of his book. "A handbag."

She rolled her eyes. "Not just any handbag. It's a Louis Vuitton Damier Speedy Alma from the canvas multicolor collection. It costs a fortune."

He put down his book. "It's very nice. So I guess your *chesed* project is going well then?"

"*Chesed* project?" she looked at him blankly.

"Designer Handbags for Terror Victims. That's what it's for, right?"

As if. She clutched it to her breast. "No, it's a gift. To me. From Joie."

"A gift? And it costs a fortune, you say? Exactly how much of a fortune are we talking about?" he asked, looking at her steadily.

"I don't know," she lied. She knew exactly how much, since she had looked it up in the on-line catalog.

"Well, if it's over a hundred dollars, you really shouldn't accept it."

"Over a hundred dollars?" she looked at him contemptuously. "You can't get a Louis Vuitton key ring for a hundred dollars."

"How much, Delilah?"

"One thousand five hundred thirty-nine dollars and fifty-three cents."

"What?" he exploded. "You can't accept a gift like that! It's going back."

"She'd be deeply hurt and offended. And embarrassed. Don't our sages tell us that embarrassing someone is almost as bad as killing them?" She tucked the handbag protectively under her arm.

"Then you'll have to add it to your *chesed* project. How many bags do you have already?"

She had a cheapo Prada pink begonia pouchette that Solange had unloaded, a *very* old classic quilted Chanel in a horrible dark blue from Mariette, and a beat-up Fendi from Amber in some weird lilac shade. Felice had been the only one who'd come across with something she'd coveted: a silver snakeskin and leather Argent bag, which was actually cute, if you liked silver snakeskin. "I've got a few," she answered defensively.

"How many, Delilah?"

"Four. So far."

"That's it?" Chaim said. "After all these months? Only four? Think about it, Delilah! How is it going to look if you suddenly show up with an expensive designer handbag in front of all these people you've been asking to donate? You are going to make us a laughingstock, or worse."

She fingered the handbag thoughtfully. She hadn't thought of that. He was right, she realized. She didn't answer him. But the next day, she told the babysitter to stay a few extra hours. She rode Amtrak to Penn Station and then took the subway to Canal Street on Manhattan's Lower East Side. She walked down the street, humming, looking into the crowded shops filled with Oriental merchandise.

It didn't take long.

"Psst. Youbyvuton?" Little Chinese women clutching cell phones accosted her on every street corner, looking like extras in one of those Japanese kung fu mafia flicks. "I ge goo pri!" they insisted, in reassuring tones. She nodded, allowing herself to be whisked off to a side street. The woman whipped out a laminated page with every Louis Vuitton handbag imaginable. She spotted the Alma.

"How much?" she said, pointing.

"Forty dolla!"

"That's high!"

"OK. Thirty dolla. Goo pri for you?"

She nodded. "I'll take one of those and one of these," she said, pointing to another model, in black with colored letters.

The woman returned with a plain plastic bag. Inside were the two handbags.

"Sixty bucks?"

The woman nodded. Money changed hands.

She knew better than to take them out and examine them on the street, in case an undercover cop was around. On the way back to the subway, she went into a store on a side street and bought three Louis Vuitton lookalike wallets. Each one cost her ten dollars. The real ones cost four hundred. Each.

When she got home, she took out her booty and examined it. Her purchases even came with their own monogrammed felt holder, just like the real ones. And inside the bags and the wallets there was a label that said LOUIS VUITTON, PARIS. She looked at the fake, and then she looked at her original. It was almost impossible to tell them apart. OK, it was *totally* impossible to tell them apart. What people never realized about Louis Vuittons until they shelled out thousands of dollars and brought them home was that most of the real models weren't even leather, just laminated cloth.

"Delilah?" Chaim said, when he saw her wearing her new purse.

"Relax. I picked up a fake on Canal Street. Pretty realistic, no?"

He looked it over. It looked exactly like the one Delilah had shown him the day before. "Are you sure this is fake?" he asked suspiciously.

"My goodness! Only a man would ask that. Of course it's a fake! It's obvious. Just look at the stitching; it's got two extra stitches. And the zipper? I mean, come on!"

He shrugged, lost. "Well, you know it's against the law to buy these. You could get arrested, Delilah. Not to mention the fact that it is totally unethical."

"The only police that would arrest me over this are the fashion police. Relax, Chaim. This is America."

"It's stealing. It's wrong. You've got to take it back."

"To whom, the Chinese Mafia?"

"Promise me you'll never do it again?"

"I promise." She meant it too. Who wanted a fake, even a very good one? It was like cubic zirconium, or a really well-dressed whore. The fact that nobody could tell the difference didn't change what they were.

The sisterhood looked over the rebbitzin's new handbag with envy. But anyone who asked was told it was a fake. From Canal Street. To salve her conscience, she added the two fakes to her collection. She couldn't see what difference it would make to victims of terror, who, she was sure, would be equally delighted with these bags, since Israelis, being over there in the Middle East, wouldn't know the difference anyway. Besides, Palestinian terrorists, those beasts, had absolutely no respect for either human life or really, really important designer handbags. It would be such a shame if a real, brand-new Damier Speedy got caught up in a terror attack.

To help speed donations to her project, Joie agreed to give a luncheon buffet at Uspekhov. Delilah was thrilled. To please Joie, she went down the synagogue list, paying personal visits to almost everyone and duly noting the size of their lots, the upkeep of their homes, the quality of their furnishings, and the cars in their garage. From these women, she received further lists of names of non–synagogue members, whom she approached and visited, until she was able to compile a true A-list of the most well-to-do people in the community and its surroundings. She went over the information with Joie, and together they prepared the guest list. The invitations were eagerly accepted, and the best-dressed, best-jeweled, richest women of Swallow Lake soon flowed through the iron gates of Uspekhov, touring the estate.

It was a huge success, Delilah's designer and almost-designer handbag collection swelling to hundreds of bags. She was thrilled. And so was Joie.

Soon after, the Shammanovs were suddenly everywhere. They were the honorees at the annual Hebrew Day School fund-raising dinner, pushing aside Arthur and Solange, who had spent years toiling to help balance the budget of that money-eater. They were announced in the highest category of the Lions of Judah circle for the UJC fund-raising campaign. They were seated to the right of the Israeli ambassador at the five-star Israel Bonds Dinner in Hartford. They were on the cover of *Lifestyles* magazine.

They were photographed with Steven Spielberg and Demi Moore and her very young husband at a benefit for the Shoah Foundation. And there was a smiling photo of them accepting a medal of honor from former President Clinton and a smiling Hillary at a B'nai Brith dinner.

Discussions were held and it was decided, although not unanimously, that Viktor and Joie Shammanov be invited to join the synagogue board.

All the while, the members of Ohel Aaron felt their hearts rise and fall, buffeted equally by waves of envy and admiration. Suddenly, their homes began to feel cramped, and they started to find contractors to add porches and finish basements. They hired landscape designers and began importing dwarf trees from Japan. They watched the fashion channel for the latest designer shows in Milan and Paris and then rushed to get their dresses made by Joie's dressmaker.

And then the community held its breath in hushed anticipation as they waited to see who among them would get an invitation to the Bar Mitzva of the Shammanovs' son, Anatoly. All over the community, wild rumors abounded. A synagogue was already under construction in Macchu Pichu, fortress city of the ancient Incas, in a high saddle between two peaks in northwest Cuzco, Peru, they whispered to each other in wonder. Llamas would bring up the kosher foie gras. Or Viktor was building his own island, like Sealand, in the middle of the ocean with the help of his oil rigs, a place where he would declare himself king and give out passports to all the guests, giving them tax-free status for the rest of their lives. The Bar Mitzva boy would be brought in by aircraft carrier, or strapped to the back of a great whale. Destiny's Child would be there, and/or Shania Twain, Michael and Janet Jackson, Celine Dion, the entire cast of the Cirque du Soleil from Las Vegas, Britney Spears, Nicole Kidman, and Natalie Portman and her Israeli boyfriend. They would argue, debate, and discuss, rumors flying, becoming more and more fantastical with every day that passed.

The hunger to be on the guest list soon became ravenous.

Delilah and Chaim were spared the suspense. Their invitation had been personal. Delilah had already begun shopping for cruise wear.

"Shorts? You're buying shorts? I'm not so sure we should even go," Chaim told her, scandalized and depressed over the whole thing.

She was stunned. "Not go? Are you insane? Why not?"

"Because I'm the rabbi, and there will be some members of the congregation who won't be invited, and they deserve services on the Sabbath. Who will provide them if I leave?"

"So for one Sabbath there will be no speech! Believe me, they'll survive."

"It's not just that. They'll probably invite all the people who run the service. The cantor and the Torah reader and the *gabbai*—"

"So what? All the synagogue needs is ten people to hold a service! Believe me, there will be more than ten who aren't getting invitations. They'll manage. For Pete's sake, you aren't going to make me miss this, are you? Because that would be cruel, Chaim, really cruel. Besides, the Bar Mitzva boy is going to need your support. You need to stand next to him as he's reading, in case he forgets."

That was certainly true, he thought morosely. Little Anatoly, with his thick Russian accent and even thicker brain, would need all the help he could get. "There is only one way that kid is going to get through this without humiliating himself and his parents: if he doesn't open his mouth."

"You're his teacher! How can you say that? He's got to read something. You just have to try harder. After all, you've got another two months, no?"

"If I had another two years I still wouldn't manage. The kid's got a wooden ear. And he doesn't remember anything."

"But he'll have it written in front of him, no? He doesn't have to memorize, does he?"

"No, thank God for that. But he does have to remember in which direction to turn the page. He can't even remember that!"

"So that's not a reason to be upset with him. He's just a kid, after all."

"I'm not upset with him. I'm upset with how this whole extravaganza is affecting the community. I know what will happen: All the women in shul will be running around in bathing suits on Shabbes, and the men will sit around the pool playing cards! I just don't understand it." He shook his head. "When I first spoke to Viktor, he seemed perfectly willing to have something modest, here in the synagogue. I don't understand where they got the idea for this circus."

Delilah cleared her throat. "Actually, it was Amber who had the idea about the circus," she murmured, examining her manicure. "Look, Chaim, isn't it better that they spend money on a religious ceremony than spending it on something else that would be more frivolous, like . . . like . . ." But she couldn't think of a single thing that would be more frivolous.

"Religious ceremony? You mean the half hour in the synagogue? The rest is just one big, ostentatious, overblown, see-how-much-money-I've-got festival! You know what? It would be better to tell everyone in the world not to have a Bar or Bat Mitzva at all. To skip it. Believe me, most of these boys and girls would have a much better chance at actually becoming thoughtful, spiritual adults without one!"

She gasped. "How can you say that? What about *hedoor mitzva*?"

"That doesn't mean spending the most money on something! You know, rabbis in certain Hasidic sects have put a ceiling on how much people can spend on weddings. They say, if the wedding has more than one hundred and fifty people and is held in too expensive a place, they won't attend or officiate. They did it because they didn't want people to go into debt or be ashamed, and because it was becoming impossible for parents to marry off their children. That's *hedoor mitzva*."

"Well, that's all very nice, but it's too late now. You can't embarrass the Shammanovs by staying away and by saying these things out loud."

"I've already said all these things out loud," he sighed, "but, obviously, no one was listening."

～～ ～

The feeling was dawning on Rabbi Chaim Levi that not only was he not doing any good, he had actually become just one more facilitator for all that was going wrong in the Jewish world. The Shammanovs' Bar Mitzva was just the tip of the iceberg.

He remembered the Bat Mitzva invitation he had gotten the month before, directing him to a Web site. He had dutifully logged on and looked it up. There he was confronted by a photo of Selma and Max Gutfreund's chubby twelve-year-old daughter Leah in a sleeveless white top, bra strap showing, who managed to give him a braces-filled come-hither look over her bare tattooed shoulder. When he clicked on her picture as instructed, she breathily announced that he was invited to her "golden girl rock concert" and invited him to click onto her video.

Mesmerized with horror and fascination, he clicked.

There he found the child wandering through a mall with a group of her prepubescent friends holding shopping bags as she wiggled her hips and threw back her hair, singing. The lyrics, which he tried hard to decipher, went something like:

If I was rich, I could be a bitch,
I'd never go slow, yo, because of my cash flow, wo!
So don't be a smarty, come to my party.

There was a picture of Leah sitting with provocatively crossed legs on a motorcycle as she sang an off-key rendition of a song that went: *Give me a chance to make you happy, your lovin' me is the key.*

And then he saw something else. There was a link entitled MY RABBI. His heart beating, he clicked on it. There he was confronted by a picture of himself and of the synagogue. *I want to thank Rabbi Levi. He's a super cool dude! Like, he's taught me everything I know.*

He felt like laughing. He felt like weeping. He was furious, mortified, and overwhelmed. He felt like retraining, becoming an electrician or a plumber or any other profession in which you can enter a situation with a competent tool box and fix the bloody problem; a profession where the people who hired you actually respected your expertise.

Instead, he allowed people to enter his synagogue week after week and to leave feeling good about themselves, whether or not they deserved to. He was unable to provide them with true values, true direction. Not that he hadn't tried.

There was that time he had talked to the congregation about the importance of shiva calls to the bereaved. A young widow had complained to him that few people had made condolence calls, and one who did had cornered her young son and told him, "Your father was so good that God needed him more," bringing the child to hysterics, lest he too behave himself into an early grave. Another shul member, who hadn't bothered to show up at all, had come over to her in the supermarket and said, "You were just so together that we didn't think you needed a shiva visit."

He had exhorted his congregation, chastised them, explained to them, entreated them to please *please* visit the bereaved during their week of mourning, not to speak unless spoken to, and to be respectful.

And what had been the result of this heartfelt sermon? A group of synagogue members, together with a sprinkling from the board, had accosted him during afternoon prayers, demanding that he apologize because certain people were now embarrassed and were thinking about leaving the synagogue altogether! And a synagogue, they explained to him ominously, can't afford to lose dues-paying members.

The days when a rabbi got a post for life, and when a congregation would not have dared to oppose him, were over, he thought. Most rabbis felt the yapping at their heels every minute of every day. They felt constantly under review, their every speech fodder for both their enemies and their friends, and that they need only say the wrong thing one too many times to turn friends into enemies and themselves out onto the unemployment lines.

But it wasn't just the fear of losing their jobs. They didn't want to leave because they were invested in the community, caring deeply about the lives of its individuals and families. They wanted to make a difference, and they felt that if only they could hang on just a little while longer, they and their congregation would turn the corner and a great expanse would open before them, a safe harbor in which to dock the ship that swayed and trembled, buffeted by heavy winds and changing tides. If they could only be good captains and navigate correctly, there was no telling what good could be accomplished, how many could be rescued from drowning in heartache or getting eaten by the reconnoitering sharks of modern vices.

He knew he was never going to be an intellectual giant, author of memorably profound works of scholarship. He was fine with that. He had a very simple plan, a very modest life's goal: to do some good. To bring to the people around him some of the largesse of their heritage, to sustain them with the fruits of goodness that came to people who knew who they were, and how they were connected to their history and culture and God. So many ills of the modern world—destroyed families, miserable single men and women looking for connection, angry directionless teenagers seeking solace and meaning in mind-altering drugs—could be healed by spirituality. The Torah had answers. He wanted so much to give them, but no one would let him.

Places of worship and communities had turned into hotbeds of strife and competition and a way to show off material wealth. And many times congregants, who were unable to keep up with the Schwartzes or the Malins or the Rollands, were pushed beyond their means into bankruptcy or worse—economic activities that bordered on the unethical or downright criminal. Perhaps it was inevitable, given the cost of day school tuition, monster mortgages, and unrelenting excesses in lifestyle adopted by many communities as the norm and relentlessly foisted upon all those wishing to remain members in good standing. The striving for excess had created a culture that dripped with excess, a culture that was the opposite of everything Judaism valued and cherished and taught.

Despite his better judgment, he had let circumstances and his wife bully him into taking on a congregation that had been blackballed by everyone he respected. Since taking the job at Swallow Lake, he'd been frozen out of alumni events at Bernstein, which had taken him off their mailing list. The heartfelt letters he had received from his grandfather's friends and colleagues, urging him to reconsider, had gone unanswered. He had placed all his eggs in the nest of Swallow Lake. If this didn't work out, he didn't know what he would do.

He wondered, for the first time, if perhaps Delilah was right. Maybe he should try his hand at something else, some little business he could work hard at and build up, a job that would supply him with what he needed to keep his wife happy in nice clothes and jewelry and household help. A job that would let him buy a roof that couldn't be whisked away the moment he failed to supply the flattery necessary to keep afloat the overblown ego of some self-important *macher*. A home he could call his own, in a neighborhood full of normal people who didn't need three thousand square feet of living space filled with in-your-face excess. A place where people took care of their own children, made their own gefilte fish for Passover, and served it by themselves to beloved family members around their own dining room tables. A place where people didn't think it was what they owned that was important, but what they gave.

Maybe, he thought, I can't create such a place in Swallow Lake. But maybe, just maybe, it already existed somewhere else in America—or in Israel—untouched, forgotten by time, and hidden off somewhere, like Brigadoon. If he could find it, perhaps there still was a chance he could manage to do some good and be happy.

But for now—he sighed—he had to get Viktor Shammanov's son ready for a Bar Mitzva that would no doubt have much bar and very little mitzva.

{ TWENTY-SIX }

*L*ike Jews on the night of the final plague, ready to pack up and leave for the Promised Land, the members of Ohel Aaron tensed, waiting for the arrival of the coveted invitation to the Shammanovs' Bar Mitzva. Soon, there arose from each household a whoop of joy, or a bitter sigh of regret, as it became clear who had gotten the golden tickets and whose home the angel had passed over.

As those fortunate enough to have experienced it related, a limousine pulled up to the house and a tuxedoed servant holding a silver tray got out and rang the bell. On the tray was a single white orchid and a handmade music box. When you opened it, it played the "Cell Block Tango" from *Chicago*. There inside was a ten-page invitation, each page describing yet another event as well as the dress code they expected (sport casual, black tie for dinner, golf and tennis wear, swimwear). The idea of swimwear in the doldrums of a freezing East Coast winter was enough to warm the hearts of every lucky invitation holder. Invitees were given the date and time they needed to arrive at the airport, but no other information. The mystery of it all thrilled them.

There began, then, a certain shift in the communal dynamics. Those preparing for the trip began to meet in groups to discuss their wardrobes and their household arrangements. They chattered over the phone and in coffee shops and over their shopping carts in supermarket aisles. How many dresses? How many shoes? What kind of hats?

Gradually, those who had not received invitations felt themselves weeded out socially. And even though it was clear that the Shammanovs could not have invited everyone nor, in the very short time that they had become active in the synagogue, could they possibly have formed a reasonable or accurate opinion of anyone, the uninvited began to think people were looking at them differently, wondering: Why not them? What had the Shammanovs perceived about them that others had not yet been alert enough to discover?

Alas, there was more than a shred of truth to these perceptions. Despite the fact that it was unclear on what basis invitations had or had not been sent out, it was nevertheless assumed by those invited that those left out were in some way to be held responsible for their fate.

The uninvited heard the communal buzz, like a chain saw, cutting down their reputations along with the community's cohesiveness. Among themselves, they began to search out answers. It was a fact that certain synagogue members had been invited to meet the Shammanovs at the rabbi's home and at the Shammanovs' home. And who had been the driving force behind both events? They all came to the same conclusion: Rebbitzin Delilah Levi, dearest friend of Joie Shammanov.

Thus there began the communal wooing of Delilah Levi. Those who hadn't thought much about her until this time suddenly remembered to invite her over for tea parties and book clubs and trips to the city. Those who had actively disliked her now donated heavily to her *chesed* project, parting with fairly new and expensive bags with a groan. They offered her their au pairs to help babysit her little boy, lent her their maids, sent flowers on her birthday, and cakes for the Sabbath. They stopped calling her at all hours of the day and night and made sure to come up to her in the synagogue and compliment her on her outfit, her hat, her husband's "brilliant" sermon, her little boy's amazing cuteness. They helped her get appointments with the best hairdressers and manicurists and cosmeticians. They showed up at sisterhood meetings. In short, they groveled.

But as time grew closer and invitations still failed to arrive, it became clear that mere hints were not enough. Like Hasidim who go to their rebbe, asking him to intercede with God on their behalf, those of a gentler nature humbly approached the rabbi's wife, pleading with her to find it in her heart to get them an invitation. This, of course, she could not do. After all, who was she to make up the Shammanovs' guest list? Besides, most of the people who were calling her had never even said two words to her before, so why should she put herself out now when they were falling all over themselves to be nice?

The others, mostly low self-esteem types, were unbearably hurt, depressed, angry, and consumed with a desire for revenge. As they could not see their way clear to being able to avenge themselves on the Shammanovs, they looked for the next best thing: either invitation holders or Rabbi Chaim and his wife, who had introduced the Shammanovs to the community in the first place. They suddenly began to find all kinds of faults with Rabbi Chaim's speeches, which in the past they had either ignored or enjoyed. They began to talk about the way the rebbitizin's hair stuck out of her hats, and the expensive new clothes she had suddenly started wearing, no doubt at the expense of dues-paying synagogue members. Rumors began to circulate about how the Levis had been run out of town in their last congregation. And someone who had known a roommate of Delilah's at Bernstein Women's College even whispered a thing or two that put all listeners into a state of delicious, openmouthed shock.

Busy choosing head coverings to match her synagogue dresses, her evening wear, her beach cover-ups, and her Sabbath afternoon clothes, Delilah was oblivious to the boiling cauldron of communal strife. But when someone left an anonymous note in the rabbi's mailbox, describing with malicious joy how they felt a religious obligation to inform him of all the things that were being said about him and his wife, Chaim finally had no choice but to interrupt her dreamy happiness.

"Who," he said, dangling a white slip of paper between his thumb and forefinger, "is Yitzie Polinsky?"

Her face lost color. "Oh, isn't that the baby crying?" She hurried up the stairs.

Slowly and deliberately, he climbed up after her. "Delilah?"

"Who's been buzzing in your ear, Chaim?"

"Would you like to see this anonymous letter someone slipped into my mail?"

She shook her head vociferously. "I went out with him once or twice in college. Rivkie fixed me up with him. But he turned out to be a yeshiva bum."

Chaim looked down at the letter in his hand, undecided. Finally, he shrugged and left the room. He didn't say another word to her until dinner, at which time he finished his veal cutlet, wiped his lips, and placed his knife and fork on his plate with careful precision. "This," he told Delilah, "has got to stop. Delilah, you've got to talk to the Shammanovs!"

"What, exactly, do you want me to say to them? That they have to invite the entire shul? What, are we in fourth grade? They'd have to charter three more planes and pay for three times the food!"

"This Bar Mitzva is destroying the community. People are bitter and jealous, and they hold us responsible!"

"Us? What do mean?"

"Well, after all, it was you who brought the Shammanovs into the community in the first place. You are the one who decided which of our neighbors would be invited to their home and to ours."

"I invited the people who have been nice to us. And the board."

"Exactly! You invited all the big shots and left out the ones who are just ordinary, good-hearted, hardworking members of my congregation!"

This, of course, was absolutely true. She'd left out the wig-wearers, the day-school PTA moms, the makeup-free mikva stalwarts, and the yentas with complaints. Delilah wasn't interested in the boring accountants and lawyers and Hebrew teachers. But then, neither were the Shammanovs.

When Joie had asked for her help in deciding the guest list, she'd seen it as a perfect opportunity to weed out the shleppers and put together a wonderful weekend with fun people who would know how to enjoy themselves without putting everyone (read: the rabbi's wife) on a big guilt trip for wearing a bikini or dancing or taking a swim. She'd suggested inviting women whom she thought would be amusing for Joie and, yes, for herself, young women who were rich and thin and sexy and who wore their designer clothes well and would know what to do at a concert by the legendary rock stars who would no doubt be entertaining them, no expense spared. Imagine: Mick Jagger, with his sneer and swagger! Or Ricky Martin with those hips, just inches away from her! She just couldn't wait.

"Chaim, what is it you want from me? You were the one who told me to go out into the community. To be friendly. To help you get new members, didn't you? So I did! *Now* what is it you want?"

He stared at her blankly. It was like shouting over the Berlin Wall. He shook his head and left, spending as much time as possible hibernating in his study until the wretched event would finally be over and peace and sanity would, hopefully, be restored to his congregation.

The day finally arrived. A limousine picked Delilah and Chaim up and drove them to the airport, where a huge refrigerated truck was loading into a cargo plane enough food to feed the U.S. Army in Iraq. A rabbi in a white coat and long beard was supervising.

"They are using Golden Caterers," Solange whispered.

"The ones that cater at the Waldorf and the Plaza?" Felice asked, surprised. "They absolutely never cater outside!"

"I've been watching the plane loading. Whole cows, dozens of them, glatt kosher; a farmload of chickens and turkeys! Pounds of caviar and kosher French foie gras—which is only produced once a year, so you have to get it just in time," Amber whispered back in awe. "And truffles, Swiss chocolate, raspberries, baking supplies. The chefs are flying out with all their pans and pots and utensils, and whole sets of dishes. They even brought along their own stoves and dishwashers, because they don't want to have to kosher the hotel's."

"Wow, what a production," Mariette marveled.

"Wait. I'm sure this is nothing compared to what they have planned," Felice predicted, something to which they all silently agreed. "Look, there's Delilah. My, doesn't she look fetching." Felice arched her brow. "If that skirt was any tighter—"

"Or shorter. Really, ever since she and Joie became such dear friends, the woman has—"

"Careful," Amber whispered.

Solange stopped abruptly, looking around her edgily.

It was like being in the Gulag. You didn't want anyone to overhear you saying anything that could even vaguely be interpreted as negative about either the rabbi or his wife. The rumor was going around that Lorraine Harris had said something in the gym to a friend on the treadmill about an outfit Delilah had dressed her baby in and almost immediately had gotten a call that the invitation had been rescinded. "The messenger actually came to Lorraine's house and asked for it back! They wouldn't even let her keep the music box!" Felice shuddered.

"All I was going to say was isn't it a wonderful thing that Delilah has become so close to the Shammanovs? For the synagogue, I mean..." Solange's voice trailed off.

They waited in smiling silence as Delilah strode up, air-kissing each of them. "Well, here we all are! What fun this is going to be!" Delilah whooped.

The women glanced at each other with strained smiles, being careful to stay politely behind Delilah and Rabbi Chaim as they joined the line of the privileged few invited to board the Shammanovs' own private jet. The rest of the guests had to content themselves with a normal charter flight.

The Shammanovs' private jet was like something out of the Victoria and Albert Museum, done up in red with lots of gold braid and oil paintings of faded pastoral scenes and nudes. There were only 50 seats on the plane, instead of the usual 120. There were private servants who prepared the meals and served them, and first-run movies.

Delilah looked around her. The entire board was there. The men were already huddled with Viktor. She noticed that each one of them made an effort to get him alone whenever they could, and that Viktor was constantly in clandestine whispered conferences with the richest people in Swallow Lake and the environs. She wondered what they were talking about, but didn't trouble her head too much about it. After all, the really important thing was that everyone was being incredibly nice to her.

She was almost ready to make her shipment of designer handbags to Israel's terror victims, and donations continued to pour in. Friends of Solange, Felice, and Amber kept asking her what she and Chaim were doing for their summer vacation; if they'd consider joining them at their private beach houses, country estates, or ranches in South America. She said she'd let them know.

She and Joie sat next to each other on the plane, talking about the latest movie-star-couple breakup, while their babies were cared for by Joie's daytime and nighttime au pairs.

"I've hired another au pair, who is waiting for us at the hotel. The concierge arranged it. She's going to be my water au pair, because you need someone to be especially careful with a baby near the water, and I get so sleepy in the sun. Also, if—God forbid!—one of the other au pairs gets sick, she can take over, because goodness knows I've got my hands full with supervising this whole shindig."

And then, before they knew it, the plane had landed, refueled, and taken off again. After hours over the open sea, it suddenly hovered above a series of incredibly green and magnificent islands. "Ooooh!" everyone gasped, third-graders on their first trip to Disneyland, as the plane came in for a landing amid palms and mountains and beaches. Dark-skinned girls in hula outfits waited on the tarmac. Hips swaying, they placed thick purple, white, and pink leis around the guests as they descended. "Don't worry about the luggage. It'll be brought to you," someone said, directing them to waiting limousines.

Delilah leaned back, sighing with contentment, as the car drove off. How far she had come from middle-income housing projects near the bay, she thought, holding her baby in her lap and threading her arm through her husband's. She rested her head against Chaim's shoulder. She felt a surge of gratitude toward him for being her partner and making all this possible.

He looked at her, surprised and touched, and patted her hand. "Happy, my love?"

She nodded. For the first time she felt it was really true. She *was* happy. She had everything she'd always dreamed about.

And it was just the beginning.

{ TWENTY-SEVEN }

*H*otel employees welcomed them tenderly, as if they were delightful friends who had been away too long. An unseen hand gently placed a tall glass filled with untold amounts of gaily colored alcohol and a little umbrella into her hand. She followed a bellboy through a spectacular outdoor lobby facing the sea until she reached her suite.

Oh! Delilah thought, looking around the suite. It was like an Entertainment Channel special featuring "celeb perks." She sank into the pillows of the couch, fingering the bows of a huge gift basket.

"Delilah!"

"Huh?"

"The baby, remember?" Chaim held out the sweating, unhappy infant to her.

She looked at him, annoyed. Little Abraham with his endless secretions and appetites. She took him reluctantly, shaking her head. "Look,

Chaim, if this weekend is going to work, I have to have someone to help me. Otherwise, I won't be able to do anything."

"What, exactly, are you planning to do?"

She thought fast. "Well, help Joie through it. Sit next to her in the synagogue during the ceremony, explaining things. You know she expects me to. And I can't do it with a crying baby."

He shrugged. "Well, I can't take care of him. I've got to be up there with the Bar Mitzva boy. He's going to need all the help he can get."

"Not you! I need an au pair."

"Can't the Shammanovs' three au pairs watch him?"

She shook her head. "Viktor wants them to concentrate on Natasha."

"Don't you have to bring one of those with you?"

"No, actually the concierge can arrange it. Joie told me all about it." She handed the baby back to him and picked up the phone.

The baby, hungry and hot, with aching ears, began to whimper.

"They say it's absolutely no problem," she said, hanging up the phone triumphantly. "They'll send us one. We can have her for the whole weekend."

"And the cost?"

She looked at him steadily. "Look, we are getting this entire vacation for free, so we can afford to splurge on this one little thing." She walked over, patting down his tie. "Come on, honey, otherwise I'll never get to go swimming or anything."

"Oh, so that's what this is really about! Delilah, it's just not appropriate for the rabbi's wife to be walking around in a bikini."

The baby was now screaming so loud he'd completely lost his breath, his face going frighteningly red. Reluctantly, she took the infant back, unbottoning her blouse and whipping out a breast. Little Abe, already familiar with the lay of the land, wasn't taking any chances; he latched on to the nipple quickly, hanging on with desperate determination.

"Ouch, that hurts! You little leech! Look, Chaim, don't be a fuddy-duddy. These are all fun people who won't mind a bit. I made sure of that."

"What?"

"I mean, Joie made sure of that."

"So it's true, then! You *did* pick the guest list."

"Don't be silly. Joie made the final decision."

"But you were the one who told her who'd be fun and who wouldn't?"

Delilah, who was holding the baby in one arm and rummaging through her luggage with the other as she looked for her bathing suit, cover-up, trendy baseball cap, flip-flops, and eyewear, looked up for a moment. "You say that as if it's a bad thing."

"Don't you understand?" he exploded. "You—no, *we*—are guilty of everything people have been accusing us of! And they are absolutely right to be furious."

"They're just jealous. You know what? Maybe they'll learn a lesson from all this. Isn't that what you always say, that God gives us troubles to open our hearts and make us repent and become better people?"

He stared. "And what, exactly, are the people back home trudging through the icy sludge supposed to learn from this, Delilah?"

She thought about it for a moment. "That they should be nicer to their rabbi's wife," she said, shrugging. "But when I get back, I promise you I'll give them every opportunity. After all, doesn't the Torah tell us not to hold a grudge?"

He shook his head, giving up.

The pool was surrounded by little three-sided tents, inside of which there were two chaise lounges. In one tent she spotted Viktor, deep in discussion with Stuart Grodin. She thought about waving to them, but they only had eyes for each other. The pool boy led her to an empty tent, handing her thick white towels and arranging her lounge covers. Delilah left the baby in his carriage and stretched out. Soon a dark-haired Hawaiian beauty came by.

"Mrs. Levi? I'm Lana, your au pair for the weekend. Aloha. Happy to meet you."

Delilah swung her legs over the side of the chaise. "And I'm *delighted* to meet you." She grinned, stretching out her hand. "Well, here he is, the baby. Abraham. Little Abe." She made appropriately maternal faces at the exhausted baby, who looked back at her, bleary-eyed. "He's a little knocked out from the flight. But here is some formula, and his bottles and pacifier, and his favorite giraffe."

And just like that, little Abe disappeared.

She leaned back, stretching out, allowing her robe to open, and cautiously peeked around to see if anyone had reacted. Seeing nothing, she took it off altogether.

It was a white suit, covered with tiny gold cross-stitch embroidery. She looked, she realized, absolutely luscious in it. Plates of pineapple were brought to her, and a bar menu. She chose a Heavenly Hawaiian Smoothee, made with frozen yogurt, fresh tropical fruits, and some kind of liquor. She wasn't an expert, but, boy, what a wallop! Considering that she was still experiencing the effects of the welcome drink, whatever inhibitions still lingered were soon sent on their way.

She leaned back, boldly lifting off the baseball cap. Covering her hair suddenly seemed ludicrous, considering the vast expanses of forbidden flesh now open for public viewing. She pushed back her sunglasses, surveying the new world. She had no idea that at the same time, the world was surveying her.

Just across the pool lay Dr. Joseph Rolland. From behind his sunglasses, he examined the rabbi's wife.

She was like a big, soft, sexy doll, he thought. Blond hair (this was definitely not a wig, he realized, delighted) lightened from darkish honey to fourteen-karat gold, the shadings competently but not expertly done. It was the kind of color a man with meticulous and expensive tastes might secretly sneer at after he'd had his good time. Her lips were full yet delicate, when not cheapened by a slash of some too-bright trendy shade as they were now. The eyes were a glorious blue but a little narrow at the corners, the only part of her face that really looked better with her obvious and carefully applied makeup. Without it, he considered, her face would look more deliberate and calculating, like an animal scurrying for escape or chasing its next meal.

The bathing suit was nice but, given his experience with keeping high-maintenance girlfriends happy, he knew it had been found on a bargain rack in an expensive department store because of some fluke of size or color or style that didn't mesh with popular taste. Yet it looked wonderful on her. She had the knack, which very few women have, of making clothes her own so that you couldn't imagine them on anyone else. No one would look at her and say, What a beautiful bathing suit! They'd say, What a beautiful woman!

He was quite surprised to see her at the pool in this state of undress. He knew she was careful never to put herself outside the religious pale. Nothing too low-cut or sleeveless or far above the knees. And her hair was always covered. He blessed his good luck as he studied her slim ankles and shapely calves, her curvy wide hips and slim waist, with just the right absence of any excess fat to make her truly delicious. She was turning to talk to the women on all sides who had gathered around her, her head high, her smile and laugh animated, her expression alternately amazed or scandalized, while all the while her eyes cast furtive, searching glances around her that acknowledged and ignored the male appreciation being beamed at her from all directions.

"Like some more sunscreen, honey?" Mariette offered her husband, as she covered her nose with white goo.

He jerked back to reality. "Huh! Oh, ah. Well. Sure. Thanks, Mariette," he murmured, allowing her to massage it into his chest. He saw Delilah glance up and stare in his direction. He nodded and waved. Mariette turned around to see who it was he was greeting. She saw Delilah lying there in her bathing suit, and her eyes narrowed.

Delilah lowered her head. Mariette had her hands full, she thought, flattered and scandalized. He was sort of cute though, she thought, in a very subdued and older-man kind of way. He looked as if he had had lots and lots of experience. But even those men eventually find their perfect match and settle down. Look at Warren Beatty. Look at Michael Douglas. Of course, they were usually close to sixty and being blown off by chorus girls when it finally happened, but *c'est la vie*. He was old enough to be her . . . *sugar daddy*, a small voice inside piped up. She gave the idea a slap to see if it would howl and go away, but it didn't. It just gave a squeak, to prove that it was real and flexible.

But even Delilah Levi had her limits, she told herself. Besides, if it was just money she was after, there were plenty of ways to get it. And plenty of younger men who had it.

She put on her robe, turning her attention to the small group that had gathered around her as the women of Ohel Aaron zeroed in on their favorite rebbitzin, the one who had made it possible for them to leave behind the freezing cold Connecticut winter for a few days on this ultimate, all-expenses-paid dream vacation in Hawaii.

Those lucky enough to find empty chairs near her sat down as if they were at the Western Wall and had finally maneuvered their way into touching distance of the holy stones. The others crowded in nearby, having no choice but to content themselves with turning their bodies in her direction so they could catch her every word and perhaps seize an opportunity to participate in the conversation. And when they looked at Delilah, they couldn't believe they'd never noticed how beautiful she was: a golden girl, her skin turning a little bronze as it tanned under expensive sun cream, supplied in the gift basket each guest had found in their room. Beautiful and young and wise. And smart! And funny! Why, they found themselves laughing and laughing at the least little roll of her eye or slightly raised inflection of her voice. They adored Delilah Levi, so kind and friendly and down-to-earth! Not one of those hypocritical fanatics whom everyone had to tiptoe around in case they bumped into her halo.

And Delilah liked them, for the most part. But not enough to put herself out. She was content to smile with noblesse oblige as she accepted offers of chocolate-covered macadamia nuts and *Cosmopolitan* magazines. She closed her eyes, letting the sunlight dance on her lids, listening to the sound of the waves crashing soothingly on the white beach sand below the pool.

As all religious people know, there are two ways to take any fortunate event that occurs in your life. The first is to accept it as a pure blessing from God, a reward for numerous good deeds. The second is to view it as God's way of emptying your mitzva-reward bank account, as He readies the roof to fall in upon your head for your sins.

But Delilah wasn't thinking about either possibility. She was simply living in the present, imagining it would go on this way forever.

{ TWENTY-EIGHT }

The next morning they gathered on the beach as instructed, waiting to be borne off to the mysterious venue of the Bar Mitzva to end all Bar Mitzvas. At that point, everyone was so psyched up, only a few would have been surprised if the ground had opened up and a rocket had emerged from an underground silo ready to launch them to the moon.

"Have you figured out the theme?" Amber asked Mariette, who shook her head.

Every Bar and Bat Mitzva has to have a theme. Becoming responsible for your deeds is such a downer. So people have a gangster theme, with each table commemorating another Jewish crook or murderer. Or a shopping theme, with each table representing a different store: Bergdorf's, Nordstrom's, Lord & Taylor. Or a Greek theme—which is a bit problematic, considering that Jews annually celebrate the victory of the Maccabees over the vicious Hellenization program that almost destroyed Judaism—but, hey, togas are so cute.

People were still not sure what the Shammanovs' theme was.

"First, I thought it would be maybe *Eighty Days Around the World*. But then you'd need a hot-air balloon, and I don't see any," Mariette said, scanning the area.

"It could be *Swiss Family Robinson*," Felice murmured.

Just then they spied the sails in the distance, as a flotilla of boats headed toward shore and landed, one by one. Burly, handsome sailors, their tanned and muscled thighs set off perfectly by white shorts, jumped out to haul the boats in. One by one, the sailors approached the women, their smiles dazzling in their sun-kissed faces, as they picked up the valises and led the wives on board, their husbands following as an afterthought. Soon the entire Bar Mitzva party had pushed off from shore into the wide ocean.

"Oh, look at the whales!" Delilah shouted, squeezing Chaim's hand.

"Where?" Mariette demanded.

"Right there! See that spray of water?" Dr. Rolland exclaimed, pointing to the horizon as he moved toward the boat railing next to Delilah. She felt his shoulder brush against hers, his hip connect for a moment, but when she turned to him with a raised eyebrow, he seemed completely oblivious, looking out to sea, his hand clasped around his wife's waist. Delilah shrugged, moving away.

Soon the sea was full of whales, dashing around the boats, thrilling them.

"I don't know, they're awfully big. Isn't this a little dangerous?" Amber pointed out. "I mean, couldn't they turn our boat over?"

Just as she said it, a huge one brushed past the boat ahead of them, dousing the passengers with water.

"Oh, my clothes are soaked!" one woman wept, very not in the spirit of the party. But Joie wasn't having any of that. Soon the woman found herself in a lifeboat, speeding back to shore. Her husband waved to her. Joie took a megaphone: "And if anyone else gets wet, don't worry. We've got plenty of clothes on board! Relax!"

"Maybe the theme is *Jaws*?" Felice said, shuddering as the poor woman faded in the distance.

"Or *Mutiny on the Bounty*," Chaim whispered.

Just then it came into view: a fabulous cruise ship flying Russian flags and flags with . . . with—no, it couldn't be—flags with the face of Anatoly Shammanov, the Bar Mitzva boy! Soon the guests were being helped from the sailboats up to the ship.

They were greeted by a group of Hawaiian musicians who began to beat their drums and play their slack-key guitars. Lovely girls in grass skirts and leis undulated all over the deck, giving out grass skirts to all the women.

"Everybody hula!" a deejay commanded them.

"Isn't this fun?" Joie shouted over to Delilah, who was busy fastening the grass skirt around her hips.

"The best!" Delilah shouted back, outswiveling the dancers as best she could.

Then the girls were replaced by men naked to the waist, juggling burning torches as hypnotic drums began to play. And then, suddenly, a loudspeaker invited them all to the right side of the boat.

They peered at the empty sea, where a tiny speck appeared in the distance. It got larger and larger.

"Look!" someone finally screamed, pointing into the sea. "Dolphins!"

There were dozens of them.

"Dolphins? Who cares about bloody fish? It's my Anatoly!" Viktor Shammanov boomed. And sure enough, seated on a little rubber throne, holding reins around the heads of the mammals and flanked by waterskiers who looked like former KGB agents, was the Bar Mitzva boy.

"Ve try to train vhale." Viktor shrugged. "But vhales not interested!"

The child looked terrified.

"Khere khe comes. King Neptune!" Victor roared, as the child shakily climbed up to the deck. He lifted the boy onto his shoulders and began to hula.

So, was that the theme? Pagan gods? Or was that just a little side remark, a joke, Rabbi Chaim wondered, looking at Viktor dancing wildly and Delilah undulating in her grass skirt. His eyes widened in alarm.

He was trapped, he thought. There wasn't a single thing he could do, cornered as he was with the entire synagogue board on a boat in shark-infested waters and a current that ended in Japan. He couldn't exactly walk out in protest, now could he? Whatever was going to be, was going to be. He looked longingly at the sailboats now casting off back to shore as the band struck up again and the hula lesson continued.

Finally, they were all given keys to their staterooms to prepare for the evening ahead. He took two aspirin and lay down, trying to compose himself for the Friday-night services still to come. His head felt like a drum on which a healthy native was pounding out an emphatic tribal message.

Services were held in the main ballroom, which had been transformed into a synagogue. It seated a thousand comfortably. Delilah looked around, realizing that they had been joined by numerous Russian-speaking families who were certainly not from Swallow Lake.

"It's all Viktor's friends and relatives." Joie rolled her eyes. "Russian families are very close."

The service went along well enough, Chaim thought. And afterward, they went to the second ballroom for dinner. Food and booze flowed incessantly like the sea down the gullets of the celebrants. And just when they were about ready to doze off, the cheerleaders came out. There were about twenty of them, healthy, voluptuous, young, in tiny skirts and sleeveless tops. They bounded onto the dance floor with their pom-poms, singing a cheer that incorporated the name Anatoly.

"Isn't great?" Viktor laughed. "Lakers' Girls."

"As in Los Angeles Lakers cheerleaders?" Arthur choked, stunned.

"Ve vant only best." Viktor smiled. "For Anatoly. Go, Anatoly, go! Girls teach you cheer."

The chubby teenager ran out into the center of the floor.

All the men got up and jockeyed for the best eyeful. Joseph, Arthur, Ari, and Stuart nudged one another. Delilah was there too, right in front, not wanting to miss anything, her arm around Joie's waist.

And then the girls disappeared and a live band began to play balalaikas and other traditional Russian instruments.

"But Viktor, I told you, Jews don't play music on the Sabbath. It's not allowed!" Chaim pleaded.

"Rabbi don't vorry! Musicians are not Jews—don't even like Jews! Are Russians. For Russians, it's not Sabbath!" Viktor laughed, linking arms with the dancers as they stamped out "Kalinka-Malinka," carrying him off.

Chaim looked over at this scene. Friday night, the beginning of the Sabbath, the holy day of rest.

"Rabbi! This is a desecration of Shabbes! You have to get that band to stop playing!" Arthur Malin demanded. "This is a disgrace! You have to talk to the Shammanovs!"

"Arthur, I tried—"

"Try again!" Arthur shouted, scandalized. "Get Delilah to talk to them!"

Chaim looked around for her. She was in the center of the dance floor, clapping. "Delilah," he hissed, taking her arm.

She turned around and looked at him. "Isn't this great?"

"What's the matter with you? It's a desecration of the Sabbath!"

"Why?"

"Because they are playing music!"

"But they're not Jewish! They can play!"

"No, they can't! Jews aren't allowed to pay people to work for them on the Sabbath. Everyone has to have a day of rest. Arthur Malin is furious."

"Arthur Malin has five maids who work for him on the Sabbath on a regular basis! All of these people have maids who work for them on the Sabbath. And besides, aren't the waiters working? Aren't the sailors who are running the boat working?"

"That's different!"

"Why?"

"It's—" He suddenly felt his head swim. He had to talk to Viktor again. To explain. He looked around for him, but his host was now in the center of an impenetrable knot of dancers, sitting on his haunches and kicking out his feet as he balanced bottles of beer on his head. Right next to him was Delilah.

He turned around, dizzy, groping his way toward the bar. "Double scotch," he said. He held the glass in his unsteady hand as he weaved his way through the long halls back to his cabin. He unlocked the door and looked in on his sleeping son.

"You can go now, thanks," he told the au pair. "I'll watch him." Then he stumbled to the veranda. The night air was mild and cool. He sat down in a deck chair, gulping down the liquor, watching the dark waves as they carried him farther into the night.

～ ⌒ ～

The next day, the guests, hung over and exhausted, dressed in their good suits, their pastel hats, their custom wigs, their spike-heeled Jimmy Choos, their diamond earrings and brooches, made their way to the ballroom-turned-synagogue to witness the Bar Mitzva of Anatoly Shammanov.

All eyes were on Delilah, who was dressed in a pink brocade suit. She sat next to Joie, who wore a little black dress and a diamond-and-onyx necklace that looked like the Crown Jewels and cascaded down her generous cleavage like a waterfall inside a cave. A pashmina, brought along because Delilah had advised her friend that cleavage in the synagogue freaked out the rabbi, lay forgotten in her lap. Delilah didn't notice. She was totally preoccupied with examining the truly amazing creation on Joie's head: a hat with a large stylized horsehair flower and striped coque feathers.

"Love the hat!" Delilah whispered.

"Thanks! Love yours," Joie giggled.

Anatoly mounted the steps that led to the bimah, stepping up to the plate, as it were, to read the scripture of the week from the Haftarah. Unlike the whiz kids who read the entire Torah portion from the unvoweled and unpunctuated scrolls of the Torah, all he had to do was remember to read the transliterated Hebrew words of a short selection from the Prophets to the tune he'd been taught.

Chaim stood next to the child, wondering which of them was more nervous.

Anatoly cleared his throat. Then he began:

"La ...... LA...... la.... la..... LA la la............ LA..... la.............. la LA la...
la LA...
.... LA LA.."

Omigod. She saw Chaim wipe beads of sweat off his brow as he whispered to the boy, probably feeding him every incoherent word. At this rate, it was going to take hours. She slid down in her seat, casting nervous glances at Joie. But Joie was just looking at the boy with a fixed smile on her face, and was that—could it be—a yawn? Delilah exhaled. As long as no one broke down in tears, or ran away, or admitted defeat, it would be fine.

Joie leaned in and whispered. "It's a shame his mother didn't come."

Delilah looked around the packed room, surprised there could be anybody left behind in the Ukraine. "Why isn't she here?"

"Because she's a bitch. Besides, she's not Jewish, so all this upsets her. I mean, she had him baptized in the Greek Orthodox Church when Viktor wasn't looking." Joie grimaced. "Can you imagine? Viktor hit the ceiling, of course. He put the kid's head under a faucet and washed it off. 'He's my son, and he's a Jew, like me!' he told her."

Delilah swallowed hard, looking up at her husband, who stood sweating next to the boy at the bimah. According to Jewish law, a person was the same religion as his mother, not his father. "So he was converted, right? Anatoly, I mean?"

"Converted? Why? His father is a Jew. Anyhow, the rabbi who converted me said it wasn't necessary."

Delilah stared at her husband, standing with his arm around the Bar Mitzva boy, a Greek Orthodox Christian.

Forty-five excruciatingly long minutes later, the torture finally ground to a halt. The child was pelted by candies, and finally, finally, the fun could begin in earnest, as soon as the pesky restrictions of the Sabbath day were over. But first, they had to sit through Chaim's sermon. Delilah leaned back, sighing.

Chaim walked up to the podium. He coughed, then wiped his glistening forehead with a tissue. "When the Jews were in the desert, God asked them to build a tabernacle. Not because God needed a sanctuary. After all, God is everywhere. No, He asked it of us, because He knows the limitations of human beings. He gives us the sun, and what does He ask of us? To light a candle. A measly little candle. That's all."

Delilah looked up, suddenly guilt-stricken, the words playing in her head like a familiar tune. She had heard this before.

"But for many, even that is too much. Remember that when you feel the sun on your face every morning, when a healthy, beautiful new child or grandchild is placed in your arms. Remember all God does for you and the little He asks.

"Place yourself at His service, Anatoly, on this your Bar Mitzva day, the day a Jew becomes responsible for his own sins before God. Your parents are absolved. They are not responsible for your sins, and you aren't responsible for theirs. Now you control your life and your relationship to God. Give Him your devotion. Accept His demands on you." He hugged the child and motioned for him to sit down. Then he turned to the congregation. "Under His guidance, let us eliminate from our public and private lives every aspect that is not worthy of our relationship with Him. Those who resist God will be shattered."

Delilah looked around at the startled faces of the audience, who shifted uncomfortably in their seats. What was Chaim doing? she thought, alarmed.

"In the words of the great Samson Raphael Hirsch, joy is only to be found in the advancement of good and right. May your sons step into your place and may *you*, the parents, be *worthy* of emulation," he said pointedly.

"Don't depend on material prosperity to save you, or the approval of other people. The future depends on ethical and dutiful conduct."

Delilah darted nervous glances at Joie, who stared straight ahead, attempting to suppress yet another yawn. Delilah tried to motion to Chaim to speed it up, but he never even glanced in her direction.

Chaim closed his book and kissed it with reverence. "Anatoly, I congratulate you. May your parents be blessed through you and may you be blessed through them."

Delilah let herself exhale in relief.

While the prayer service continued, most of the women filed out. They strolled slowly around the deck, waiting for the men to finish so they could go into the dining room and partake of a magnificent kiddush, to be followed by a still more elaborate lunch, whose combined caloric intake would be enough to wipe out famine in a small African village. In the afternoon, they would groaningly fall into bed, sleeping through the numerous, annoying constraints of the Sabbath day until the sun sank into the sea, and the party they had flown halfway around the world to attend could begin.

Delilah found she was too excited to nap.

"Where are you going?" Chaim called after her sleepily.

"I'll be back soon. I just need to walk some of this food off."

She closed the door behind her.

"Well, hello," she heard over her shoulder. She turned. It was Joseph Rolland.

"Oh, Shabbat Shalom," she said primly. "Where's Mariette?"

"Now, now, we don't want to talk about Mariette, do we, Delilah?" He smiled at her, a smile he used confidently, whipping it out and dusting it off like a faithful surgical tool that had performed miracles numerous times, even on the comatose and half dead. Delilah, who had been hoping to run into Mick Jagger or Keith Richards, gave him a respectful nod-to-older-man, which—had it been taped and shown to the morality police—would have proclaimed her innocence.

This surprised and wounded Dr. Rolland, who was used to the magic of his white coat immediately transforming women into eager contestants on the win-a-night-with-Joseph-Rolland game show. It made him feel that he was losing it, that he was getting . . . old. He looked her over, her image suddenly transformed from an amusing dalliance into a seriously important project upon which much depended.

"Mind if I walk with you?"

She hesitated, then shrugged. What could she say?

"You know, I've been wanting a few moments alone with you for some time."

She looked down at her shoes. "Really? Why?"

"Well." He thought fast. "I don't think enough people really appreciate how difficult your job is."

"Oh, that's certainly true. It's really nice of you to say so."

Encouraged, he kept going. "I mean, the constant visitors, the politics, the catering to everyone's needs. And you are so young! It doesn't seem fair that those soft fine shoulders should have to bear so much."

Delilah straightened her back, feeling almost as if he'd caressed her. Where was this leading? she wondered. "No one forced me into it."

He inhaled, surprised by her resistance. He wasn't used to working very hard where women were concerned. But he liked a challenge, and his ego was involved, so he was willing to put up with it. "No, no, that's true. But sometimes our lives take turns that we don't expect. We drift along until one day, we wake up and find ourselves so far from where we thought we'd be, with so many needs that have gone unmet for so long. . . ." He stopped, his hands gripping the guardrails, as his eyes looked with what he hoped was mysterious longing off into the sea.

Delilah stood still. Was he for real? Rich, attractive Dr. Joseph Rolland, with the international jet-setting career and the wondrous mansion with its own gazebo, outdoor pool, and tennis courts overlooking the lake, had "unmet needs" that Mrs. Perfect didn't have a clue about? And he was standing here, opening his heart to . . . her?

She was, above all, flattered. "I know what it's like not to be understood."

He turned his full attention to her. "I sensed that in you from the moment I met you. That . . . yearning. That desire for something . . . better, deeper."

She began to protest mildly. He raised both hands, finding hers. "Sssh. Don't say anything, Delilah. I'm not asking anything of you. Just to be near you, when I can. To speak to you, when you'll let me. I've never met anyone like you. Don't try to talk me out of it. We're like two rivers, you and I, flowing along, and some force of nature has brought us together. There's something in our souls that are propelling us, making it happen."

She bit her lip, trying to hide a smile, considering the idea. It was all very well and good and might even be fun, she thought, like some after-noon soap. But quite aside from the whole morality of the thing, the Ten Commandments "adulteresses shall be stoned" issue, she did not want Mariette Rolland as an enemy.

"I am Mariette's friend," she murmured.

"And I am her husband and lover and the father of her children. This is much more difficult for me than it is for you."

Couldn't argue with that, although something was askew with the rea-soning, she understood. "It's immoral."

"Morality! God tells the Jews to murder every last person in Amalek, men, women, children, even the cows and sheep. What's moral about that? A person has to listen to his God-given brains, his heart, not follow rules blindly! I mean, Abraham was willing to slit the throat of his only son. That's where blind faith leads you. . . . Some things are above morality."

Now she was thoroughly confused. The willingness of Abraham to sacrifice his only, beloved son when God asked it of him was considered the ultimate test, and Abraham had passed it with flying colors. His will-ingness was the foundation stone of the Jewish faith. "Above morality? Like what, for instance?"

"Like love, Delilah. Like once-in-a-lifetime, true, take-it-or-leave-it-because-it-won't-return-again love." This was his big finale. The title of his hit song. After discreetly surveying the area, he reached out and took her hand in his in wild abandon, pressing it to his heart.

She grabbed it back, massaging it as if it had been injured. "Are you crazy?" she whispered, giggling.

He smiled at her. "I haven't offended you, Rebbitzin Levi, have I?" He arched his brow.

She glanced at him sideways, in silence.

Going for broke, he reached out and put his hands around her waist. "Please, Delilah. Have mercy!"

Just then, a couple from the shul came jogging around the corner. Delilah turned her back on Joseph Rolland, whose hands fell limply to his sides. "Good Shabbes!" She smiled at them.

"Good Shabbes, Rebbitzin, Dr. Rolland." They smiled back, not slow-ing their pace but looking curiously over their shoulders.

Delilah and Joseph stood still, waiting for them to disappear.

"Come with me for a minute!" Joseph whispered to her urgently, tak-ing her by the hand.

"You are insane! What if Mariette sees us?"

"She's snoring for the next two hours at least. Believe me, I know Mariette."

She followed him down the stairs into a small private alcove hidden behind a giant potted palm. He sat down, his hands on his knees, then leaned forward, pulling her onto his lap. She smelled his good cologne—she was a sucker for musk—and the dab of something lemony in his hair. A small feeling began in the pit of her stomach, as she remembered her days with Yitzi Polinsky and Benjamin, those sweet, powerful feelings that kept her in a state of drama and excitement, making her feel young, beautiful, and endlessly desirable.

She thought of her husband, also snoring away in bed, and the little boy who was all needs and wants who didn't see her at all. She thought of Mariette, always so superior, so perfect, and so full of advice, who'd stabbed her in the back with her criticism. She heaved herself up and walked away, back out to the deck, her nostrils flaring as she took deep, heady breaths of the sea air. She felt dizzy, grabbing onto the railing to steady herself. She looked out at the endless sea to where it met the endless sky. She was a tiny mote in the fleeting turnover of creation, insignificant and worthless as dust. Life was so incredibly short, and death so incredibly long. It was startling to her that only a little while ago, she thought Joseph Rolland a lecherous old jerk. And now? She looked up at his face that was close beside her. Here was a man who saved lives. A man who could hold a living human heart in his hands, putting it inside a heartless human being and allowing him to live.

Those hands, those wondrous hands, had touched her own. He wanted her. Loved her. He saw something in her that was worthwhile, a prize to be attained. She felt desired in a way that she had not felt for a very long time.

Inside, the raw unruly pull of passion slugged it out with reason, while all the while in the corner of her mind she was aware of Joseph's puzzled face close beside her, waiting.

She didn't want this to be like the others. She wanted something real out of this. Something serious and life-changing. She had to be sure that's what he wanted too.

"Can I ask you something?"

"Anything, my sweet."

"If I say no, will you just go on to your next conquest?"

He was startled. He hadn't given it any thought, although that was a pretty fair and accurate description. Still, if it was really fun, he might delay the inevitable.

"Is that what you think of me?" His eyes were tender, full of hurt.

"I'm sorry, Joseph." She reached up and touched his face. He took her hand, kissing the palm. Instinctively, she curled it into a fist.

She looked over his shoulder into a mirrored column, studying her face. Never had her eyes seemed more lovely and tender. Never had her lips seemed more tempting and desirable. This, this, was what life was all about. The excitement of the new conquest. The ability to test one's charms. The gift of mesmerizing and alluring.

Chaim treated her like he did one of his congregants: He paid attention to her in the hope that he could solve the problem and send her on her way. Most of the time, all he really wanted was to be left alone in his study to read. Of course, when he got the itch, she was suddenly remembered, or if she'd just come back from the *mikva* and it was his religious obligation. She didn't want to be some man's religious obligation. Not with those eyes. Not with those lips. She wanted someone who would fling the world over the abyss for her. All the novels she had read—*Anna Karenina*, *The Thorn Birds*—all the movies she had seen, were swirling through her head. They all made adultery seem funny and charming, exciting and interesting. And the husbands in these books and films were always so dull, so painfully clueless that one couldn't help feeling sympathy for the free spirit that wandered.

A person can only pretend to be something they're not for just so long.

Who had said that? Tzippy, she remembered, shuddering a little. Maybe she'd been right. Why should she not be the heroine of her own production? Why should she be stuck in the drab existence that had been forced upon her through no fault of her own when she had the ability, the talent, the looks, the daring, to hand herself another chance, another life?

He moved back. "Can you sneak away tonight? During the party? I know a place—"

"It's much too dangerous!"

"Life is full of worthwhile dangers, Delilah," he whispered, prying open her fingers one by one until her palm was once more naked and exposed. He pressed his lips full inside it.

"Not on the boat," she whispered.

{ TWENTY-NINE }

Saturday night on the calmest ocean in the world, Rabbi Chaim stood outside the magnificent ballroom of a cruise ship, holding a cup of wine in his shaking hands, while two men beside him held a burning candle of twisted wicks and a bag of fragrant spices. As hundreds watched, Chaim closed his eyes and concluded the recitation of Havdalah, the traditional prayer that denotes the end of the Sabbath day and the beginning of a new week: "Blessed be You, God our God, King of the Universe, Who has made a distinction between holy and profane." He had a feeling the profane would be taking over in record time.

The ballroom doors flung open. Silver lanterns wreathed in white roses hung from birch branches. Trapeze artists flew through the air, turning somersaults and catching each other by the wrists. And who was that on stage? Three voluptuous Black girls wearing . . . well, one couldn't be quite sure, but something with strands of material and feathers and Lord knows what else, that covered roughly eighteen percent or less of what needed to be covered. They began to sing a song specially written for the Bar Mitzva boy, who was invited onstage. And then, as the child looked on, they began to bump and grind and wiggle their behinds in their signature way, moves that had earned them millions, international fame, and even music awards.

"No, no, no!" Chaim moaned, closing his eyes.

He felt someone hug him. "What's wrong, Rabbi? You don't like girls?" Viktor Shammanov grinned cynically, putting his arm around him. His eyes were bugging out of his head, drinking in the girls' bodies as if they were water and he was dying of thirst. It was then he realized Victor Shammanov was not the man he was pretending to be.

Chaim got up abruptly. "Excuse me." He weaved his way unsteadily through the crowd, drunk with shame and disappointment and helplessness. The party swirled around him, the serving stations, the huge video screens, the thousands of flowers, the noise from the stage, as one famous act followed another. Was that a white horse? Was that a small elephant? Was that David Copperfield, the magician?

Maybe, just maybe, he could get him to make the whole shebang disappear.

A very skinny, extremely long-haired, vastly tattooed guitarist was jumping up and down in black leather pants. The drums were something out of deepest Africa. And the guests, his congregants? They were all out on the dance floor, gyrating and bumping and grinding. There was one in particular, some blond bimbo in a really tight gown, her hair whipping from side to side as she shook, and wriggled, and boogied, practically lap-dancing her partner right on the dance floor. Who was she with? Could it be Dr. Rolland? He was also going wild . . . and the woman was definitely not Mariette. Chaim moved closer, angling for a better view.

No. It just couldn't be! He found a chair and collapsed into it, putting his hands over his face and feeling the blood rush into his head in shame and humiliation. Without another look, he got up and walked quietly back to his cabin.

"I can go now?" the babysitter asked, before he opened his mouth. He nodded, and she took off like a homing pigeon, thrilled, to find the source of the vibrating booms that filled the ship. Maybe she'd enjoy it, he thought, and he could claim *that* as a good deed when he stood before God and was grilled on how he could have let all this happen.

Like Aaron facing Moses just after the Golden Calf debacle, he thought desperately of some way to exculpate himself and transfer the blame, something along the lines of "What could I do, Moses? You know what these people are like. All I did was throw the gold into the fire, and oops, out came a calf!"

Not particularly convincing, was it? he thought, ashamed to face God.

And as Chaim Levi sat there in the dark, rocking his baby son in his arms, looking out at the dark sea for answers, many thoughts went through his head, many questions. Like chemical elements poured into a beaker, disparate ideas began to churn and fizzle and send up strange odors.

He thought about Benjamin. How strange a coincidence it had been that he lived in the same building with his grandfather's chiropractor. And how, after his grandfather's stroke, he never once telephoned or even paid a shiva call, simply vanishing. How Delilah had wanted him to go to the theater with her that night, and how she had come home so late and acted so strangely. He thought about the color in his grandfather's cheeks when Delilah walked into his hospital room, and how he had tried to sit up and pull out his tubes. How old Mrs. Schreiberman had physically attacked his wife and had to be hospitalized. And how Delilah had met the woman on the subway while she was sitting next to Benjamin, and how nervous she had been about it.

The ideas sloshed around in his head, bubbling, congealing, and changing colors as they began to react.

～ ⌒ ～

"Delilah, have you seen the rabbi?" Joie asked.

For the first time that evening, Delilah looked around for her husband. "I don't see him."

"Can you find him, please? Viktor has a spectacular surprise for everyone, but he wants the rabbi to be there! Hurry."

Delilah didn't ask any questions. She wandered through the ballroom, then finally went back to their cabin.

As she opened the door, she saw the back of his head.

"Chaim?" She walked around. He had the baby in his arms. His eyes fluttered open. "Joie sent me to get you. Viktor has some important announcement to make and he wants to be sure you're there. Put the baby down and come. Where's the au pair?"

He didn't move.

"What's the matter with you?"

"Do you love me, Delilah?"

She stared at him. "How much have you been drinking?"

"Just answer me. For once in your life, tell me the truth."

She studied her nails. "I had your son, didn't I? I became a rebbitzin, didn't I?"

"Answer me!"

Oh, gee whiz, what now? "Chaim, I love you. Now, can we *please* just go back to the party? The entire ship is waiting for us."

"You don't, do you? I think I always really knew that, deep down. You think I'm ridiculous. I bore you."

Her mouth dropped open. "What's gotten into you?"

"I saw you out there on the dance floor, with Dr. Rolland."

Uh-oh. She tossed her head. "Dr. Rolland? So?"

"So? So a woman who loves her husband wouldn't dance with another man that way."

"Oh, grow up! I was just having a little fun!"

"I know all about it, Delilah."

"It?" For some reason, she started to get nervous.

"Yitzie Polinsky."

Her jaw dropped. Oh, boy. "There's nothing to know."

"Josh told me all about it before we were married."

"What? That sanctimonious piece of—!"

Chaim smiled sadly. "I was also angry at him. I didn't want to know." He looked into her eyes. His face was somber. "I don't care about that, Delilah. You didn't know me then. You were single. I want to know about Benjamin."

Her face went white. "Benjamin?"

"Why didn't he come to pay a shiva call? You knew him so well. He took the train with you every morning—"

"Oh, I get it. It's the old Schreiberman subway business! You're mad so you are bringing up ancient history. Is that it?"

"I went to see her, Delilah."

"Schreiberman? In the mentally challenged ward?"

"She told me some things that don't sound so crazy. That make everything fit together."

She inhaled, wondering what part to play. Outraged and Insulted? Hurt? Amused? (Harder to pull off but infinitely more fun as a part, she thought.) She decided on Innocent-Until-Proven-Guilty.

"You know, the Torah says if a person makes accusations, they have to back them up with facts."

"Oh, it would be easy to back up. All I have to do is find out if you really worked late that night. All I have to do is call your boss when we get back."

There went Innocent-Until-Proven-Guilty. "You wouldn't embarrass me by doing that!"

He looked at her shocked face. "Are you sure?"

She took a deep breath. "Look, Chaim, I can see you're upset. And you probably have every right to be. I agree with you that we need to have a long talk. But please, the Shammanovs are waiting. It's going to be humiliating for them if we don't show up soon. Please, please, can we just talk about all this later? After all, *they* haven't done anything to deserve being embarrassed in public."

"They've embarrassed themselves with this ridiculous, tasteless display of excess."

"Chaim, promise me you won't hurt their feelings? They're my friends!"

He thought about it. He got up and handed her the baby. He straightened his tie and tapped the top of his head with his cupped palm, checking that his skullcap hadn't slid off. He tucked in his shirt and buttoned his jacket and then, without turning around to look at her, walked out of the cabin.

Realizing the au pair had probably been let go for the night, Delilah groaningly put the baby down in his carriage, praying he wouldn't wake up and ruin her evening. Then she wheeled him into the banquet hall.

"There khe is!" Viktor boomed when Chaim walked in. "Rabbi, please, please, come up khere!" Viktor waved enthusiastically. "I vant to tell you, every one of you, I luff this man. Khe is a true friend. Khe take my son, my Anatoly, teaches him. Khe brings me khonor, pride, brings me back my grandfather's kheritage." He pounded his chest. "I am Jew. I am proud! Thank you, Rabbi!" He gave Chaim a bear hug.

"You're welcome," Chaim gasped.

"And my Joie, where is my Joie? And Delilah? Where is Delilah?" He motioned urgently for them to join him onstage. "I have announcement. In honor of son's Bar Mitzva, I build for Svallo Lake new synagogue. Not like tepee, like palace! I build new house for rabbi—beautiful house, with swimming pool. Until is ready, I give you extra house on Uspekhov for synagogue! Khere, I khave surprise."

The lights dimmed, and a huge screen was lowered. "*Khere it is!*"

The crowd gasped as the screen projected the image of a magnificent synagogue about three times the size of their present one. There were land-scaped grounds and a sculpture garden. The screen flashed pictures of the new social hall, which looked like the lobby of the Bellagio Hotel in Las Vegas. He pounded his chest. "No donations! No fund-raising. I do this myself, for Grandfather!" Wild applause rang out. Confetti fell from the ceiling and the boom of a fireworks display lit up the windows with ma-genta and orange.

Delilah looked at the plans for her new house as they flashed on the huge screen, thrilled. Again and again, the drawings of the new synagogue, the banquet hall, the landscaped grounds flashed on, almost hypnotically. There was a moment of mass hysteria, as the drunk, exhausted crowd ap-plauded and applauded and applauded until their fingers felt numb. Chaim looked around. Arthur Malin, his rage at Sabbath desecration for-gotten, clapped along with the rest. Then Viktor took the microphone in hand once more.

"And vun more thing: I khave Superbowl tickets for all men. You come as guest of Viktor Shammanov. New England Patriots vill vin!"

A shout arose from the luxurious deck as it plowed into the calm wa-ters of the night, a cry of surprise and awe the likes of which had not been heard on a cruise ship since the *Titanic*.

{ THIRTY }

*B*ack home in Swallow Lake, Chaim and Delilah settled the baby and unpacked their suitcases. They felt hung over, exhausted, and emotionally drained. Both were eager to avoid conflict. Ever since the Bar Mitzva banquet, they had been polite and distant, like bus passengers thrown together on a crowded Greyhound going from New York to California, wishing only to travel along pleasantly without additional stress.

Chaim had no time to deal with his personal life, because members of the synagogue had been calling him nonstop ever since Viktor's dramatic announcement, wanting to hear him gush about what a saint Viktor Shammanov was.

"I mean, it's just wonderful, don't you think?" rich accountants and lawyers and businessmen would blather through the phone lines, the same way those who had been to the Bar Mitzva had done in person on the plane all the way home from Hawaii.

"Well, it certainly is a generous offer that we should consider" had been his usual cautious answer.

This infuriated his listeners.

"Consider? What's to consider? A billionaire falls into our laps and wants to redo our shul, saving us millions; what's there to think about?"

"Well, first of all, do we really need a new synagogue?"

This incensed them even more. "We've been saying for years that the social hall is tiny. And the kitchen—no decent caterer would set foot inside it! Why should we look a gift horse in the mouth?"

Ask the Trojans, Chaim thought. But all he said was, "Well, I'm sure that the board will make the right decision. It's not up to me. I'm only the rabbi, after all."

"But Rabbi, with all due respect, I just don't understand! You and the rebbitzin should be thrilled! After all, you are the ones who brought the Shammanovs into the community! You introduced them and made them feel at home! None of this would have happened if not for you! Besides, hasn't he also promised to build you a new house?"

Something in those words, meant as praise, struck Chaim like a blow. He took a deep breath. "Perhaps we shouldn't accept such a generous gift. There are so many worthy causes that need support: terror victims in Israel, handicapped children, the poor, the aged. Just because there are resources to buy something doesn't mean one should buy it. Perhaps we should redirect Mr. Shammanov's generosity elsewhere."

At this point, the questioner usually gave up, exasperated, casting baleful and uncomprehending looks at the telephone or the rabbi, as the case might be, followed by an explanation of some unexpected and urgent reason to end the conversation.

Chaim locked himself in his study, writing furiously. He must write the sermon of his life, he exhorted himself. He must bring some sanity back to this community, before it drowned in its own Olympic-sized ego. Patiently, he sieved through the sources.

Was a man permitted to live excessively if he could afford it? Judaism, he found, was not in favor of asceticism. The Rambam had said, "No one should, by vows and oaths, forbid to himself the use of things otherwise permitted." In the Talmud it was written, "In the future world, a man will have to give an accounting for every good thing his eyes saw, but of which he did not eat."

There would always be poverty in the world. There would always be the suffering caused by disease and the malice of humans toward one another. The Torah commanded people to set aside ten percent of their wealth for charity, but the other ninety percent, a person was free to enjoy in any permissible way he saw fit.

Yes, all this was true. But who decided what was a fit way to enjoy God's blessings? Was it not the society in which one lived? One's neighbors? Should not the synagogue set the standard for moderation and being happy with what one has? For as it is written in Ethics of the Fathers: "Who is wealthy? He who rejoices in his lot in life."

Why shouldn't this community which had everything, including a perfectly adequate synagogue, simply rejoice in what it already had? Would Viktor Shammanov's gift really make anyone happier? Or would it feed into the community's ever-burgeoning demands upon itself, making each congregant mourn all those things they imagined they lacked, instead of praising God for the abundance that was already theirs?

The first rule of fund-raising is to know how to say no to a donor who wishes to donate something you don't want: the million-dollar statue of the late Herbert Cohen, to be placed at the entrance to the town's meeting hall; the Hospital for Stray Raccoons; the soccer stadium for ultra-Orthodox Jerusalem.

This is very difficult, because for the fund-raiser it means deliberately reducing your bottom line. But sometimes less really is more. This too, he thought, was a time to say: No, thank you very much. We have what we need. We should not be concentrating on walls and floors. We should be concentrating on how to fill the shells that are our homes and places of worship with the richness of meaning, values, and generosity toward our wives and children and neighbors and friends and employees that is expressed in the expenditure of time, and words, and caring personal acts, not the purchase of more things. Enough with the remote-controlled toilets, the three-hundred-dollar rubber beach sandals for three-year-olds, the infinity pools, the midget trees, the au pairs day and night, the ten-thousand-dollar koi fish, the army of servants you treat like slaves. Enough! Learn to find pleasure in your relationships with your family and your God. Learn to cherish what you have, not to pile on more junk you'll need to unload: things that will clog your basements and attics and brains and arteries, like plaque choking off the flow of lifeblood to the heart; things that will block and obscure what really matters in life!

He wrote furiously, nonstop, his armpits wet, his forehead glistening, his hands shaking.

Yes, Chaim thought, his chronic stomach pains leaving him for the first time since he got the invitation to the Shammanovs' Bar Mitzva. This is the speech he would make. Let them fire him! Let Delilah leave him! As he had once read on the door of a toilet stall in a vegetarian restaurant: *It is never too late to be what you might have been.* This is what he would say to them all. For once in his life, he would be a real rabbi, a mentor.

A week after the Bar Mitzva, Viktor Shammanov gathered up the men of Swallow Lake and took them on his private jet to witness the triumph of the New England Patriots in the Superbowl. While Chaim too was invited, he gently declined, claiming an inability to take off more time from his congregational work. Surprisingly, he got no special phone call from Viktor—or any of the other invitees—urging him to reconsider, a circumstance Chaim viewed with a mixture of relief and foreboding.

Delilah had come home with leis around her neck and a feeling of heaviness in her heart. The words that had passed between herself and her husband revealed to her how flimsy a structure her marriage really was. More a sukkah than a brick house set on concrete. She had never given her marriage—as a marriage—the least thought, viewing Chaim as she viewed the anchor person for the evening news: Whatever happened in the world, he would be there with his well-pressed suit and toothpaste commercial smile. The idea that her bond with Chaim could ever dissolve or disappear had not occurred to her.

Until now.

She pondered the unthinkable. What would it be like, she wondered, to dump Rabbi Chaim and run off with some rich, sexy, irreverent playboy, who knew how to dance and drink and do more than a quick close-your-eyes-and-wait-twenty-seconds-it-will-all-soon-be-over in bed? She thought about life with Joseph Rolland or even Viktor Shammanov. Joie didn't really appreciate her luck. A man that extravagant and adventurous. A man looking for meaning in his life. She finally had to admit to herself that was what she wanted, what she had always wanted: a Yitzie Polinsky, someone dark and dangerous who lived on the edge and took the world on his own terms. Not some scared rabbit hiding in some sunless warren, always a terrified hop, skip, and jump in front of some plodding hunter. This was all frighteningly new, thrilling information for Delilah as it bubbled up from her subconscious into her daydreams.

Yet despite the newfound clarity that her husband held few attractions for her, that he—in fact—bored her silly, she, like many women, was terrified of the idea of losing the roof over her head and the social acceptance and respectability that was the ground beneath her feet. Did she really want to go from "rebbitzin" to "divorcee" and "single mom" with a weekly Parents without Partners meeting in downtown Hartford after a day of scraping goo off the teeth of strangers?

To leap from Chaim into the sheltering arms of another man was one thing, to take a flying leap into the unknown, quite something else again. Chaim, as a rabbi, had adequate reason to send her on her way. No rabbinical court in the world would back her up once he revealed what he knew about Yitzie Polinsky, his suspicions about her relationship with Benjamin, and what he had witnessed between herself and Joseph Rolland. It wouldn't even matter if in the end he had not a single shred of evidence to back him up. Rabbinical court judges were notorious for their one-sided rulings in favor of husbands; they were all hanging judges when it came to even the merest appearance of impropriety on the part of the wife. This was based firmly on Torah law, which even had a special-Divine category called "the jealous husband." A man didn't need proof. All he needed were his suspicions in order to put a wife through humiliating and life-threatening trials. If she was innocent, of course, the bitter waters she was forced to drink made her fertile. But if she was guilty, they caused her "belly to swell and her thighs to waste away."

There was nothing remotely similar for the philandering husband unless he was involved with another man's wife, in which case both he and his paramour earned themselves a mandatory death by stoning. These days, of course, such a verdict was unenforceable. The result was that the man went scot free while the woman got divorced and ostracized.

If, one day, time and chance provided her with an opportunity she just couldn't turn down, in the form of a desirable suitor willing to provide for her the kind of life she had seen all around her since coming to Swallow Lake, she might willingly open the door and walk out. Until then, she had no intention of letting Chaim open it for her, kicking her out into a world of uncertainty, homelessness, poverty, and calumny. She wanted the decision—and the timing—to be hers. That being so, she felt she had no choice but to mend her ways and earn her way back into her husband's good graces.

The first thing she did was to talk to her former boss at the Riverdale dental clinic. He had been most understanding. That taken care of, she decided to start dealing seriously with her *chesed* project. She began to go through her handbags and pack them up for shipping. She contacted a number of well-known charitable agencies dealing with terror victims. But, for some reason that she couldn't figure out, none of them had any interest in becoming involved. In fact, unless she was imagining it, she heard muffled laughter in the background during her phone conversations with them, which she found shocking, considering that the subject was no laughing matter. She chalked it up to pressure. Anyone involved with such tragedies had to crack sometime.

She now possessed two hundred and seventy-four used—but more or less still very nice—designer handbags and nothing to do with them. She put in a call to the Israeli embassy. A very nice girl, whose English left much to be desired, explained that if she shipped them to Israel she'd have to pay tax on them, even if they were a charitable donation. Something about putting the local used handbag stores out of business.

"But Israel doesn't have any used handbag stores!"

"That's not entirely true," the girl said, getting a bit snooty. "Anyway, we don't think a designer handbag is the most important thing a terror victim lacks. Especially the ones that are still in the hospital, or orphaned, or widowed."

Well, she couldn't solve *all* their problems.

A bit desperate, she decided, very reluctantly, to call Rivkie, with whom she had had no contact at all since the doula businesss. But times were desperate; besides, Delilah wasn't the type to hold a grudge, especially if the person involved could still be useful.

"Hi, Rivkie, you'll never guess!"

She could tell Rivkie wasn't exactly thrilled to hear from her, but being Rivkie she was polite and kind. She had relatives in Israel who could give them out, she agreed, but Delilah would have to raise the money for taxes and shipping.

"How much do you think that will be?" she asked.

"Well, it depends on how much they estimate the bags are worth."

"Look, between you and me, some of them are fakes that are worth thirty bucks, and some are worth two thousand."

"Well, the tax on a two-thousand-dollar bag is going to be a lot of money, believe me. But if you get it together, let me know."

"Thanks, Rivkie." She hesitated. "Sorry I haven't been in touch. It was just so awkward and all. I mean, after the doula business. How is she?"

There was silence. "Her hand has healed."

"Oh. I'm glad to hear it. And how are things going with the two of you?"

"Fine, fine. Josh has just accepted a position as rabbi of the Lincoln Center Synagogue on the Upper West Side."

"Wow, Manhattan!"

"It's a nice congregation. Look, Delilah, I've got to run. Take care of yourself, and let me know if I can help you. 'Bye."

" 'Bye, Rivkie. And thanks. For everything. Oh, by the way, you don't happen to have any friends or relatives that live in Swallow Lake, do you? Someone you might have spoken to about me?"

There was dead silence on the other end. Then a tiny voice. "Why do you ask?"

"Because someone wrote Chaim an anonymous letter about Yitzie Polinsky."

"Delilah, I—I'm . . . well, I have to ask *mechilah*."

The traditional request for forgiveness that went around before the high holidays and Yom Kippur was rarely used at other times of the year, unless the penitent truly feared for their eternal soul.

"*Mechilah*?" Delilah asked suspiciously. "For what?"

"Delilah, I swear I didn't know it would get back to Chaim. Mariette Rolland is friends with my mother. And I might have mentioned it to my mother years ago."

"Rivkie, I have something to tell you."

"Yes?"

"Your clothes? They never actually fit me. They were too big, especially around the butt! And you can forget about *mechilah*. You can kiss my little ass, and that goes for your husband too!" She slammed down the phone.

Mariette Rolland. How appropriate, Delilah thought. She looked at the boxes and boxes of handbags. What to do with them? She picked up a Chanel and turned it over. Not bad. Someone would pay good money for it on eBay. A little light clicked on in her head. She piled them into cartons and put them down in the basement. Every day, she'd auction off one of them, until she had enough money to pay the taxes and shipping costs for the rest.

She got busy. She started cleaning the house, taking the baby out for walks. She skipped her aerobics classes and, instead, baked fattening cakes for myriad Sabbath guests.

"Chaim?" She poked her head into his study.

He looked up from his open books, eyeing her silently.

"I thought you might be hungry. I made a little snack." She placed a mug of hot freshly brewed coffee on his desk with a blueberry muffin, warm from the oven. "And Chaim?"

His eyes shifted from the food to her face, which was settled in pleasant docile lines. "I have made up lists of people we should invite over soon. Can you check them over and see if I've left anyone out?"

He looked down at the neatly typed pages, holding dozens and dozens of names.

"This looks fine, Delilah." He nodded correctly. "Now, if you'll just excuse me, I have some work. . . ."

"Oh, sure, of course. Sorry." She smiled, looking chastened and pathetic, he thought, as she closed the door behind her.

He looked down at the food. He couldn't bring himself to touch it.

{ THIRTY-ONE }

The Sabbath following the Superbowl, Chaim sat nervously in his chair, waiting impatiently for the moment he could rise and approach the podium. All the while, he anxiously patted his jacket pocket, like a best man fingering the rings, to make sure the pages of his speech hadn't somehow disappeared. Finally, the Torah reading was completed, along with all the post-reading blessings. This was his cue. He rose, taking the papers out of his pocket, and strode purposefully down the aisle and up toward the podium.

Just as he was about to mount the first step, Arthur Malin reached out and touched his arm. "Rabbi? I want to ask your kind permission to address the congregation this Shabbes. The board has something very special to tell them. Would you mind?"

Chaim looked down at the speech clutched in his hand. He had opened his mouth to object when he realized all the members of the board had now risen and were standing in front of him like an opposing football team, ready to tackle him to the ground.

"You don't mind, Rabbi, just this once?" Stuart smiled affably.

"Really, Rabbi, do us this favor?" Joseph nodded.

"You'll understand why in a minute." Ari rubbed his hands together.

Chaim looked at them and at the congregation. It was, after all, their synagogue. He was just the hired help. He bowed, turning around and walking back to his seat. He sat down heavily, crumpling the pages in his fist as he rammed them back inside his pocket.

"I thank the rabbi for giving up his pulpit for me. Thank you, Rabbi Chaim! I have wonderful news!" Standing in the front of the synagogue surrounded by the other male members of the board, a huge smile on his face, Arthur Malin announced: "The board held an extraordinary meeting after the Superbowl and agreed to accept the fantastically generous gift of the Shammanovs to build us a new synagogue and a new rabbi's house. We signed the papers yesterday. The new synagogue will have sixty-five-thousand square feet! A catering hall that is fifteen thousand square feet! It will have twenty-eight classrooms, a two-thousand-square-foot library, recreation rooms, screening rooms, a swimming pool, and a cafeteria—so you can eat after every minyan! In addition, there will be a fifty-six-foot-high waterfall in the lobby with a reflection pool that will symbolize our new theme: Mayim Chayim, living waters—and I must say, since this whole thing started off the coast of Maui, it's particularly apt." He chuckled.

The privileged ones who had been to Maui chuckled with him, while the others stared in shocked, morose silence.

"Construction begins next week and we should be enjoying—well, I don't know if that's the right word exactly, heh-heh—our Rosh Hashanah and Yom Kippur prayers in our new space. For his unbelievable gift, we would like to present Viktor Shammanov with a token of our community's thanks. Viktor, would you come up here, please?"

Viktor, seated in the front pew, bounded up to the podium, a huge smile on his face. "I luff this man! You are so kind to me and my family! Who vould have thought little Viktor from Turdistan would be in America, an American, in a synagogue? That khe would build synagogue in khonor of khis grandfather, such a kholy man!"

Arthur wiped his eyes, reaching out to hug the man. Viktor hugged him back. When Arthur was able to breathe again, he said, "On behalf of

Ohel Aaron, we wish to present you with this silver pointer that is used by the Torah reader. We think it is appropriate, Viktor, because in all you do you help point the way for our congregation, showing us what we all want to be."

Shouts of "Mazel tov!" "Bless you!" "*Yashar koach!*" "Wonderful!" rang out from every corner, or so it seemed to Chaim, who turned around, staring at the congregation. The truth was, he realized, that the well-wishers were strategically seated all over the synagogue to give the appearance of overwhelming adulation. In fact, the synagogue was deeply divided, an equal number of congregants sitting stone-faced, their hands clenched in their laps. For a moment, a swell of hope rose in his chest. Just then, he heard his name called: "Vere is khe? My rabbi?" Viktor shouted. "Khere khe is! Come khere, come khere." He waved. Reluctantly, Chaim got up and walked toward him. "This is reason I came to your synagogue. This man. Khe is responsible for everything!"

Select members of the synagogue broke out into a fury of foot stamping and applause. And even those unwilling to applaud the new synagogue, found it in themselves to unclench their fists and slap their palms together, joining in the adulation for their rabbi, with whom they felt they enjoyed a special bond, especially since he had been willing to forgo his Superbowl ticket to be with them. Still others sat facing forward without moving a muscle or changing their expression as they lifted their eyes to Chaim Levi, the man who had brought Viktor Shammanov to Ohel Aaron.

Chaim stood firmly sandwiched between Arthur and Viktor, facing the congregation, his physical presence blessing the enterprise, the speech in his pocket crumpling and growing moist from the sweat that now drained from every one of his pores.

In the women's section, Delilah sat shaking hands and air-kissing furiously, like a queen. She had done it. Pulled it off! Her husband was safe in his job. She was safe in hers. There would be no wandering now, no fear of unemployment. There would be a brand-new, huge, custom-designed house with every luxury, to rival those of even the richest members of the congregation. Chaim would forgive and forget. Their lives would be blessed, floating on calm waters forevermore. She glanced up eagerly at her husband.

He looked back at her, expressionless, then turned away. This small gesture landed in her stomach like a rock.

She looked at the fawning smiles of the women who surrounded her, women wearing clacking, pointed designer shoes, wildly expensive hats, and custom-made suits, suddenly remembering the bored eyes of the captains of the punchball teams when they finally turned in her direction, having no one left to choose. Finally on the team, she had fumbled the ball, let it drop, lost the point, and they had all turned their backs on her, pretending not to know her. Her heart froze. What did it matter how these women looked at her now, when her own husband looked away?

Why did everything she dream of, lean on, depend on, turn to straw the instant it came to fruition, collapsing beneath the weight of reality? she wondered. Was there truly no happiness in the world? Was everything, then, a lie? Love, faith, joy, constancy, sincerity? All those kissing her now, would they still love her tomorrow? Would they love her husband? Or was it a merry-go-round that constantly stopped and made you get off, forcing you to pay for new tickets if you wanted another little ride, another little taste of success?

She wanted someone to take her off the carousel, someone with strong firm arms who would lift her up and let her rest her weary head against his shoulder, whispering compliments and extravagant promises in her ear with unconditional love. She wanted to exhale and be safe and secure at last, she told herself, without conviction.

No, she realized, that wasn't it at all. That would be supremely boring.

And then the truth finally hit her. As Emma Bovary had finally figured out in the end, there was nothing worth having, nothing that lasted: "Every smile hid a yawn, every happiness, a misery. Every pleasure began to curdle, and every embrace left behind a baffled longing for a more intense delight."

An image arose in her mind: the neat little figure, the dark passionate eyes, a woman who had driven herself to madness and suicide, who had betrayed and been betrayed. An unfaithful wife, a bad mother, a silly self-destructive fool. And yet, a dreamer who was not afraid to envision a different life, no matter how others condemned her for it.

She took a deep breath and straightened her back. There would be a huge house. Her husband would be head of one of the largest synagogues in the area. People would point to her and say, "Rebbitzin Levi!" And all the punch ball captains and rabbi's daughters who had lived in Tudor mansions in the Five Towns would think of her when they sat alone, divorced or on their way to teach special ed in hellholes in Brooklyn. And when her name and her husband's popped up in the social columns with flattering pictures of her in dazzling dresses at charity events, they would envy her and be sorry they hadn't been nicer to her. They would understand that all along she had been playing the game alongside them, that she had been a good player, a worthy teammate, and that she too had won. Even if she didn't feel that way now, she told herself, she was sure she would feel that way tomorrow. After all, as someone much smarter and more successful than Emma Bovary had pointed out: "Tomorrow is another day."

⌒ ⌒

The bulldozers came the following week. All the furniture, the sacred Torah scrolls and the prayer books had been moved temporarily into the spare house on the Shammanovs' property, where the synagogue would continue meeting until the construction ended.

People stood around in awe, a bit horrified, as the metal teeth bit into the side of the building, bringing down the concrete tepee with its ribbons of stained glass. With amazing ease, where the synagogue once stood, there was only a pile of chalky rubble, twisted metal, shards of brightly colored glass, and splintered wood. Billowing clouds of choking dust filled the air, fogging the windows and whitening the plants of the expensive homes in Swallow Lake. Maids and cleaning services would spend weeks of backbreaking labor erasing the evidence of the collapse.

Chaim stood outside, mesmerized, watching it fall, his heart filled with mixed emotions: horror, regret, and a tiny twinge of strange joy.

Delilah spent the morning at the country club, anxious to talk to Joie about the plans for the new rabbi's residence. To her surprise, Joie wasn't there. And when the congregation showed up at the Shammanov estate that Friday night to attend services, they found the gates locked and nobody home.

EPILOGUE

The collapse of the Ohel Aaron Congregation on Swallow Lake created a mushroom cloud reminiscent of those hovering over unlucky cities at the close of World War II, filled with controversy, heartbreak, and conjecture. The story, featured in every major newspaper and magazine in America, included photos of the bulldozed synagogue with a furious Solange Malin shaking her fist. Both *Newsweek* and *Time*, on the other hand, chose to use photos of Viktor Shammanov at the airport, ushering his blond wife and baby into a private jet just before they flew off to God knows where.

The whole convoluted tale of Viktor's business dealings—which turned out to be one huge international con job—was fodder for exposés in both *Fortune* and *Business Week*, which debunked all the facts, the same facts they had written about him earlier—which had convinced people to trust him in the first place. As it turned out, Viktor was selling shares in an oil company that the government of Turdistan declared belonged to them, denouncing Viktor and his company as worthless. But then, the entire government of Turdistan had also been declared a scam, the elections having been rigged and the opposition candidates fed disfiguring poison.

Viktor, of course, had done it all through a tangled web of companies incorporated in places like the Cayman Islands, the Seychelles, and other accommodating sun-kissed shelters. The Four Seasons Hotel in Maui was suing him, as were the cruise line, the catering services, the Lakers cheerleaders, Mick, Christina, Michael, and hundreds more, many of whom were forced into declaring bankruptcy.

And then, just as the dust was about to settle, the true, horrifying dimensions of the scam came to light. It was not just the synagogue that Victor Shammanov had bulldozed in Swallow Lake, but the lives of its most prominent inhabitants as well. From quiet conversations between accountants, lawyers, and financial planners, who shared the painful truth back and forth on cell phones and over alcohol-soaked dinners, the story came out. Unbeknownst to one another, the wealthiest residents, those who had been courted by Victor and his wife, invited to their home and their Bar Mitzva, had one by one persuaded Viktor Shammanov to overlook the rules and allow them to purchase shares in his company. Swearing each to secrecy, and with a great show of reluctance, Viktor had done them the great favor of accepting the substantial investments they pressed upon him.

Many of those defrauded were too embarrassed to admit it. And those who tried to claim a tax deduction on their losses aroused the interest of the Internal Revenue Service, who wondered where all that money had come from, prompting them to do a thorough audit going back many years, resulting in huge reassessments, fines, and even criminal charges.

Soon after, many FOR SALE signs began to appear on Swallow Lake's largest estates. Many were quietly repossessed by the banks or sold at auction. The kind of people who bought the homes were quite different from the original residents—local small businessmen and white-collar workers who smelled a fire sale and lined up for bargains.

The land where the synagogue had once stood became embroiled in lawsuits and countersuits because Viktor had managed to sell it several times over. The legal wrangling kept it a pile of weeds and rubble, an eyesore, for years to come. Eventually it was rezoned, and some builder put up condos and then a Baptist church.

In the beginning, Ohel Aaron members used the auditorium in the day school for services, until the dwindling student body forced the school to close its doors. Without a synagogue or a day school, the remaining Jewish families trickled out of the community to places like New York, Boston, and Hartford. Solange and Arthur wound up in San Diego, where they started a new day school. Ari and Felice quietly divorced. Ari is now working in a high-tech company in Ramat Aviv and was recently drafted into the Israeli army.

Amber and Stuart, who were hit worst of all, having invested every penny they owned with Viktor, declared bankruptcy, losing control of their teddy bear empire. But they managed to bounce back, designing a new doll that shakes its behind when you press a button, and reportedly have made countless millions with it.

Only Joseph and Mariette stayed behind in Swallow Lake. She stopped wearing her hats, and they no longer call themselves Orthodox. Her house, they say, is as beautiful as ever, and so is she. Still, she is alone much of the time.

As for Chaim and Delilah, they've become somewhat of a legend, the subject of rabbinical sermons from Johannesburg to Jerusalem and all points in between. Someone even made a movie about a hapless rabbi and his scheming wife, which everyone knew was based on all the newspaper articles about them. It poked a lot of fun at Orthodox Jews and was roundly condemned by embarrassed congregations everywhere, who accused the screenwriter and the producers of being "Jewish anti-Semites." It got Reese Witherspoon another Oscar nomination.

As for what really happened to Chaim and Delilah, stories—like Elvis sightings—continue to surface every few years, claiming to be the true, the only, authoritative version. What everyone agrees on is this: Immediately after the Sabbath when they were turned away from the ornate gates of Uspekhov, a furious crowd of shul members showed up at the home of their rabbi and rebbitzin, who, fairly or unfairly, were held entirely responsible for the disaster. Holding buckets of concrete, glass, and wooden rubble, they poured the contents on Rabbi Chaim's front lawn, all the while waving flashlights and screaming insults. Someone marked their front door with an X, and others ran after their speeding car with a bucket of tar and feathers.

After that, it all depends on whom you want to rely. One widely circulated report, published in the *Jewish Daily Press* (known by all as the *Jewish Mess*) had them driving directly to Tijuana, where they got a quickie civil divorce and an even quicker religious divorce, or *get*. Never did anyone get a *get* as fast as Delilah Levi, the story claimed. And Chaim, instead of gently tossing the scroll into her hands, as is the custom, pitched it so hard she wound up having to duck. Subsequent reports in that same paper had Chaim remarried a year later to a short, dark-haired Torah teacher with whom he went on to have other children in addition to little Abraham, over whom Delilah was only too happy to relinquish custody. Years later, another story about a Rabbi Chaim Levi appeared, describing the life of the Orthodox rabbi of a large, prosperous synagogue in Bogotá, Colombia. It described how he had learned Spanish and how he and his wife—a second marriage for both—lived in luxury with their eight children, surrounded by an adoring, respectful congregation and full-time personal bodyguards, who protected them from drug-crazed kidnappers.

Soon after that, someone who looked exactly like Delilah surfaced on the cover of a California business journal. She wore a very chic and modest black suit as she smilingly accepted an award for running the most successful new eBay venture, a Web site selling "gently pre-owned designer handbags." In the article, the woman accepting the award—who called herself Marlene Gold—talked about how she had begun her business after surviving a devastating divorce and losing custody of her only child to her vindictive ex.

She described how she'd started at the bottom and worked her way up. She talked about her mansion in Beverly Hills with its pool, her shopping trips to Paris and Milan for the shows, her fabulous vacations in sunny spots all over the globe. Despite the fact that she wore a magnificent wedding ring, she refused to give any details about her personal life, saying only that "she had a very handsome young husband, and two beautiful blond daughters." She had everything she wanted in life, she said, and moreover, she had earned it herself. Someone scanned the magazine cover and article, and for a while it circulated through the Internet to millions. Everyone who saw it and who had known Delilah agreed that, if it really was her, she looked fabulous and thin, and sexier than ever.

But the most recent article, which you must have read—everybody did—was the one in *New York* magazine. The reporter, a crack investigative journalist and a Gentile, tracked down a former classmate of Chaim's who had sent out the following shocking revelation to everyone on the Bernstein alumni e-mail list.

Dear Friends:
In light of the terrible sin of gossip and scandalmongering of which we have all been guilty over the years concerning our friend and colleague Rabbi Chaim Levi, who defied the ban on the Swallow Lake congregation, I would like to set the record straight once and for all. Chaim and Delilah Levi are still married, baruch Hashem, and the parents of five children. They are the rabbi and rebbitzin of a tiny shteibel somewhere in North Dakota, consisting of thirteen families, who all meet in the rabbi's basement for Sabbath and holiday prayers. Because the town is snowed in most of the year, the entire congregation regularly has not only kiddush but lunch and holiday meals at the rabbi's house, which the rebbitzin prepares, although congregants often bring homemade contributions. I know because I spent the Sabbath with them.

In the magazine interview, the classmate tried hard to convey the great joy and serenity the Levis had found in living in such a tiny Jewish community, as well as the great love of the congregation for their rabbi and rebbitzin. He described Rebbitzin Levi as

the picture of the matriarch of an older generation, dressed in the modest clothing one would expect of a pious wife and mother, her dress loose and midcalf, her hair completely covered by a snood where only her blond bangs were visible, like those pious women of Boro Park and Meah Shearim. Numerous small children tugged at her dress as she ate with a healthy appetite from the heaps of cholent, kugel, and potato salad arrayed in plastic serving plates on a plastic tablecloth. There was much sincere laughter and the singing of many Sabbath hymns, as the children played board games and the adults conversed.

She looked, the classmate claimed, *perfectly content.*
The reporter, however, was not convinced. He wrote:

The classmate, a very pious Jew who lowers his eyes when he meets other men's wives, is a man who seems to be defending the Orthodox world. It is not impossible that he views the creation and publication of this fairy-tale ending to a scandalous tale that has rocked the religious world for years as a good deed, a mitzva.

Furthermore, the classmate could not, or would not, provide an address and phone number for them, claiming he wished to protect their privacy, as they had "suffered so much from public scrutiny."

The reporter's cynicism produced a furor. Hundreds of letters to the editor arrived at the magazine. Those who defended the classmate's tale said they found it perfectly feasible that the Levis, having undergone such terrible trials, had stayed together and learned to love each other. Delilah's repentance and reformation further confirmed to them the beauty of the Jewish religion, which allows people to change and grow and learn from their mistakes.

But most people, including a good number who had actually known the Levis, were inclined to share the reporter's skepticism. They said they found the classmate's story *hard to believe*, either because they couldn't bear to think of Chaim still saddled with Delilah or vice versa. They also took issue with the idea that anyone, particularly a weekend house guest, could possibly know if someone was *perfectly content*.

But the best letter of all, people agreed, was from a woman claiming to be Delilah's former roommate and the rebbitzin of a large congregation. Her sentiments spoke to many when she wrote:

> It is not easy to be a rebbitzin. There are so many demands on your time, such a constant intrusion into your private life, and sometimes not much appreciation. Some people are just not suited to it. Wherever she is, we hope that Delilah has come to terms with the limitations of our lives and the impossibility of having all our dreams come true. If she has been forced, or has chosen, to live a simple pious life, we hope that the serenity to be happy with such a choice has come her way as well. And if she really has found the overabundance she craved, we hope that it doesn't give her high cholesterol or make her mean-spirited and that she is nice to her household help and takes care of her own children, at least some of the time. And that she remembers to say her prayers as sincerely and as often as she can.

THE SATURDAY WIFE

by Naomi Ragen

About the Author

- A Conversation with Naomi Ragen

In Her Own Words

- "The Boulders in the River: A Thousand Years of Jewish Women's Achievements"
  An Original Essay by the Author

Keep on Reading

- Recommended Reading
- Reading Group Questions

For more reading group suggestions
visit www.readinggroupgold.com

ST. MARTIN'S GRIFFIN

A Conversation with Naomi Ragen

In a recent *Jewish News* article, you mentioned that with your novels, you "hope to open hearts and minds and make people more compassionate by helping them to live a little while in someone else's shoes." What inspired you to walk in Delilah Levi's shoes? Also, was it risky to showcase the footsteps of such an admittedly unsympathetic character?

I was at a kosher-club weekend in the Dominican Republic at a resort that had been turned into a mecca for Orthodox Jews for Chanukah vacation. We were all there because we observed the laws of the Torah—eating kosher food, observing the Sabbath rituals, reciting daily prayers, etc. Well, one evening I happened to wander over to the "entertainment." And there, lo and behold, was a blonde in a miniskirt and halter top dancing on stage together with the toddlers. She was there supposedly to help her three-year-old, who didn't seem to need any help. And one could see she was enjoying the attention immensely.

This woman fascinated me. What was she doing there among the kosher food eaters and Sabbath observers? It didn't seem a comfortable fit. So I followed her around shamelessly, eavesdropping on her poolside conversations, her interactions with her husband and children. I actually came to feel great sympathy for her. She reminded me of the character in the book I was reading, *Madame Bovary,* who also had the potential for breaking with the rules of her society and doing something mad.

I viewed the book *Madame Bovary* as a wonderful satire, a send-up of bourgeois French society. And I thought: why not do something similar to my own social group, modern Orthodox Jews? In a way, it was an opportunity to make fun of myself, which I think every writer who has written books critical of others should eventually do.

"I am horrified by Delilah. But she also makes me laugh."

In deciding to do a satire, I don't think I was actually concerned enough with my readers' reactions. I just assumed if I made the character over-the-top enough, and funny enough, it would be clear to all this was a portrait that was not to be taken seriously. Like Swift's "A Modest Proposal," an essay in which he suggested that the problem of famine in Ireland could be solved by encouraging the Irish to eat their babies, I felt Delilah was such an outrageous portrait of a rabbi's wife, no one could possibly take her seriously.

Alas, that was not the case. Some people did, and as with Swift, they were horrified and offended by my characterization of Rebbitzin Delilah Levi. Such are the pitfalls one faces when assuming others' sense of humor matches one's own.

Yes, I am horrified by Delilah. But she also makes me laugh. And I think, in the end, she is more sinned against than sinning.

Your previous two novels, *The Covenant* and *The Ghost of Hannah Mendes* (also available from St. Martin's Press) concern the lives of contemporary Jewish women. Can you take a moment to talk about your own cultural identity? Also, what is it like being an American Jewish woman living in Israel?

I was born into a traditional family of Polish-Russian ancestry. Not a Sephardic forebear in the lot, as far as I know. But I have always admired the Sephardim. Their customs and observance manage to avoid the extremes to which my own Eastern European heritage is prone. I especially admire how they survived the Inquisition, which was in its way worse than the Holocaust, and lasted hundreds of years.

About the Author

As an American who decided to move to Israel in my early twenties, I'm always a bit torn between both worlds, and my books reflect this dual cultural heritage. My reason for making the move was originally religious: "Leave your father's house and your birthplace and go to the land I will show you," G-d tells Abraham. I took that personally. I had never been to Israel when I moved there with my husband in 1971. I was just a starry-eyed kid. But the interesting thing is I never got disillusioned. It's an amazing place to spend your life if you are a Jew, especially a religious Jew. But while I've never looked back, I know that I will always feel like an American living in a foreign country, even though I've lived in Israel now longer than I lived in America.

How do you balance the demands of the religious and the secular as both an observant Jew and a commercial novelist?

I try, as best I can, to always remember the larger picture. My work is an avocation, not just a vocation. In my books I explore the ideals and conflicts that religious women face. I try never to cross my own red lines, which is to denigrate my religion or make G-d's laws appear cruel. I always separate Divine commandments from the behavior of the divinely-commanded, who don't always live up to their obligations. I criticize religious people, but never my religion as such. My own view of my religion is that there is vast room for the individual to serve G-d with his or her particular talents. And so, having been given my own gift, I try to use it well. Being religious and being a novelist is something I share with many other writers. I think of Pope and Donne, and many others who were actually clergymen. The love of G-d and the clear grounding in identity and history that comes from knowing who you are and what you believe in is a gift for any artist.

"I will always feel like an American living in a foreign country, even though I've lived in Israel now longer than I lived in America."

In the opening chapter of *The Saturday Wife,* the first
thing we learn about our heroine is that she "always
considered herself the victim of a painfully disadvantaged childhood." You have discussed—in interviews
and lectures, and in your autobiographical novel
Chains Around the Grass—your own "disadvantaged"
upbringing. Can you share some stories about your
childhood in New York City during the 1950s? How,
if at all, did it inspire Delilah's story?

Actually, that line is meant to poke fun at our heroine. Unlike Delilah, who has two perfectly nice parents who, while not wealthy, provide her with a perfectly adequate childhood, I was not as fortunate.
There is a big difference between bemoaning your
fate if you have to buy clothes on sale, and not being
able to afford to buy clothes at all. My childhood
was overshadowed by a father's untimely death, and
the struggles of my widowed mother to keep off welfare—which she did, to her great credit. Like Delilah,
I too went to an upscale Orthodox Hebrew Day
School. But I was a scholarship student, unlike
Delilah, whose parents had to scrape together the
tuition. I sympathize with Delilah out on the punchball fields wanting to play. I was more like the narra-
tor, "permanently relieved of hope." The Delilahs in
my class were one rung up the social and economic
ladder from me. But from vantage point of rock bottom, I could see clearly all the way up to the top. I've
tried to convey this.

**Please share a few words about the writing process.
Also, did you face any particular challenges while
working on *The Saturday Wife*?**

The process of figuring out a character is a journey
you take sitting next to a stranger on a long ride,
who slowly opens up to you. By the time the ride is
over and you've reached your destination, you know

absolutely everything there is to know about them, from the things they've told you, and of course and, most important, from the things they've desperately tried to hide. I never know more about my characters than the initial handshake at a party would tell you about the guests, along with some whispered rumors you've heard before they've arrived. So it's really more like reading a book than writing it. And always full of surprises.

Delilah was a particular challenge because she just kept telling me these awful things about herself. She was sacreligious in a way I found shocking. I've had characters who were evil, like Isaac in *Jepthe's Daughter*, and characters who are noble, like Josh in *The Covenant*. But I never had a main character who was an airhead with absolutely nothing admirable about her. Keeping the reader interested enough not to throw down the book in disgust was a challenge. I think I succeeded because she has so many of the faults we recognize in ourselves (except she is blessed with far more than most). And she is always getting into trouble. It's so much fun to see how she slides her way out. And of course, we enjoy laughing at her and at ourselves.

Who are some of your favorite Jewish female literary figures—fictional, historical, even biblical—and why?

I adore Abigail, the woman in the Bible who was married to a cheapskate named Nabal. She was resourceful, beautiful, and intelligent, and managed through her cleverness not only to dissuade an angry King David from justifiably destroying her home in response to her husband's stinginess, but also managed to win the King's heart and give her husband a heart attack, in roughly that order. In the end, she became David's wife.

"Delilah was sacreligious in a way I found shocking."

One of my other favorite Jewish women is the late Professor Nechama Leibowitz, who taught the Bible for seventy years or more, and who wrote and gave out study sheets on the Bible to factory workers, so they too could learn. She spent her spare time checking answers and replying to hundreds, even thousands of students who mailed the sheets to her home in Jerusalem. Of course, she never asked to be paid either for the sheets, or for her time. I remember her telling us in class that she'd gotten a phone call at 2 a.m. from someone who wanted to discuss the answer to a question on one of her Bible study sheets. Far from being furious, she politely asked why he was calling at such an hour. "I'm a street cleaner," the man told her. "This is the only time I have to study." She answered his question, and then told him how much she admired him.

(Note to reader: See author's essay for more information about Professor Nechama Leibowitz.)

And what are you working on now?

I'm working on a book about a mother and daughter whose wonderful lives face sudden destruction, and how the experience makes them reexamine everything they thought they knew about life, with startling results.

The Boulders in the River: A Thousand Years of Women's Achievements
An Original Essay by the Author

If we are going to talk about the history of women, Jewish women, over the last thousand years, let's start with the tale of Gertrude B. Elion, who won the 1988 Nobel Prize for her work in medical research.

Born in New York City in 1918, to a long line of rabbis, Trudy spoke Yiddish at home. A good student, she was forced to attend a free city college when her father lost his money in the stock market crash of 1929.

"Others ... rose above the barriers by simply sprouting wings and flying..."

Although she majored in chemistry and graduated Phi Beta Kappa, she couldn't get the financial aid of an assistantship to continue her studies. Professors told her that a pretty young woman like herself would be a distracting influence in the labs. She enrolled in secretarial school instead, and worked seven years as a secretary to save the $450 she needed to attend graduate school. Working on her master's degree, she continued to work part-time as a receptionist in a doctor's office. In 1942, when male chemists were all drafted, she was hired by a British pharmaceutical company, Burroughs Wellcome.

Within two years, her revolutionary work altered the way drugs are discovered. In a major breakthrough, she developed drugs that interfered with the development of abnormal cells, and left healthy cells alone. Attempting to earn her doctorate by attending school after work, her professors insisted she quit her job. She refused. Because of her discoveries, today 80% of children with childhood leukemia survive. When Trudy began her work, half of all such children died within two or three months, and fewer than a third lived a year. Her work in the development of AZT, the main drug used to combat the AIDS virus, was rewarded with the Nobel Prize in 1988. She never did get her Ph.D.

And one cannot help but wonder what would have happened if Trudy Elion hadn't been able to type.

Over the last thousand years, the history of women in general, and Jewish women in particular, can be compared to a mighty river of talent, ability, and creativity willfully dammed by huge boulders of prejudice and social and religious strictures. And yet, despite the choking impediments, a small trickle has still managed to flow around and through, reaching us in the form of cultural, literary, and scientific achievements.

What all these women achievers seem to have in common is the ability to somehow free themselves from a male-dominated society by either never marrying, or through a fortunate birth which conferred on them by proxy the powerful, unique status held by noteworthy fathers or brothers.

Others, like Trudy Elion, rose above the barriers by simply sprouting wings and flying when their climb up the ladder of success was permanently blocked, achieving such spectacular successes that they became simply impossible to ignore. It is interesting that some of our earliest information about such women comes from the Talmud, that bastion of male intellectual hegemony.

Despite its own dictum that "women are lightheaded," it is from the Talmud that we learn of Beruriah, the second-century wife of Rabbi Meir, who actually corrected a misinterpretation of ritual law, and is thanked for it in the Talmud (Mesechta Kelim, Chapter 1). We learn of Yalta, Rabbi Nachman's wife, and the daughter of Rabbi Chanina Ben Tardyon, who disagreed with her father on a point of law and her view is accepted (Tosephta Kelim). And from the Talmud Yerushalmi, Chagigah, 2:1, we discover that the daughter of Elisha Ben Avuyah refuted the arguments of Rabbi Yehuda HaNasi and forced him to admit this mistake.

In Her Own Words

One of the rishonim, Rabbi Eliezer of Mainz, praised his wife, saying "Her mouth opens with wisdom and she is fluent in all the laws of issur v'heter and on Shabbat she sits and expounds the law....." Rav Shmuel HaLevi of Bagdad had an only daughter who was fluent in chumash and Talmud and would deliver lectures to men from behind a curtain.

The Maharshal reported that his grandmother, Rebbitzen Miriam, directed a yeshiva for many years. Also sitting behind a curtain, she would lecture advanced students. There is also Osnat, the only child of a rabbi in Kurdistan, who, in the 1500s, ran her own yeshiva.

In other cases, the unique conjunction of the particular needs of the age and personal circumstances opened up unique opportunities for women to reach prominence. In the sixteenth century, the terrors of the Inquisition and the death of her husband gave Portuguese converso Dona Gracia Mendes the opportunity and the power to use the vast wealth of her spice trading empire to spirit Jews out of the hands of the Inquisition. She bought land in Tiberias and her plan was to give the Jews of her time a place of refuge.

It is noteworthy that male historians have often tried to credit her achievements to her nephew, Don Joseph. However, archival material point clearly to Dona Gracia as the moving force through that moment in history.

Another unique opportunity for women came along after the death of the Baal Shem Tov, founder of Chassidim, whose void was filled by other charismatic leaders, some of them women. The most famous was Hannah Rachel, renowned as the "Maid of Ludomir." Her story is illustrative of the kind of pressures brought to bear on outstanding women to force them into a more stereotypical existence. Born in 1815, the only child of a prosperous merchant, Hannah had an

"The idea of a school for religious girls was revolutionary... less than seventy years ago."

ecstatic experience and thereafter began praying with tallith and teffilin. After her father's death, she said Kaddish for him and used her inheritance to build a Bet Medrash in which she delivered scholarly discourses attended by thousands from all over Europe, including many prominent rabbis. Eventually, rabbis accused her of being possessed by the devil. To counter this, her friends urged her into a disastrous marriage which soon ended in divorce. After that, her influence declined and she soon left the country, becoming the first Chassidic leader to settle in Israel.

In contrast, Sara Schnerir, founder of the Beit Yaakov school system, rose to prominence with the blessing of the rabbinical establishment. The idea of a school for religious girls was revolutionary in its day, a time when girls received no education at all or were sent to Christian schools. This was less than seventy years ago.

Born in 1883 in Cracow, Poland, Sara was the pious daughter of Belz Chassidim. Troubled that religious girls would not follow in the path of their pious fathers if they continued to be ignored, she asked the blessing of the Belzer Rebbe, the Rebbe of Ger, and the Chafetz Chaim, to turn her sewing workroom into the first religious school for girls. The leaders, reluctantly acknowledging that it was only fair to teach Jewish girls that which non-Jewish girls wishing to convert needed to know, i.e. laws, rituals, etc., gave her their blessing. At first, young women refused to attend, and she was forced to teach children. But by 1935 there were 248 Bet Yaakov schools in Poland alone, comprising 35,000 students. It is perhaps ironic that today Beth Jacob schools educate girls to marry early and bear many children. Sara Schnerir herself was divorced and childless.

A true pioneer in Torah study for men and women was Professor Nechama Leibowitz. Born in 1905 in Riga, Latvia, Nechama's father took the rare step of hiring

*In Her
Own Words*

private tutors to teach his daughter Hebrew and religious studies. Professor Leibowitz became the world's greatest teacher of the Bible, pioneering a completely unique method of biblical analysis and emphasizing the moral teachings and practical application of biblical texts. She also popularized Torah study for the masses through her weekly Bible sheets, beginning the program after giving a Bible class to vacationing women factory workers, who expressed a strong desire to continue studying when they went back to work.

Nevertheless, despite her unique achievements, when Rabbi Shlomo Riskin asked her to teach students in his yeshiva in 1987, he was condemned by haredi rabbis for inviting a woman to teach his students. Rav Ovadia Yosef actually proposed that Professor Leibowitz teach the class behind a curtain! Proffesor Leibowitz taught the class, without curtains.

"Even today, (religious) barriers ... continue to interfere with women's ability to share their unique gifts."

For some women, the ticket to greater accomplishment came with illness, or with immigration, both of which conferred on them a freedom from the strictures women suffered under normal circumstances. Writer Grace Aguilar's delicate health earned her private tutors and the ability to devote her time to literature. She wrote seven books, both novels and nonfiction, and was considered a champion of the Jewish faith.

For writer Mary Antin, born in 1881 in Plotzk, Russia, the catalyst to freedom was immigration to America, where her strictly Orthodox family quickly Americanized and Mary benefited from public school. Attending Columbia University and Barnard College, she published the first American bestseller, *The Promised Land* which went into 34 printings and sold 85,000 copies.

Another Nobel Prize winner was Rosalyn S. Yalow, born in New York in 1921. She, like Trudy Elion, also graduated from Hunter College, but was awarded an assistantship and eventually received her Ph.D. Her

revolutionary work with radioisotopes in medical research was awarded the Nobel Prize in 1977. Nevertheless, her mother would always admonish her: "No self-respecting woman goes to work and leaves two small children at home with just a maid." Speaking to authors Bob and Elinor Slater for their 1994 book *Great Jewish Women,* Ms. Yalow said, "If women are ever to move upwards, we must demonstrate competence, courage, and determination to succeed and must be prepared to challenge and take our place in the establishment."

These fleeting glimpses of the achievements of Jewish women over the last thousand years is remarkable more for what it tells us about what has been lost rather than gained. From these drops of accomplishments, we learn of the huge reservoir of ability and talent lost to the human race because of all the man-made dikes and breakwaters that hold it back, barriers which even today continue to interfere with women's ability to share their unique gifts.

In Her Own Words

The following is a case in point. Israeli filmmaker Elena Chaplin documented a remarkable haredi women's rock group called Tofaaha, filming the women's lives as well as their performances. At every step, the women in the group encountered another obstacle. They needed to care for their children, one of whom was severely handicapped. Another battled health problems. All of them were circumscribed by strict rabbinical decrees which dictated who they could perform for, what kind of material they could use, what clothes they could wear, and how they could advertise their show.

And always, there was the catch-22, an unexpected rabbinical ruling that threw a wrench into the works at the last minute: a rabbi, who had originally given them a ruling permitting them to be filmed, suddenly told them that their mouths couldn't be filmed while they were singing. And so, they appear on screen with large crayon scratchs mark where their mouths should be. A little bigger, I thought, and the rabbis will have achieved their ultimate goal: to erase these women completely.

And yet, despite it all, the women, bursting with musical skills, songwriting talent, remarkable voices, and amazing energy, lit up the screen.

It made me want to cry.

O Pioneers!
Willa Cather
This author is one of my favorites. I've read everything she's written and find that despite the fact that we lived in different centuries, had different religious beliefs, and completely different cultural backgrounds, her voice touches my heart and illuminates the human condition.

Hunger
Knut Hamsun
The quintessential artist starving in the attic. It's a book that you can't forget (and remember to take along a snack while you read!).

Two Old Women
Velma Wallis
A book I picked up in Alaska. The legend of survival of two old women left by the tribe. Really wise, and important.

Madame Bovary
Gustave Flaubert
This was the book that inspired *The Saturday Wife*. Loved it.

A Death in the Family
James Agee
This simple, classic tale of loss and childhood tragedy taught me a great deal about what it means to write a book with universal themes. No literate person should miss reading this masterpiece.

*Keep on
Reading*

The Selection Committee
Rabbi Marc Angel
A recent novel by the Rabbi Emeritus of the
Spanish and Portuguese Synagogue in Manhattan.
A brilliant examination of what is happening to the
religious Jewish world through the words of the
rabbis, their wives, donors, and students as they are
interviewed by the selection committee charged with
choosing the next head of a prestigious
Talmudical Academy in Brooklyn.

Crisis, Covenant, and Creativity
Rabbi Nathan Lopes Cardozo
A very wise examination of the rapid changes
overtaking our world, and how it affects our
lives and our faith, by one of my favorite
rabbinical thinkers.

Because They Hate
Brigitte Gabriel
A Lebanese Christian woman who suffered from
terrorism makes us understand what is at stake
in the war against terror.

(Available from St. Martin's Griffin)

Reading Group Questions

1. *The Saturday Wife* has been described as a satire. Do you agree or disagree? If you agree, what is the author satirizing, and why?

2. Describe what you think would be the perfect ending for this book and why.

3. What do you think is the role of a good spiritual leader?

4. Describe the perfect spiritual leader for Swallow Lake.

5. Do you think Chaim failed the congregation, or did the congregation fail him?

6. In what way could Delilah be described as a comic figure? In what way a tragic one?

7. In her acknowledgments, the author says she was inspired by the book *Madame Bovary*. Can you find some parallels between the two books?

8. Do you think Delilah jumped over the edge, or was she pushed?

9. Describe the kind of life that would have really made Delilah happy.

10. If you had to write a sequel to this book, describe chapter one.

Keep on Reading

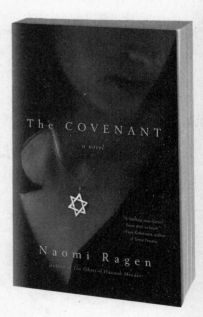